DEMONS &

DAMNATION

SHADOWED SOULS SAGA
BOOK 1
C.J. LAURENCE

For all those with their own troubled minds.
You're not alone.

Reader Information

The characters you are about to meet walk the lines of right and wrong, precariously tilting one way or the other depending on their mood and the situation. They have all suffered in their past and they bring that here with them.

However, what one person finds horrifying is like water off a duck's back to another. If you like it dark and have no triggers, carry on. If you're uncertain and want some reassurance, please head over to my website for a full list of trigger warnings www.cjlauthor.com

CHAPTER I

A ZAZEL GRINNED, A TRUE, ear to ear sadistic grin, one that painted him as the demon he was. He'd perfected it to the ideal mix of his human form and his demonic form, keeping his appearance human save for his 'this is your end' grin where he showed off his mouthful of needlepoint teeth, glistening and stained dark red. It filled each and every subject with nothing but fear.

His current subject, a man in his mid-fifties, damned to Hell for the worst crime possible, sat in Azazel's leather dentist chair, strapped down by his forehead, chin, wrists, stomach, and ankles. For three days already, Azazel had tortured him to the brink of death, revived him, and repeated the process. With nothing but pleasure.

Glancing down at the man's freshly repaired body, Azazel gave him his signature grin and asked, "Are you ready for round four, Gerald?"

Gerald's silvery blue eyes filled with terror. He tensed his entire body and attempted to shake his head. "Please," he said, all but spluttering, struggling to speak with the chin strap so tightly pressing against him.

Azazel loosened the strap and gestured his arms outwards. "Please, continue," he said. "Plead your case. I'm eager to hear your justifications."

Gerald moved his jaw up and down, loosening the muscles. He glanced down at his feet, a stainless-steel table at the end of the chair, lined with a hundred different tools that were each designed to bring maximum pain but not kill. Knives, saws, picks, scissors, scalpels—he'd had them all used on him, repeatedly.

Flicking his eyes back to Azazel, Gerald smiled at him. "Please. If you're going to torture me again, at least give me something to watch, take my mind off it."

Azazel narrowed his eyes. "But that only pleases you, not me. Where's my fun in that? I need you focused on your pain, on your suffering." Azazel let out a sigh. "But I'm feeling jovial. Humour me, what would you choose to watch if I did allow it?"

A predatory spark ignited in Gerald's eyes. He replied, "The video I took of me and Eva." He closed his eyes and licked his lips. "Oh, that girl. She was so sweet, so innocent, so *pure*, and I had her. All of her. She's mine. Forever."

Rage fired through Azazel's veins. Paedophiles were his favourite to torture. He kept them all alive for weeks, sometimes months at a time, suffering the same excruciating agony over and over again. An eternity of torture would never be enough for one of these scumbags.

He looked down at Gerald, placing a hand either side of his head, looming over the old man's weathered face. "Is Eva really the last thing you want to see?"

Hunger filled Gerald's eyes and he squirmed against the hold of the straps. "More than you know."

Azazel lifted his right hand and pressed his index finger to the middle of Gerald's forehead. That single touch gave Azazel a 'window' into Gerald's memories, instantly filling his mind with images of a young girl no more than eight or nine. Long curly chocolate brown hair, pastel pink lips, and beautiful big brown bambi eyes, she was an adorable little thing.

Was being the operative word.

Taking his finger back, Azazel kept the man's eye contact as he focused his mind on the image of Eva, letting his magic take over. In a matter of seconds, Azazel's short blonde hair grew out into long brown curls, his green eyes shading over to dark brown and his red lips lightening to pastel pink. His bulky six-foot one muscled frame shrunk to a petite three feet.

Gerald's eyes filled with horror as he watched the demon shrinking at the side of him. "No, no!" he yelled. "You can't taint my last memory of her, no, I won't allow it." He squeezed his eyes shut.

Azazel altered his voice, mimicking Eva's honey laden sing song tone. "I'm afraid you don't get a choice."

Walking to the other side of the room, Azazel grabbed a small three step step-ladder and dragged it over to the side of the chair. He opened it out and climbed up it, peering down at Gerald.

"Gerald, come now, you wanted me to be the last thing you see."

Gerald shook his head and kept his eyes firmly closed. "Not like this. You're not capable of doing horrible things to me. You're too good."

"You should be careful what you wish for, Gerald. This is what you wanted."

Gerald said nothing, concentrating only on keeping his eyes shut.

Azazel looked over at his table, spotting the exact thing that would solve this problem. Hopping down off the step ladder, he picked up the suture needle and thread and headed back to Gerald's side.

"Last chance, Gerald. Keep your eyes open willingly or I will force them open."

"You wouldn't force anyone to do anything, you sweet, sweet girl." He slid his tongue out and wet his lips. "I can still taste you, you know."

Azazel felt his stomach churn. Placing his left hand on the man's forehead, he kept his head still whilst pinning his eyelid back with his right hand, holding the long, curved suture needle right in Gerald's line of sight.

"I will sew your eyelids open, Gerald. Last chance."

Water filled Gerald's eyes. "Eva, don't do this, sweetheart. I carry your innocence in me. It's ok if you're lost, all you need to do is be with me and you'll find it again."

Azazel pressed his lips together whilst running through a list of expletives in his mind to describe the despicable excuse for a man in front of him. Realising he needed to reapply the chin strap, Azazel stabbed the suture needle into Gerald's right bicep, using him as a pin cushion.

Gerald hissed and strained against the straps. Using both of his hands to align his head perfectly straight, Azazel reapplied the chin strap and made it one hole tighter than what it had been previously. Threading the needle, he used his left hand to pin the eyelid open as he aimed the needle at the inside corner of Gerald's right eye.

Right at that moment, the heavy metal door to Azazel's torture room burst open, his brother, Balthazar, standing in the doorway.

Balthazar raised his dark eyebrows as he took in the scene before him—his burly evil brother as an eight-year-old girl leaning over an old man with a needle and thread at his eye. "What *are* you doing?"

Azazel glanced up and rolled his eyes. "I'm busy. Come back later."

"It's March twenty-first, Azazel. Midnight. It's time to go."

Azazel glanced up at the Grim Reaper clock hanging above the doorway, the scythe and one skeletal arm acting as the hands of the clock with thigh bones marking the hours. Sure enough, the scythe and one of his arms were both pointing straight up at midnight.

"Damn it," he said, letting out a long sigh. "I was about to have some fun here."

"Well, he can wait. We're due a holiday. Come on."

Azazel looked back down at Gerald. "To be continued, Gerald."

Gerald's eyes softened as he looked up at the face he treasured so dearly. Just as a wistful gaze glistened over his eyes, Azazel switched his form back, going full demon mode mere inches from the old man's face.

Upon the sight of jet-black eyes, purple-coloured veins, and a mouthful of needle-sharp canines stained crimson red, Gerald sucked in a sharp breath, his eyes widening as he startled at the stark, instant transformation.

"Maybe Eva will enjoy tasting you when she's back," Azazel said, giving the old man a wink and a smirk.

Gerald squeezed his eyes shut and clenched his hands, willing the demon to leave.

"See you in three months, Gerald. It's holiday time."

Azazel strode towards his brother, slinging an arm around his younger sibling's shoulders as he guided them out of his torture chamber. "Have you decided where we're going this year?"

Balthazar nodded, allowing Azazel to dictate their leisurely pace towards the portal. As they meandered through the small, stone passageways, lit only by oil lamps every few feet, the lingering stench of death and decay reminding them of their situation, Balthazar focused on only one thing—keeping his mind shielded from his brother.

If Azazel were to find out his intentions for their annual three month break this year, he knew without a doubt that all hell would break loose.

CHAPTER 2

A S THEY REACHED THE old mahogany door that hid the Earthly portal behind it, Balthazar sucked in a deep breath. *It's now or never,* he thought to himself. *Do or die.*

"You're being very mysterious about the destination this year, Balti," Azazel said, grabbing the black wrought iron door handle and shoving the heavy old door open.

As the silence around them filled with the creaking of the ornate iron hinges, Balthazar took the couple of seconds to choose his words carefully.

"It's a surprise."

Azazel quirked a sandy coloured eyebrow up, his jade green eyes filling with mischief. "I remember the last time you said that we ended up in Thailand. What an adventure *that* was."

Balthazar allowed himself a small smile. "This will definitely beat that," he said. "Don't you worry."

Azazel stole a quick look at his brother, scanning his coffee-coloured eyes for any kind of a hint as to where they were going. In his mind's eye, he reached out with a long tendril of pulsating green energy, gently pushing at his brother's mind, trying to break inside and peek at what

11

was going on in there. All he met was a fortified wall of steel.

"Keeping your secrets close to your chest, hey? I like the mystery of it. Very good."

They stepped through the doorway, scanning the long, narrow room for any potential intruders. Around ten feet wide and sixty feet long, the room itself was nothing but chunky grey stone bricks all around. At the very end sat the portal itself – a ball of rainbow coloured energy pulsating as if it had its own heartbeat.

"I don't see why we have to use this still. It's ridiculous. It's been over a thousand years already," Azazel said, rolling his eyes. "We're more than capable of going straight to Earth without having to use this thing."

Balthazar shot his brother a sideways glance as he ran a hand through his dark hair, trying his best to hide the fact his hands were shaking. "One breach of the threshold was one too many, Azazel," Balthazar replied. "You only have yourself to blame for this."

Azazel pressed his lips together and frowned. "It was one momentary lapse of concentration, that's all. Now I know humans can follow us through our own portals, it won't happen again." He shrugged his shoulders like an innocent boy. "Scouts honour."

"Azazel, you allowed an entire tribe of Amazonian warriors to follow us here...whilst you were...*copulating*...with their queen through the portal itself. I really don't think your 'scouts honour' carries much weight in that respect."

Azazel closed his eyes and let out a groan of satisfaction. "Oh, Acantha...my, I've not thought about her in a *long* time. She was as sweet as honey. Tasted like morning dew on fresh grass."

"And worth you complaining about this every year?" Balthazar asked, pointing at the portal.

Flashing his brother a mischievous grin, Azazel replied, "If you knew the things that woman could do with her tongue, you wouldn't have even asked that."

Balthazar sighed and marched forwards to the portal. "It would be nice if you could have just one thought, one sentence, without it involving your dick or some woman."

"But where's the fun in that?"

Balthazar didn't dignify his brother with an answer. Instead, he placed his hands either side of the portal, feeling its energy latch onto his, surrounding him in what felt like a magnetic field. As it spread over him like water seeking an edge, it made a small 'pop' as it engulfed him completely. Then, an instant later, Balthazar disappeared from Azazel's sight.

The three seconds spent inside the portal were the most peaceful three seconds of Balthazar's year. All that surrounded him was beautiful silence encompassed by a myriad of colourful geometric shapes. As the portal pushed him through its tubular length at five times the speed of light, Balthazar kept his eyes wide open to soak in as much detail as possible. It was nothing short of a celestial wonder.

Azazel, left on his own in the room, took a deep breath, muttered a few curse words, and then followed his brother, his mind only remembering what he and the Amazonian queen had been doing all those hundreds of years ago.

In the icy waters of the North Sea, a lone fishing boat bobbed along the gentle waves, the captain and his men paying little attention to their vessel as they stared above them in awe at the spectacular light show of the aurora borealis. They were seeing for free what would cost anyone else thousands of pounds.

Completely entranced by the glimmering radiance, like moths bewitched by a flame, they noticed nothing of the shadowed island they floated past. The tiny piece of land last encountered humans in Norse times. On the eastern side of the Shetland isles, the mere eighty hectares of Balta provided no use for anything except a lighthouse.

And a pair of demons.

If the fishermen had not been so captivated by the rainbow-coloured lights reaching down to earth, they would have seen two figures shimmer into existence. But as soon as the hypnotic polar lights touched the ground, they recoiled as if in pain, leaving their hitchhikers alone in the darkened landscape.

Azazel sucked in a deep breath, closed his eyes, and let his breath out with an appreciative groan. "Can you smell it, Balti? Can you smell the sweet scent of all those mortal females?"

A muscle in Balthazar's cheek twitched as he narrowed his eyes at his brother. "Don't call me that." Choking almost to death on a spicy Indian dish over thirty years ago had been nothing but humiliating for Balthazar and only pure entertainment for Azazel ever since. "The joke's getting a little old now, Azazel. Grow up. A bit of maturity once in a while wouldn't hurt, you know. *Zay Zay.*"

Azazel curled his top lip back at hearing the stupid nickname given to him by the Lamia, the lethal female temptresses of Lucifer's lair. He closed the gap between them in the blink of an eye, staring his brother down with narrowed eyes. "Me grow up?" Azazel snorted. "That's rich coming from you. Every year do you, without fail, fall in love with some poor girl, wrap her up in a whirlwind romance for three months and then disappear. If you're such the romantic, as you claim to be, where's the romance in breaking a different woman's heart every year?"

Balthazar folded his arms over his broad chest and squared his shoulders. "Has your pea sized brain got the capacity to think that maybe I want these twelve weeks of freedom to give me a glimpse of something I've yearned for for centuries? That it allows me to temporarily live a life I never had, and probably never will have. As for the woman, she remembers nothing of it. My last kiss goodbye wipes their memory of me."

A twinge of empathy coursed through Azazel before burying itself back in the darkness. "Why would you torture yourself every year like that? Reality check, *brother*. We're not going to be human again. Ever. So, in between now and eternity, loosen up and enjoy what you can."

The two glared at each other, neither one wanting to back down. A strained silence fell between them, the atmosphere thickening with emotion, secrets of old tales threatening to re-surface.

"Need I remind you," Balthazar said, stabbing his index finger into his brother's solid chest. "That we are stuck like this because of *you*. You're a damn curse—always have been. If you want to cause misery to everything and everyone you come into contact with for all eternity, go ahead and be my guest, but don't drag me down with you. Asshole."

Azazel quirked up a sandy coloured eyebrow, delight filtering through his eyes at the taste of a challenge. "You're kidding me, right? You think we're stuck like this because of *me?*" He poked Balthazar in the chest with two fingers, causing his brother to stumble back a step. "You might want to re-think that little statement, *Octavio.*"

Balthazar's brown eyes swirled with flecks of blackness, the hint of his demonic form scratching just beneath the surface, ready to unleash at any moment. "That. Is. Not. My. Name."

"No?" Azazel asked, giving his younger sibling a smug smile. "Let's follow your little ideals for a moment, shall we? Let's say you find that person, that special one, your *demi*-soul. You know what you need to do to have that love confirmed. And it involves everything you were as Octavio. *Everything.*"

Balthazar tilted his chin up with a defiant flick. "I'm fully aware of the rules. There's someone for everyone, Azazel. Every year we come here is my chance to find her. The right one will love me despite my past. I know that. It matters what I am here and now, not what I was or have been."

Azazel chuckled. "You're nothing but a soppy hearted idiot with idealistic views of love. I would have thought after two millennia, you might have learned something."

"I have learned something, you infantile moron. I know I don't want to continue much longer without feeling love. Unlike some."

Tipping his head back, Azazel laughed so loud it echoed through the dark skies. "But that's where you're wrong. I do feel love—" Azazel grabbed his groin in a crude gesture, looked back at his brother and grinned "—I feel it right here."

"And what would *Cassia* think of you if she could see you right now, hmmm?"

In the blink of an eye, fuelled by fury, chiselled cheek bones became lost under a sea of dark purple veins as Azazel's demonic form came to the surface. Jade green eyes gave way to obsidian depths, the gleam in them nothing but dangerous. "Don't you dare speak her name, you vile piece of—"

Blessed with feline reflexes, Balthazar hurled a clenched fist at his brother's face. The crunch of bone splintering bone thundered through the sky. Turning away from his uncouth brother, a whispered curse left Balthazar as he walked across the frosted grass, chastising himself for being drawn into another physical fight. He drew a deep breath and re-focused his mind on this year's destination.

Azazel shook his head, his demonic features evaporating as quickly as they'd appeared. He shouted a stream of curse words as his broken nose realigned itself, each shattered piece of bone clicking back into place.

"Why can't you just accept that we're different?" Balthazar asked, glancing briefly at his brother over his shoulder. "Why do my ideals of love bother you so much?"

Azazel paused for a moment, thinking over his brother's question. "Because we have immense power and magick, more knowledge than any amount of books could ever contain, and an eternity to enjoy it all with. Why would you want to give that up just to live eighty years with some human whose looks will fade after twenty years anyway?"

"But that's my choice. Not yours."

"I want what's best for you," Azazel said, the feeble tone to his voice not quite passing off his sincerity.

Balthazar chuckled. "No, you don't. You just can't stand the thought of me finding happiness before you."

Azazel pressed his lips together and stared at the grass beneath his feet. His brother had hit the nail on the head.

Seeing Azazel lost in his thoughts, Balthazar took his opportunity and lifted his hands, tracing his fingers through the crisp night sky. He drew a large triangle, his fingers leaving behind a shimmering glow of silver and purple specks hovering in the air, like a plane leaving vapour trails.

"Transporto," he said, giving his brother a quick sideways glance before he said the next two words. The stillness around them began to change, a slight breeze strengthening into a powerful vortex. Spinning in all directions, the turbulent energy ripped a hole in time and space. A sharp crack, as if the sound barrier had been broken, signified the completion of the closet-sized magickal doorway being opened.

Sucking in a deep breath, Balthazar spoke his final words as fast as possible. "Amor aeternus."

Azazel snapped his head up, his face contorting into a picture of horror as he glared at his brother. "What the fuck did you just do?" He launched himself at Balthazar, rugby tackling him to the ground. "You fucking bastard!"

CHAPTER 3

THE TWO BROTHERS ROLLED around on the damp earth, grunting as they hit each other with enough force to cause an earthquake. Shouted curses echoed around them as they fought. After a brief wrestle and some quick moves, Azazel pinned his brother to the ground with his hands around his throat. He glared down at him, spitting in rabid fury at the implications those two little words would now cause.

"I don't want my fucking demi-soul. It's all a damn lie anyway. A stupid urban myth made up by Lucifer to keep idiots like you hanging on to nothing. Change it," he yelled, his green eyes nothing but black holes of hatred. "Change it now."

Balthazar chuckled and shook his head. He couldn't resist the fact his demi-soul, the other half of him that would make him feel whole for the first time ever, was just a few steps away through a magickal portal. He knew Azazel wanted the same thing, deep down, it was merely a matter of making him accept it.

A roar of frustration left Azazel. He'd wanted to travel to a remote village in China, spice life up a little for the locals and give them some tales of demons to spin for the next few centuries. He couldn't alter the doorway himself—meddling with another demon's magick was as lethal as poking around with biological warfare.

The option to go somewhere on his own didn't exist. Their deal with Lucifer, for their three months of freedom per year, was on the condition they took their 'vacation' together. If they didn't, no time off. Simple.

'Amor aeternus' rattled around in Azazel's mind, it's meaning of eternal love on repeat in his brain. His head whirled in a thousand different directions. An unfamiliar tightness gripped his heart. He loosened his hold on Balthazar enough for his brother to overthrow him.

Eager to arrive in this year's twelve-week temporary home, Balthazar stood up and stepped inside the black hole gaping before them. He glanced back at Azazel and shrugged his shoulders. "Shut up and get in."

Azazel glared at him. "Whatever happens from here on out is your fault. You get that?"

"Shut up and get in."

For the first time this century, Azazel had no words. He loved having the last say, always the one to end an argument, but now he was helpless. And he didn't like it.

Sulking like a petulant child, he stumbled to his feet and shuffled in next to his brother. The deep frown creasing his forehead made his displeasure obvious and the shadows still lurking beneath his skin told of his underlying rage.

The split in the air sealed behind them like a set of elevator doors. It closed with a definitive smack that rumbled like thunder through the empty night. As it reached its crescendo, their destination appeared before them, and the portal opened once more to allow their exit.

Balthazar hopped out, smiling as he inhaled the fresh, earthy scent surrounding him. He closed his eyes, and for a brief second, revelled in the smallest feeling of peace flowering inside him.

"For fucks sake," Azazel said, wrinkling his nose up in disgust.

Still stood inside the magickal doorway, he showed no signs of stepping out any time soon. Balthazar shot him a steely stare. Leaves, twigs, a discarded plastic bag, and someone's clean bedsheets were in a tornado around them. But not a hair on their heads moved.

"Get out," Balthazar said, all but growling. "Before you draw attention to us."

Azazel snorted. "From who?" He opened his arms, gesturing at the quiet village they were in. Not a soul could be seen or heard in the sleepy place. "There's no-one around if you hadn't noticed. What is this—a retirement village?"

Sighing in exasperation, Balthazar clapped his hands together once. The whirlpool of energy harbouring his brother changed shape into a small circle. The edges squeezed around Azazel's muscled body, trying to push him out. Folding his arms over his chest, Azazel glared at his brother and stuck it out until the bitter end when the powerful energy forced him out like a cork from a bottle.

"Exactly where are we staying, genius? Just to clarify—I'm not feeling the older woman, granny thing this year, so we may need to move."

Balthazar walked away. Focusing on nothing but where the worldly energies were guiding him, it didn't take long for him to put some distance between them both.

Reading energies happened to be one of the more fun things for a demon to do. It took Azazel a while to master the art due to his impatience and jovial nature, but Balthazar caught on quickly. The necessity to stop and empty the mind for a few seconds proved almost impossible for Azazel. A constant merry-go-round of sex, food, torture, and more sex kept his mind constantly active.

However, for Balthazar, the need to imagine his hands turning into long, twisty vines, reaching out and touching physical objects made sense. Everything past, present, and future, only existed, or would exist, because of energy. In order to feel it, and read it, he had to believe he was a part of it.

Azazel only relished in the ability to see human's dirty little secrets, observe their past, gather information that could be useful to use against them, and of course, get a front row seat to any sexual encounters.

Distance didn't affect how far their mindful tentacles could go. Only their own mental limitations inhibited their capabilities. Azazel's main interest focused mostly on areas that burned with a bright red aura—the tell-tale sign of residual sexual energy.

The quaint setting of Grimsthorpe, nestled away in the east of England, held a serene beauty shrouded in a time capsule. Class divide from a century ago seemed still so obvious here—old houses, grossly large but stunning sat within their own grounds and away from the other smaller houses all clustered together in terraced rows. However, the cobbled, sandy bricks and promises of cosy mystery erased the dislike for such close neighbours.

A traditional butchers, greengrocer, and milkman all still thrived in the village, making the feeling of stepping back in time that little bit more realistic. A newsagent tagged onto the end of an old barn, right at the edge of the main street, giving away the only push into modern day customs. Even family from the workers who had worked at the nearby beautiful castle still lived here, stories of ghosts and other strange happenings being passed down from generation to generation.

Whilst the castle itself belonged to The National Trust, the surrounding land and remaining estate attached to it—including the former workmen's quarters—were left untouched, a taste of days gone by to whoever passed through.

"Doesn't anyone have sex around here?" Azazel said, wrinkling his nose up in disgust. "Balthazar, I'm serious. I'm not staying here."

"Shut up moaning, Azazel."

Scanning his eyes over the fields behind him, Azazel let out a growl of frustration. "I'm not moaning, Balthazar. I'm pointing out a key survival factor here."

"I've never heard of a human dying from a lack of sex, so I think the chances of us doing so are nil. Now, get a move on and follow me."

Balthazar crossed the empty road, eyeing up the local pub as he walked past it. Lights were on, and a horrible screech sounded over a microphone as someone tried to sing. He ignored it, more interested in following the narrow gravel lined track running alongside it. A thick privet hedge, neatly trimmed at head height, provided a good amount of privacy for whoever ventured down the small lane.

After a few hundred yards, the track opened out into a magnificent carriageway style driveway. An ornate, grey stone fountain sat in the middle, the once stunning equine feature now covered in patches of algae, bird faeces, and years of dirt. The water in the large base around it resembled nothing but a green slime topped with layers of dead leaves.

When Balthazar set eyes on the house, a warm smile warmed his handsome face. *Now, this feels like a home*, he thought.

Dark red bricks and brown timber window frames gave away the age of the house. Two sides, both sprawling across the extensive grounds, joined together by an awe-inspiring archway entrance porch. The brickwork above the porch had once been white but now held a yellow, aged tinge.

For the first time in years, Balthazar felt the small buzz of excitement deep inside his gut. Even without his magickal abilities, he would have known that this time would be different. This time would be *the* time for him. He closed his eyes and drew in a deep breath, immersing himself in the reality of this moment.

A long, low whistle cut through his peaceful moment. "Now, this is a house for a party. You done good, little bro." Azazel clamped his hands down on Balthazar's shoulders and shook him with excitement. "And we each get a wing to ourselves. An entire wing full of women...I really can't think of anything better."

Balthazar shook off his brother's grip and stalked towards the front door. Trying to hide his irritation failed when he motioned a hand at the solid wooden door, sending it flying backwards on its squeaky hinges like it weighed nothing.

Consumed once again by ill feelings towards his brother, Balthazar missed the friendly, sky-blue energy trying to connect with him. It wasn't until he stomped his first footstep on the thick wooden floor that the energy materialised in front of him.

"Welcome to the Worthington house. I'm Mildred. I will be your maid during your stay. How can I help you?"

Balthazar stopped dead, his anger notching up a level as yet again, his brother put him off something that could have been vitally important. He stared at the sweet old woman stood in front of him. Boasting the smile of a loving grandmother but wearing the black and white uniform of a maid, she bowed before him.

"Oh, there's two of you. How lovely. Would you like a cup of tea?"

Peering over his younger brother's shoulder, Azazel looked at the sight before him. The tight bun on her head pulled her grey hair back off her face. Even edged with wrinkles, her eyes still shone a brilliant blue. Her skin appeared smooth, plump, and full of life.

"Well, hello, Mildred," Azazel said. "And what might you be hanging around for?"

A sly smile passed over her pale lips. "I am 'hanging around' in my home, dear boy."

"Boy? Really?" He snorted in disgust. "Have you any idea—"

"I know full well *what* and *who* you are, Azazel. To be quite frank, if you wish to stay under my roof, you *will* abide by my rules. I'm afraid that extends to an entire wing of female company, of which I'm sure you won't be surprised by my forbidding it." A glassy stare hardened over her eyes. "This is not a brothel, and I shall not have a lady of the night tainting my house under any circumstances. Do I make myself clear?"

Azazel grinned. "Yes, you're making yourself very clear. Your manifestation is quite remarkable. I've never seen one of you in such detail. If I didn't know better, I'd say you were live and kickin'."

Mildred smiled. In one swift, fluid movement, she reached up to her neck, slipping her aged fingers beneath her high frilled collar.

"You know," Azazel said, pointing his index finger at her and grinning. "I can tell you're the kind of old bird who was a fine piece of ass in her day."

In response, Mildred pulled her hand back from beneath her clothes. A gold chain fell down on her chest, its centre point settling between her breasts.

Azazel fell silent when he saw the intricate detail of a pentagram nestled inside a hexagram. "Ah," he said, scratching his head.

Clasping her hands in front of her once more, Mildred nodded. "I believe we have an understanding?"

Azazel nodded, a sheepish look sweeping across his features.

"Good boy. Now, how about that tea?"

CHAPTER 4

K YLA MARSHALL GLANCED UP into the night sky, admiring the vibrant stars twinkling above her. Leaning back against the cool bricks of the pub where she worked, she gave in to her nicotine craving. Grabbing the last cigarette from the battered silver packet in her hand, she grumbled about the cost of the damn things these days.

As soon as she lit it and took the first drag, she tried to breathe out all of her negative thoughts with it. The sweet rush of nicotine surged around her body, tingling through her veins. She dared to think back over her mere thirty years of life. Working in *The Phantom Horse*, and still being single at this age hadn't been her plan, but since when did life care about plans?

Staring at the old oak tree on the boundary line between the pub and the mansion behind, Kyla found herself lost in thought. Daydreams of sitting in an oak-lined office with a psychopath offering up his mind for dissection brought a small smile to her lips. Her idealistic dreams of becoming a criminal psychologist seemed like a whole lifetime ago and belonged to someone she no longer knew.

Still, her morbid fascination of serial killers and the inner workings of the mind had never faded and even now she relaxed to murder documentaries and read whatever books she could on anything murder related.

A violent shudder ran through her, bringing her back to the present and leaving goosebumps in its wake. From out of nowhere, a powerful gust of wind whipped around the empty garden, knocking her sideways. Dropping her fag when she used her hands to steady herself against the wall, she frantically looked around for it.

"For fucks sake," she said, chasing it across the grass.

She grabbed after it like it was a long-lost piece of treasure. Being her last one, she didn't want to have to traipse into town when her shift finished. She could moan about needing to do that in the morning instead.

Fishing around in her pocket for her lighter, she placed her fag back between her lips and relit it. She'd barely finished inhaling her next hit before a clap of thunder and another strong burst of wind took it from her again.

"Are you freakin' kiddin' me?" she yelled, looking up into the vast dark sky.

With the threat of a storm lingering, she felt more than grateful she'd chosen laziness today and driven the two miles to work instead of taking her usual walk. Chasing after her fag again, she plucked it from its place near the hedge lining the boundary of the pub's land.

"Kyla. Where are you?"

The high-pitched voice of Kyla's boss, Keith, echoed through the shadowed garden. She closed her eyes, took a deep breath, and counted to ten.

"Coming," she shouted back, trying to sound as sweet as possible.

Chewing on her tongue to stop a flow of curse words from spilling out, she threw her ill-fated cigarette over the hedge into the abandoned garden on the other side and stomped back to work. Reminding herself she only had two hours to go until she could go home, she plastered a smile on her face and played nice to the customers.

Several of the regulars were leaning on the bar with empty glasses, bored expressions on their faces. Wondering to herself what the hell Keith was doing and why he couldn't serve them, she remembered that her boss was nothing but a lazy bastard and expected all of his staff to do everything. Regardless of whether they were legally entitled to breaks or not.

The man disgusted her, but to be fair even that didn't describe the skin-crawling revulsion that swamped her every time she so much as thought of him. She couldn't pinpoint anything specific that made her feel that way, it was just the whole package. Short, bald, fat, blackened teeth—the few he had left anyway, and small, piggy eyes, his entire demeanour made her cringe. That and the fact he perved over anything with breasts.

If he'd been a nice guy, she could have excused him for being the same height as her ample chest and not having anywhere else to look at eye level, but he wasn't. The best word to describe him would be a leech. He only ever employed young, single women.

As Kyla was halfway through pulling a pint for the last thirsty guy, Keith scurried through from the kitchen.

Sweat glistened all over his bright red face, and his belly heaved up and down.

"Fire," he said, gasping for breath.

Kyla's mouth dropped open and her heart stopped dead. "What? Where?"

He pointed to the back of the pub. "The garden!"

Without a second thought, Kyla ran past him, ignoring the nausea swirling in her stomach as she brushed against him. Bolting outside, she stopped dead when the blazing heat hit her several feet from the hedge. Sure enough, bright orange flames were consuming the ancient oak tree that had sat on the boundary line since before she was born. Charred black pieces of tree floated through the illuminated air. Every passing second only ensured the tree trunk would be nothing but a crispy log.

Dread hit her. It could only have been her fag. So certain it'd been blown out by the wind, she'd thought nothing of tossing it over the hedge.

"I've already rung the fire brigade."

Kyla jumped, not having realised Keith was stood next to her. When his greasy hand clamped around her forearm, she shook her arm free and shuffled backwards. She couldn't help but shiver when she registered the fact his flesh had touched hers. Thoughts of how much he would have enjoyed those few seconds of skin on skin contact sprung to mind but she pushed them away before she made herself sick.

Glancing around her, it seemed the entire village had now piled into the back garden to watch the slow, miserable death of what had been a rather magnificent tree. The wail of sirens sounded in the distance, surprising her with how fast they'd responded. But as she thought about it, it'd probably taken Keith a good couple of minutes to waddle through from the back room where the phone sat.

"Right, people. Come on, move along please. The fire brigade will need room." Kyla clapped her hands together and shouted over the low hum of excited chatter. "NOW, please."

Painfully slow, the crowd began to move out of the garden, congregating on a small patch of grass across the road, outside the village hall. It really said something about village life when the highlight of their year was watching an old tree burning down.

Still, it'd gotten her off work early.

A minute later, the firefighters arrived on site, each man seeming to go on auto pilot with his own job to do in the team chain. Aware of giving them space, Kyla headed back inside the pub to tidy up, lock up, and shut everything down.

As she gave the bar a final wipe down, the rustle of a jacket caught her attention. Seconds later, a young, dark-haired fireman appeared. His bright green eyes were the first thing she noticed. Combined with high cheekbones and tanned skin, he was more than easy on the eye.

"All sorted," he said. "Unfortunately, there isn't much left of the tree. Do you know the owners of the land?"

"Kinda," she said. "Old man Worthington died a couple of years ago. He didn't have any family except for two nephews he'd not seen since they were toddlers. He left them the estate, but they've been travelling ever since, pissing the family fortune up the wall."

He nodded and pulled a thin smile. "I see. Well, I guess that's lucky for you then."

Kyla frowned. "How's that?"

"Because it was your cigarette that started it."

Biting back a smirk, Kyla couldn't help but play with him. He was cute and she loved a bit of flirting. Feigning hurt, she slapped a hand over her chest. "Excuse me? How dare you accuse me. There are plenty of people who smoke around here. What brings you to the conclusion it was me?"

Grinning, he ran his tongue over his lips. "The fact your lighter is hanging out of your back pocket. And your boss said you were out there only minutes before it happened."

She sauntered back along the bar, wiping the mahogany surface as she eyed the young man, deciding he was in early twenties at the most. Coming closer to her prey, she raised an eyebrow at him as she ran her tongue over her bottom lip. "Have you been staring at my ass?"

He glanced towards the doorway, checking for his colleagues, looked back at her and smiled. "And what if I have?"

"Well, I think I'd have to ask for your opinion." She stepped towards him and ran her index finger down his navy-blue jacket. Noticing it was unzipped, she slid her hand under it, surprised at the hard chest beneath his cotton t-shirt. "So what do you think then?"

"It's lovely," he said, his voice a hoarse whisper.

Grinning, she turned slightly, placing her ass just in front of his hand hanging by his side. "Why don't you see if it feels as good as it looks?"

His eyes lit up with hunger, the temptation of such easy meat taking over any rational thought. He pressed his hand to her ass and when he squeezed, a small groan slipped through his lips.

"My boss will kill me if he sees me in here," he said, almost breathless.

"Really? Taking risks for me already?" She pushed back into his hand and looked back at him over her shoulder. "I like that."

He slid his hand up to her lower back, slipped his arm around her hips and pulled her against him. "You're hot, you know that?"

"Hot enough to burn a tree down?"

"And some."

A man's voice shouted from outside, sounding very close to the back door. Kyla flickered her eyes towards the open doorway they stood in front of. One glance down the corridor and she knew they'd be caught.

Stepping away from him, she tugged on his jacket for him to follow. He needed no encouragement. A few strides and they were out of direct sight.

"So is my naughty little secret safe with you?" Kyla asked in a voice so sweet, it would rival any angel. Placing both of her hands on his solid torso, she revelled in the feeling of his hard body beneath her palms. She could feel his pecs beneath his thin t-shirt and the temptation of ripping his shirt off was becoming harder to resist by the second.

Backing her up against the bar, he leaned into her ear and whispered, "That depends."

"On what exactly?"

"If you're free for a drink or dinner one evening?"

Trailing her fingers down to the waistband of his trousers, Kyla peeked up at him from beneath her lashes and whispered back, "Skip the pleasantries. No point in beating around the bush." She flashed him a wicked smile. "Not that I have a bush. If you get my meaning," she said, giving him a cheeky wink.

A pink flush spread over his chiselled cheeks. "What...what time do you get off tonight?"

Kyla leaned into him, inching towards his ear. Gently placing his ear lobe between her teeth, she nibbled on it. "That depends what time you come and get me off."

The young lad swallowed, his Adam's apple bobbing up and down. "Jeeze, lady. You'll give a man a heart attack."

"I'd rather give him a hard on." Kyla moved her hand down and grabbed his crotch, smiling as she felt the bulky handful through his trousers.

"Jesus," he said, jumping backwards and pushing her away.

"Oh, sweetie. I don't think you're man enough for me yet." She pulled away from him and winked. "I'd eat you for breakfast."

A deep voice yelled down the corridor, "Matt, get yourself here. We're going."

Seemingly dazed, he smiled at her before wandering back to his team. Kyla couldn't help but grin to herself. At least she'd managed to have some fun this evening.

CHAPTER 5

K YLA CHECKED FOR DRUNKEN customers lingering in the corners, then turned off the lights, all whilst giggling to herself about her interaction with the fireman. Heading down the corridor, towards the back door, she had her mind set on one thing only—home.

However, it seemed the universe had other ideas as a familiar Oompa Loompa shaped person blocked the narrow passageway and her way out.

"Kyla, dear," Keith said, huffing and puffing as he attempted to run to her. "I was worried about you."

Kyla took a step back and had to consciously stop herself from recoiling her top lip. "I'm fine. I've cleaned everything, checked for stragglers, and turned everything off."

"Oh you are a love," Keith said, reaching a hand out towards her arm. "I don't know what I'd do without you."

As Keith's podgy fingers clamped down around Kyla's left forearm, she found herself in an immediate battle between being polite or snapping every damn one of his disgusting sausage like digits. His need to touch some part of her every time he saw her was starting to wear more than a bit thin. Revulsion and rage ignited inside her and for a brief moment, she could understand how killers lost their control and did things they could never take back.

"I'm just doing my job," she replied, moving her arm back, trying to release his grip.

"Were you on your way home?" he asked, squeezing her arm tighter and taking a step forward.

"You don't need me anymore tonight?"

"No, no, no. You go home and get some rest. Unless of course, you're a little bit too shaken to be on your own. You're more than welcome to stay on my sofa. Or I can have the sofa and you have my bed."

With it being past eleven p.m., the only illumination pouring in down the dark, narrow passageway came from slivers of moonlight sneaking through the open back door. Kyla flickered her eyes up from Keith, staring straight over his fat, bald head at her exit route.

Hundreds of black and orange embers floated in the air, swirling around completely carefree, nothing but ashes in the spring breeze. A few voices muttered inaudible words from outside and a couple of firemen were still walking the grounds, checking everything had been dealt with.

"I'm fine. Thank you, though," she replied, looking back at him.

"Are you sure? I don't mind. I'll even change the sheets for you," Keith said.

Even through the poor light, the glisten in his predatory eyes was hard to miss as he said this, leaving Kyla with a cold chill.

"I'm good, Keith, thank you. I just want to go home."

"Or maybe you want some company at yours?" he asked, tapping his index finger against her skin.

Kyla bit her lip, struggling to hold back the torrent of abuse that danced around on the tip of her tongue. *I need to pay my mortgage. I need to pay my mortgage*, she reminded herself, over and over. "Keith," she said, her voice loud and her tone full of authority. "I'm fine. I just want to go home if I'm no longer needed here."

"Ok, ok. Very well," he said, finally releasing his hold on her. He turned to the side, which didn't open up anymore room than when he faced her. "Squeeze past me then and off you pop."

Nausea and distaste clashed together inside Kyla's stomach. She knew exactly what he was playing at. "I'll back up," she said, already taking steps back before he could protest.

Kyla walked backwards, taking long strides to keep the creep as far away from her as possible. When she made it back out into the bar area, she hopped to the side and waited for him to emerge. He pushed himself through the small opening, his hands grabbing either side of the doorway, like an octopus forcing itself through a hole half the size of its body.

"You didn't need to do that, dear," Keith said, wiping his sweaty forehead with the back of his hand.

Kyla said nothing, instead offering him a thin smile, before rushing towards the exit. She stepped outside and breathed in a lungful of fresh air. As the wandering firemen gave the thumbs up to their colleagues and headed back towards their truck, Kyla fished her car keys from her pocket and made her way around the front to the car park.

The small car park at the front of the pub now only held her car, which meant she wouldn't have to manoeuvre a twenty-point turn because some ass in a huge truck parked too close, as was usually the case.

With two old stable blocks flanking both the left and right-hand boundary lines of the pub's land, and a neat little fence marking the edges of the car park, it meant that, unfortunately, there was only one way in and one way out which was by a ten-foot gap at the bottom right hand corner.

Unlocking her car, Kyla collapsed in the driver's seat, switched the engine on, and pressed the brake pedal. Ten seconds later, the clunk of the locks battening down had her breathe a sigh of relief.

A final shudder shot down her spine at the thought of Keith having touched her. Deciding she needed a shower, she shoved the car in reverse and turned to face the exit. Realising she'd forgotten to turn her lights on, she flicked the switch. The bright beams of light cut through the darkness, showing her the way out.

And the solid silhouettes of two men blocking the exit.

Was this the cute fireman? she wondered. *Had he brought a wingman with him?*

She smirked to herself and drove over, stopping just a few feet short of hitting them. As she came closer, she could tell it wasn't the fireman. The athletic, defined shape of both of these shadows combined with their six-foot plus height immediately knocked out any man she knew. Then when she saw a hint of golden hair gleaming in the edges of her lights, curiosity killed the cat.

Opening the car door, she stepped out with one foot, using the door as a shield. "Hey, could you move please? You're kinda in the way of me getting home."

The guy on the left, the one with the golden hair, flashed her a smile. For the first time in a long time, Kyla found herself a little unnerved. It wasn't a warm, friendly smile or a sadistic, serial killer smile either. It was just...cold. No emotion attached to it at all, just a motion to perform.

He took a few steps towards her, skirting around the edges of her lights, making sure he stayed in the shadows. When he came level with her front wheel, he stopped. Jade green eyes sparkled at her like gems under moonlight. As she took in the depth of colours glimmering through his eyes, she sucked in a sharp breath. The colours were so deep and mesmerising, it seemed as if the iris was actually moving and the colour within it shimmering as a result.

An image of a book she had at home sprung to her mind, one with a cover that had a bright green tree python wrapped around a red apple, poised, ready to bite.

His eyes are as vivid and green as that snake, she thought to herself.

With his chiselled cheeks, pink lips, broad shoulders, and his mysterious with a touch of danger aura, it all added up to the complete package of a drop-dead gorgeous man. Who was he? Why had she never seen him around before? And why was every cell within her screaming bright red danger alerts?

Kyla licked her lips and tried not to let her mind wander as to what exactly was underneath that tight black t-shirt. The definition of his pecs couldn't be missed—the guy didn't have an ounce of fat on him. If there was one thing Kyla loved, it was a guy with a proper six pack and pecs. The desire pooling between her legs as she thought of the last chiselled body she'd licked every inch of almost distracted her completely from the current situation.

"Are you going to pay for that?" he asked, flicking his gaze behind her for the briefest of seconds.

The deep, raw husk to his voice only heightened the craving gathering between her thighs. She'd had some guys affect her in some ways but never like this, never from sight alone and one mere sentence. This guy screamed macho male and Kyla's body seemed to be begging for his attention.

Excitement clashed together with confusion deep inside her. This was new territory for her and she wouldn't explore it until she was sure where she was going. Keeping her cool around the opposite sex and always being two steps in front was Kyla's forte. But this guy, this guy was a whole other level.

You've met your match, she thought to herself, before then pushing the intrusive words away.

Ignoring her intensifying feeling of being vulnerable, Kyla carried on in her usual bullish way. "I'm sorry," she said, frowning. "What?"

"The damage you did to our garden."

Just look down, just a few inches. See what he's packing...

Kyla had to fight to keep her eyes from straying down to his groin. The curiosity to see what bulge, or lack of, was down there almost became too great. If it were to match his body and arrogant air of confidence, it would be enough to split a woman in half. But, there was no way he had the whole package. There was always a compromise with a guy and if he had the whole package thus far, chances were he'd have a micro-penis for sure.

Ignoring her need to look down there, Kyla snorted in disbelief. "I know what you're talking about. I meant could you please repeat the question because I swear I heard you say you expected me to pay for some antique tree being used for firewood."

A gleeful chuckle sounded from the other guy, who still stood in the shadows. The golden-haired man in front of her glared at her, his green eyes swirling with displeasure. He shifted from foot to foot as he folded his arms over his chest.

"Who are you anyway?" Kyla asked. "No one has been in that place for years."

The other guy took his opportunity to step forwards. "Ah, come on. You remember us. We're the nephews. I'm Ben and this is Adam. We've just got back and decided to see what sort of restoration Uncle Henry's place needed."

Ben was almost the mirror of Adam. Maybe an inch taller and a little stockier, but just as much of a hunk. Except he owned the whole tall, dark, handsome man thing with his raven black hair and eyes as dark as coco.

Kyla's mouth dropped open. "No way. No way is that you guys." A quick thought sprung to mind and she decided to test if they remembered how long it had been since they last saw each other. "You were definitely not this fit the last time I saw you."

"And when would that have been?" Ben said, smiling in amusement. "When we left college over ten years ago?"

Kyla laughed. Her test had been passed. "I've heard of people growing into their bodies, but jeeze, you two. What the hell have you been doing whilst you've been away?"

"It's a secret," Ben replied. His dark eyes glistened in such a way, it seemed as if the colour in his eyes swirled like melting chocolate, inviting her in further, deeper, to drown her in their depths.

Kyla shook her head slightly, refusing to believe she'd just almost been hypnotised by his eyes. *What is going on with these two?* Her heart started racing and her palms became sweaty as she realised she was alone in the dark with two gorgeous men. She needed to get out of here, fast, before she did something really bad. Even if it was the good kind of bad.

Seeing that they were both stood by her car and her way out was no longer blocked, Kyla regained her equilibrium and threw them both a triumphant grin. "I am now going home seeing as you two have finally decided you don't want to be run over tonight."

Patting her car door, she hopped back in, slammed it shut and put her foot on the accelerator before either of them had any cute ideas about blocking her way again.

Grinning like a Cheshire cat as she sped out of there, she dialled the number for her best friend, Sam.

"Oh my God," she said, as soon as Sam answered. "You are not going to believe who I just saw."

CHAPTER 6

B ALTHAZAR COULDN'T RESIST THE giant smirk crossing his face. As the red taillights of Kyla's Audi S3 disappeared into the night, he patted his brother on the back, and chuckled.

"Think it's safe to say you've met your match there."

Azazel turned and shoved his brother away from him. "I think it's safe to say that you clearly underestimate me. What the hell was with you claiming we know her already?"

"If you'd bothered to actually do some reading around here, then you'd know that she knows the family and went to college with the real nephews. Thankfully they're three years older than her which nicely explains how we've 'grown into our bodies'."

"Bal, why bother? Why bother with all the familiarisation crap? We're demons. We influence people, compel them to do what we want, use them as our little playthings. Why waste time and energy with all that energy reading when there's no need? All we need to do is fuck them up, fuck them, and fuck off."

Dark eyes narrowed in on Azazel. "Really? Is that what you really want or is it you thinking that's what we should want?"

Azazel laughed. "You are kidding me, right? You remember this is me you're talking to?"

"Unfortunately, yes."

"Then I think you can answer your own stupid questions."

"I *know* this isn't you. How long are you going to keep up this...façade?"

Silence fell around them, deafening the immediate area. Bright green eyes began to cloud with dark shadows. "That was a whole other lifetime. That person doesn't exist anymore."

Balthazar stepped closer, relaxing and softening his body language as much as he could. "Yes, he does." He pointed his index finger to the middle of Azazel's chest. "Lucius is still in there, somewhere. Changing names, defying mortality—it doesn't alter who we originally were."

"No, I guess you're right. Our DNA is still the same as it was two thousand years ago. The people who brought us into the world are still dead, and the people we all loved in that life, are still dead, too. Oh, except for the fact they lived their 'lives' without a single memory of us." Losing his grip on his temper, he grabbed his brother's outstretched finger and yanked on it hard. "So, in a case of nature versus nurture, which matters? The demons we've lived as for two millennia, or the thirty-odd years we had as humans—which are only remembered by us?"

Refusing to wince under the crushing grip around his finger, Balthazar decided to switch tactics. "So when I become mortal again, what are you going to do? Just goof around as a solo act? Or suddenly buddy up with Lucifer's next babysitting job?"

An insidious smile spread across Azazel's face. "If you're mortal, and I'm still a demon, what do you think I'm going to do?"

Balthazar narrowed his eyes, veils of darkness turning chocolate to coal. "What are you saying? That if I want to live out my life, like I should have done all those years ago, that you're going to kill me?"

"Kill?" Azazel chuckled, and with one swift move, ripped off Balthazar's index finger. "No, kill is too good for you, *brother*. You're forgetting all the fun I can have first—maim, torture, disembowel—" he tapped his brother's temples with his broken off finger "—let alone all the fun I can have in here. For three wonderful months. And then I'll put you back together, so you can wait for my next annual visit. Over and over again."

Balthazar gave him a sad smile. "Have you ever wanted something so much you physically ache? Your heart literally feels like it's going to burst with burning desire. Your insides, deep inside, in the core of your soul, cries to be complete, and sometimes the cries become so loud they send you crazy." Balthazar felt every ounce of fight leave him as if he were a balloon popped by a needle. "And then the very cause of all that walks right to you—it's as if the universe has answered your prayers." He glanced down at the floor, trying to fight back the flood of tears welling up inside him. "She was so beautiful, so thoughtful, caring, intelligent. She was a—"

"SHE WAS MY WIFE!" Azazel roared, grabbing his sibling's throat. Fury ignited inside him, releasing his demonic form. "She was my wife. And you...—" he gulped back a choking sob "—...took her from me. YOU TOOK HER FROM ME!"

Razor sharp nails dug into Balthazar's flesh. The soft pink skin broke beneath Azazel's vice-like hold. Blood rushed to the surface, flowing out in a steady trickle.

"I didn't want to," Balthazar said, his voice barely a whisper. "I didn't mean to. I just...I couldn't fight it anymore. I'm sorry, Azazel. You know I am. I can't even guess at how many times I've said sorry to you over the years."

"It doesn't matter though, does it?" Azazel said, his voice vibrating with the threat of a growl. He stuck his face right in Balthazar's, their noses now touching. "Your apologies don't bring her back, do they? Nor do they take away the last two thousand years I've had to spend with you."

The tearing of muscle and tendons filled the air as Azazel inched his fingers through his brother's neck. Blood poured over both of them as if Balthazar's neck were a sponge being squeezed dry of water.

"But I guess there's one thing I'm grateful of," Azazel said, sneering in his brother's face. "And that's knowing she'd rather stab herself in the gut than bear your child."

Before Balthazar could even make sense of what he'd just heard, the sickening crunch of his neck being snapped rang through the empty night.

CHAPTER 7

A ZAZEL TOOK OFF AFTER killing his younger brother for the thousandth time. Luckily for Mildred, Balthazar, and the rest of the village, the pub grounds still belonged to the Worthington estate, meaning Mildred could hide the evidence of the horror that just took place in *The Phantom Horse* car park.

Being a ghost had its advantages, but also its disadvantages. In order for Mildred to remain what humans call an 'intelligent haunting' as opposed to a 'residual haunting,' she had to bind her soul to one place in order to use its physical presence as an anchor for her existence.

Having worked all her life serving the respected Worthington family, it made sense to Mildred to remain within its boundaries. At least the extent of the estate stretched over many acres, so she wasn't confined to the house.

Using some brown sugar and strawberry jam, Mildred summoned an army of ants to her aide. Seeing Balthazar's bulk floating millimetres off the ground as her small soldiers carried him to the house made Mildred smile. She could have used a simple levitation spell or cast some blue-flower petal powder to make the entire scene invisible, but years of boredom and loneliness had led Mildred to turn her attention to means outside of spells. Perhaps the casting of a complicated spell to enable her to interact with nature had helped, but aside from that, her spell usage these days was becoming as decayed as her physical body in the local graveyard.

With the thought in her mind of where she wanted Balthazar's broken body putting, the ants marched into the house, down the hallway, and into the huge living room. In front of the open fireplace, which housed a small, active fire, Balthazar's limp mass came to rest on the carpet, head first, with each ant then working its way backwards so as not to be crushed under his deadweight limbs.

Like a synchronised human army, the troop of ants moved across the red carpet and onto the dark wooden floor in the hallway like a living shadow sweeping through the old house. They stopped in unison at Mildred's feet, waiting for their payment.

A sheet of greaseproof paper lay on the floor, covered in pea-sized balls of brown sugar mixed with strawberry jam. Each ant took one tiny ball, before scurrying out of the door and back into the surrounding grounds. Mildred mentally thanked them all again for their help before closing the door and heading to Balthazar's side.

From the mess Azazel had made, she roughly calculated how long it would take the younger brother to re-awaken. Judging from the re-aligned bones, and connective tissue re-working itself into place, she estimated around thirty more minutes before Balthazar would be awake again. By then, he would be hungry. Perhaps she should sort him out a little dinner.

Azazel sat at the edge of the lake in the local nature reserve. Shrouded with tall reeds and covered in hundreds of frog-bit, the only thing that gave away the demon's presence was the splash that happened every minute or so from the loose dirt he threw into the water.

He hated bringing up the past, picking over old scabs and re-opening wounds. But somewhere deep down inside him, he just couldn't quite completely forgive his brother for what he'd done.

Allowing himself to drift back into memories of Cassia, his heart became weighted like a ships anchor when he pictured her deep copper coloured hair, vibrant blue eyes that would rival any Egyptian shade of blue, and the dazzling smile she always gave when he walked through the door.

A ghost of a kiss tickled his lips as he remained locked inside his world with his former wife. Behind closed eyes and a soft heart, Azazel barely kept his fractured soul together. He didn't permit himself many moments like this, but his brother's persistent whining of wanting to find himself a woman had scratched deeper than Azazel had realised.

Over the years, he'd tried thousands of times to step into Cassia's world; a world where she knew nothing of Lucius or Octavio, but each time he attempted to follow every moment of the life she lived, he was kicked out like it was some sort of bucking bronco and he was the failed cowboy trying to tame it.

Desperation had risen and fallen in swells over the first millennia, but as time went by, the ability to live with the past became easier. As far as he and Balthazar were concerned, well, that was a curse both were damned to for eternity. They'd struggled along this far, trapped in a concurrent pattern of one drowning the other in a river of dark emotion before allowing him up for air and then sinking himself into the murky depths.

It was toxic, lethal for any being that got in their way, and ultimately a habit that needed to end.

Now.

As the moon sat high above him, casting a silvery glow onto the earth around him, he picked out the faint sound of a heartbeat and footsteps from behind him. He knew instantly from the rhythm it was his brother, now all healed and back to brand new. He could have taken his head off but that wouldn't have killed him. He'd done it before and quite clearly failed. The next day he'd been more than surprised when Balthazar reappeared at Lucifer's side, who explained that demons are immortal, and only *he* can extinguish a soul, no one else.

Minutes later, Balthazar sat down on the damp grass next to his brother and let out a sigh. "Are you ok?"

Azazel shrugged his shoulders. "Of course."

"I think we need to talk."

Azazel turned his head and stared at his brother. "About?"

"About what you said before you snapped my neck."

Azazel glanced down at the ground, sadness washing through him. He'd managed to keep that little secret to himself for two thousand years. "You heard what I said, Balthazar."

"Cassia was pregnant? With my child?"

Azazel squeezed his eyes shut, fighting back a torrent of emotions that clawed at his heart to be set free, to be rid of the festering storm they stayed in, century after century. "I'd been away for months, Balthazar. It definitely wasn't mine, was it?"

Balthazar looked away from his brother, processing this information. "Why didn't you tell me before?"

Azazel lifted his head and narrowed his eyes at him. "And what would that have gained exactly? You can't go back and change anything, can you?"

"At least I could have had the chance to mourn the loss of my child."

Azazel jumped to his feet and clenched his fists. "You amaze me. You really fucking do."

"Why am I not allowed to have sad feelings about this as well, Azazel?" Balthazar stood up and forced his brother to make eye contact. "It's not all about you."

Azazel stabbed a finger into his brother's chest. "You were the bad guy. Why do you get to feel sad?"

Balthazar sighed and stepped back. "It's not like it was planned, Azazel. It was just an awful lapse in judgement, a moment of weakness. I don't know what to say or do. My apologies aren't good enough. I don't know what you want from me."

Azazel lowered his hand and turned his back on Balthazar. "Some loyalty, Balthazar. Look at what you've done to us this year. You've potentially set a course of events in motion that will be nothing but history repeating itself." He turned around and glared at his brother, a streak of fire burning through his green eyes. "Only this time, now you're getting your demi-soul, you'll have *me* to worry about."

CHAPTER 8

"I 'M REALLY NOT IN the mood," Kyla said, letting out a sigh as she pulled up on her drive. "Sorry, Sam. I just want to strip off, get a glass of wine, and indulge in a volcanic bath."

Sam groaned down the phone like a child being told no to sweets. "But Kyla, pleaseee, I really want to go dancing."

Kyla rolled her eyes, not that it made any difference as Sam couldn't see her. "Sorry, but no. I'm being selfish tonight. Maybe tomorrow night?"

"Deal," Sam said, almost shouting down the phone in her excitement. "You've committed to it, there's no backing out now."

"I'll speak to you tomorrow," Kyla said, laughing and shaking her head as she hung up the phone.

Dragging herself from the car, she walked up her driveway and stood in front of her white front door, fiddling with her keys, trying to find the correct one to unlock it. Muttering curses to herself about having too many keys, she finally found the right one and let herself in.

She stepped through the door, slamming it closed with her left foot, and then leaned back against it, letting out a long breath. Closing her eyes, a grin crossed her face as she remembered her fun with the fireman. If only he'd had the balls to follow through.

"Your house is far too easy to get into," a deep, rough male voice said.

Kyla sprung her eyes open, squinting in an effort to peer into the darkness of her house. Her heart started pounding as her mouth ran dry. Reaching out with her left hand to flick the light switch on, her fingertips just brushed against the plastic switch as a large hand grabbed her wrist.

"I don't think so," he said, dropping his voice to a hoarse whisper.

In one swift move, he pinned her left arm above her head and pressed his six-foot three, bulky body against hers, trapping her against the door.

Kyla bit her bottom lip, her knees trembling, and her mind racing. "Please," she whispered.

The man leaned in closer, brushing his cheek against hers as he leaned into her ear and asked, "Please what?"

Kyla reached out with her free hand and grabbed his groin, smiling as she felt his hardness through his jeans. "Fuck me."

He nipped at her ear lobe with his teeth, sending a shiver down her spine. "Fuck me what?"

Feeling the desire pooling between her legs already, Kyla squeezed his dick, licking her lips as she remembered the last time she'd had him. "Fuck me...*Daddy*."

He let out a groan as he slid his lips down to her neck, biting into her soft flesh and sucking on it. "Mine," he said, letting her skin release from his mouth with a pop.

Kyla scrabbled with the button on his jeans, desperate to get inside and feel him, skin on skin. Pushing her hand inside his boxers, she wrapped her hand around his hard length and let out a moan of relief. "So fuck me like I'm yours," she said. "Come on, Dylan, it's been three months."

Dylan tore at her jeans, ripping the button off and pushing the light-coloured denim down her legs, using his feet to force them down. Kyla slipped her legs out of them completely and grabbed at him, curling her right arm around his neck as she jumped up, coiling her legs around his waist. Tearing her lacy thong clean off, Dylan then pushed his jeans and boxers down to his ankles and thrust himself inside her.

"Fucking hell," she said, leaning her head back against the door and letting out a groan of relief. "Finally."

Dylan took her free hand and threw it back against the door above her head, forcing both of her wrists into one of his shovel sized hands. With his free hand, he slid an arm around her lower back, angling her ass slightly off the door.

"Better," she said, panting. "But I need it harder, Dylan. Fuck me like you've missed me."

Dylan pounded into her, staring down at himself sliding in and out of her, the moonlight through the small half-moon shaped frosted glass window giving him just enough light to see. Her juices glistened on his cock, her pussy like a tight, velvet glove he couldn't ever bury himself deep enough inside of.

Kyla emptied her mind of everything but the feel of Dylan fucking her, his long thick cock sliding in and out of her at a pace only a pornstar could be proud of. As his hand tightened around her wrists and his breathing became shorter and shallower, Kyla knew what was about to happen.

"Don't you fucking dare," she said, her voice all but a growl.

Dylan looked up at her and pressed his forehead to hers. "You feel so good," he panted. "It's been three months." He took a breath and then said, "Give a guy a break."

Feeling more than a little devilish, Kyla whispered back in the sweetest childlike voice she could muster, "But *Daddy*, that's not fair."

Dylan plunged himself deep inside her and stilled, moving his head and resting it against the door. He trembled from head to toe as he sucked in a deep breath. "Play fair," he said, his voice low and full of authority.

Kyla leaned forwards and nipped at his ear with her teeth. "Come on, *Daddy*," she said, whispering in his ear. "Make me happy."

Dylan pressed his lips together and sucked in a deep breath. Lifting his head, he locked eye contact with her and inched his face towards hers. With their noses touching, he took his arm from around her back, letting out a low growl as she tightened her legs around his waist, pulling him in closer, driving him deeper inside her.

With his hand now free, he moved it to Kyla's throat, curling his fingers against her warm skin. Applying just a little bit of pressure, stopping when he heard her breath hitch, he asked in a dangerously low voice, "Who's in charge here?"

Every inch of Kyla's body tingled with excitement. She knew the correct answer if she wanted to finish this and give them both their relief, but she'd missed their power play sexual antics and she wanted nothing more than to test his patience, to bring him to the edge over and over until he gave in and let himself go.

Kyla squeezed her pelvic floor muscles, gripping him even tighter. A flash of danger flitted through his dark eyes. "I don't know," she whispered. "But I definitely don't think it's you."

Dylan licked his lips in a slow, teasing move. "You wanna play that game, huh?" He gave her a single nod. "Ok, fair enough."

Dylan moved his hand slightly upwards, giving him just enough length to slide his index finger against Kyla's lips whilst still holding her throat. Kyla opened her mouth and bit his finger, moving her ass up and down as she did so, silently begging him to move.

Moving a step towards the door, Dylan pressed Kyla flat against it, taking her favourite angle of pleasure away from her. Before she could say a word, he started moving at a furious pace, plunging himself in and out of her at a rate that left her breathless.

When his fingers tightened around her throat, Kyla knew she'd lost. As Dylan let out a groan and stilled inside her, his pulsing cock all too telling at his release, Kyla felt nothing but at a total loss. Completely inebriated by the furious sex but frustrated at her lack of orgasm, Kyla didn't know whether to feel pleased at having had sex after three months or angry at her failure to have a happy ending.

Dylan loosened his hand from her throat, moving it down to her back. "Was that as good for you as it was for me?"

Kyla narrowed her eyes at him. Uncurling her legs from his waist, she placed both of her feet on each of his thighs and shoved him away from her with a hard kick. "Bastard," she said.

A devilish grin unfolded across his thick, pink lips. "Told you I was in charge."

"Let me go," she said, looking up at where he still had her hands pinned against the door. "I need the toilet."

Dylan obliged, ready to catch her as she lowered herself to the floor, but the hardened glare she settled on him told him he shouldn't even try.

Kyla flicked on the upstairs light as she hit the first step. "Thank fuck for vibrating shower heads," she said, looking back over her shoulder at Dylan.

From the glow of the upstairs light, she could see the realisation in his eyes clashing together with fury and stubborn determination as he registered what she was saying. As he turned to give chase, stopping her from giving herself her own sweet release, he forgot his trousers were still around his ankles and fell face first onto Kyla's laminate floor.

Kyla giggled as she took the stairs two at a time before locking herself in the bathroom with her magic shower head. Jumping straight in, not even bothering to let the water heat up, Kyla grabbed the shower head and switched it on.

"Fuck," she hissed, as the vibrations coursed through her.

"Kyla," Dylan yelled, pounding on the door so hard, the doorframe jumped. "Don't you dare."

"Who's in charge now?" she replied, moving the shower head into a better position.

"I *will* break this door down." Heavy panting followed for a few seconds before he lowered his voice and said, "And I will *not* pay for the damage."

Kyla ignored him, focusing too much on the tightening ball in her core. Her body trembled as her heart raced, her mind filled only with one sole thought. *Just a few more seconds...*

The bathroom door burst open, splinters of wood exploding all over the bathroom. Kyla shrieked in surprise and dropped the shower head. As she stood naked in front of him, taking in his broad shoulders, his ripped arms, his chiselled chest, and those perfect lines heading in a V right down into his dark jeans, Kyla couldn't help but grin.

"What are you grinning at exactly?" he asked, his voice deep and husky, danger and threat glistening in his eyes.

Kyla gave him her sweetest smile and fluttered her eyelashes at him. "Because I know Daddy's come to spank me."

Dylan stared at her, keeping his dark eyes locked on hers as his gaze clouded over with nothing but carnal desire. "For what you've done, you won't be able to sit for a week."

Kyla let out a sweet little giggle. "Just a week? Is that all?"

Without a further word, Dylan marched over to her, picked her up, and slung her over his shoulder. Heading towards her bedroom, he said, "I'm gonna fuck you silent."

CHAPTER 9

KYLA WOKE THE NEXT morning feeling deliciously sore, exhausted, but oh so satisfied. Dylan had taken off in the middle of the night, as per his usual M.O.

The two of them had had a fling going for years but it had never been anything more than sex, a mutual recognition of being attracted to each other and trying to wear it out with red hot sex. So far, all that had happened was their sex had become nothing but a game, a constant clash of control of who could better the other.

Kyla had had her fair share of others, but none of them quite understood her like Dylan did. He knew exactly what to say and when to say it. He also knew exactly what to do and when to do it. The problem was, he was hardly ever around to satiate Kyla's borderline nymphomaniac tendencies.

He would stick around for a month or so and then disappear for three months or more. The longest he'd ever been gone was a year. Even then, he'd strolled back into her life and fucked her brains out like he'd never been away at all. Their dynamic was odd, but it worked for them.

As she looked over at the empty space next to her, smiling at the rumpled sheets, she realised she wouldn't have things any other way. She had the best of both worlds—singledom and a drop-dead gorgeous fuck buddy.

Kyla's phone sprang to life, pulling her from her daydreams of Dylan. Grabbing it from her bedside table, she turned it over to see Sam calling her.

"S'up, homie?" she said, answering the call.

"Are you up for some breakfast at the café?"

"Sure. What time?"

"I'll meet you there in thirty?"

Kyla held the phone away from her ear to see the time on the top right of her phone screen. Nine thirty-two. "Sure, I can do that."

"Cool. See you then." Sam paused and then said, "Oh. My shithead brother is back so he might join us, he's still deciding. That ok?"

Kyla's heart skipped a beat. "Yeah, no worries at all."

"Great. See you in a bit."

Kyla hung up the phone and tried to ignore the gnawing feelings of guilt biting at her conscience. Throwing back the duvet and heading for the shower, Kyla stopped dead in her tracks when she saw the carnage from last night laid out all over the landing and bathroom floor.

Her phone pinged with a text message. Looking down at her hand, she turned her phone over to see a message.

Dylan: I mean it, I'm not paying for it. That's what you get for being a brat.

Kyla couldn't help but grin. She loved being a brat to him. The way it set off his dom side turned her legs to jelly every time.

68

Kyla: I don't need a bathroom door anyway *shrug shoulders emoji* I live alone and even if I didn't, I've got a hot enough body to walk around naked *grinning face emoji*

She hit the send button and grinned to herself. Dylan knew she had sex with other people, but he didn't like it. The thought of her walking around naked and the implication of not living alone would have him seething for the rest of the day. Which, of course, would only make for a good fucking tonight.

He replied almost instantly.

Dylan: I'll break down all the other doors in your house as well then, shall I?

Kyla: Go for it, Daddy. It'll be like an advent calendar—you won't know what toy you'll find me with behind each door.

Dylan: There's only so many doors in your house, Kyla.

Kyla: I love it when you first name me, Daddy *winky face emoji*

Dylan: Carry on and I'll fuck you silent again x

Kyla: I'd rather you fuck me til I pass out but maybe you might need some help with that...*winky face emoji*

Kyla held her breath. Her comment was dodgy territory, like walking through a live minefield blindfolded. It could go one of two ways—very well, or very fucking bad. Years ago, when they'd first started sleeping together, Dylan had teased Kyla with the idea of a threesome with him and a friend. Kyla had jumped at the idea—two hot guys willing to pleasure her, hell yes, why not? Except when it came down to it, Dylan hadn't been able to handle it. The instant his friend laid a finger on Kyla, he'd pulled the plug on it and told his friend to leave.

Every now and again, Kyla would have a dig at him about it, which usually ended with Dylan getting defensive or shitty, and they wouldn't speak for a couple of days. The meaning behind that happening had always niggled at her. Did Dylan want something more? Did he have feelings for her that he couldn't express for one reason or another?

Dylan: I can fuck you until you pass out. No help needed.

Kyla let her breath out and grinned. He'd bitten but not fully. Picking her way in between the shards of wood, she reached the shower and set her phone down on the side. There was nothing more to be said to Dylan—she'd given him his challenge and now she just needed to wait for the challenge to be completed.

Kyla pulled up at Hattie's café at quarter past ten. Seeing Sam's black golf TDI in the car park already, Kyla couldn't help but wonder if she'd come alone or not.

Parking her Audi A3 next to Sam's car, she switched the engine off, jumped out, and rushed inside, ready to be scolded for being late.

"Afternoon," Sam said, grinning up at her from the table.

Kyla rolled her eyes. "I had to shower before I left the house."

Sam wiggled her eyebrows up and down suggestively. "Oh, really? Had a visitor last night, did we?"

"I wish," Kyla said, taking the seat opposite her friend. "Is your brother here?"

Sam nodded. "He's in the toilet."

Kyla's heart did a backflip as heat rushed to her cheeks. She couldn't say anything more about him though or it would look odd. "What are you having?"

"Usual full English I think. You?"

"Same," she said. "So, where are you torturing me with going tonight?"

Sam's green eyes lit up. "So you're going to keep your promise then?"

"Yes, of course. Unfortunately."

Sam launched into a full-on excited chat about all the different clubs in the neighbouring cities and who had what on and all the varying prices. As she chattered on, Kyla found herself thinking how blessed she was to have a friend like Sam in her life. Struggling with her own breakup at the moment, Sam was still powering on through and being Kyla's constant. Sam was the only person who had been Kyla's unfaltering rock, right from when they met at playschool. Suffering a night out in a trashy local club was the least Kyla could do to repay her for what she had done, and still did, for her.

"Hi," said a familiar, deep male voice.

Kyla jumped out of her thoughts and glanced up into a pair of dark eyes she knew all too well. "Hey."

"Dylan," Sam said. "Can you go and order us two full English breakfasts please. And of course, whatever you want."

Dylan looked at his little sister and nodded. "Sure. What drinks?"

"Orange juice for me, please," Kyla said.

Sam nodded. "Same for me."

Dylan gave Kyla a brief look with a hint of a smile before heading over to the counter to order.

"Don't do that," Sam said, dropping her voice to a whisper.

Kyla frowned. "Do what?"

"Look at my brother like you're undressing him with your eyes."

Kyla sucked in a sharp breath, almost choking on it. "What?"

Sam rolled her eyes and laughed, leaning back in her chair. "Please. I know that look on you, Kyla."

Kyla couldn't deny it. The guy was freakishly hot. If she denied it, Sam would know something was up. Kyla grinned at her. "The guy is smoking hot, Sam. I know he's your brother but Jesus, even you've got to admit if you weren't related, you totally would."

Sam quirked an eyebrow up. "I'm not even having this hypothetical conversation with you. It's got so many icks attached to it, it's unreal. He's my brother and I think he's gross. End of."

Kyla smirked at her and decided to test the water. She had never lied to Sam about anything. Except Dylan. And it killed her. Every time they were around each other, with Dylan present especially, Kyla couldn't help but feel like the world's worst friend.

"But he's not my brother," Kyla said, licking her lips and wiggling her eyebrows in a suggestive manner.

Sam opened her mouth, then closed it. After a few seconds, she said, "I'd do anything to see you happy, you know that, even if that meant you shacking up with my brother. But you can't give him what he wants, Kyla, and that's where my issue is...would be, if it were ever a thing."

A tsunami of sadness hit Kyla square in my chest, completely consuming her heart and filling her stomach with nausea. With water hazing over her vision, she faked a smile and shrugged her shoulders. "Good job it's not even a thing then, isn't it?"

Sam faltered for a second before nodding. "I'm sorry," she said, leaning over the table and reaching for her friend's hand but Kyla moved her hand away. "I shouldn't have said anything. Me and my big mouth." She buried her face in her hands and shook her head. "I'm a terrible friend."

Kyla's mind was racing, wondering if she knew about her and Dylan and was fishing for information or warning her away from him in a subtle way. If she knew Kyla had been lying to her...Kyla stopped that thought as her stomach churned.

It will all come out in the wash sooner or later, the little voice in the back of her mind told her. *Dirty laundry has to be washed at some point.*

Kyla didn't know what would happen if Sam found out about her and her brother. Being an only child, Kyla had never shared a sibling bond or been privy to its deep roots, but her relationship with Sam was founded on something so old and loyal, she looked at Sam as if she were her own sister.

They had never had to worry about going after each other's men as Sam had a tendency for liking the older gentlemen, whilst Kyla preferred them her own age or younger. Sam always claimed if Kyla found an older guy, she'd never look back, but Kyla wholeheartedly disagreed.

"There's nothing like experience," Sam would say, with a cheeky wink. "And they know how to be gentlemen. None of this baggy jeans crap with the crotch hanging around their knees and taking you to McDonald's for a first date."

However Sam liked to see it, it was as simple as she loved a sugar daddy and liked being taken care of. Kyla could take care of herself and only wanted a man for one thing.

"I think I'll drive tonight," Kyla said, smiling at Sam.

Sam pouted. "Why? What fun are we supposed to have if you're not drinking? Is this because of what I said? I didn't mean it. You know I didn't."

Kyla shook her head and waved her hand dismissively through the air. "Water off a ducks back. It's just close to pay day and we'll save a fortune in taxis if I drive." Kyla shrugged her shoulders. "It's as simple as that."

Sam's green eyes clouded over with worry. "Are you struggling? Do you need some money? I have plenty left from Melvin still."

Kyla chuckled and shook her head. "I'm good, Sam. I'm being an adult and budgeting accordingly."

Sam shrugged her shoulders. "Come over to the dark-side, Ky, you don't know the freedom you're missing out on." She gave her friend a mischievous wink. "No pervy bosses, no restrictions on what I can do, no one telling me what to wear or who I can see. It's the best of both worlds."

Kyla grinned. "Until you take their trousers off. Then you get the worst of it all."

"Nothing a little blue pill can't fix." Sam dropped her voice and leaned forwards. "Plus, then when they've finished, they can still go some more."

Kyla laughed. "But then I'll just get bored. The whole excitement is getting him to finish."

Sam rolled her eyes. "Different strokes for different folks. I prefer to indulge."

Dylan placed three glasses of fresh orange juice down on the table, the glasses covered in water droplets. "And I think that's the end of that conversation," Dylan said, narrowing his eyes at his sister. "You keep your girl talk for when I'm well out of ear shot."

Sam glared at her brother and snatched her glass of juice, her fingers slipping on the condensation and nearly tipping the glass over. "Spoil sport. Anyway, change of topic," Sam said, taking a sip of her juice and quirking an eyebrow up at Kyla. "I wonder if we'll see you know who out tonight."

Kyla frowned. "Who?"

"Have you forgotten the two hunks you bumped into last night?"

Kyla's heart froze. She could feel the burn of Dylan's eyes boring into her, but she couldn't look at him, not after the conversation her and Sam had had only moments ago. "Ah yes," Kyla said, clearing her throat. "How could I forget them?" She giggled and reached for a glass of juice, daring to catch Dylan's eye as she did. Nothing but a cool, hard stare glared back at her. "I guess it depends on where we go as to whether we'll see them or not."

"You think they'll stay local?"

Kyla nodded. "Definitely. They're only just back. They'll stick with what they know."

Sam ran her tongue over her bottom lip. "I could just be tempted to try your age range of men you know."

"I saw them first so I get first dibs," Kyla said, grinning at her friend. "I quite like Adam but Ben has this whole quiet, sultry thing going on. They're both hot...maybe I'll just have them both." She gave Sam a wink.

Sam laughed. "Nothing would surprise me with you. We'll see what happens later. I guess if we're going by your theory, we need to go to The Black Iris then."

Kyla nodded. "Sounds good to me. I'll pick you up at what, eight?"

"Good for me. I might even go shopping this afternoon, find a new hot little dress to wear. You never know, I might be the one taking them both home."

Dylan cleared his throat and shot his sister a look that could kill. "Enough. Both of you. I didn't come here to listen to you two talk about men and sex like a pair of teenage girls."

"If you don't like it, you know where the door is," Kyla said, staring right at him with a playful smirk tweaking at her lips.

The waitress appeared at that point with three plates of full English breakfasts. Her appearance cut through the growing tension somewhat, settling Dylan back into his box with the distraction of food.

When the waitress left, Sam laughed and said, "I guess we need to save our chat for later, Ky."

I grinned and bit into my toast, looking over at Dylan. "I think we definitely do."

CHAPTER 10

A FTER BREAKFAST, KYLA HEADED home. She'd
barely made it half a mile down the road before her
phone chimed with a text message. A grin unfolded over
her lips. She knew exactly who that would be and what the
message would say.

Pulling up on her driveway fifteen minutes later, she
didn't even switch her engine off before reaching for her
phone.

Dylan: Going out with my sister? Check. No problem. Pulling some hot dude? Not cool. Having a 3some with 2 hot dudes? I'll lock you in your house and never let you leave again.

Kyla chuckled to herself. She'd really set off his dominant possessive side. This could escalate into some proper fun.

Kyla: Needing your permission to do anything? Check. No problem. We're not together so *middle finger emoji*

Dylan: ...and what if I wanted to change that?

Kyla's heart froze in her chest. What? She stared at that simple sentence for several seconds, her mind completely blank. In a daze, she got out of her car and went to her front door, only to realise she'd left her keys in the car. And the engine was still running.

Switching the car off and grabbing her keys, she wandered inside her house, shut the door, and walked into the living room, finally collapsing onto her plush grey sofa.

Her phone pinged again with another message.

Dylan: I know it would be complicated, Kyla. But I don't care about any of that.

Kyla knew she couldn't ignore him. She had to reply with something.

Kyla: We can't, Dylan. I'm pretty sure Sam knows about us as it is. She all but warned me off you.

Dylan: When? What did she say?

Kyla: At the café this morning. She said she'd do anything to see me happy, even if it meant being with you, but I can't give you what you want and that's where her issue would be.

The message turned from delivered to read. The three little dots bounced around at the bottom of the screen for a few seconds then stopped.

Several seconds passed.

Then a minute.

Finally, he replied.

Dylan: Leave this with me. She doesn't get to decide my life, only me.

Kyla: Dylan, don't cause problems, please. Just leave it. It's not worth it.

Dylan: It is to me.

Kyla: I can't give you what you want, Dylan, leave it be. Please. Trust me. It's better this way.

Dylan: There are ways around everything, Kyla. Where there's a will, there's a way. And where there's a Dylan, there's gonna be shit that happens.

Kyla let out a sigh. Just how bad were things about to get? Anxiety and fear mixed around inside her, leaving her desperate to just have things left as they were. What if Dylan said something to Sam today?

Dylan was a doer. That was his thing. People asked him to action things and he did it, no questions asked. Whatever Dylan wanted, Dylan got, regardless of the carnage in the middle. Being a private contractor for the military came with a certain attitude and mindset that didn't always merge seamlessly with civvy street.

Kyla: Dylan, please. Let me speak to her first. She might take it better coming from me.

Dylan: What are you saying?

Kyla's heart pounded against her ribcage so hard she could feel the thud of it in her ears.

Kyla: I'm saying if we're going to admit this to Sam, let me do it.

Dylan: And then what?

Kyla hesitated for a minute. He was pushing her to say she would be his, that she wouldn't ever be with another man again. That she would commit herself to him and him only. That didn't sit well with Kyla. She liked her freedom, her lack of answering to anyone. If anyone ever did tempt her to commit, it certainly wouldn't be over a damn text message either.

Kyla: And then nothing. I'm not doing this over a text message. And you can man the fuck up and ask me to my face.

Dylan: I'll be there in ten.

Kyla sighed and rolled her eyes.

Kyla: No. Not everything has to be done right now, at a hundred miles an hour. Wait.

The message delivered. Two minutes later, it still hadn't been read. Kyla started chewing on her fingernails. Was he coming over? Had he not read it because he was driving? Or had he read it on his notifications bar and decided to ignore her?

She headed into the kitchen to make herself a cup of tea. Tea always calmed her nerves, or perhaps it was all the sugar she poured into it. Flicking the kettle into life, she stared mindlessly at the blue light, watching and listening to the kettle heat itself up.

As the water boiled, and the switch finally flicked itself off, her front door burst open to reveal none other than Dylan Mohun standing in her doorway. A gust of spring air blew through the open door, ruffling his finger length chocolate coloured hair into a sexy ruffle.

Kyla whirled around and folded her arms over her chest. "I told you not to come. And I swear to God if you've damaged *that* door," she said, pointing at her front door. "You *are* paying for it."

His dark eyes softened with a touch of care, compassion almost, something Kyla had never seen on him. "I don't care," he said, his voice low, barely above a whisper. "I'm tired of playing games, Kyla."

Kyla's heart jumped inside her chest, did a triple somersault, and then leapt into a galloping rhythm. Even his tone of voice was soft, his words careful. He'd opened up a door inside him that Kyla wanted nothing more than to close.

"Shut the door please. You're letting all the heat out and I've spent enough money trying to keep this place warm."

Dylan swallowed, his Adam's apple bobbing up and down as shock and surprise filtered across his handsome face. Without a word, he did as asked, closing the door. He walked into the kitchen, his eyes fixed on Kyla, watching, waiting for her reaction, wondering if she would be receptive or tell him to leave.

He stopped at the kitchen doorway, leaning his bulky muscled body against the doorframe. Folding his arms across his broad chest, Kyla couldn't help but let her eyes rove over his fine form.

Wearing a charcoal-coloured shirt that stretched across his pecs and clung to his torso like a second skin, the various tattoos adorning both of his arms were only highlighted further by his tense muscles. This did nothing but distract Kyla from the current problem and only made her want to run her tongue in all the grooves, maybe with an ice cube or two. She'd licked the sweat from his body on more than one occasion.

"I can see the fear on your face," Dylan said, keeping his voice low and quiet.

Kyla snorted. "Then you clearly can't read me very well because right now all I'm thinking about is running ice all over your body with my tongue."

Dylan dropped his arms to his side and closed the distance between them in three quick strides. Grabbing Kyla's upper arms, he gripped her tight and kept their eyes locked. "Don't do that," he whispered.

"Do what?"

"Turn everything sexual to avoid the real problem."

Kyla rolled her eyes and looked away, staring at her white kitchen tiles. She noticed that some of the grout had started to gain a yellowish tint and made a mental note to add grout whitener to her next Amazon shopping spree.

"Kyla," Dylan said, squeezing her arms. "Look at me."

Kyla waited a few seconds before turning her attention back to him. "What?"

"Did you think this was just fun to me?"

"Well, yeah. Why would I think any different? We both agreed NSA at the beginning, remember?"

Dylan pressed his lips together and let out a sigh. "No strings attached. Yeah, I remember. But you didn't think that after all these years it might have developed into something more? Hell, surely that night with Jack proved that."

Kyla raised an eyebrow as her breath hitched in her throat. "But...but we'd only been having sex for a few months back then...that was years ago."

Dylan shrugged his shoulders. "I was hoping you would eventually start to feel something."

Water pricked at Kyla's eyes, burning its way to the front of her vision. "I can't," she whispered, glancing down at her feet. "You know I can't allow myself to do that."

"Kyla," he whispered, letting go of her left arm and tilting her chin up with his index finger. "Yes, you can. You trust me, right?"

Kyla squeezed her eyes shut as he lifted her face up. She could feel the wall of water building behind her eyelids and she knew the instant she lifted the barrier, a river of tears would stream down her face. "You're asking me for a different kind of trust, Dylan," she replied, her voice cracking.

Dylan released her other arm and touched his thumb to her left eyelid, wiping over it. A sliver of water touched his skin, confirming what he knew. "Open your eyes, Kyla," he said, his voice soft, as if speaking to a child.

Kyla bit her bottom lip and shook her head.

Lowering his voice into a gruff command, he said, "Open them. Now."

Kyla sucked in a deep breath, letting out a sob at the same time, shaking her whole body. She opened her eyes, allowing her tears to run free. "Are you happy now?" she asked, her voice laced with sarcasm as she wiped at her cheeks with the back of her hand.

Dylan took her hand and pushed it back to her side. Cupping her cheeks with both of his huge hands, he brushed her tears away with his thumbs whilst forcing her to look at him. "I'll be happy when you trust me."

"Why?" she asked, her face screwing up into a ball of anger and confusion. "Is this some kind of game to you, Dylan? Is it some sort of challenge to get me to hand over my heart and soul to you so you can toy with it and do as you please? So you can break me all over again? Is that it? Is that what you want?"

Dylan frowned, his eyebrows furrowing together. "Do you really think that of me? That I would ask for your trust, for your heart, only to view it as a trophy and not as something to treasure?" He dropped his hands from her face and sighed. "I thought you knew me better than that, Kyla."

Kyla shook her head. "We don't *know* each other, Dylan. We know each other's bodies, sure. We know how to have great sex, but we don't *know* each other. You don't know my favourite colour or my favourite food, my most hated actor or my most hated smell. And I don't know those things about you either."

"Purple. Chinese. Ben Affleck. Cherries."

Kyla held her breath. Her head spinning at a million miles an hour she didn't know what to think. He'd shocked her for sure. "Well," she whispered. "You didn't have to fuck me silent that time."

"I don't want to hurt you, Kyla. I just want to love you."

Kyla dropped her head and closed her eyes. Huge racking sobs took control of her body. Wrapping her arms around her middle, she cuddled herself. "You need to leave," she said.

Dylan ignored her completely, instead enveloping her in a crushing bear hug. "If you want me to leave," he whispered. "Then you need to force me out of that door yourself."

As Kyla felt Dylan's arms encompass her and block out the world around her, a little shard of ice melted from her frost hardened heart. The way Dylan held her, with a tender yet strong embrace, sent shivers straight to her soul. She knew he cared for her more than either of them had anticipated.

For the first time in a decade, Kyla crumpled and allowed her sorrow to be comforted by someone else. What scared her even more was the fact that she liked knowing she had a rock of stability willing, and wanting, to be hers.

CHAPTER 11

K YLA CRIED HERSELF DRY. Until her eyes were red and the size of golfballs and she had no more energy left to give.

Dylan lifted her up and carried her upstairs. When he reached the top of the stairs and saw the wood from last nights antics still all over the place, he headed into Kyla's bedroom and set her on the bed, pressing a kiss to her forehead.

Picking his way towards the bathroom, he put the plug in the bath, turned the hot tap on full blast, the cold tap a quarter of the way, and poured in half a bottle of Radox, just how she liked it.

As the tub filled, he made swift work of clearing the wood. When most of the chunky parts were to one side, the bath had filled already. He switched the taps off and went back to Kyla. He found her laying on her back, eyes wide open, staring up at the ceiling, not even blinking. The gentle rise and fall of her chest told him she was still alive. He couldn't deny he had thought the worst for a brief second.

Without a word, he picked her up and carried her to the bathroom. Whispering to her, he said, "Can you undress yourself or do you want me to do it?"

Kyla blinked at him but said nothing. Her pretty blue eyes looked at him, but she wasn't there. She stared straight through him, almost as if the lights were on but no one was home.

A chill ran down Dylan's spine. He'd seen this before. On Kyla. And in men he worked with. His heart cracked in two as he realised he might have to ring his sister. But that would bring with it its own mess of questions and a further complicated situation. He'd leave Sam out of it until absolutely necessary.

Stripping Kyla's jeans, socks, and thong off, he picked her up and set her down in the volcanic water she loved being in so much. As the water rose and swallowed her body up to her perfectly round breasts, Dylan swiftly took her bra and t shirt off and eased her back against the end of the tub.

As the bubbles converged underneath her chin, she blinked a few more times, as if she were slowly coming back around out of her catatonic state. She looked up at Dylan, her eyes full of fear of shame and whispered, "Thank you."

"You don't need to thank me," he said, bending down and kissing her forehead. Stroking her red hair, he said, "I'm going to clean this mess up but if you need me, I'm here."

She nodded and closed her eyes, enjoying the feel of the warm water soaking into her body. Dylan hurried to clear the mess, wanting it clean and safe for her to walk across the carpet whenever she decided to emerge from the bath.

Within half an hour, he'd cleared the mess and hoovered every last splinter from the carpet. He returned to the bathroom and sat down on the bathmat, facing Kyla.

"How are you feeling?" he asked.

Kyla stared into space, not moving a muscle, not even blinking. Her eyes were glazed over as if she were not even conscious. Dylan reached out and touched her shoulder, making her jump. She blinked several times and turned her head slightly to face him.

"Sorry, did you say something?"

He nodded. "How are you feeling?"

Kyla let out a long sigh and then closed her eyes before sliding under the water, immersing herself completely. Dylan raised an eyebrow, wondering if this was her response he was supposed to somehow decode.

After several seconds, Kyla resurfaced with a big smile. "I'm good. I feel like a brand-new penny."

Dylan pressed his lips together and said nothing for several seconds. "Good. I'll give you some peace whilst you finish up. I'll wait downstairs for you."

Dylan headed downstairs, flicking on the TV in an attempt to distract his wandering mind from worrying about Kyla.

Half an hour later, Kyla emerged, wrapped up in her purple fluffy dressing gown and her long red locks held up in a towel on her head.

"You didn't need to stay," she said, flopping down on the sofa next to him.

"Yes, I did," he replied, pressing the mute button on the TV. "You ok?"

Kyla shrugged her shoulders. "I'm fine."

Dylan sighed. "If there's one thing I've learned as a man, it's that where it concerns women and the phrase 'I'm fine', things are usually never 'fine'."

"Well, in that case then, I'm good. That better?"

Dylan let out a light chuckle. "It'll suffice. Look, if you want to talk about it, I'm always here for you." He settled a hand on her knee and squeezed it. "I mean it. Night or day, rain or shine, screaming, crying, or laughing. Pick up the phone and call me, I'll be here faster than you can blink."

Kyla shrugged her shoulders again and grabbed the TV remote, turning the sound back on. "I told you, I'm fi—good. I'm good. There's nothing to talk about. Besides, it's not like you're just around the corner all the time, is it? I never know how long you're going to be here for. How long this time?"

"Kyla," Dylan said, snatching the remote back from her and letting out a sigh. "You're far from fine and there definitely is something to talk about. As for my job, you know what the deal is with that. I have to earn money somehow. I'm good at what I do, and I enjoy it."

"You didn't answer my question," she said, narrowing her eyes at him.

Dylan pressed his lips together and indulged in her staring contest for several seconds, debating his options. She was pressing him, backing him into a corner she knew he couldn't back out of. The worst thing was he knew what she was doing and the direction this conversation would take next.

Backing down, he glanced away and sighed. "I'm back for six weeks."

Kyla nodded. "And then you're away for how long again?"

Dylan moved his right arm, resting his elbow on his thigh before dropping his head into his hand and pinching the bridge of his nose. Squeezing his eyes shut, he debated not even answering her. She'd forced him into a checkmate, again. He knew their power play dynamics from the bedroom were spilling over into reality, and that wasn't necessarily a good thing either.

"Four months," he whispered, holding his breath after he spoke.

Kyla felt the blood beginning to boil in her veins. The audacity of him astounded her. How could he come back here for six weeks, ask her to commit to him, and then disappear for four months, no contact? He sat next to her asking her to bare her soul to him anytime she wanted, anytime she needed, making promises he couldn't keep by saying he'd be at her door whenever she asked, and yet, he wouldn't even be able to uphold his side of the deal.

Anger simmered in her core. She wrestled with her conscience as to whether to obliterate him with her words, hit out at him and cure the pain prickling through her veins, or whether to, for once, be an adult about it.

She wanted to gloat. She wanted to say, "See? I told you. There's no point in this. In any of it. We're just fuck buddies," but saying that would just be pointing out the obvious. He could already see his loss. Did she really need to dig the knife further in?

Kyla moved her left hand and slid it under her thigh, clenching it into a fist. Taking a deep breath, she said in a shaky voice, "Do I really need to say anything at this point?"

Dylan let out the breath he'd been holding and opened his eyes. After a couple of seconds, he lifted his head from his hand and asked, "It's not a matter of needing to say anything. What do you want to say?"

A sinister smile curled up the edges of Kyla's mouth. "Are you sure you want to swat at that wasp's nest?"

He shrugged his shoulders. "You need to get it off your chest so go for it."

Kyla debated her options. He'd never welcomed her to share her thoughts before. He knew a torrent of abuse sat poised on her tongue, nothing but an attack of poison barbs that once set free, could never be taken back. Was he pulling her into a trap, trying to win the argument in some way?

Or was he genuinely trying to show her that he could, and would, be there for her? That opened up a whole other can of worms that Kyla knew was a bad idea to even contemplate ripping open. Trying to cram those buggers back in the can would not be an easy job once he disappeared again in six weeks time.

"It's not a trap, Kyla," Dylan said. "I can take it. Say whatever you want to say. Hell, dealing with you every time I come back makes me realise how easy my job is.

Dodging fifty cal bullets and snipers is child's play compared to you."

Kyla didn't know whether to laugh or be insulted. "Not funny, Dylan. Is that supposed to be some sort of backhanded compliment?"

He gave her a cheesy grin and chuckled. "You take it however you want to take it. Come on, what do you want to say?"

Fuck it, she thought. *After that shitty comment, you can have both barrels, mate. Make you pleased to go back to your sand and blood.*

"Alright," she said. "You want to know what I think? I think you've got a damn bloody fucking cheek to come here and demand this of me. Eight years we've been fucking and you've not once made any attempt to make this anything more. Now you come here, after three months, and ask me to not only commit to you, but to hold you up on some sort of fucking pedestal and pour my heart and soul out to you?" She laughed. "Are you insane? Have you overheated out in that fucking desert? Because, by God, Dylan, I would rather shove hot pins in my eyes than ever give my heart to you. You don't get to demand this of me. You don't get to make me feel how I'm currently feeling, and to be quite frank, you have no fucking right to make me question myself and take me back to that place I spent so long crawling my way out of. You, Dylan fucking Mohun, are no better than the damn Devil himself. Not after today. So no, I don't want to be with you, and thanks but no thanks, I am not going to be talking to you about anything more than where I want your tongue or your dick." Kyla stopped and took a shaky breath. "Have I made myself clear?"

Only when she stopped did Kyla realise she was trembling from head to foot. It wasn't anger though, it was adrenaline, the sort that releases through your veins when you're terrified to your very soul.

Dylan sucked in a deep breath and nodded. Her words had hurt, more than hurt, they'd cut real deep, but he couldn't yell at her, he couldn't complain—he'd asked her to spill her thoughts, three times. Instead he just replied, "Yep, more than crystal clear."

Hot water burned at her eyes, clouding over her vision. "I can't believe you think you had the right to do this, Dylan. Why?" She jumped to her feet and stormed over to the other side of the room. "Why would you do this to me? I don't understand. Everything was perfect as it was." Her tears streamed down her face only heightening her anger even more. She hated feeling so weak and vulnerable. "If it's not broke, don't fix it. Why did you have to do this? Do you hate me? Is that it?"

Dylan stood and strode over to her, his arms out, ready to envelope her in another hug. "I don't hate you, Kyla, quite the opposite. If hating me heals a little part of you then go ahead and do it, I don't care. I'm here however you need me to be."

As he approached her with his arms outstretched, saying these caring, compassionate things, Kyla lost control of her last bit of restraint. She pushed his arms away, letting out a primal scream only a warrior could be proud of.

Dylan let his arms drop to his side and simply stood in front of her, waiting for her to blow her own steam out.

Kyla closed the gap between them, her hands balled into fists, molten tears cascading down her cheeks, her face as red as a hot poker. Without any hesitation, she hammered her fists on his chest, ignoring the vibrations of pain shooting up her arm as she put all of her might into hurting him.

"You're a bastard, Dylan," she screamed. "I fucking hate you."

Dylan said nothing. He merely stood and let her beat his chest, not moving a muscle. Seeing her lose herself like this tore into him like nothing he'd ever felt. He knew her secrets, he knew her past, and he also knew that every day was nothing more than survival for her. Every morning she opened her eyes was a victory that she hadn't taken her own life. He knew that despite her years of counselling and the endless pills the doctors had shoved down her in order to subdue her, he knew that she was still bottling things up, letting the bad thoughts intrude and fester, allowing her emotions and her life to be ruled by something that had been so out of her control.

She slapped his face, leaving a bright red hand imprint across his left cheek. He blinked twice but said nothing. Seeing his lack of reaction only angered her further and she slapped him again but this time across his right cheek.

"I hate you so much," she yelled. "I hope you burn in Hell."

Kyla raised her right hand, ready to slap him across the face again, but seeing his stoic reaction at her threat, after everything up to this point, popped her balloon of rage in an instant. Like water pouring from a shattered mug, her fury fell away into nothing, leaving her stood in front of Dylan as nothing more than a broken shell.

When she hung her head and stared at the floor, sobbing, Dylan stepped forwards and folded her into his body, wrapping his arms around her so tight he could feel every breath she took and let out.

Several minutes passed before she whispered, "Why are you still here?"

Dylan lowered his head and pressed a kiss to the side of her head. "Because you need me."

CHAPTER 12

S AM HAD EXHAUSTED HER feet and her bank card after hours of shopping. Coming home with three new pairs of shoes and four new dresses made her aching feet more than worth it. Pulling up to a stop outside her house, it took only one glance to know that her parents and Dylan were both out.

Their six bedroomed old red bricked farmhouse sat in the middle of six acres, surrounded by a small wood. The dark wooden window frames were something her and Dylan both disliked, but their parents loved. Of course, as their parents paid the bills, they had the final say.

All the windows were covered by curtains and the landing light along with the kitchen light had been left on—the signal to each other that the house was empty. Whoever arrived home first would open the living room curtains and switch on the living room lamp—the signal that someone was in, and everything was ok.

If, by some chance, someone broke into the house and switched on different lights, or opened different sets of curtains, whoever arrived home would know something was up. It had never been an issue but being prepared, especially living in the middle of nowhere in a large house, could never be a bad thing.

Just as Sam unlocked their red front door, the sound of tyres crunching on gravel stopped her from pushing the door open. Looking back over her shoulder, Sam saw Dylan speeding up the driveway, as per usual, in his gorgeous to die for black C63 AMG Mercedes. Sam knew nothing about cars but the grumble coming from that engine combined with its looks made her want to date the next old guy who owned one.

Satisfied the only threat was her annoying brother, Sam kicked the front door with her left foot as she picked up her bags of goodies. Dylan skidded to a stop on the drive, showering gravel everywhere but on his immaculate car. Sam rolled her eyes and sighed. That guy could fall into a heap of shit and still come out smelling of roses.

"How much of sugar daddy's money have you spent today?" Dylan asked, hopping out of his car and striding up behind his little sister.

Sam marched into the kitchen, dropping her bags onto the oak topped kitchen island. "I earned that money, thank you very much, so it's *my* money."

Dylan headed over to the fridge and pulled out a carton of orange juice. He snorted at his sister. "Sure. Earned it by sucking dick."

Sam whirled around and faced her brother with her hands on her hips, anger flashing through her green eyes. "I don't care for your insinuation."

Dylan finished drinking the orange juice, putting the empty box back in the fridge with all but a dribble left in the bottom. "I couldn't care less what you think to be quite frank. The fact is you fuck old guys, and they give you money."

Sam ignored his remark, which was nothing other than him wanting to pick a fight. Instead, she stared at the fridge door as it closed shut, then looked at her brother. "Because you couldn't have finished that last little bit and put it in the bin, could you?"

Dylan gave her a mischievous grin. "Nope. Because then it wouldn't annoy you, would it?"

As Dylan walked across the kitchen, the yellow lighting from the spotlights in the ceiling caught his left cheek, highlighting a red imprint across it.

Sam raised an eyebrow and cleared her throat. "Uh-hum."

Dylan stopped. "What?"

"What is that?" she asked, pointing her index finger at his cheek.

Dylan shrugged his shoulders. "I was falling asleep driving so I slapped myself to stay awake."

"Please," Sam said, rolling her eyes in exasperation. "I may be blonde, but I'm not that stupid. Quite clearly that handprint is not yours. It's half the size for a start, never mind the fact that it's the wrong way round for it to be your left hand."

"Since when did you turn into Miss Marple? It's nothing, leave it be."

Sam opened her mouth to argue back but then thought better of it. A sly smirk crossed her pink lips as she decided to hit him another way. Her heart pounding and her palms sweaty, she was purely calling his bluff, but she felt ninety percent certain she was right.

"I know about you and Kyla," she said.

Dylan stopped dead. He drew himself up to his full height and glared down at her. "Excuse me?"

Sam folded her arms over her chest and jutted her chin out in nothing but complete defiance. "You heard me."

Dylan quirked an eyebrow up. "You're delusional."

"That's not a no."

Dylan ran through his options quickly. He could continue to lie to his sister and battle on with Kyla alone, or he could confess everything and have Sam on side to help Kyla when he wasn't here.

As the light bulb flicked on in his head, he realised that was his answer to convincing Kyla to be with him. She was scared about being alone when he was gone, but with Sam on side, everything would fall into place perfectly, like a seamless jigsaw puzzle.

Dylan let out a sigh. "How long have you known?"

Sam grinned at him. "I suspected. I called your bluff. My, my, soldier boy, you wouldn't hold up well under torture, would you?"

Biting his tongue and refusing to be drawn into another sibling argument, he ignored her last comment and rephrased his question. "How long have you suspected?"

She shrugged her shoulders. "I started suspecting the last time you were back. You and her were MIA at the same time more than once. Then the way she looked at you today...your early morning arrival, her being late for breakfast...all seemed a little too convenient."

"I see," he replied, a muscle in his neck twitching. "And how exactly do you feel about that?"

Sam took a black leather bar stool out from the side of the kitchen island and sat down on it. "I told Kyla earlier how I felt about that. I want nothing more than for the pair of you to be happy, even if that means putting up with the grossness of you two being a thing, but she can't give you what you want, Dylan. That's the end of it."

Dylan walked around to the other side of the island and bent over, resting his forearms on the oak top, meeting his sister at eye level. "That's the end of your opinion, yes. That's not the end of me and her."

Sam narrowed her eyes at him. "I'm going to gloss over the fact that the pair of you have been lying to me for at least six months. That's another conversation. You have a responsibility to this family, Dylan, you've known about that from day one. Kyla cannot help you uphold that responsibility. Whatever this is going on with you two is completely pointless and will only end in heartbreak. It's best to cut it off now before it becomes anything more." Sam inclined her head towards her brother's cheek. "That from her?"

Dylan pressed his lips together but said nothing.

"Dylan...what did you do? Do I need to be worried about her?"

Letting a long breath out, Dylan prepared himself to be yelled at by a second woman in the space of two hours. "Look, you don't need to know the ins and out of me and Kyla. It's been nothing but sex from the beginning. We both agreed NSA. It was just a...a fling. We both found each other hot and decided to screw it out but, well, here we are this far down the line."

"And? I know there's more."

"And I want more. I told her today that I want more. I asked her to commit to me, to trust me, to turn to me when she needs someone."

Sam let out a groan and buried her face in her hands. "You're a fucking moron," she said, lifting her head. "And that's when you got that?" she asked, looking at the fading mark on his cheek.

"More or less."

"More or less? What do you mean by that?" Sam jumped off the stool, her heart pounding as a million possibilities of Kyla's delicate state of mind ran through her thoughts like a carousel on hyper speed. "Is she ok?"

"She's fine. She's sleeping. I think...I think she kind of had a bit of a PTSD episode earlier. I put her in the bath, and all was fine. Then she came downstairs, and we revisited our previous chat and she just had a complete and utter meltdown. She beat me." He stood up and lifted his shirt to reveal fading red marks across his upper torso. "But I think she's fine now. She got it all out and I put her to bed."

"Oh my God," Sam said, running her hands through her hair. "You don't even realise the damage you've done, do you? You absolute blundering buffoon."

Dylan frowned. "What am I missing here? I figured by now she'd be wanting some stability and some sense of normality. She knows me, you, our family, we get on well, there's no nasty surprises in the bedroom department either." He shrugged his shoulders. "What am I not getting?"

Sam cocked her head to one side as she racked her brains trying to think of an appropriate analogy to use on her simple brother to make him understand. "Do you remember when you were little? When you were scared of pigeons and clowns?"

Dylan narrowed his eyes at her and folded his arms over his chest. "What's your point?"

"Did locking you in a room with a flock of pigeons or a bunch of clowns help?"

"No..."

"What happened? How did you get over it?"

He shrugged his shoulders. "As I grew older, I understood things more and I learned they weren't a threat."

Sam widened her eyes at him, as if saying 'duh'.

"Are you telling me she needs to grow up?"

Sam laughed. "Not in so many words. Her body is obviously a thirty-year-old woman, but her mind, trapped in this permanent PTSD state, is stuck back ten years ago when it all happened. And with that, her emotions too. You've just asked her to lock herself in a room with a bunch of clowns playing falconry with a hundred pigeons."

Dylan unfolded his arms, let out a sigh, and ran a hand through his hair. Staring down at the floor, he felt nothing but a complete idiot. "I get it," he said. "I didn't think of it like that." He looked back up at his sister and asked, "So what do I do now? How do I fix it?"

Sam sat back down on the stool and let out a long breath. "You don't. We do nothing. She doesn't know that

I know about you two. If I go over there now, after your mess this morning, she's going to know that I know. I think that will just make her worse."

"How will she know you know if you just pop over for a cup of tea or something?"

"Because we're seeing each other later when we go out. I've no need to go see her now for a cup of tea. She'll know something's up. Knowing Kyla how I do, she'll sleep it off, pull herself together, and soldier on like nothing's ever happened." Sam shrugged her shoulders. "That's what she does. It's how she survives."

"By ignoring it?"

Sam rolled her eyes. "Dylan, she can't ever ignore what happened to her. It's in her thoughts all day every day, from the minute she wakes up to the minute she goes to sleep. She lives with it. She confronts it head on and refuses to let it get the better of her, but sometimes, sometimes there is a weak spot where the defences break under the pressure, even if just for a minute, and unfortunately, today, you made that happen."

Dylan said nothing more and left the kitchen, wandering upstairs to his bedroom. Thinking over his sister's words of wisdom, he realised he had two ways of looking at this—he either pressured Kyla to the point that she broke, or Kyla broke under the pressure that was already there and he happened to be there to comfort her.

"Definitely the latter," he muttered to himself.

CHAPTER 13

EIGHT P.M. SHARP, KYLA rolled up at Sam's house, feeling brand new. She'd had a long sleep until late afternoon, rolling out of bed at four thirty. After fixing herself some tangy tomato prawn pasta, she took a long bubble bath before slowly getting herself ready for her night out with Sam.

Sam all but ran out of the front door the second she heard tyres on gravel. Her new red midi dress clung to her body like a second skin. Paired with a pair of stiletto heeled black suede ankle boots and a black diamante clutch bag, she looked, and felt, like a million dollars.

As she sat down in the passenger seat of Kyla's Audi, Kyla raised an eyebrow at the rather daring keyhole neckline of her friend's dress. Stretching from the bottom of her neck to the bottom of her cleavage and yawning over the side of both boobs, it was more than a little tease.

"That's a little more revealing than normal for you," Kyla said.

Sam glanced down and patted the yawning oval shaped hole baring her chest. "I know but the rest of the dress is perfect. Maybe it's time I switched up my fashion a little. What do you think?"

Kyla tore down the driveway, the sadistic part of her wishing for the stones to hit Dylan's impeccable car. "I think you look hot as always. You could wear a bin bag and somehow make it look hot."

Sam giggled and took in Kyla's choice of dress for the evening—a forest green wrap dress with a slit up one thigh, currently revealing her left leg as she worked the clutch on her car. With a deep sweetheart neckline, it didn't leave much to the imagination for her chest either.

"Someone looks dressed to kill tonight," Sam said, winking at her friend. "Anyone would think you were on the pull."

Kyla laughed. "When you see those two, no amount of rich old men will take your interest, trust me."

Sam tipped her head back and laughed. "There is no man on this earth hot enough to pull me away from rich old men. Trust me."

Kyla grinned. "With how those two look, I'm tempted to say they're not of this earth. Just wait and see."

"Well, I came dressed for the part," Sam said smoothing her dress down. "So we'll see if they're Sam Mohun worthy."

"Oh they are," Kyla replied, clicking her tongue. "We just need to agree who takes who."

"What if they both want me?"

Kyla laughed. "Then you get both. I can find my own entertainment for the night."

Sam bit her lip. Now would be the perfect time to tell her friend she knew about her and her brother, but seeing Kyla as her normal self, not a word mentioned of her horrific day, Sam knew this was not the time to pick her battle.

"Ky," Sam said, keeping her voice quiet and calm. "Can I ask you a question?"

Kyla frowned and looked at her friend out of the corner of her eye. "Why are you being all serious? I hate it when you get like this."

"Just humour me. Please."

Kyla pressed her lips together and sighed. "Ok. Go for it."

"Do you ever think about the future? You know, old age, and wonder what it holds?"

Kyla held her breath as a shot of adrenaline burst free from her heart. "Why are you asking me that?"

Sam swore at herself mentally. She should have just kept her mouth shut. Trying her best to be casual, Sam replied, "I was just thinking about things, you know? We're thirty and—"

"I can do maths, Sam," Kyla said, her tone sharp. "And I'm perfectly aware of how old I am."

"Well, I was just thinking it would be nice to actually settle into a stable relationship, none of this chasing around on a Saturday night, looking for the next euphoric hit. Do you know what I mean?"

Kyla fixed her eyes on the road ahead, her heart pounding, her veins tingling, and her mind racing. Pressing her foot down further on the accelerator, she hurled them around the country road corners, her tyres squealing as they scrabbled for grip on the damp roads.

"I just wondered," Sam said, trying to fill the awkward silence. "If you'd had any thoughts about your life going forwards?"

Without warning, Kyla stomped on the brake pedal. Both of them jerked forwards, their seatbelts snatching back at them as the car skidded sideways across the road, its headlights pointing out over flat, empty waterlogged fields.

Glaring at her friend, Kyla stared Sam straight in the eye, and asked, "Where is this coming from?"

Sam sucked in a deep breath, trying to quickly figure out the best answer here. Ignoring the rising fear in her body, Sam mustered up her most innocent voice and replied, "I've just been thinking about things. I scrolled through Facebook earlier and saw some posts from our old school friends, Jenny, Nicole, Becky, remember them?"

Kyla scanned her eyes across Sam's face, trying to guess her next move. "Yes, of course I do."

"They're all married now. Jenny has three kids, Nicole has just gotten married in Dubai, and Becky has two kids with a doctor." Sam shrugged her shoulders. "It just made me wonder about life in general and why neither of us have that. It made me reevaluate things shall we say."

Kyla eyed Sam for several seconds, then deciding this was nothing more than Sam having her head in the clouds again, she pushed the car forwards again, straightening it up as she eased it back up to the speed limit.

"So what are you saying?" Kyla asked.

"I don't know," Sam said. "Just that it might be nice to have someone permanent as opposed to temporary. Sure, the money is good and all, but money doesn't keep me warm on a cold winter night or give me a proper soul deep laugh. It doesn't make me feel loved or appreciated, you know?"

Kyla snorted. "You know my opinion on this, Sam. Given the alternative, I'd rather stay as I am."

"But forever? Do you really think you'll be still going out on a Saturday night in another ten years, twenty years? Come on, Ky, you're worth more than that."

But not worth enough to be with your brother, Kyla thought to herself, then shook the thought away. "I don't know, Sam. It's a big thing. You know it is. I don't feel like I'm quite there yet."

Sam wrung her hands together as she said, "I mean this with *all* due respect, Ky, but it's been ten years...there's got to come a point where it gets left behind. You're living in the past, you're never in the present, and you're missing out on the future."

Kyla fell silent as she soaked in the meaning of her friend's words. As they drove closer to town, hedges and field edges turned into pavements and streetlights, then house after house, lining the streets. The unspoken words between the two hung in the air, an ever-growing palpable ball of tension that could explode at any moment.

Thinking back over the day's events, Kyla couldn't help but realise that she'd lost a day of her life to being stuck in her head and living in her past. It was only a day, but it wasn't the first. If there was one thing Kyla knew for sure, it was that time can never be gotten back. How much longer would she allow her demons to steal her life from her?

"Am I that bad?" Kyla asked, turning into a car park near the town bridge.

Sam let out a breath quietly, relieved her friend hadn't erupted like a volcano. "I'm not saying you're bad, Ky. God knows that what you've lived through is hell itself, but I want to see you happy. I want to see you *living,* not just surviving. Do you understand what I'm getting at?"

Guilt gnawed at Kyla. She knew exactly what Sam was referring to. "You mean being grateful for more than just managing to not top myself every day?"

Sam held her breath, then after a few seconds, she nodded.

Kyla parked the car and switched the engine off, her hands still on the steering wheel as she stared blankly straight ahead at the brick wall in front of her.

A good two minutes passed, in complete silence. Sam watched her friend's eyes glaze over as she zoned out, becoming lost in that dark abyss in her head again.

"Ky," Sam said, touching her forearm. "I didn't mean to upset you. I only want the best for you."

Kyla snapped back to the present and turned to look at Sam, plastering a smile on her face. "I know. I just...I don't know how to stop it, Sam. I don't know how to not let it affect every part of my life. It feels like I'm not me anymore, I'm just...I...I'm not me, *it's* me. Kyla Marshall isn't a person anymore. The thing that happened to her is her. Does that make any sense?"

Sam squeezed her arm and gave her friend a sympathetic smile. "I get it, Ky, I do. I want to help you. Will you let me help you?"

"How are you going to do that?"

Sam took a deep breath and then said, "I know about you and Dylan." Kyla's eyes widened, filling with shock and apologies. As she opened her mouth, Sam held her hand up to silence her. "Let's not get into the details of it tonight. My point of this conversation was to tell you that you're not alone. I want to see you happy, and so does Dylan. I want you to know that you can trust us both and lean on us both as much as you need, but I think it's time, Ky, to start moving on."

Kyla's head whirled with her friend's admission. Foolish didn't even come close to how she felt. She had done the one thing she prayed every day would never happen to her again—betray the trust of the person she loved most. And yet, here she was, still offering to help Kyla, be her continued crutch for her miserable existence, to drag her up out of her wallowing self-pity.

"Sam...I...I'm so sorry...we never meant it to happen, it just kinda did..."

"Save it for another day. For now, it's out in the open, you know we're both here for you, and now you can start thinking about your life in the present and the future. Yes?"

Kyla nodded. She reached over and grabbed Sam's hand. "You are the best friend anyone could ever have. I literally wouldn't be here if it weren't for you. I can never thank you enough for that. If that means I have to leave your hot brother alone, I will. Cross my heart, hope to die, I swear if you tell me to never touch him again, I won't." A cheeky grin passed over her lips as she then said, "But I can't promise to not think about our times together."

Sam laughed. "So are you two a thing? Are you official?"

Kyla shook her head. "No. I don't think he's got the nerve to ask me that again after I let loose on him earlier."

"I saw."

"What do you mean you saw?"

"Your handprint on his cheek."

Heat flushed Kyla's face. "Yeah...I might have said a few things as well. He's a good guy, Sam, and the sex, wow."

"Stop it," Sam said, unclipping her seatbelt. "I'm not having this conversation with you when the man is my brother. It's just...ewww. To me, he's a eunich, ok?"

Kyla laughed. "Believe me, he is far from a eunich."

"KY!"

Still chuckling, Kyla said, "Look, all I want to say is, I can't give him a one-word answer, click my fingers, and jump into something intense, something so committed. You know me, I'll end up feeling like a caged animal, and I'll do anything to sabotage my way out. He doesn't deserve that."

Sam nodded. "I can't disagree with that at all. What I will say is I'm so glad that you've been honest about it. Most women wouldn't think twice because they'd just see the end prize of him." Sam opened her door and then said, "Besides, you're still single which means we still get to party, right?"

Kyla undid her own seatbelt, grabbed her bag from the passenger footwell, and opened her own door. "Too damn right."

CHAPTER 14

A s THE TWO WOMEN walked towards the exit of the car park, two tall, broad male figures strode down the street on the opposite side, making a beeline for the side entrance door of *The Black Iris*, the town's only nightclub. Their faces obscured by shadows, Kyla couldn't be sure it was them, but the silhouette of their bulky bodies only brought back memories of the previous night.

"I'm pretty sure that's them," she said, pointing at them both turning down the narrow alleyway that led to the side entrance.

Sam squinted and then said, "No...it can't be. They were never that tall. Or muscly."

"I saw them last night in darkness. I'd recognise those fine male forms anywhere. I'm telling you that's them."

Sam ran her tongue over her bottom lip and giggled. "Well, I may be swayed from older men after all."

Not needing any further encouragement, Sam dragged Kyla across the road, all but running down the alley towards the club entrance. A queue had already started forming to get to the check in desk, but the two hunks they'd both seen come down here were nowhere to be seen.

"Where are they?" Sam asked, looking around the grey entrance lobby and the dozen people in front of them, waiting to pay to enter.

Kyla shrugged her shoulders. "Maybe gone for a smoke round the back?"

"Maybe. I hope they're here."

Kyla grinned. "You're like a teenager all over again. I remember Mr Duvall's social economics class and you drooling over them back then."

Sam blushed, redness sweeping from her neck right up to her forehead, flushing her tanned skin to a deep red colour. "But then I met Harry and my course of life was set. It was like comparing diamonds to cubic zirconia. A proper man next to two boys."

Kyla rolled her eyes. "Well, now the boys are men."

Sam licked her lips and gave her friend a wink. "I'll be the judge of that."

The queue moved forwards and soon enough, the pair had paid and were clattering up the stairs to head into the dark world of booze, good music, and promiscuous predators. Foggy memories clouded Kyla's mind as she thought back to the first time her and Sam had come here. So much had happened since then.

As a shudder ran down her spine, Kyla pushed her thoughts away, forcing herself to live in the present, not the past. Reaching the top of the stairs, a set of light-coloured wooden double doors stood between them and the two hot brothers.

Sam yanked the doors open, enveloping them both in thumping dance music, the bass vibrating right through their bodies. Stepping inside, they took a moment to let their eyes adjust. Almost immediately, Kyla spotted a lone figure at the bar on the other side of the room. Easily a head taller than anyone else, he was easy to spot. The broad bulk of his body and the confidence oozing from him made him stand out like an apple amongst oranges.

"Wow," Sam said, her mouth dropping open. "He is just...I don't remember either of them being this fit. Which one is that?"

"I don't know," Kyla replied. "I think..." She waited for one of the spinning lights to cast its beam over him and highlight his hair. "I think that's Adam, the blonde one."

Right on cue, as if he heard her, the lonesome brother turned around and looked right at them. Sparkling green eyes locked onto hers, flecks of gold flitting through them every few seconds, making Kyla think of jade crystal and gold. Even from this distance, his eyes were as vibrant and mesmerising as if he were stood right in front of her.

A sickening lurch clenched around Kyla's heart as their eyes met. Something whispered in the back of her mind that this was more than just her body reacting to him. As much as she appreciated his fine form, she found herself wondering what his story was, not just wanting to know what he was hiding in his boxers.

Trying to battle her thoughts and figure out why she was thinking so differently about him, Kyla didn't notice Sam pushing her way through the crowds until she had nearly reached him. Feeling like a rabbit caught in headlights, Kyla couldn't take her eyes from him. Whatever spell he had cast over her with one look broke the instant he looked down to find Sam touching his well-defined bicep.

Kyla stood, watching with curiosity, to see how he would react to Sam. As the lights twirled around, bathing the room in various shades of colour, Kyla could have sworn she saw a swirl of black dissipate through his eyes as he looked at her friend. The obvious recoil and the disdain in his features was nothing short of as if he'd just sucked on a lemon.

Taking a step towards them, Kyla jumped out of her skin when a hand touched the middle of her back. Spinning around to see whose wrist she would be breaking, she found herself stunned to see the handsome Ben Worthington stood next to her.

"Sorry," he said, withdrawing his hand and holding both up in a surrender sign. "I didn't mean to scare you." He gestured his head towards the bar. "Would you like a drink?"

She stared back at him, falling into the darkness of his eyes. Just like his brother's had done moments ago, Kyla found herself lost, hypnotised by him. His chocolate eyes speckled with glints of light, silver and purple, and Kyla couldn't help but feel like she was falling into a bottomless abyss.

"Are you ok?" he asked.

His deep voice brought her back to reality with a snap. "Yes, sorry. I just..." Heat flushed through her body, and she laughed. "Your eyes are really pretty. Have you seen the film *Men in Black*?"

Giving her a lopsided grin, he nodded. "Of course. Who hasn't?"

"You remember the bit with the cat and the galaxy on its collar? When the woman stares into it, she gets lost?"

He nodded.

"Your eyes remind me of that. I don't know why."

He leaned down and whispered into her ear, "Because I'm full of mystery, that's why."

Goosebumps popped up all over Kyla, causing her to shiver. She smiled back at him but said nothing, finding herself thinking over and over about his eyes. It unnerved her that she could be so lost in something as simple as someone's eyes. And not just one person's either, both of them.

The eyes are the window to the soul, sprang forwards from her memory. It was one of her gran's most favourite sayings about people. From the depths she had seen of Ben Worthington's eyes in just a few seconds, he had a soul buried so deep, someone would lose theirs trying to find it.

"Still want that drink?" he asked.

"Sure," she replied. "But I'm driving so just a coke for me please."

"Of course. At least I know you'll remember this in the morning and there's no risk of you throwing up on me."

Kyla laughed and allowed him to lead her to the bar. As they walked, she couldn't ignore the throng of thirsty, drunken people seeming to move around them like he was Moses parting the Red Sea. The Worthington's were a highly respected local family, but she hadn't expected anyone to remember the two nephews, nor immediately know that Ben was one of them. The change in them was just phenomenal.

The bartender ignored the people who had been stood there for minutes longer and came straight to Ben for his order, much to the disproval of those around them. Within a minute, Kyla had a pint of coke in her hand, complete with clinking ice and a blue straw. Ben bought himself a glass of whiskey—neat. As full as her own glass, Kyla started doubting her choice to entertain him in any way.

Placing his hand on the small of her back, Ben guided her towards the overcrowded booths that edged the dancefloor. Blue velvet bench seats and wooden tables were always a welcome place for drinks that got in the way of dancing, or throbbing feet that needed a brief reprieve from high heels, body weight, and twisty moves.

Kyla didn't need to look to know that there would be no spare places. These were usually the first things claimed by the early birds that came in the instant the club opened. As luck would have it, a group of young lads cleared out of one as the pair approached it.

"Perfect timing," Kyla said, grinning at him as she sat down.

"It's a knack of mine," he replied, sitting down opposite her and taking a sip of his drink.

Kyla pulled a face at him. "How can you drink that?"

He shrugged his shoulders. "The same way you drink your coke. It's refreshing, and I like the taste of it."

She burst out laughing. "I've never heard whiskey described as refreshing when it's mixed with something, let alone when it's not."

"Well," he said, lifting his glass. "Now you have. You know what they say—first time for everything."

Watching him take a proper gulp of it, Kyla shivered. "So where did you end up on your travels?"

He flashed her a dazzling smile. "Everywhere."

"That's...specific," she replied, already trying to think of how to escape him. Sam could gladly have this one. "Excellent conversation starter."

"Sorry," he said, grinning at her. "A decade of travelling makes it hard to pick out exact details."

Giving him the benefit of the doubt, Kyla tried to help him along. "Surely you must have had a favourite place? Somewhere that you really loved and didn't want to leave?"

"Oh yeah, for definite." A warm smile tugged at his pink lips. "That would be Pompeii."

Now he had her attention. Kyla couldn't help the gasp that escaped her. "You went to Pompeii?"

"Yeah. Several times," he said, shrugging his shoulders as if it were something nonchalant. "Absolutely amazing place. It's coated in this deathly silence that's somehow peaceful and beautiful. The way everything has been preserved so perfectly for all these years...words can't describe it. I'd give anything to go back."

Kyla couldn't miss the water glistening over his eyes as emotion clearly overwhelmed him. She began to wonder if it were true when people reported feeling extreme sadness when visiting places steeped in so much tragedy.

"Are you going back?" she asked.

The corners of his mouth tweaked up with a twinge of sadness. "No, not again. That's all in the past now."

Kyla wanted to dig a bit deeper into his cryptic words. What was all in the past? His travelling? Or visiting Pompeii? Seeing his eyes glaze over, something she knew all too well herself, she tried to distract him with something else. "Was there anywhere you really hated?"

Blinking the water from his eyes, he looked back at her and chuckled, before taking a large swig of his whiskey. "Plenty. There was this one particular place I couldn't stand but Adam loved it. Had to drag him away from it." Shaking his head, he finished the rest of his drink in one gulp, slamming the empty glass down on the table. "He'd go back there right now if he could."

"Where was it?"

For just a second, he hesitated. "Down under."

"Down under? As in Aus—"

A shot glass banged down on the table, making Kyla jump. "Couldn't take the heat, could you, little bro?"

The sarcasm dripping from Adam's words couldn't be missed. Adam sat down next to Kyla, sprawling his arms across the back of the seats. He glared at Ben with such hatred, Kyla squirmed in her seat, feeling like she really needed to move and let them work out whatever issue they seemed to be having but she couldn't go anywhere, trapped between a wooden board and the bulky body of Adam Worthington.

"Oh, it wasn't the heat," Ben replied, smiling back at his brother. "It was more the people."

Leaning forwards, Adam grinned. "Never did quite fit in, did you? Couldn't quite make your own way in life so you thought it'd be best to just take someone else's, hmmm?"

Kyla picked up her drink and sipped at it as she widened her eyes in shock at the two brothers jabbing at each other with words. The atmosphere between them started to charge, the air becoming almost electrified, as if taking on its own physical form.

Becoming acutely aware that things were escalating, Kyla shrunk into her corner, pressing herself up against the wooden partition as much as possible, wishing she could sidle her way out of this now.

"Well," Ben replied, his skin seeming to turn a shade of onyx. "Whose life would be better to take than that of someone who makes everyone around him miserable because he's such a selfish bastard."

As the dancing lights continued to spin around the room, casting moving shadows over everything and everyone, Kyla couldn't quite work out if the darkening of Ben's skin was from the lights or not. Narrowing her eyes to try and zoom in on him, Kyla couldn't quite register what her eyes were reporting back to her. It lookcd as if all of Ben's veins were popping from his skin, creating ridges in his blackening skin tone.

As quickly as the illusion had appeared, it disappeared, leaving Kyla wondering if Ben had snuck some alcohol in her coke after all.

"I'd love to rip your heart out," Adam said. His icy tone combined with his flat, emotionless stare sent chills down Kyla's spine. "But I prefer watching you torture yourself every day."

Kyla's eyes widened. Where the fuck was Sam? Clearly, these siblings had some deep-rooted issues that needed working out. Remembering her thought from last night of Adam most likely having a micro-penis, she bit the inside of her lip and stifled a giggle. She then realised the catch with this pair wasn't their lack of manhood but the freight train of baggage they obviously had.

"She was too good for you," Ben said, resting back against the velvet bench with a sadistic smile. "You didn't appreciate her at all."

Adam jumped up and slammed his fists down on the table. The noise reverberated around the entire building, instantly silencing everything. Music stopped. Lights stilled. People froze. Chatter ceased.

Kyla held her breath and kept her focus on the large indents his fists had left in the table wondering what the hell was happening right now.

"You know nothing," Adam said, his top lip curling back as he sneered at his brother. "You were a curse to us, always hanging around like a lost puppy. It was almost like you couldn't let me have the perfect life unless you had it as well. Even when you did the most unspeakable thing, you took the cowards way out. You couldn't even face your own reflection, could you? Did the demon within you smile back at you then, *Octavio?*"

With cat-like reflexes, Ben sprung to his feet and knocked the table clean out of the booth. Kyla shrieked and curled her legs to her chest, trying to make herself as small as possible. With clenched fists, Ben invaded his brother's personal space, literally going head-to-head with him. Kyla felt like she had been caught between two warring bulls and had no way out.

"I did it to save you the pain of doing it. You really are a stupid fuck sometimes, Azazel. Get your head out of your ass and actually pay attention to what goes on around you. Some day you might just realise people do things because they care—" Ben's chest heaved up and down with his laboured breaths "—about you."

Kyla froze. *Azazel? Who the fuck was Azazel?*

Adam threw his head back and laughed. When he looked back at his brother, Kyla's heart stopped dead. The trick of light she thought she'd seen earlier was now confirmed to her as reality. Adam's eyes were no longer the colour of jade crystal but that of the deepest shadows of night. His flesh bulged with wine-coloured veins and his teeth had turned into a mouthful of lethal canines. The energy around him pulsed with menace, the promise of blood being spilled hanging in the air.

As Kyla took in the perilous sight before her, something deep inside her stirred, coming alive. A fire she'd smothered years ago that tried relighting every day suddenly reignited with a roaring flame. Whatever betrayal Adam spoke of, Kyla understood that pain, the agony of family, of your own blood deceiving you.

Kyla knew that kind of anguish never lessened, it was just something that had to be lived with. Some days, it could be plastered over, but it could never be aired because it would never heal. Because it would never heal, it was always there, pulsing, throbbing for attention.

Watching such a magnificent, terrifying kindred spirit feel emotions just as raw as Kyla did bewitched her. But that wasn't the scary part.

The scary part was the more she watched, waiting, expecting, relishing in it, the more turned on she became.

CHAPTER 15

"**A**RE YOU OK?" BEN asked Kyla, rubbing his hands up and down her upper arms.

Kyla, completely dazed, stared back up at him, blank, numb. "What? What just happened?"

"You drove, right?" Ben said, taking her hand. "Where's your car?"

As the cold spring air bit at her skin, Kyla found herself pulled back to reality. Looking around her, she felt nothing but confused. Standing on the opposite side of the river, on the wrong side of the river to where her car sat, Kyla stared at *The Black Iris* crumpled into an unrecognisable heap of bricks.

Sirens and blue lights lit up the town like Christmas as ambulance, police, and fire crew attended the chaotic scene.

"Sam...," Kyla said, looking around her frantically. "Where is she?"

"I'm here, don't panic," Sam said, putting her hands on Kyla's shoulders from behind. "I called Dylan, he's coming to get us."

Kyla stared at the car park outside the club, where she'd parked her car. "But my car..."

"I think most of the cars in that car park have been destroyed, sadly," Adam said, stepping in front of her. "Sorry."

Kyla looked up at him, something inside her jolting when their eyes locked, unfurling a sense of unease combined with a heady mix of excitement. "Why are you saying sorry? Did you damage my car?"

Adam took a step back and grinned. "No, I most certainly did not."

"I don't remember anything," Kyla said, trying her hardest to remember what happened.

She remembered the sickening lurch in her chest when she'd locked eyes with Adam in the club, then Sam going to him. Then Ben had taken her to the bar for a drink and they'd sat down, chatting.

"I remember you banging a shot glass down on the table," she said, narrowing her eyes at Adam. "Then nothing. What happened?" She turned around to face Sam and said, "Where were you?"

"I went to the loo. The queue was huge. I'd literally just sat on the toilet when the earthquake hit."

Kyla's jaw dropped. "Earthquake?" She turned back to the club and gasped. "Is that what did that?"

Adam nodded. "It most certainly is."

Kyla shook her head, confused. "Why don't I remember anything after you putting the shot glass on the table?"

Adam shrugged his shoulders. "Everything went pretty mental. Trauma, shock."

Kyla frowned at him. "How does running out of a building cause trauma?"

"I don't know," he said, snapping at her. "Do I look like a doctor?"

Kyla raised her eyebrow at his short tone. "With that attitude, you certainly wouldn't have many patients."

Ben chuckled. Sam giggled. Adam folded his muscled arms over his chest and stared down at Kyla, his green eyes hard and impassive.

With all the lights from the emergency services in the area, the darkness of the night had been illuminated into all but daylight, allowing Kyla to study the men's features for the first time without shadows hiding them.

Dylan worked out religiously. He pushed his body to the limits, he had to for his job, and he had not an ounce of fat on him. Chiselled, ripped, whatever you wanted to call it, Dylan was poster worthy. But these guys, these guys were a whole other level. The way their clothes clung to them, highlighting every ripple and bulge, it was as if someone had photoshopped them in real life and carved them out with a paintbrush.

The way they elicited feelings with a single look only spoke of the energy surrounding them and the ease of confidence they lived with. Ben seemed rather laid back, thoughtful, and from what Kyla remembered of their conversation, he seemed sensitive and emotional.

Adam, on the other hand, seemed antagonistic and arrogant. The tilt to his chin as he glared at Kyla for challenging him spoke only of disapproval.

The roar of Dylan's car cut through the buzz of chatter from the crowd of people converging near the river. Swinging into the road full throttle, Dylan flicked the car round, sending it sideways across the street as he came to a stop next to the pavement. He jumped out of the car and ran to Sam, his eyes never leaving Kyla.

Silence surrounded everyone, only interrupted by the sound of the fan kicking in to cool his engine down, which he'd left running.

"Are you ok?" he asked Sam, finally looking down at her.

Sam nodded. "I'm fine. We're both fine. We got out, thanks to these two."

Dylan glanced up at Ben, casting his eyes down to his hand wrapped around Kyla's. When he diverted his eyes to Adam, he met a mischievous smirk and glinting green eyes.

Dylan narrowed his eyes at him for the briefest of seconds before faking a smile, giving him a single nod, and saying, "Thanks. Both of you."

"No problem at all," Ben said. "It's a shame our evening was cut short. We were having a good time, right, Kyla?"

"From what I remember," she replied, taking her hand from Ben's and walking towards Dylan.

"I can walk you to the car if you like," Ben said, taking a step forwards.

"I got her," Dylan replied, slipping an arm around Kyla's waist as she reached his side.

Sam stifled a giggle as Kyla rolled her eyes.

Kyla turned to look at Ben over her shoulder. "Thank you. See you soon maybe."

"I hope so," Ben replied, smiling at her.

Kyla turned her attention back to the car as Dylan opened the front passenger door for her. After she'd sat down and settled herself in, Dylan closed the door, gifting the two brothers one final glance.

"I'll sort myself then, yeah?" Sam said, snorting at her brother's lack of care for her door to be opened.

"You're a big girl," Dylan replied. "You can work a door."

Jogging around to the driver's side, Dylan got in and immediately feathered the throttle, revving the engine to warn gathering spectators he would be moving. As they cleared a path and allowed him through, he saw a clear, straight road and gunned it, filling the air with the noise of his V8 engine.

"Was that necessary?" Kyla asked, looking at him.

A muscle in his neck and another in his cheek twitched. His shoulders were tense, his knuckles white from where he gripped the steering wheel so tight. "You know how I drive, Kyla."

Kyla rolled her eyes. "That was nothing more than you being the last dog to piss up the lamp post. You may as well have all got your dicks out and argued over whose is bigger."

"You're lucky the cops are all busy, driving through town like that," Sam said. "I wouldn't be surprised if we get a visit tomorrow."

Dylan responded to his sister by accelerating. He hurtled them around the country roads at speeds that even Kyla wouldn't dare drive at, at least not on these roads.

Three minutes later, he pulled up outside his and Sam's house, the fan on his engine still whirring.

"Do you know what Mum and Dad will say if I tell them you drove five miles in three minutes?"

Dylan rolled his eyes. "Do you know I don't give a flying fuck?"

Sam's jaw dropped. "Wow. You really are something else, Dylan." She touched Kyla on the shoulder and said, "I would say you're welcome to stay but I don't particularly want to hear you two fucking all night and I suspect he needs some tension easing."

"It's fine," she said, patting Sam's hand. "I think he needs to mark his territory."

"I'm right fucking here," Dylan said, his voice all but a growl. He stared straight ahead, his carotid artery pulsing underneath his skin. "And if I fuck you hard enough, you might remember where you're better off."

Kyla glared at him. She knew the green-eyed monster had gotten a hold of him, real good. Still, his ego needed taking down a peg or two. "It's not about fucking me hard, Dylan. It's about fucking me right."

He turned to look at Kyla, his eyes wide with shock. "What?"

"Ok," Sam said, opening her door. "I'm out. See you two tomorrow."

Sam jumped out of the car, running for the safety of her house. As the door slammed shut, silence encompassed Kyla and Dylan, every ticking second raising the tension by ten levels.

"Are you telling me I'm not fucking you right?" Dylan asked.

Kyla bit her bottom lip and looked away. "I shouldn't have said that. I'm sorry."

"My question still stands."

"You know our sex is good, Dylan. I have no complaints."

"Good?" He snorted and floored the car down the driveway, heading back out onto the road. "Good is like a B grade, Kyla. Some would argue even a C grade. I don't want good. I want fucking mind blowing amazing. The kind of sex that you think about when I'm not there."

Wow, Kyla thought to herself. *Really dented his ego with this one.*

"And what's our sex to you?" she asked him. "Is it mind blowing amazing?"

He cleared his throat and loosened his grip on the steering wheel, his knuckles returning to a normal colour. "It is, yes."

"I can feel a but there."

"But sometimes it would be nice to not just, you know, fuck like animals that can't control themselves."

Kyla's heart started pounding. She had a horrible feeling this conversation was going to go somewhere she didn't know how to process. "What are you saying?"

Dylan let out a long breath. "I'm saying that as much as I love our banter and our power play dynamics, sometimes it would be nice to just be, you know...*nice.*"

"I've had a fucking day from hell, Dylan. Please don't push me back to where I was twelve hours ago."

Dylan nodded. "Understood. End of topic."

CHAPTER 16

THE REMAINDER OF THE two-minute journey to Kyla's house happened in utter silence. Dylan only felt a growing frustration at his desire to be with her and her lack of acceptance of it. Kyla only felt angry, furious that Dylan felt he could cage her in and take away her freedom, wanting her to rely on only him.

As he pulled up on her driveway, he let the engine run, allowing it to cool down. He'd barely put it in park before Kyla jumped out of the car, slamming the door shut. Marching to her front door, keys already in hand, she unlocked it and threw it back on its hinges.

The more she thought about this situation, and his ridiculous behaviour when picking her and Sam up, the more the blood boiled in her veins.

"You're mad, aren't you?" Dylan asked, standing in her open doorway.

Kyla threw her bag up the stairs and whirled around to face him. She glared at him, her hands on her hips, and cocked her head to one side. "You think?"

Dylan closed his eyes for a few seconds, then opened them. "What have I done now?"

"You know damn well what you did. Don't act all innocent with me. You were so rude to those guys. The guys that saved mine and your sister's lives, might I add."

"Look, you wouldn't understand it, it's a guy thing." He shrugged his shoulders. "We know when another man is sniffing around—"

"Sniffing around what, Dylan? Don't you dare say what's yours because I'm no one's."

Dylan checked back over his shoulder, looking at his car. "I need to switch the car off. I'll be back in a sec."

Kyla folded her arms over her chest and sat down on the stairs, resting her feet on the bottom step. Leaning down, she fiddled with the buckle on her high heels, trying to undo the strap.

Dylan reappeared and stepped through into the hallway, closing the front door behind him and locking it. He watched her struggle with the buckle, the delicate little pin wobbling and refusing to leave the small hole it had been shoved through in a hurry earlier that evening.

"For fucks sake," she yelled, yanking at her shoe and forcing it off her foot without undoing it.

"Do you want some help?" Dylan asked.

Kyla threw her shoe away from her, not in any intended direction, just away from her. It smacked Dylan square in the knee, but he said nothing.

"Ky?"

"No," she said, wrenching her other shoe off without undoing it. When the pin snapped, she launched the shoe at the front door, hoping the damn thing would break.

Dylan resisted the urge to smile. He knew that would be the end of him if he did. "I think someone else needs some tension easing."

Kyla snapped her eyes to his, narrowing them at him. "The only thing I need easing is the fucking pressure you're putting on me. You're like Gordon fucking Ramsey cranking the heat up in this frickin' pressure cooker, Dylan. You've got to stop it."

Dylan raised an eyebrow at her. "Ky, I've said nothing since this morning. This is all in your head."

Kyla jumped to her feet and took two steps back, standing on the step that allowed her to be at the same head height as him. "Don't you fucking gaslight me, Mohun. I am not crazy, I know damn well what's happened today."

Dylan lifted his hands in a surrender sign and took a step back. "Ky, I've said nothing more since I left you this afternoon. Have I?"

Thinking over the day's events, over and over, Kyla said nothing for a good two minutes before she realised she had to admit defeat. "No," she said, her voice quiet. "You haven't."

"So all this pressure you're feeling in your head, it's not from me, sweetheart. My foot is firmly off the accelerator. You made your feelings very clear earlier today. If all I get of you is this then I'm happy with that because it's better than nothing."

"But your behaviour earlier, Dylan, you looked like a jealous boyfriend. Those guys didn't deserve that."

Dylan sucked in a deep breath and let it out slowly as he contemplated his words, picking them very carefully. "Did

I look like a jealous boyfriend? Or did I look like a protective friend who wants something more? Kyla, you don't know those two guys. They clearly are very interested in you, and my sister, and I don't like the energy they give off. There's something not right with them. Above all else, I don't want you to end up with another Tony." He took a breath and continued. "And those guys, Ky, those guys have all the feels of Tony, and then some. So yeah, I did the whole protective thing. Not because I want them to think you're mine, but because I want them to know that if they even think of doing something to hurt you, they will have hell to pay, and then me."

Kyla let his words soak in, letting them register one by one. She didn't know what to respond to first. Her defensive, aggressive part wanted to pick at him and argue he was twisting her frame of mind, trying to manipulate her into thinking his agenda was neutral and innocent when it was the opposite.

However, her other side, the side Dylan seemed to be slowly chipping away at, believed him completely and softened even more at the sentiment his words carried.

"I don't know what to say to that," she whispered.

"I'm not asking you to say anything. I'm just asking you to listen...with this," he said, tapping his index finger over his heart.

Tears sprung to her eyes in an instant. "I can't," she whispered.

Dylan closed the gap between them, his toes meeting the bottom step. "Why not?"

Kyla closed her eyes, squeezing her tears free. "Because if I do, I'll end up broken all over again."

Dylan climbed the stairs and wrapped his arms around her, nuzzling his face into her hair. He inhaled deeply, revelling in her familiar pomegranate shampoo. "I think you're still broken, sweetheart. I think you're still waiting for someone to put you back together but you're afraid if you let them close enough to do that then they'll be close enough for you to fall in love with."

Kyla nestled her head on his shoulder, resting her left cheek on his broad muscles, staring numbly at her hallway wall. His words struck a chord deep in her soul. He was right, without a doubt he'd hit the nail on the head.

After a minute or so, she said, "I can't do that to you, Dylan."

"Do what?" He squeezed her tighter.

"I can't let you fix me."

Pressing a kiss to the side of her head, he asked, "Why?"

Lifting her head from his shoulder, she touched their noses together and replied, "Because then you'll be broken too."

Dylan couldn't ignore the stab of pain that hit him square in the chest upon hearing her words. It pained him to see her in so much agony, not just for herself, but for others too. "The only thing that could break me," he said, brushing her hair back from her face. "Is not having you in my life."

Kyla scanned his eyes, trying to read his soul through his beautiful brown windows. "I literally don't know why you stick around when I'm such an awkward bitch ninety percent of the time."

Dylan grinned at her. "Ah, is this you admitting you're awkward to test my boundaries? See how far you can push me before I snap?"

"Maybe," she said, shrugging her shoulders. "Subconsciously, I mean. I would never do such a thing on purpose."

"Of course not."

She shook her head. "Of course not."

Dylan slid one hand down underneath her ass and in one swift move, he lifted her in his arms and ran up the stairs to her bedroom. Kyla let out a shriek and started to giggle at the unexpected move. He laid her down on the bed before removing his top and his jeans in the blink of an eye, leaving just his boxers on.

Watching him come back towards her with a glint of mischief in his eyes that Kyla knew all too well, she couldn't help but think how her mood had been flipped in a matter of minutes. From the simmering rage in her veins when she first arrived home to now, Dylan had managed to turn her mood around.

And not for the first time.

Don't even go there, said the voice in the back of her mind. *You can't afford to let your guard down again.*

Dylan climbed on top of her, trapping her between his thick, muscled legs. Placing one hand either side of her head and staring down at her with a primal hunger drifting through his eyes, Kyla couldn't help but grin.

"Come on, *daddy*, I'm all yours."

Dylan smiled at her, his eyes softening. "Let's leave that out of it tonight, hmmm?"

Kyla narrowed her eyes at him, her mind racing with ideas of what their sex would be like without the fight for dominance, without her sass pushing his buttons. "And replace it with what, Dylan?"

"Just trust me," he said, leaning down towards her neck. "Lay back and relax."

Kyla closed her eyes and tried to relax. Dylan pressed soft, gentle kisses across her collarbone, slowly creeping his way to the crook of her neck. He nipped at her skin with his teeth, sending a shiver down her spine and tingles straight between her legs. As he kissed his way up her neck towards her ear, he trailed his fingertips across her stomach, sliding his hand down towards the edge of her dress.

Dylan nibbled on the bottom of her earlobe, making her gasp at the change in sensation. Potent throbs fizzed over her clit leaving her yearning for more. Lifting the bottom of her dress up, Dylan pushed the fabric up her body before removing it from her completely. Staring at her underneath him in nothing but her black lacy bra and thong, Dylan couldn't help the smile that unfolded over his face.

"You're so beautiful," he whispered, looking back at her, willing her to open her eyes.

Kyla fluttered her eyes open, her vision blurred momentarily as she came back to reality from her moment of utter decadence. She smiled at him but said nothing.

Dylan moved down to her stomach, the one area that she hated to be touched. Pressing kisses along the line of her thong from one hip bone to the other, Dylan traced his fingers up and down her inner thigh, watching with satisfaction as goosebumps followed his touch.

Kyla closed her eyes again, emptying her mind and focusing only on his touch. As he kissed his way from her thong, across her stomach, up to the bottom of her breasts, Kyla arched her back, silently begging him to take her bra off.

Dylan reached behind her back and undid her bra with one swift move before pulling it off her. He kissed between her breasts before stroking his tongue up her cleavage, watching her shiver beneath him. Tracing his tongue towards her nipple, he skirted all around the soft edge, taking delight in her rosy pink bud shrinking.

As he gripped her hard nipple gently between his teeth, Kyla revelled in the intoxicating buzz filtering through her body and let out a moan. Dylan slid his fingers underneath the fabric of her thong feeling her excitement for him already leaking out of her.

Moving his focus to her other nipple, Dylan inched her thong down her legs, removing it with his foot as he skimmed his fingers up her inner thigh, eager to feel her wet warmth around his fingers. Slipping his index and middle finger inside her, Dylan let out a groan at feeling how ready for him she was.

Kyla let out a gasp as she felt his fingers ease inside her. Feeling him slide inside her at the same time his tongue teased her nipples had her floating on a cloud of utter ecstasy.

Dylan took his hand back, smiling as Kyla let out a moan of protest. Removing his boxers in the blink of an eye, Dylan nestled himself between her legs. Still licking and nibbling at her nipple, he wrapped his arms around her back and cradled her against him as he pushed himself inside.

Kyla moaned his name in relief, her satiation on the horizon. Feeling his lazy, slow moves as he moved in and out of her, Kyla became lost in a sea of overwhelming pleasure.

Dylan took his mouth from her nipple and pressed his lips to her, slipping his tongue between her lips. Kissing her deep, entwining their tongues together in a tender, gentle dance, Kyla lost herself to him, a single thought of *This is nice* crossing her mind. The way he held her so tenderly, so carefully, whilst he caressed her in so many different ways, Kyla could feel the love pouring from him, surrounding her, enveloping her.

A barb of panic lodged itself in her heart as she remembered his words from earlier about sex being nice and not just fucking. She knew exactly what his end game was now, and she couldn't let it happen. She just couldn't. Because if he did that, if he *made love* to her, it would mean something so much more. Something she wasn't ready for.

In that single second of realisation, her pleasure didn't matter one bit. She needed out from this situation. Now.

"Dylan, stop, stop now," Kyla said, placing her hands on his chest and squirming her way up the bed, away from him.

Dylan lifted himself from her straight away, pulling out. "What's wrong?"

"I know what you're doing," she replied, scrambling into a sitting position. She grabbed the duvet and wrapped it around herself, as if it were some sort of comfort blanket. "I can *feel* it from you." She shook her head. "It's not what I want, Dylan. Please don't ruin this."

"How am I ruining this?"

"I asked you not to push me back to where you put me this morning. Don't try and wriggle out of this. I *know* what you were doing. It's not happening. You either fuck me or you don't. There's no being nice, no 'making love'," she said, motioning with air quotes.

Dylan pressed his lips together and let out a sigh. After a few seconds, he nodded. "Sure, ok, fine." He shrugged his shoulders. "But one day, Kyla, you're going to have to realise that not everything can be your way. One day you will have to give in and compromise."

A seductive smirk tweaked at her lips as she whispered, "Make me." Then she breathed, *"Daddy."*

Dylan's eyes darkened in an instant. He crawled towards her, yanking the duvet from her before grabbing her ankle and dragging her back towards him. In one swift move, he flipped her over onto her stomach, slapped her ass, and said "Ass up. Now."

Kyla bit her lip and smiled. Now he was talking. Keeping her face down on the bed, she lifted her ass up into the air, creating that perfect angle she knew he loved.

Placing his hands on her hips, Dylan thrust himself back inside her, digging his fingers into her skin as he fucked her hard and deep, just how she liked it in this position. After a minute or so, he took one hand and grabbed a hold of her hair, wrapping it around his wrist, arching her head back.

Kyla sucked in a deep breath as she quivered with excitement. Reaching down to her clit, she started playing with herself, wanting to feel as many sensations as possible, anything to remind her she was alive and didn't need to think about reality.

As the sound of their skin smacking filled the air, Kyla closed her eyes as she picked up the rhythm, chasing an orgasm. She closed her eyes as the feeling in her core built, waiting for that cascading moment where she could spiral down on a cloud of ecstasy.

Right as she tumbled over the edge, her body twitching with its sweet release, Kyla's mind filled with the image of swirling jade green eyes, blonde hair, and hard as steel muscles.

CHAPTER 17

T HE NEXT MORNING, HAPPY, satisfied, and relieved to be alive, Kyla and Sam indulged in breakfast at the café. It had to be done after a night out.

"It measured six-point-six on the Richter scale," Sam said. "We were at the epicentre apparently."

"It's crazy," Kyla replied, biting into a bit of toast. "I mean, we've felt tremors before, but nothing like that. That was something else."

Sam nodded and sipped at her tea. "That's global warming for you."

Kyla chewed her toast, glancing out of the window as a grey Porsche pulled up outside, its occupants two very familiar faces. Her jaw dropped open, almost spilling her partially eaten toast.

"Is that who I think it is?" Sam asked.

"Uh-huh," Kyla said, coming back to reality and closing her mouth. "Not only do they come back hotter than ever, but they're now rich enough to own a Porsche. Of course they fucking do."

Sam laughed. "Are you forgetting Henry had more money than our local bank branch? And they've inherited the lot."

The car doors opened simultaneously, the two hot as hell brothers climbing out of the little sports car, Adam from the driver's side. As he closed the door, he looked directly at Kyla.

A sudden dizzy fog descended over Kyla as their eyes met, making her grip onto the side of the table for some sort of stability. The feeling of déjà vu hit her like a violent of gust of wind, leaving her grabbing at pieces of memory that simply evaporated whenever she got too close.

"He's intense," Sam whispered. "And intensely hot." She looked Ben up and down as he walked to the café door, a pink blush sweeping up her neck and to her cheeks. "Ben is something else. He's like a divine hot chocolate. You know, the sugary rich cup of oh so good badness that you want to curl up with on your sofa."

Kyla laughed. "The sugary rich cup of what?"

"So good badness," Sam replied, giggling like a teenage girl. "You know, when it's so good it's bad."

"I thought you wanted Adam when you made a bee-line for him last night." Kyla's heart skipped a beat as she waited for her friend's response.

Sam lifted one shoulder in a casual shrug. "You know tall, dark, and handsome is my thing. I was just curious what Adam was like after all these years. Ben, is well...you've seen him."

Kyla laughed. "I have, yes. He's nice but I think I prefer his brother."

Sam wiggled her eyebrows up and down and grinned. "So we've decided who's having who then?"

Kyla cleared her throat and lowered her voice. "Shouldn't you be telling me to stay loyal to your brother?"

Sam let out a sigh and rolled her eyes. "Are you two official?"

Kyla shook her head.

Sam shrugged her shoulders. "Then what happens between you two is between you two. I'm not getting involved."

Before Kyla could think of a response, the café door opened and the two men breezed through with an air of authority that had the middle-aged waitress, Miranda, flustered in an instant.

Pushing her shoulder length brown hair back behind her ears, Miranda scurried out from behind the counter. "Hi, where would you like to sit?" She hurried over to the table opposite Sam and Kyla. "Is here ok?"

Adam glanced over at Sam and Kyla, a mischievous smirk tweaking at the corners of his mouth. "Well, well, well. Fancy seeing you here. If I didn't know better, I'd say you two were stalking us."

Kyla snorted. "Don't flatter yourself. And just remember who came here first. Stalkers follow, not lead."

Jade green eyes illuminated with joy, relishing a challenge. "Wow. I see someone forgot their happy pills this morning."

Ben pointed at the two empty chairs on their table of four. "Can we sit with you two?"

Sam widened her eyes at Kyla, sending a silent message of 'hell yes'.

Kyla shrugged her shoulders and took a swig of her orange juice. "Sure. I guess it's the least we owe you after saving us from the club."

"Oh, ok," Miranda said, shuffling from foot to foot. "Um, I'll be back in a minute for your orders?"

Adam nodded at her. "Sure. Thanks."

Ben pulled the chair out next to Sam, leaving Adam to seat himself next to Kyla.

Leaning back in his chair and turning to look at Kyla, Adam asked, "So who was the jealous jerk that picked you up last night?"

"That would be my brother," Sam replied, raising an eyebrow at him. "Why do you ask?"

Not even the slightest bit bothered he'd just insulted her brother, Adam looked at her and grinned. "No reason. Just good to know who's likely to try and take me on."

Sam snorted. "If Dylan wanted to take you on, he certainly wouldn't make a point of making himself memorable to you. Besides, you wouldn't even know he was there. You'd be dead before you knew it."

Adam smirked. "Is that so?"

"He's a private contractor for the military," Sam continued. "Whatever they don't want their lads to do, he does, off the books."

"I see," he replied, nodding. "I'd better sleep with one eye open then."

Ben shot his brother a glare of 'shut the fuck up' before clearing his throat and changing the topic. "I hope you both managed to sleep last night?" He turned to Kyla and asked, "Have you done anything about your car yet?"

She shook her head. "It's Sunday. My insurance company is closed. It'll be my first job tomorrow before I go to work."

"At that pub, right?" Adam asked. "That's where you work?"

Kyla nodded.

"Full time?"

"Yes. Why?"

He shrugged his broad shoulders, a speck of glee lighting up in his eyes. "Just asking. Making conversation. Nothing more."

Kyla narrowed her eyes at him. "Before you get all judgemental that I 'only work in a pub' just remember that I have bills to pay like any other person around here. Me working in a pub is no different to people working in McDonald's or a supermarket. It all helps the world go round."

Adam quirked an eyebrow up. "I never said a word."

"You didn't need to. Your face said it all."

Miranda reappeared then, asking Adam and Ben if they were ready to order. They both ordered a full English with black coffee.

Just as Miranda walked away, Kyla's phone rang. When she saw **Keith** flash up on the screen, she let out a groan of frustration.

"Everything ok?" Sam asked.

Kyla showed her who was calling. "He's going to want me to go in. I want a weekend off. Just one whole weekend. Is that too much to ask?"

Sam giggled. "He can't bear to not see you for more than twenty-four hours."

Kyla flipped the bird at her unsupportive friend before pressing the green answer button on her phone.

"Hello? Kyla?" Keith said.

"Yes, Keith. Hello."

"Um, I'm terribly sorry to intrude on your weekend but is there any chance you could cover Amy's shift today? The poor dear was in that club last night when it collapsed and she's terribly distraught. Such a near death experience has shaken the poor little lamb up."

Kyla rolled her eyes. "I was in the club when it happened, too, Keith."

"Oh, oh my goodness. How awfully frightening that must have been. Are you ok?"

"I'm alive, Keith, yes."

"Well, you have always been such a strong girl, never one to be beaten by anything, hey?" He let out a nervous laugh, all but barking into Kyla's ear. "Do you think you can be here in the next half an hour?"

Kyla let out a sigh. She didn't want to go in. Sunday's were the worst day. The pub was always overflowing with people, people who were delusional enough to think that Keith's cooking was the bees knees and his carveries were the best for miles around. That meant a sweaty, stressed Keith who would have a pub full until close. However, extra shifts meant extra cash and she definitely needed more of that.

"Do I have a choice?"

"Wonderful, Kyla. Thank you so much, dear. I'll see you soon."

Kyla ended the call and threw her phone down on the table, letting out a sigh.

"Why agree to it if you don't want to do it?" Sam asked. "You moan about him all the time but whenever he asks for more, you're always there. I don't get it? I thought you'd avoid him as much as possible."

Kyla pressed her lips together. She quickly debated whether to be honest or not. Had Adam and Ben not been present, it wouldn't have been an issue, but admitting the truth in front of two smoking hot guys was nothing short of embarrassing.

"Is it money?" Sam asked, reaching her hand across the table. "Just let me lend you some. Please."

Kyla shook her head. "No, Sam. This is my mess and my issue. I can't keep going through life relying on your handouts when I fuck things up. One day, you'll need all that money for yourself and you won't be able to give it to me so just keep it, ok?"

Sam grinned. "Exactly. So take it whilst I offer it."

Kyla smiled. "Like I said, my mess, let me figure it out. Thank you though."

Sam pushed her car keys over the table. "Take my car. I'll get Dylan to come pick me up."

"Thank you. I appreciate it."

Kyla finished her breakfast in a hurry before grabbing Sam's keys and standing to head out. Just as she stood up, Miranda came over with Adam and Ben's food.

"Thank you," Kyla said, looking between the pair. "For saving us last night. We owe you."

Adam grinned, a mischievous glint flashing through his eyes. "Yes, you do."

Kyla ignored him and headed out to work.

As soon as the café door shut, Adam said to Sam, "She's quite the fiery one, isn't she?"

Sam nodded. "She's not had an easy life so far. She is the way she is for a reason. Deep down, she has a heart of gold. You've just got to give her time to show it."

"That," Adam said, biting into a mushroom. "Sounds like a polite way of saying she's a bitch."

"Stop it," Ben said, narrowing his eyes at his brother. "Stop it now."

"I'm not wrong, though, am I?" Adam asked, looking at Sam.

"That woman is my best friend. She's my sister from another mister. She can be challenging at times, yes, but you just have to understand her, that's all. She had another setback recently and it's kind of put her on edge." Sam's eyes glistened over with water. "I'm actually quite worried about her."

"What's happened then to make her life so horrible? Her pet goldfish die or something?"

Sam glared at Adam, mentally cursing him to high heaven. "As if I'm going to tell you, an all but stranger, my best friend's deepest darkest secrets." Sam took a sip of her tea. "And especially with your attitude."

Ben placed his hand on Sam's forearm, causing her to look at him. When their eyes met, her breath hitched in her throat. Her heart started pounding as a cold sweat broke out all over her body. A shiver ran down her spine as she stared into Ben's chocolate eyes, instantly captivated by his dark, swirling depths.

"Ignore him," he said. "We just want to understand you both better, nothing more. We're going to be sticking around for a while yet and I would like to think we'll become quite good friends."

Warmth and hope flowered inside Sam, filling her stomach with butterflies. "I'd really like that," she said, her face flushing bright red.

"So please, help us understand Kyla a little better."

Sam nodded, and after a few seconds, she tore her eyes from Ben's and took a deep breath, her voice shaking as she spoke. "Kyla started dating this sleaze ball called Tony Wilkins. He's three years older than us, which to a young eighteen-year-old girl is a big deal. Not only was he highly desired by most women because his father is an MP, but he was also her first love." Sam squeezed her eyes shut and ran her hands over her face. Wringing her hands together on the table, she continued. "And he was also her last. She's damaged not only physically, but mentally, too. The last time I ever saw this attitude on her was when she had a meltdown."

"A meltdown?" Ben asked.

"As in she ended up in a straight jacket and locked in a psychiatric unit for six weeks. She's been in intense therapy and under strict psychiatric care until eighteen months ago. Everything's been fine. Medication hasn't been needed for two years. She's done so well."

Feeling overwhelmed and utterly hopeless, Sam couldn't hold back the wave of tears any longer. Ben looked to the table behind him, hoping to find some napkins. Seeing none, he glanced around quickly before deciding to manifest his own.

He slid a hand under the table. A brief, but affirmative thought of what he wanted appeared in his mind's eye. Blocking everything else out for just that second, he focused his energy on white napkins in his open hand. Hot tingles heated his palm before the white tissues pieced themselves together on top of his skin, as soft as velvet and as thick as a winter duvet.

In less than a second, he was offering the crying woman just what she needed. Grabbing at them without another thought, Sam blew her nose into one and wiped her eyes with another.

"Sorry," she said, keeping her eyes down in embarrassment. "I just don't know what to do to help her. I never expected her to go back there..."

Annoyed at the cryptic conversation and having no juicy gossip, Adam drummed his fingers on the table and sighed. "Some detail here might help, you know. All we know so far is that her first love was a politician's son and him dumping her sent her into a decade worth of pills and shrinks. Not seeing anything traumatic there, honey. Welcome to 'love'."

When he said the word 'love', Adam couldn't resist looking at his brother as he mimicked the quotes with his fingers. Love was a load of horse shit in his eyes. Ben glared at his brother, rage boiling up inside him at his blatant disregard for anyone else.

Sam snapped her head up and narrowed her eyes at Adam. When she spoke, the venom dripping from her words would have killed a King Cobra. "I never said he dumped her, asshat. This isn't some sad tale of a first love breaking up. It's so horrific you couldn't even dream this up."

"Oh, I don't know," Adam said, smiling. "I bet I know a situation or two that would fit that title."

"Really?" Ire bubbled inside her at his sheer arrogance. "You might have a pretty face, Adam Worthington, but there's definitely nothing deeper than that, is there? I bet if I had a black dog, yours would be blacker, wouldn't it? If I'd...skydived twice, you'd have done it three times—"

"Six, actually."

Sensing the tension building up inside her, Ben acted before Sam reacted. He punched his stoic brother on his upper arm, sending him sprawling across the floor.

So emotional, Sam didn't even find it funny. She simply looked at Ben and said, "Thank you."

"Would you rather go somewhere else to talk?" Ben asked, wondering if the openness of the café made her feel uncomfortable.

All too aware a break would make her chicken out of revealing her best friend's sordid tale, Sam declined. Apart from an elderly couple across the other side of the room, they were the only ones in here now the breakfast rush had left.

She took a deep breath and continued. "All was fine for the first eighteen months or so. Then he got her pregnant," she said. Folding her arms across her chest, she managed to hide her clenched fists. "And insisted she had an abortion. Kyla refused. Not because of how in love with him she was or anything like that but because she didn't see it as fair that their carelessness had created a life. To her, that gave her no right to extinguish it. She was prepared to carry to term and give it up for adoption."

The clatter of Adam's wooden chair being righted cut through her explanation. Not even daring to look at his brother for fear of exploding, Adam sat back down and forced himself to pay attention.

"But that wasn't an option for Tony's father. It would be nothing but an embarrassment for his son to have an illegitimate child palmed off on other people, so he piled on the pressure. Kyla ended up taking a couple of trips down the stairs. When that didn't work, Tony got desperate."

For the first time in years, Adam felt nausea churning around in his gut. Whatever Sam would say next would be sickening. He could feel it. He suddenly felt more than foolish for his mocking comments.

"He drugged her one night, put some rohypnol in her drink." She choked back a sob. "It was me who found her—" Sam took a deep breath before carrying on "—there was so much blood. God, I've never seen so much blood." She took a swig of tea, not caring it was cold, her throat raw with dryness. "He'd attempted to give her a home abortion with a coat hanger. Needless to say, it'd gone horrifically wrong and he'd ripped...inside. She nearly died. If I'd been any longer—"

She burst into tears. Whilst supporting Kyla through all of her turbulent times, not once had Sam given thought to the fact she might need some help too. Nightmares were frequent and always involved the sickly grey face of her best friend dying in puddles of her own blood.

Without even thinking, Ben wrapped an arm around Sam's shoulders, unsure of the best way to comfort her. Truly shocked by what he'd just heard, he looked up to see his brother's features paling. Was he actually feeling something from hearing this harrowing tale?

"Shhh," Ben said, rubbing the tops of her arms. "You weren't any longer though and you did save her. It's all ok."

Sam shook her head, tears flying from her flushed face. "No, you don't understand. That's not the worst of it."

The brothers looked at each other, exchanging part worried, part enquiring thoughts.

"It's ok," Ben said. "I get that she probably can't have kids now. Is that right?"

"No," Sam said. "I mean, yes, you're right. He did so much damage to her that it's pretty much all scar tissue in her womb. If by some miracle she ever fell pregnant, chances are she wouldn't be able to carry to term anyway." She shook her head. "But that's not what I meant. Haven't you wondered why I found her and not one of her parents?"

That queasy feeling hit Adam's gut again. He wasn't used to feeling human things...not the bad side anyway. He enjoyed pleasures of the flesh but blocked everything else out. Except, somehow, this had snuck up on him from nowhere.

"Her father skipped out years ago, but her mother...ha." Sam wiped at her eyes and sat up straight again, filling with irate defiance. "Her mother had been having an affair with Tony. Whilst Kyla was in hospital, the pair of them took off. She's never seen or heard from her mother since."

CHAPTER 18

KYLA WAS NOT IN the mood for a twelve-hour shift, and especially not twelve hours of Keith. When she arrived at the pub, as per usual for Sunday's, the place was heaving. Darren, Keith's only friend, ran around behind the bar trying to serve everyone their drinks in a timely manner.

Why Keith couldn't hire one or two more staff for weekends, Kyla couldn't fathom. Well, she could. She guessed he'd rather keep the money in his bank account ready for his monthly visits to the local prostitute. A cold chill ran down Kyla's spine as she mentally praised the woman bold enough to take Keith's clothes off for any amount of money.

Keith stayed away from Kyla for the first couple of hours, run ragged in the kitchen cooking meals, his tiny little brain couldn't cope with more than one thing at once. By three p.m., most of the lunch crowd had disappeared, no doubt to go home and collapse on the sofa. The pace would pick up again around teatime when others would come in for an evening meal.

Just before three thirty, Lloyd, Keith's most loyal customer, ordered his usual grilled sandwich and sweet potato fries. Kyla served him his usual pint of ale before heading into the kitchen to give Keith the order.

Kyla opened the kitchen door to see Keith wiping a mixing bowl clean with his finger, then sucking it. She stood staring at him, letting the door slam shut behind her. Keith jumped, dropped the bowl, and wiped his podgy little hands all over his dirty white apron.

"Kyla, dear. I didn't expect you back here with more orders just yet."

"Evidently," she replied, sarcasm dripping from that one word.

"Is there a problem?"

"Lloyd wants his ham and cheese grilled sandwich with the sweet fries."

He nodded. "I don't suppose you could be a doll could you please and get the sweet potatoes off the shelf for me?"

Kyla glanced over to her left, at the walk-in pantry. Tucked away in the far corner on the top shelf, were the sweet potatoes. Keith's short little ass would struggle without a stool, but Kyla knew there was one in there.

Still, in the spirit of being a good employee, she did as she was asked. As she grabbed hold of the plastic bag with the last of the potatoes inside, a greasy fat hand settled on her hip.

"Careful, dear. I'm behind you getting the bread."

The repulsion that swept through her at feeling his touch made her stomach swell with nausea. Fury ignited in her veins. Taking a deep breath, she closed her eyes and mentally counted to ten.

However, as Keith stretched forwards to take the bread from the lower shelf, his hand, of course, happened to slip and rest on her ass.

Her fury boiled over into rage. Three years of working for this slobbery, grimy pervert who took any opportunity to touch her came to a head.

Kyla spun around so fast, his hand ended up resting over her groin. The vile man grinned, thinking she was finally giving in to his advances. Kyla recognised the predatory glint in his eyes, abhorrent distaste flooding her in a split second.

Taking his hand, she put her thumb on his and her fingers on top of his wrist. She piled on the pressure, forcing his chubby digit back to the underneath of his forearm. He ran backwards from the pain, squealing like a pig.

But she wasn't done. The horrible creature needed to learn a lesson—this had all gone on too long.

Keith bumped into the shelving behind him, and Kyla grabbed a hold of his throat with her other hand, digging her fingernails into the sweaty folds of his neck.

"Stop fucking touching me," she said, her top lip curling back as she all but snarled. "You're nothing but a sleazy pervert with nothing better to do than wank himself silly over his bar staff. You will NOT touch me, or any of the other girls EVER again. Do I make myself clear?"

The arrogant man grinned at her. "You love it," he said, snaking his tongue out to lick his lips. "You're all little whores who love the idea of a man jacking off to thoughts of you."

Those words were nothing more than a red rag to a bull. Her body started burning with hatred, her wrath erupting inside her like a volcano ready to release its rampage. Her mind went blank as she allowed herself to be controlled only by her sheer loathing for this man.

She let go of his hand and throttled him with both hands. With all the force she could muster, she pulled him forwards a couple of inches, and then slammed him back, his egg-shaped head smashing into the thick wooden shelf. The hollow thud should have sickened her, stopped her, but instead it spurred her on.

As if he were a rag doll, Kyla did it again and again, until his beady eyes glazed over. He murmured something. A bit of drool trickled out of the corner of his mouth and his head lolled forwards.

She took a hand from his throat and using the palm of her hand on his forehead, pushed his head back upright. "Are you getting it yet, you bastard?"

His eyes rolled in the back of his head. Kyla slapped his forehead repeatedly, but she knew he was slipping into unconsciousness as he became more and more limp with each second.

She screamed her question at him over and over, only becoming more and more irate the less conscious he became.

With her throat raw and her voice breaking, Kyla didn't hear the kitchen door banging shut.

"Ok, ok, time to let go," said a deep, male voice.

Two shovel sized hands tried prising her fingers from Keith's throat but without success. Less than a second later, a whirling sensation of déjà vu had her world spinning once again. When she finally grasped a hold of reality, she found herself pinned to the stone-cold wall of the pantry, her arms outstretched like Jesus, with the handsome face of Adam Worthington mere inches from her own.

Except it wasn't Adam Worthington.

It was something else.

A gothic mix of jet-black eyes, dark purple veins, and razor-sharp canines stared back at her, shaking her into a whole new horrifying reality.

Chapter 19

Kyla didn't know how to react. That was more than an understatement. After all, what the hell do you do when the monsters from your nightmares come to life right before you? But not only are they the terrifying creatures from beyond the veil, but they're also menacingly hot and give you shivers where they really shouldn't.

With her chest heaving, her heart pounding, and her mind racing, Kyla was nothing but a jumble of every emotion going. Highly charged didn't quite describe it. Everything tingled with energy, *everything,* and she needed to do something, *anything.*

"Adam?" she breathed, raking her eyes over his demonic face. Her fuzzy memories from the previous night suddenly shattered, becoming crystal clear. "Oh my," she said, sucking in a sharp breath. "You guys caused the earthquake..."

The pressure pinning her to the wall released instantly. The monster from the deepest recesses of her dreams bolted back inside its hole in the blink of an eye. And there, just like nothing had ever happened, stood the smoking hot Adam Worthington.

"Name's Azazel," he replied. "Pleasure to meet you."

His green eyes gleamed with joy as a playful smirk unfolded over his pink lips. Kyla couldn't help but stare at his mouth, his plump silky lips just there, inviting her to touch, to kiss.

Kyla threw herself forwards, grabbing each of his cheeks with her hands and planting her lips on his. A split second of shock stunned him before he wrapped his arms around her, pressing her against him. Azazel couldn't help but groan. The feel of warmth from a woman compared to nothing else on earth, or in Hell.

As their tongues clashed together in a furious battle of passion and dominance, Kyla dropped her hands from his face and started grabbing at his shirt. Desire pooled between her legs, the intense throbbing driving her need for relief.

Azazel pushed her back against the icy wall, trapping her beneath his bulky, solid body. Kyla found the edge of his shirt and slid her hands up underneath it, letting out a moan of pleasure as she felt her way over his washboard abs.

More than satisfied with that, she moved her hands down, desperate to see what he was hiding beneath his layers.

"Wait, wait, wait," she said, turning her mouth away from him. "It's not got like spikes or anything on it, has it?"

Azazel stared back at her, disbelief running through his eyes. "What? No." He chuckled. "I'm all but perfectly human, just with a few upgrades."

Kyla delved deeper inside his jeans, feeling his long, thick length already hard. As she wrapped her hand around his cock, her thumb and fingers barely touching, she licked her lips. "Definitely with an upgrade."

As she started moving her hand up and down his length, already yearning to feel him inside her, Keith let out a groan, bringing her rather sharply back to the present.

In the mayhem of Azazel bursting in and taking Kyla away from Keith, he had collapsed into a round heap on the stone-cold floor.

"Fuck," Kyla whispered, taking her hand away from Azazel, the passionate moment gone as if a bucket of ice had been chucked over her. "I'd forgotten about him. Why did you pull me off him?"

"I couldn't just let you kill him. To take a life is something even the strongest of men struggle with."

Kyla leaned her head back against the wall, needing some solidity and some grounding of her current reality. The last few minutes had been a whirlwind.

"You're a...a thing, a monster," she said. "And you're worried about me killing someone?"

"A demon would be the correct term," Azazel replied, rearranging himself in his jeans. "And I'm not worried about him being killed, I'm worried about you being the one to do it."

Kyla frowned. "But why?"

He shrugged his shoulders. "The first kill is hard for any man. The more you do, the more numb you become to it. But for a woman? It's different. They're more emotional."

Kyla snorted. "I beg your pardon?"

A lopsided grin tugged at his lips. "Females of all species are more emotional than males. I'm afraid it's the way nature works. As a result, there is a significant impact on a woman when she kills someone as opposed to a man."

"Wow. You know nothing about me, Azazel. I can handle anything. Especially oxygen thieves like that wanker," she said, pointing at Keith.

Azazel cocked his head to one side, the grin falling from his face. "Do you really want to kill him?"

"Too right. He's a menace to society and a threat to all females."

Azazel held his hand out to her. "Come with me."

Eyeing up his offer with trepidation, wondering if there was some sort of trick or a contract she'd be unwittingly signing, Kyla finally gave in and took his hand.

Azazel led her over to Keith and bent down, pulling her down with him. "Keep your hand in mine," he said. "And close your eyes. Focus on what you can feel. Tell me what you can feel."

Kyla closed her eyes and took a deep breath. Thinking about her hand connected with Azazel's, she concentrated on her sense of touch. After a few seconds, a faint beat, a pulse, thrummed through her skin.

"I can feel a pulse, faint, but it's there."

"Good," Azazel said. "That's Keith's pulse. Now, I'm going to ask you this one last time. Do you really want to kill him?"

"He's a vile piece of shit," she replied.

"I just need to say, take it from someone who knows all too well the damage such an act can leave in your mind. Think very carefully."

Kyla opened her eyes and smiled at him. "And take it from someone who knows all too well the damage *their* kind of acts leave in your mind. Can you imagine a teenage girl trying to defend herself against him? Do you think I want to be the person who could have done something to prevent it, but didn't? I've been through a lot worse than death, trust me. Killing a piece of vermin like him won't keep me up at night."

Azazel sighed. "Has he got any family or anything?"

"Not that I know of. No woman worth her salt would marry him. As far as I know he was a runaway in London, landed a job with a brewery, and here he is."

"So he doesn't own the pub?"

Kyla shook her head.

"Very well," Azazel said. "Focus on your hand again."

Kyla didn't close her eyes this time. She watched as Azazel placed his index and middle finger on Keith's chubby neck. Seconds later, the faint pulse she'd felt through her hand stopped, just as Keith's limbs jerked violently.

"That's it," Azazel said, dropping Kyla's hand and standing up.

Kyla frowned. "What do you mean that's it?"

"He's dead."

"Just like that?"

"Pretty much."

Kyla fell silent. Her mind was at war. She should be happy Keith was no longer living. His reign of terror had ended. Every woman in the world could finally breathe a sigh of relief. But his death seemed too peaceful for what he deserved. She wanted something more fitting, more suited to her emptying herself of all her rage and giving him back the fear and pain he'd caused to others.

"Are you ok?" Azazel asked, watching her with curiosity.

Kyla nodded. "I need that power."

"No, you don't."

She laughed. "Yeah, I really do. And I think you've just volunteered for the job of teaching me."

Azazel laughed, the deep husk emanating from his chest vibrating right through her. "No, Kyla, I have not. Nice try. Whatever issues you've got going on in that pretty little head of yours need dealing with in a human way."

Thinking over his words for a moment, Kyla nodded and folded her arms over her chest with a broad grin. "You know what? You're absolutely, one hundred percent right."

CHAPTER 20

WITH A DEAD KEITH and a pub half full of customers with more expected shortly, Kyla couldn't exactly drag his body out, chop it up, and dispose of it. She would have to make a call and ride it out, hoping and praying that whatever Azazel had done to kill him wouldn't be pinned on her.

Azazel stuck around but made himself invisible, sitting on the countertop in the far corner of the kitchen, watching the drama unfold.

Kyla called the emergency services then cleared the pub out, asking people to leave in respect of Keith, which of course they did. By the time the paramedics arrived, only a few stragglers remained, hanging around on the street outside.

Kyla stayed in the kitchen, near Azazel, watching the two female paramedics work on Keith, trying to revive him. Her heart pounding and her body covered in a cold sweat, Kyla couldn't help but gnaw on her nails as her anxiety bested her. The thought that they just might bring the old pervert back to life worried her beyond belief.

Ten minutes later, they called time. "I'm terribly sorry," said the younger of the two ladies. "But he's gone. Does he have any family?"

Kyla shook her head.

"Ok. We'll call the coroner and sort things out. Are you ok? You look very pale."

Kyla nodded. "I'm ok. Do I need to stay or can I go?"

"Let me take your details first and then you can go. Is there someone to lock this place up?"

"I can come back later and do it."

The lady nodded before handing Kyla a small black notepad and a pen to write her details down on. Without a further word, Kyla ran out of there, her entire body shaking and her mind whirring with endless possibilities.

Azazel reappeared at her side as she stepped out of the back door. "Are you ok?"

"No," Kyla replied. "I'm really not."

Azazel grinned at her. "Is now the right time to say I told you so?"

Kyla turned and glared at him. "About what exactly?"

"I told you how you would feel about it, didn't I?"

Rolling her eyes, Kyla fished the keys for Sam's car out of her pocket and marched around to the car park at the front. "It's not that," she said, keeping her voice quiet. "It's the hand marks around his neck I'm worried about. That they'll come back and pin this on me somehow."

"You don't need to worry about that," Azazel said, giving her a mischievous smile. "His autopsy will find he died of a heart attack and that's that. Case closed."

Kyla stopped next to Sam's car, scanning her eyes over Azazel. "Just like that?"

"Yep. Just like that. Trust me."

Kyla snorted. "That's a funny enough phrase coming from a human, let alone a demon."

"We're not all bad, you know. The media never portrays us nicely."

"To the media, you're fictional."

He took a step closer to her, his eyes locked on hers. It was impossible to ignore the hitch in her breath and the instant spike in her heartrate as he invaded her personal space. Lowering his voice to a deep husk, he whispered, "Do I look fictional to you?"

Kyla pressed her lips together, her legs trembling, her heart racing like a herd of wild horses, and her mind running riot with the thought of kissing him again. She couldn't help but think of what she knew he was hiding in his trousers and how amazing he would feel inside her.

"No," Kyla breathed, unable to take her eyes from his. "Definitely not."

Azazel took the last of the space between them. He reached out and settled a hand on her hip, teasing up the edge of her shirt and brushing her skin ever so softly with his thumb. "Did you like what you felt earlier?"

Kyla licked her lips, a piercing throb settling straight between her legs as she thought about that moment. "Yes," she whispered.

Keeping his eyes on hers, Azazel took a second to poke around at her energy, feeling with his mental tendrils for weak spots in her mind, any softness where he might squeeze in and flood her consciousness with his thoughts.

As Kyla stared into his jade green eyes, mesmerised by the tiny gold flecks swirling around like gold dust, she found herself relaxing, a sense of warmth and happiness flowing through her.

The second she relaxed, Azazel found his in, sending his tentacles through her brain, searching for everything there was to know about Kyla Marshall. Flashes of her childhood like a picture book on hyper speed raced through his mind, memories of school, of gymnastics classes, memory after memory of Sam, teenage years, more school—her entire life to date filled his mind in less than ten seconds.

But he wasn't interested in that right now. He could sift through all of that later. What he wanted right now was her sharing his mind, knowing what he was thinking, he wanted her brain to be crammed full only with thoughts of him.

Kyla gasped as her mind filled with thoughts, thoughts of him and her having sex, hard, rough sex. An image of them both naked, hot, sweaty, flooded her brain. He grabbed her hair and wrapped it around his wrist before turning her around and bending her over, pounding into her from behind. The slapping of skin on skin resounded through her, echoing in her ears almost, as if it were really happening.

Her body reacted to the images in her mind, her desire heightening as the throbbing between her legs intensified, picturing how his girthy cock would feel sliding in and out of her, fast and deep.

The instant Azazel saw the spark of hunger in her eyes, he shut the mental image down, withdrawing from her mind as quickly as he'd invaded it.

"How...how did you do that?" Kyla asked, her voice all but a breathless whisper.

"Tricks of the trade," Azazel replied, giving her a cheeky wink.

Completely dazed, Kyla had no response. Utterly turned on and full of emotion after the day's events, she didn't know what to do for the best.

"After what you've discovered about me today, I'm amazed you're not screaming or fainted in shock," Azazel said.

Kyla shook her head. "I should be screaming or have run as far away from you possible. I mean, you are pretty scary when you, you know, turn into...that. But..."

Azazel quirked a sandy eyebrow up. "But?"

A hot blush crept up Kyla's neck, spreading over her cheeks and turning her face bright red. "But there's something about you...you fascinate me...and I..." She sucked in a breath and let it out slowly. "I can't stop thinking about you fucking me."

A triumphant grin spread over Azazel's face. "My little mind trick always works wonders. Quite realistic don't you think?"

Kyla tore her eyes from him, staring at the gravel beneath her feet. "I need to go home. I need to chill out after today."

"Would you like some company?"

Kyla bit her bottom lip. Oh, did she ever. After what she'd held in her hand less than an hour ago and the buzz currently running through her veins, Kyla wanted nothing more than to rip his clothes off and devour him entirely.

But something niggled at her. Something that told her not to be so easily manipulated, especially by a demon.

"No," she said, giving him a sweet smile. "No, thank you. Not today."

Azazel dropped his hand from her hip and took a step back. Shock and confusion spread through his eyes like wildfire as the reality of his first ever rejection settled deep in his soul, slicing him in two.

"Oh," he said, his voice quiet. "Of course, no problem. Are you ok getting home?"

Kyla smiled, wondering if this was his second attempt at trying again or if he just really wanted to be rejected again. "I can drive a couple of miles, Azazel. Thank you." She pressed the unlock button on her key and turned to open the door, then stopped. "Just wondering, your brother...is he actually your brother?"

"Unfortunately. His name isn't Ben though."

Kyla laughed. "No shit. Really?"

Azazel grinned at her. "His name is Balthazar. He's a hopeless romantic and a blundering idiot but you'll figure that out yourself soon enough."

"Well, Azazel. It's been a pleasure today, in a weird way. I'll um...I'll see you soon, maybe."

Nodding, Azazel watched her sit down in the car. "Don't worry about coming back to lock this place up. I'll sort it. Take some time and chill out. You've had a hell of a day."

"But you've got no keys," Kyla replied, frowning. A second later, she realised what she'd said and slapped a hand over her mouth, giggling. "Sorry, stupid thing to say, considering," she said, waving a hand at him.

"It'll take some getting used to. Don't worry about anything, ok?"

Kyla nodded and reached for the car door to close it. "Thanks. See you soon."

As she started the car and drove off, Azazel couldn't help but feel a little piece of himself went with her.

CHAPTER 21

A FTER KYLA LEFT, AZAZEL wandered back to the mansion, his mind in a constant whir of what he'd learned about Kyla and what had happened today.

Being a demon, Azazel had seen, heard, and done, some rather macabre things in his time, but what Tony and Kyla's mother had done to her was something that not even he would have ever thought possible. Exactly like Sam said—you couldn't even dream it up.

Aimlessly walking around the gardens, kicking bits of dirt and stones out of his way, Azazel tried to understand where his head was at and why this bothered him so much. Usually, for him, things entered his head for all of a minute, max, then left again, leaving not a trace behind. If it served him to store it to memory, then he would, but no scenarios had ever left a scar on his mind that caused him to overthink like this.

Had it been Sam that affected him? Sure, she'd been emotional recalling the story, but that hadn't bothered him. He'd had plenty of women in tears in his time and not one of them had ever broken through his steel layers to prick an ounce of sympathy from him.

By process of elimination, if it wasn't Sam's teary tale telling that had filtered through to his conscience then the only conclusion left was that it was who the tale was about.

But why? What was so special about Kyla that hearing such a ghastly story pained him so much? Somehow, she had managed to evoke emotions in him that hadn't stirred for thousands of years. How?

Amor aeternus sprung to his mind, reminding him of the spell Balthazar had cast when he brought them here.

A ball of dread settled in his stomach as his heart lurched. *No, no, no,* he thought to himself. *This isn't possible. Balthazar wanted this, not me.*

"Rule number one and the most important rule," Lucifer had said, when he'd first recruited them both. "Professional emotional detachment. Absolutely vital if you have any chance of surviving around here."

This was the first time in all his years of serving Lucifer he had ever encountered a problem with this rule. His life as a demon, up to now, had been pretty much as you'd expect—full of torture, mischief, and all things grisly. It was his job, after all. But all being said, even a demon had rules to follow. They didn't kill innocents or create chaos for anyone that didn't deserve karma.

The souls in Hell that they tortured were there for a reason and Azazel and his brother were there to carry out the sentences delivered. To inflict Hell punishments on someone who had done nothing to deserve it went against Lucifer's rules. Doing that was something not even a demon would do.

For two humans who were supposed to love and care for Kyla to actively premeditate something as horrific as what they did sparked a fire in him. For them to betray her as they did, what kind of people were they?

A slow malicious grin spread over his face as he looked forward to the day their souls ended up on his torture table. What fun he would have.

Then he questioned himself as to why he wanted revenge for Kyla. Some of the souls he'd torn to pieces were worthy of their pain—child murderers, child molesters, rapists, they all deserved whatever Azazel had done to them, but he'd never actively thought about one human and wanted to singularly avenge what happened to her specifically.

The further he delved inside himself and his thoughts, the more of a mangled mess he became. By the time the skies turned dark, the stars winking at him from the black velvet above, Azazel hadn't achieved anything other than wearing a path in the damp grass.

"Where did you go?" Balthazar asked, striding across the grass to his brother.

"I went to see Kyla at the pub."

Balthazar studied his brother for a few seconds before asking, "Why?"

Azazel shrugged his shoulders. "I don't know. When Sam told me what happened, I just couldn't stop thinking about her. Sam saying she was worried about her, I wanted to make sure she was ok. Turns out she wasn't."

"How so?"

"Well, when I found her, she was strangling her boss to death in the pantry."

Balthazar widened his eyes. "What? For real?" He then narrowed his eyes and took a step towards his brother. "Did you influence her to do that?"

Azazel shoved him in his shoulder, pushing him back two steps. "No. That's what she was doing when I turned up. Anyway, to cut a long story short, he's dead, the pub is closed, and Kyla's at home."

"Did you kill him or did she?"

"I did but only after asking her if that's what she really wanted." Azazel took a breath and thought back over that moment, the gleam in her ocean blue eyes as she'd watched Keith die gave him pleasant chills. "She's a loose cannon, Balthazar. Sam's right—she's right on the edge."

Balthazar folded his arms over his chest and grinned at his brother. "Ok. And?"

"And I'm worried."

Silence fell between the two. Balthazar stared at his older brother, waiting for the penny to drop. Azazel stared back at him, trying to figure out what his younger brother was thinking.

"What?" Azazel asked. "What are you staring at?"

"You. Wondering when you're going to figure out what's happening here."

Azazel shot his sibling a murderous glare before replying, "Fuck. Off."

Balthazar chuckled and took a step back, holding his hands up in a surrender sign. "I'm just saying the Azazel from twelve hours ago is a very different Azazel to now.

There's only one reason that's happened. Just think about it."

With that, Balthazar turned and left, heading back to the house. He walked in and headed straight to the living room, wanting to sit on the sofa in front of the fire and think back over his day with a nice glass of whiskey. He strode over to the crystal decanter in the corner of the room and poured himself a glass of much needed alcohol. He'd had a fantastic day with Sam, one he hoped would soon be repeated.

Walking over to the sofa, daydreaming of the blonde beauty, Mildred shimmered into existence in front of him just as he sat down. "Don't worry about him, he will be fine. I believe he may be facing his inner demons."

"If it weren't for the fact he's just told me he's worried about a human, and we've just managed a normal conversation without his egotistical arrogance getting in the way, I'd be laughing at you. But as it happens, I'm dumbfounded and also rather relieved that there is still a speck of humanity left in him."

Mildred chuckled. "Perhaps I need not point out that to utilise this to your advantage would be the best course of action here. Whilst he is feeling weakened and soft, use it to show him the ideals of love."

"He will only ever accept what he wants to, Mildred. And if I force it on him, he'll reject it. He needs to embrace this at his own pace."

Mildred clasped her hands together in front of her and smiled. "He may find his pace quickened by his desire for the girl. His body will react before his mind. He will need you to keep his mind up to speed."

"Noted," he said, inclining his head towards her. "Thank you."

"And I presume you are aware of the one who completes you being near?"

Balthazar nodded. "I think so. I initially thought my connection was potentially with one, but I feel a strangely strong connection to another." Balthazar thought over what had happened with Sam today, a feeling of serene peace settling inside him. "I'm certain it's her."

Mildred said, "The one often comes along from a place not expected. I am not surprised that she has appeared whilst your attention was drifting towards another. I presume you are aware of what you must do in order to confirm your suspicions regarding your demi-soul?"

Balthazar nodded and took a swig of whiskey. "I am."

"Be careful, Balthazar. Sometimes the answer we crave is not the one given."

With nothing but a sly smirk to follow her words, Mildred disappeared, leaving a thoughtful demon to wonder what exactly she meant.

Chapter 22

SHORTLY AFTER AZAZEL'S ABRUPT departure from the café, Sam had felt nothing but treacherous for revealing Kyla's secrets. How had she given all of that up so easily? Was it her need to share the burden or was it her desire for Kyla to be understood?

She could come across bold and brash, always on the offensive and cold hearted, but it all came from a place of fear. A fear of being loved and a fear of loving. The only love Kyla knew and felt comfortable with was that between her and Sam.

And Sam now felt that she had betrayed that. Sure, they'd gone to school with the Worthington brothers but they were older than them, they'd never been close, and they'd vanished for years. Spilling those things after a few hours in their company was something Sam never expected to do.

"I apologise for my brother," Ben said. "He can be a little temperamental."

"It's ok," Sam replied, wiping her nose. "No harm done."

"That's a truly horrific thing what happened to her. I can't even comprehend it. Some humans are just...I can't even think of the word."

Sam nodded. "I know." She looked down at her empty plate and saw the time ticking on to midday. "I want to get out of here. I need to walk or do something. Sorry."

Ben jumped straight to his feet. "Of course, no problem." He cleared his throat and then asked, "Would you perhaps like some company?"

Sam slid her phone in her pocket and looked up at him, taking in his handsome face and the genuine care rolling through his dark eyes. "Sure. Why not?" She scratched her head and then said, "Maybe the woods? We could have a wander around the woods?"

Ben grabbed his car keys and nodded. "That sounds perfect."

As the pair headed out towards the Porsche, Sam couldn't help but feel a tiny piece of hope settling inside her. She even wondered if her liking for older men might even be cured by this one man. But how would he feel about her and her past? About her liking for sugar daddies and wanting to be taken care of?

Ben opened the car door for her, waiting for her to settle into the seat before closing the door and heading around to his side. Sam liked that. She liked it a lot. Part of her attraction to older men was the fact that they were gentlemen and treated her like a lady, such as opening doors, pulling out chairs, walking roadside on the pavement. It was all the little things like that which added up to making Sam feel special and that's all any woman wanted, right?

"So what's your next plans?" Sam asked, as Ben reversed out onto the road. "Are you going travelling again or looking for work?"

Ben put the car into drive and headed out of town, quickly considering the best response. "I think we may travel for a couple more months then come back and settle down, I'm not sure. We're still debating whether to keep or sell the house."

"It's a beautiful house," Sam said, picturing the sprawling mansion in her mind. "It's been in your family for so long, it would be dreadful to sell it. Maybe one of you can live in it and raise your family in it."

Ben smiled. "To be fair, it would be big enough for both of us to do that. Twelve bedrooms, five bathrooms, a living room the size of an apartment, it could have two families in it. The biggest question would be whether me and Az...asshole would be able to not kill each other."

Sam giggled. "You two are very opposites from what I've seen. Like chalk and cheese. You seem very grounded, sensible, capable of empathy for sure, but your brother?" Sam let out a long breath. "He's antagonistic, lacks any emotion whatsoever, and seems like a bit of a wild card. I'm sure I don't remember him being like that at school."

Ben shifted in his seat as he smiled. "Well, who is still the same from their school days?"

"Fair point," Sam said. "Kyla said you had been to Pompeii, is that right?"

He nodded. "Several times. It's beautiful. You should definitely put it on your bucket list."

"I think half of the world is on my bucket list," she said, laughing. "St Lucia, Barbados, Mauritius, Maldives, Hawaii, Dominican—"

"All the affordable places, I see," Ben said, chuckling.

Sam shrugged her shoulders. "I have high expectations and I want a good life. What's wrong with that?"

"Nothing at all. If you know what you want, go get it. Life is too short to not do that."

"What about your bucket list?"

Ben pursed his lips for a few seconds, thinking if there was anything he could say that wouldn't make him look an idiot. All that remained on his bucket list was to settle down with a woman, live a human life, and finally end his days as he should have done two thousand years ago.

"I think we've crossed most of it off on our travels to be fair. The world is such a huge, picturesque place. I have a million memories to keep me happy every day. What else is on your bucket list? Apart from places to see, I mean."

A heated blush swept over Sam's face. She kept her eyes pinned straight ahead, watching the road in front of them. "Well, you know, the usual. Find a nice husband, have a gorgeous house, and fill it with mini me's."

Balthazar turned to look at her, his chocolate eyes filling with warmth and longing. "Really?"

Sam nodded, then dared to look at him, her cheeks still carrying a pink flush of heat. "I know it sounds silly and men don't get it but that's really all I want in life. A good, stable family and to see some luxurious places before I die. I'm quite easily pleased."

Ben looked back at the road, all too aware their turning for the woods was fast approaching. "I think that actually sounds quite nice to be honest. Simple but fulfilling." He nodded and smiled. "From a man's point of view, I think that's more than enough to be happy with."

Sam's tiny bud of hope blossomed a little, her mind already flowering with ideas of her being married to Ben and living together inside his mansion. Then it suddenly struck her that he might already have a girlfriend. *No,* she thought to herself. *He currently wouldn't be driving you to the woods if he did. Would he?*

"I'm aware of your overprotective brother," Ben said, a playful smirk tweaking up the corner of his mouth. "But are there any overprotective boyfriends I should be aware of?"

Sam shook her head, all the while smiling at how their trains of thought seemed to be aligning already. "No, I don't. What about you? Any jealous girlfriends?"

"No," he replied. "I've been single for a long time."

Excitement started unfurling in Sam's gut, endless possibilities running through her mind. Could she find herself with someone her own age after all? "It's funny where life leads you, isn't it?"

"What do you mean?"

"Well, thinking back to all those years ago at school, I never would have guessed that we'd be here right now."

"I'm a big believer in if it's meant to be, it will be."

Sam nodded. "I completely agree."

Ben pulled into the car park for the woods, various other cars with kids and dogs getting ready to set out for their own adventures. He turned the car off, jumped out, and ran around to Sam's side, offering his hand to help her out of the low sprung car.

As Sam put her hand in his, an electric shock passed between them, albeit a small one, but definitely there. Sam snatched her hand back and shook it, trying to dissipate the tingling feeling from her skin.

"Sorry," Ben said, shaking his own hand. "Not sure what that was."

Sam giggled. "It's fine. It didn't hurt, I just wasn't expecting it."

"This way," Balthazar said, gesturing his arm towards a large green sign with an up facing arrow painted on it in white.

As the two meandered around the sandy trails, making mindless chit chat about anything and everything from movies and TV shows to interests in history and music tastes, Sam couldn't ignore the feeling of belonging blooming inside her.

The more time she spent with Ben, the more comfortable and more at home she felt, almost as if she'd known him all her life and they'd never spent a day apart.

Nearing the centre of the woods, they had a choice of four different routes, or a fifth that wasn't signposted but had been worn down to the ground by the looks of the narrow dusty path winding through the spindly tree trunks.

"Which way?" he asked.

Sam pointed at the narrow trail that had no sign. "The fun way of course," she said, smiling. "I want to see if there's anything down there worth going off trail for."

Admiring her sense of adventure, Ben let her go first, following closely behind. As the path wound around trees and bushes, over fallen branches, and down a little hill, Sam began to wonder if they would end up lost.

At the bottom of the hill they'd just descended was a narrow stream, now dried up, its bed nothing but a muddy, leafy mess and the only sign it had ever existed. Sam picked her way through it before heading up the hill the other side.

Just as she neared the top of the hill, a loud bark echoed through the air. Sam turned her head to locate the source of the sound, wondering what furry friend would rush to greet her. As she looked to her left, a huge white Alsatian launched itself at her, its eyes hard and fixed on her. Sam screamed and stumbled back on instinct, forgetting she was at the top of a hill.

The dog locked onto her left forearm, snarling and grinding its teeth into her flesh. Its swinging weight toppled Sam from her feet, sending them both sprawling down the hill. As they hit the bottom, Sam fell on her back, hitting a tree stump, all the air being knocked from her body. The dog jumped straight back up and hurled itself at her, aiming for her neck.

With not even enough air to scream, she could do nothing but watch as the menacing form of the dog loomed over her. She squeezed her eyes shut, waiting for the final bite, when out of nowhere, a blur of Ben's bulky body rushed over the top of her, rugby tackling the dog away from her.

The dog growled, then whimpered and squealed before falling silent. Sam turned her head to the left, seeing Ben kneeling over the dog's limp body.

As Ben turned to look back at Sam, to check on her, he forgot himself. Seeing her emerald eyes fill with panic and confusion snapped him back to reality.

But it was too late.

Sam had seen him.

In all his demonic glory.

CHAPTER 23

B EN SCRAMBLED OVER TO Sam, his concern for her being ok overtaking his fear of her discovering his truth.

"Are you ok?" he asked, bending down at her side.

Sam sucked in a deep breath and with shaking hands, pushed herself into a sitting position. "What the..." she said, all but breathless. "What did I..." she waited a second to catch her breath "...just see?"

The image of Ben's handsome face twisted and contorted into something so evil stuck in the forefront of her mind as if she'd been staring at the sun for too long, leaving an imprint burned in her eyes that wouldn't go away no matter how many times she blinked.

Ben took her hand, stroking the back of it with his thumb. "I..." He looked away, staring at the leaves beneath him "...I have no explanation."

Sam, still dazed by images of Ben's face darkened by purple veins, jet black eyes, and a mouthful of razor-sharp teeth, stared at him as if he'd just introduced her to running water.

"Are you hurt anywhere?" Ben asked, picking her left arm up and examining where the dog had bitten her. He twisted her arm over, looking for bite marks, but he found none. "I swear that dog bit you," he said, dropping her left arm and reaching over for her right, looking again for any marks. "But there's not a scratch on you."

Sam jumped to her feet, her breath back, and feeling rather like a rabbit in headlights. She settled her hands on her hips and cocked her head to one side as she looked down at Ben. "I guess I'm not the only one keeping secrets, huh?"

Ben stood up, eyeing her with curiosity. "What do you mean?"

"Well, you're clearly not human." She looked down at her jeans and brushed some dirt off them. "And neither am I. But I guess you've figured that by now."

When she looked back up at him, her eyes sparkling with life, Ben knew he'd met his match. He knew in that instant, without a doubt, she was his missing piece, his demi-soul, the missing part that would finally complete him.

"But...but I sensed nothing," Ben said. "I should have sensed something if you weren't human. I don't get it." He frowned and shook his head, questioning his own abilities.

Sam grinned. "You first. What are you? And who are you?"

He stared at her for a good few seconds before letting out a sigh and giving in. "My name is Balthazar. My brother is Azazel, and yes, he is actually my brother. We are..." He waved his hand through the air as if searching for the right word "...demons. We work for Lucifer and once a year for three months we get a holiday." He lifted his arms up and gestured around him. "This year, we're here."

Sam nodded, pursing her lips. After a few seconds, she said, "I guess Dylan was right when he said something was off with you two."

Balthazar frowned, giving her a questioning look. "How did he know? What *are* you?"

Sam grinned. "Werewolf, of course."

Dawning realisation swirled through Balthazar's eyes. "That's why it attacked you. And you, not being a mum yet, don't have full access to your powers."

Sam shrugged her shoulders. "You got me."

The two stared at each other for a good minute or more, silent, working out their options from here. Sam couldn't help but think that actually, the universe had now given her everything she wanted—an older man, who was hot as hell, packed with money, and could give her everything she wanted. All wrapped up in this beautiful package. No compromise needed. He looked her age but had the experience and everything else of a proper gentleman.

Balthazar couldn't help but wonder how his demi-soul had turned out to be a werewolf. What a curve ball. Could he give up his supernatural life to be a part of someone else's? The supernatural world was dark and dangerous, he wouldn't be able to protect her without his magic. But if he wanted to be with her, he would have to forfeit it.

Then a dawning realisation hit him, Mildred's words coursing through his mind—*Be careful, Balthazar. Sometimes the answer we crave is not the one given.* Sam, being a werewolf, would live a much longer life than any human. At least two hundred years. If Balthazar gave up his demonic ways to be with her, he would still only get the mere eighty odd years of a human.

What a twist of fate.

"What next?" Sam asked, pulling him from his thoughts. "Are we just carrying on as normal or are we drawing a line in the sand?"

Balthazar ran a hand through his dark hair, letting out a sigh. "I'll be frank, no more airs and graces. Is that ok?"

"Sure."

"I think you're exactly who I've been looking for. When I cast the spell for our holiday this year, I asked to be brought to the place where my demi-soul is." He ran his tongue over his lips. "And I'm ninety nine percent sure that's you."

"Demi-soul? What the hell is that?"

"You might be more familiar with the term soulmate. We call it demi-soul because it's half a soul. One complete soul is made up of two halves. You are my missing half."

Sam took in his words for a few seconds before bursting out into laughter. When she saw the serious look on his face, she stopped. "Wait, you're serious?"

He nodded. "Yes."

She narrowed her eyes at him and said, "You think that's going to get me into bed or something?"

Balthazar rolled his eyes. "Please, I'm not my brother. I would wait years for that if I needed to."

Sam folded her arms across her chest and studied the handsome demon before her, trying to decide what his end game here might be. After a few seconds, she asked, "And what makes you so sure I'm who you're looking for?"

"Without risking sounding cheesy, it's the way I feel when I'm around you. Everything is as easy as breathing. I feel calm and relaxed..." He tapped his fingers over his chest "...in here. I feel like..." He took a deep breath and then said, "...I feel like I'm home when I'm around you."

Sam bit her bottom lip and soaked in his words for several seconds. In a split second she realised there was only one way to know if his words had an ounce of truth in them.

Closing the gap between them, Sam pressed herself against Balthazar's firm body, cupping his face in both of her hands. She touched her lips to his, marvelling at the soft velvet brushing back against her mouth.

Balthazar wrapped his arms around her, holding her against him with all the strength he dare without breaking her bones. When he parted his lips, Sam took her opportunity and tangled her tongue with his in a slow, passionate dance.

An involuntary shudder coursed through her body, settling in a potent bundle of tingles straight between her legs. Her mind filled with images of her stripping him naked, kissing every inch of his fine form.

Balthazar deepened the kiss, his hungry desire for her surging through him as he quickened the slow waltz of their tongues to a spicy tango. Sam took her hands from his face and wound her arms around his neck, pushing the palm of one hand against the back of his head, keeping him locked in place against her mouth.

When Balthazar let out a groan, he stilled for a second, then pulled back, moving his hands down to Sam's hips and keeping her at arms length. His chest rising and falling with short breaths, he looked at the beautiful woman before him and reminded himself that control was the key.

"What's wrong?" Sam asked, frowning. "Was it not good?"

Balthazar shook his head. "No. I mean, yes, of course it was good. I mean that's not the issue. I just need to stop before I get carried away."

Sam licked her lips. "Maybe I want you to."

"No," he said, dropping his hands and shaking his head. "No, you don't."

"You're holding back," Sam said. "What are you afraid of?"

Balthazar looked down at the floor, his mind racing with possible answers but all of them would be a lie except one. And that one was the one sentence he never wanted to utter. Ever.

"Balthazar?" Sam said, reaching out and tugging at his t-shirt. "Look, I'm sorry if I overstepped the mark. I just...if there's one thing I've learned in all my years it's that as Betty Everett once said, it's in his kiss." She touched her index finger to her lips. "And boy, can I tell a lot from yours."

"I really like you, Sam," he said, his voice almost a whisper. He lifted his gaze back to hers. "And there are lots of complications to us being together, but I don't want to face them yet until you're sure about me."

"What complications? How could anything be more complicated than you being a demon and me being a werewolf?"

Balthazar let a small smile play out over his lips. "Believe me, that's the least of our problems."

Sam let out a sigh and dropped her hand from his t-shirt. "Maybe we don't think of the bigger picture right now. Maybe we think of one step at a time."

"What are you suggesting?"

Sam shrugged her shoulders. "That just for now we get to know each other and spend time together. It can't get any more simple than that right? Then if we want to bite off a bigger chunk, we move onto the first problem."

Balthazar gave her a smile, trying his best to hide his doubts. How would this woman still want him when she learned the wicked truth?

"Hey," Sam said. "I can see you wandering off into your thoughts there. Don't do that. Unless you're a child killer or a paedophile then you don't have much to worry about."

"I'm definitely neither of those," Balthazar said.

"Good," Sam said, clapping her hands together. "Then we're all good." She held her hand out, waiting for him to take it. "Now take me back to the car and take me for a milkshake."

Balthazar gladly took her hand, gently brushing his thumb over the back of her hand. He knew these moments were precious. If she eventually rejected him, at least he would have had these moments and would have a small selection of memories to comfort him for the rest of his eternity.

CHAPTER 24

K YLA WOKE AROUND MIDNIGHT, restless, her mind full of thoughts, replaying the days events over and over again. She didn't know what was more troubling—the fact she'd killed Keith, the fact she'd discovered that demons were a real thing and she wasn't even scared, or the fact that she'd enjoyed hurting Keith so much.

Flicking the TV on to have some mindless noise in the background, Kyla almost choked when the romcom *Knocked Up* flashed onto the screen.

For years now, Kyla had harboured the bitter, sour jealousy of hating any woman who fell pregnant, wanted to be pregnant, or had been pregnant. She'd hated them all with such wrath, it almost ate her alive. Even the sight of babies and swollen bellies was something she'd only come to accept around four years ago, nearing the end of her therapy. She knew it wasn't their fault for their situation, just like it wasn't her fault for her situation.

However, for some reason, seeing Kathryn Heigl struggle through pregnancy with a man she barely knew but that still supported her filled Kyla with anger. She could feel the fire in her veins, the burning desire for revenge, justice, vengeance.

Itching from the dark energy brewing inside her, Kyla flung the covers back and hopped out of bed. Heading downstairs, she went into her kitchen and stood staring at a cupboard door, one that sat above the built-in microwave.

Full of odds and sods such as painkillers, plasters, sun-screen, air freshener refills, takeaway menus and anything else that had no other home, Kyla found herself itching to delve into the back of the cupboard, to pull out that piece of paper she knew sat in there. Waiting.

Kyla stood rock still, staring at the cupboard door, debating her options. She knew if she opened it and pulled that piece of paper out, she would spiral back to where she'd spent so long trying to claw her way out of.

But the feelings she'd experienced today, the blind rage and the power fuelling her to take Keith's life, the sheer exhilaration afterwards where she'd nearly had sex with Azazel, it all culminated into a hedonistic mix of something she wanted to revisit.

After agonising over her choices for several minutes, she threw caution to the wind and opened the cupboard door. Reaching inside, she felt around in the back right hand corner, her heart pounding as she waited to feel the crisp edge of laminated paper.

When it crunched beneath her fingertips, a wicked grin spread over her face. She'd forgotten the joy this simple piece of reprocessed tree could give her. Pulling it out, she shut the cupboard, sat on the worktop, and scanned over her words from years earlier.

Shoot.

Stab.
Hang.
Drown.
Set on fire.
Slit throat.
Slit wrists.
Cut off balls.
Feed to sharks.
Feed to crocodiles.
Feed to piranhas.
Throw from plane.
Push off building.
Poison.
Gas.
Inject air bubble.
Suffocate.

Kyla smiled, remembering when she'd written this all down and how the ideas had just flowed out of her like water. They were only the immediate thoughts of how to rob Tony of his life.

Next came a little more detail.

Torture—smash kneecaps, remove toes one by one, remove fingers one by one, pull teeth, pluck eyes, sever Achilles tendons, cut off ears, flog with barbed wire whip, pour sea salt into wounds, slit scrotum and remove testicles, bamboo canes into urethra, *research organ removal and adrenaline shots*

Lower into tank of hydrochloric acid—mechanical winch, no more than two centimetres at a time, toes first.

Bury alive in cement—will need to drug in order to handle him to relevant place *research current possibilities and security outside of daylight hours*

And then some undeveloped ideas that needed more research.

Find abandoned building, tie up, leave to starve.

Tie to train tracks.

Stake to the ground and run over with steamroller.

Tie legs to one thing (tree, building), arms to back of lorry/tractor/truck, and pull.

Feed to fighting dogs.

Pin to tree, cover in fish guts and leave for carrion birds.

Bury alive.

Feed to pigs.

Hang upside down, pierce jugular with minute hole.

The further she'd delved into murderous ways, the more enraged she'd become, caring less for detail and only chasing the agony that she could force him to endure.

However, she'd never gotten as far as to think about her mother. As Kyla stared at the paper, debating her options, she wondered if now was that time.

Today was the first time in years she'd felt alive, that the buzz in her veins filled her with something she couldn't control, where she could release herself and do as she pleased. Raging out at Keith had lessened some of her pent-up anger, relieving her to an extent that was not dissimilar to squeezing a spot. Most of the infection had been released but all that remained was an empty hole surrounded by angry, red skin harbouring an uneasy soreness beneath it.

Kyla knew, in that moment, that unless she faced and dealt with this hidden fury, her life would never be settled. At some point, it would always come back to haunt her, no matter where she was or what she did.

Her issue was how to deal with it, or rather more how to deal with other people who would have issues with her chosen methods. Nothing of her life had been easy since that day, not one bit, but her mother and Tony hadn't even given her a second thought. Did they know, or even care, that he'd ripped her to shreds, leaving her incapable of bearing children? With this darkness lingering inside her, should she even be thinking about that anyway? Thinking about murdering your own mother was hardly maternal instinct number one.

She knew right from wrong, her mother had taught her that, but then came the question of if she could teach Kyla right from wrong, how could she then do this to her?

Kyla only knew one person who could give her all the answers, who could be the balm to soothe the pain gnawing away at her. What she didn't know was how she would be received. Would they even want to speak to her?

Chewing her lip, Kyla scrolled through the contact list in her phone. When she reached the number she wanted, she hovered her thumb over it, hesitant if it would be a good idea or not. It had been nearly a decade after all.

Was a phone call after all this time really an appropriate thing to do? Or should she just go see them? Or completely forget about it?

Kyla took herself back to bed, vowing to sleep before making any big decisions. Everything was always better after a sleep.

CHAPTER 25

W HEN KYLA WOKE THE next morning, around eight a.m., her mind immediately filled with memories from last night, from her piece of paper. Feeling more than revitalised and rather excited about her new lease of life, Kyla leapt out of bed, showered, and dressed in less than half an hour.

Taking a deep breath, she grabbed the keys for Sam's car and headed out, intent on fixing this mess once and for all.

Her entire thirty-minute drive was nothing but a pounding heart, sweaty palms, and a racing mind, her knuckles white as she gripped the steering wheel. A whisper of a thought to call her insurance company sprang to mind but that was not important right now. Other things were far more pressing.

Pulling up outside the quaint, traditional English cottage, Kyla felt her mouth run dry. Ivy covered everything, including the wooden archway framing the small gate. Roses bloomed all around the busy little garden—red, white, yellow, orange, and even shades of purple. Bees and insects buzzed around on the warm spring day, surrounding Kyla in an idyllic scene. It was such a shame that her reason for being here was only shrouded in sadness and tragedy.

Minutes ticked by as she tried to find the courage to step out of the car and knock on the door. Her mind whirled with thoughts of what to even say. What if they slammed the door in her face?

Kyla closed her eyes and took a deep breath, telling herself she could do this. After everything she'd been through and battled against already, knocking on a door was nothing but a trivial task.

It's just knocking on a door. Deal with who answers it afterwards. Knock on the door first. Just knock on the door.

Repeating those words over and over to herself, she psyched herself up to the point of grabbing the car door handle. A sharp rap from her passenger window startled her, making her jump.

Staring back at her was the friendly, warm smile she'd always remembered, and she couldn't help but breathe a sigh of relief.

"Are you coming inside or cooking in your car all day?"

Tears welled in her eyes. "Hey, Gran."

Kyla couldn't help but notice that her gran looked like she hadn't aged a day. Her dark red hair now had highlights of grey here and there, her eyes had gathered a wrinkle or two at the corners, but otherwise, she still looked not a day over fifty, let alone her real age of seventy-two. She still carried the same calm, confident grace of energy that reflected in her beautiful name—Lily.

As her gran smiled at her, Kyla couldn't help but feel a stab of pain in her heart. Her piercing blue eyes were the most painful part of her gran to look at because her mother had the exact same eyes.

Walking inside the low-ceilinged kitchen, Kyla saw her grandad sat at the small round table in the middle of the room. His dark bushy eyebrows were furrowed together as he stared at the jigsaw puzzle in front of him.

Glancing quickly at the box lid, propped up against the teapot, Kyla frowned. *Since when did Grandad do jigsaw puzzles? Especially ones of Finding Nemo?*

"There is no age limit on animated characters, you know."

The familiar deep boom of his voice vibrated around her, making her smile. The fear and respect commanded from even the kindest words he spoke hadn't lessened any. His physical appearance alone frightened most people. Being over six feet tall and built like he'd been a contestant in *World's Strongest Man*, Malcolm could only be described as a big guy. His hands were almost the size of Kyla's head. How on earth her slim, petite framed gran coped with him still baffled her.

"What would you like to drink, dear?" Lily asked, heading to the old Aga on the far side of the kitchen.

Processing everything slowly, and piece by piece, it took Kyla a few seconds to register the fact that her grandad had answered her question—the one she'd asked herself in her head.

"What did you just say?" Kyla asked, trying to ignore the tremble taking over her body.

"You heard me," he said, still not looking up. Hovering a piece of puzzle over a particular spot, he slotted it in place and grinned when it fit. "Have that ya bugger." He finally looked up at his granddaughter, stretched out his shoulders, and smiled. "Been a long time, Marmalade."

An overwhelming sense of ease unfurled in Kyla's stomach. His nickname for her had been born from her love of her gran's delicious homemade marmalade. If she was ever with her grandparents, it was guaranteed she'd have sticky, marmalade covered fingers and cheeks. Memories of her childhood sprang forwards, making Kyla ache for the easy, carefree life of a child. Everything was so simple and innocent. Where and when did it all become so complicated?

"You're as capable of picking up the phone as much as I am," Kyla quipped back.

As soon as the words left her mouth, dread swirled inside her. She'd never spoken to her grandad with such a sassy attitude. She wouldn't dare.

Barely two seconds passed by, but they felt like an eternity as she waited for his reaction. When the corners of his eyes creased upwards and his chest jostled with a husky chuckle, Kyla breathed a sigh of relief.

"Well, you've certainly got some attitude on you, girl. You definitely didn't get that from your female lineage."

Kyla shrugged her shoulders. "No point in beating around the bush. I don't believe in politics."

He flickered his eyes to her gran then back to her. "Well, in that case then, let's not hold back any further. We know you've met Balthazar and Azazel. And we know this because your gran is a witch and I'm a former General of Hell."

The laugh that burst out of her was nothing but instinctual. And a pinch of nerves. Deep down, she knew it wasn't a joke. She'd been so consumed in her own mental war that processing Azazel's true identity had fallen way down the priority list.

Silence fell around them, only saved a minute or so later when her gran's old kettle whistled with its boiling water.

"Tea or coffee, dear?" she asked, giving Kyla the same loving smile she'd always known her to wear.

"I'm not thirsty, thank you."

"Water? Juice?"

Kyla shook her head.

"Oh, come on now. How about one of my special hot chocolates you used to love?"

"Gran, I'm not six anymore," Kyla said, her tone sharp and condescending. When she saw the flash of pain in her gran's eyes, her heart twisted with guilt. "I'm sorry. I just...no, thank you."

Lily glanced down at the floor and turned her back to Kyla, busying herself with making drinks for her and Malcolm.

"Sit your rude ass in that chair!" The unexpected bellow from her grandad made Kyla jump, sending her pulse racing. Fear grabbed her when she saw he'd stood up, knocking his chair over onto the porcelain tiles. "Don't you dare speak to your grandmother in that tone of voice. EVER. Do I make myself clear?"

Kyla nodded and mumbled an apology. Scuttling to the chair closest to the door, she sat down and swallowed several times in a bid to moisten her dry throat. Malcolm went over to Lily, his long legs only needing two strides to reach her side. He slipped an arm around her waist, pulled her in close to him, and kissed the side of her head.

The sweet yet simple gesture tore open a new wound inside Kyla. Why didn't she have that with someone? Why couldn't anyone love her so much as to comfort her when the smallest of things upset her day? Kyla realised then that she literally had nothing and no one.

For the first time in her life, she realised she was well and truly alone. Through all the pain, heartbreak, and tears she'd battled through, Sam had been at her side, being her rock. But in witnessing intimate moments like this between a man and a woman, it dawned on Kyla that actually, her life was more of a mess than she'd been willing to admit. She'd been shutting everyone out for nearly ten years.

Dylan could give you that, whispered the voice in the back of her mind. *Every day.*

Kyla thought about that for a second, her resolve nearly breaking as she realised that yes, he would, without a doubt.

But how long would it last? she whispered back. *Before he found someone else to give that to?*

You'll never know if you don't try.

I don't want to try if there's no certainty at the end.

The voice quietened, leaving Kyla alone in her dilemma. How on earth was she supposed to get past this?

Chapter 26

A ZAZEL LOST HIMSELF TO his thoughts for the remainder of the night. When Balthazar left him, he wandered over to the pond at the bottom of the garden, staring at the green stagnant water for hours, lost to his mind.

By the time he snapped out of it enough to head inside, he felt nothing but completely depleted of all energy. All he wanted was to shut his eyes and sleep, to feel nothing, to think nothing, just sleep all the pain away.

When he fell into bed just after midnight, Azazel soon found himself somewhere much worse than in reality.

Memories as clear as yesterday flooded his mind, images of Cassia flashed by, the clinking of swords battling, the metallic smell of blood lingering in the air, the dusty, cobbled streets being stained red, a tsunami of emotions and a lifetime of unspoken words.

The raw anguish he kept bottled up minute after minute, that weighed him down day after day, that had burned a hole in his soul for two thousand years released itself into his subconscious, poisoning his sweet relief of sleep.

Azazel tossed and turned, his body sweating as his mind took control, coating him in the bitter, empty feeling of helplessness that he so hated, that reminded him that humans are just as monstrous as the creatures born of Hell.

As images of Cassia faded away, they were replaced with pictures of Kyla, her striking blue eyes piercing something deep down in his very core. Knowing what he did of Kyla's story stirred emotions in him he'd buried long ago. Sensing her pain matched his, Azazel knew he couldn't let her fall into the downward spiral of where this dangerous mix of emotions would take her.

Fluttering his eyes open, Azazel stared straight up at the ceiling as realisation sunk into his reality. He had willingly slid down his path, grasped it with both hands and wrapped his arms around it as he found something to sink all of his wrath into. Kyla, however, didn't deserve to take the route he had taken. She was better than that.

With his heart pounding and the bed sheets sticking to his body, Azazel realised that if she was to him what he feared she was, he would need to save her. And maybe in saving her, he would save himself.

"I have warmed the shower for you," Mildred said.

Azazel startled and sat bolt upright to see the old maid stood to his left, next to the bed.

Glass of water in one hand and a navy-blue flannel in the other, she offered him a warm smile. "Go and clean yourself whilst I sort your bed."

Stepping into the steamed-up bathroom, Azazel tore off his clothes and jumped under the boiling water, letting it scald his skin. He stared at the water swirling down the plug hole, watching the dirt and grime flow away, taking all of his hatred and negativity with it.

Scrubbed raw, feeling refreshed and full of energy, Azazel turned the shower off and grabbed a fluffy white bath sheet from the heated towel rail. As he set his feet down on the marble tiles outside of the shower cubicle, in the blink of an eye he found himself flat on his back, looking up at the bright white ceiling, a yellow spotlight glaring straight into his vision.

His head had cracked the floor, splintering the expensive tile into a spider web pattern underneath him. Just as he wondered if he'd created a puddle of water he hadn't seen, a second rush of powerful, fizzing energy engulfed him, stealing all the breath from his body, making him realise how he ended up on his ass in the first place.

Every nerve ending tingled in his body and goosebumps popped up all over his skin sending his demonic senses into overdrive. He sat upright and placed his hand on the floor, palm down, spreading his fingers as widely as possible. He closed his eyes and imagined his fingers digging into the earth, desperate to find remnants of energy residue to see what had knocked him over.

But no residue was in sight.

This energy pulsed with life, warning of the power still running within it. Bright blue electric lines fizzled and crackled with raw power. He imagined himself looking down on the scene from metres above, albeit with one incredibly long arm still buried in the ground. The lightning bolt shaped lines spread as far as the eye could see, rooted into the depths of the earth and intricately woven like a spider's web.

He didn't need to touch that energy to know this was nothing but one hell of a witch. The fact their energy spread as far as any horizon meant whoever it was had to have access to higher magic. The energy stretched for miles but not a flicker of weakness could be seen anywhere in the power. That meant whoever it was could only be an elemental witch.

Azazel muttered a curse word and scrabbled to his feet. Now he and Balthazar had a problem. A real fucking problem.

Balthazar, Azazel yelled in his mind, frantically searching for his brother's mind in the darkness of the psychic world. *You there?*

I felt it too. What is going on?

We've got a big problem. Get here now.

I'm downstairs, Azazel.

Running into his room, Azazel nearly collided into Mildred who stood at the bottom of his bed, her hands clasped in front of her stomach, a sickly-sweet smile on her face.

"Did you feel that?" he asked her, heading for his draws for some clothes.

"Yes, Azazel. I did."

Her cool, calm tone sent a shiver down his spine. He turned around to see she had moved, silently, now inches from him. Her whole persona seemed lighter, as if a weight had been lifted from her shoulders. Her sparkling blue eyes seemed to glisten with life and her physical appearance seemed much more...touchable, as if she were a real person again.

"Are you alright?" he asked, narrowing his eyes at her. "You look...different."

"Good different?"

"Well, yes, if you ghosts are supposed to appear life-like."

Mildred gave him a sly smile. "Indeed. After all, what is life if not but a state of mind? A mere perception of being?"

A long pause ensued as Azazel processed her words, then, "Eh?"

"Can you imagine, Azazel, being free from your body? Having no limitations on anything you could think of?"

The wistful, faraway look in her eyes kicked Azazel's demonic senses into overload. He needed to get his clothes on, find his brother, and get a grip of whatever situation was unfolding rapidly in front of them.

CHAPTER 27

KYLA GAVE IN AND asked her gran for a hot chocolate, for old times sake. Seeing the sparkle in her eyes as she busied herself preparing it, complete with squirty cream, marshmallows, and grated chocolate, Kyla wished she could go back to being a kid again, when everything was easy, innocent, and uncomplicated.

Taking the large beige mug from her gran, Kyla licked the top of the squirty cream tower off before setting the mug down on the table.

"It looks like we've got some talking to do," Kyla said, letting out a sigh. "I have some questions."

Lily sat down in front of Kyla with a steaming cup of green tea and smiled at her granddaughter. "Fire away."

"So demons are a thing?" Kyla asked.

Lily nodded. "Yes, dear. And every other supernatural creature you can think of."

"Witches?"

"Yes, dear. Like your grandfather said, I am one."

"Werewolves?"

"Yes, dear."

"Ghosts?"

"Indeed."

"Vampires?"

"Unfortunately."

Kyla frowned, scratching her head for a second before carrying on. "Goblins?"

Lily chuckled. "Yes, dear."

"Angels?"

"Yes, dear."

"Pixies, elves, leprechauns...?"

"All of them."

"Gargoyles?"

"Very much so."

"It doesn't matter what I think of, does it? It's going to exist, isn't it?"

"Yes, dear." Lily took a sip of her tea and smiled at Kyla. "The world as you know it no longer exists now you are aware of your true place on this earth. Are you ready for that?"

Kyla frowned. "How does it not exist? I'm still here, my car is still outside, you still live in an idyllic crooked cottage, and my mother is still a bitch. I don't see what's changed?"

A twinge of pain shot across Lily's face, almost as if she cringed at Kyla's words. "Your mother is something we need to talk about."

"You need to understand, Kyla—" Malcolm said, reaching over to his wife and placing one of his hands over hers "—we had to be seen to be impartial. We couldn't choose between our daughter and our granddaughter. I hope you understand that?"

"Yes, I do, but what I don't get is why you never picked up the phone to even see how I was? You just wiped your hands of me like I was a piece of rubbish."

Lily gave her granddaughter a sad smile, her brilliant blue eyes washing with tears. "I'm so sorry, Kyla. That's not what we intended. Everything was so raw and emotional, we both agreed if we spoke to either one of you, we'd be running the risk of taking sides. If we kept out of it, it was no longer a possible complication."

A spark of irritation enflamed Kyla's insides. "Taking sides? Surely there is no side to take but mine. Do you even remember what she did to me? What he did to me?"

"I know it's a hard thing for you to understand because you're in the thick of it, dear, but you also need to see it from your mother's point of view. Since your father, she's been alone, and to finally meet someone and fall in love is a very special thing. Surely you can't deny her that?"

"HE WAS MY BOYFRIEND! How can you be ok with that?"

As soon as Kyla finished shouting, she cowered back into her chair, afraid of the repercussions from her grandad.

But none came.

Shock, confusion, and dawning reality creased her grandparent's faces into looks of regret and trepidation. They shared a look between them for several seconds, as if words were being exchanged in silence.

Lily turned to Kyla and reached over, taking her hand and squeezing it tight. "We understood that Tony was your best friend who you were madly in love with."

Kyla's mouth dropped open. "Is that what she told you?"

Malcolm cleared his throat. "They both did. They told us how they met and once you were introduced to Tony you became infatuated with him. The reason they moved and hid was to stop your advances on Tony from ruining their relationship."

Hot water pricked at Kyla's eyes, her heart pounded against her ribcage like a madman screaming to be let out of a padded cell. How could this be happening?

"But..." Kyla said, tripping over the words in her mind, too many thoughts racing around at once. "They left me to die...surely you knew that?"

"Kyla," Malcolm said, pulling his lips into a thin line. "Attempting to take your own life was a decision that you made. You shouldn't lay the blame at your mother's door for something you decided to do. You pushed them into a corner and then expected them to pull you out of it."

Ire boiling in her veins, Kyla couldn't handle this situation anymore. She shot up so fast from her chair it hurtled back against the kitchen wall, breaking apart. "Suicide?" she yelled, not caring for her grandfather's consequences at her raised voice. "You think I tried to kill myself?" All the odd pieces of the years gone by finally clicked together as to why her grandparents had remained so impartial and outside of the situation. "If you're supposed to be some super demon and a witch, how the hell could you not know the truth?"

Lily lowered her gaze to Kyla's left hand and the ring sat on her middle finger—a family heirloom she'd been given for her seventeenth birthday. "Do you ever take that ring off?"

Kyla glanced down at the double banded gold and silver ring. An amethyst and an emerald nestled against each other, two teardrops sat end to end with an intricate line of diamonds between the two. "No. I was told its pretty much indestructible, which in all fairness, I think it is, so it's always on me. It's never moved since my seventeenth birthday."

"Seventeen." Lily smirked and exchanged a saddened look with Malcolm. "Can you take it off for me please?"

Kyla frowned, confused. "I don't see what that has to do with this current situation?"

"Just humour me, please."

Kyla shrugged her shoulders and sighed. "Ok, sure. Whatever."

Taking the ring off and placing it on the table, the second Kyla's skin parted from the precious metals, Lily doubled over, screaming in agony. Malcolm scooped his wife up in his arms and cuddled her to his chest as she sobbed and writhed in pain.

Kyla looked at her grandad, her eyes widened, terror streaming through her body. "What's going on?"

Malcolm held a hand up, urging Kyla to be silent as he comforted his wife. Minutes passed by, feeling like eternity as her piercing screams lessened into sobs, then into quiet.

Eventually, after what seemed like forever but was more likely twenty minutes, Lily picked her head up and looked up at her husband. Her face streaked with tears, her cheeks flushed pink, she said, "We've been lied to, Malcolm." Lily turned to her granddaughter and said, "Tell us what happened."

Kyla looked down at the ring sat on the kitchen table. How could something so innocent be the cause of whatever had just happened? What would happen if she put the ring back on? "I started a relationship with Tony when I was eighteen. Around a year and a half later the doctors changed my pill and for whatever reason, it failed. I fell pregnant." Kyla took a breath, trying to dislodge the lump in her throat. "Tony was livid. He tried pushing me down the stairs, his dad tried paying me off to get it aborted, but I refused." Closing her eyes, Kyla wrung her hands together, willing herself not to cry. "As far as I was concerned, it shouldn't suffer because of something that was out of our control. I wanted to have it and give it up for adoption, but Tony wouldn't allow it."

Lily climbed off Malcolm's lap and moved her chair next to Kyla's. Putting her arms around Kyla's shoulders, she drew her granddaughter in close for a warm, comforting hug.

"He got desperate and one night he drugged my tea. He attempted a home abortion with a coat hanger."

Malcolm sucked in a sharp breath, muttering curse words under his breath.

"The next thing I remember is Sam and then hospital. If Sam hadn't found me, I'd have died. Whilst I was in hospital, him and Mum took off. I'm damaged forever—I can't have kids because of what he did."

"Marmalade," Malcolm said, his voice soft and quiet. "I promise you, if we'd known that, things would have been so much different." He reached out and took one of Kyla's hands. "I will rip him apart with my own hands, I swear to God."

Kyla listened to her grandad's words, fury at the lies her mother and Tony had spun bubbled in her veins, heating her skin from the inside out. Any anger she had towards her grandparents evaporated, replaced only by more disgust at her mother. A dire, burning need for justice licked at the edges of her consciousness.

Her memories from the day before came rushing forwards, black eyes, purple throbbing veins, and needle like teeth. Deep down inside her, something clicked, like an old lock finally opening for the right key.

Azazel knew her pain. Balthazar too. She'd seen them drowning in their own murky depths, desperate for freedom and resolve from their suffering. Would she end up a demon too if she carried on as she was?

In that instant, she knew she needed to sort this mess out. Once and for all.

"I think I need some air," Kyla said, letting out a long breath. "I'm a bit overwhelmed to say the least."

"Of course, dear," Lily said. "Why don't you head on home, take a bath, relax, and we'll pick this up again tomorrow?"

Nothing but numb, Kyla nodded, put her ring back on, and headed out, saying her goodbyes. She felt more than relieved that she'd repaired one part of her life at least.

The thought of going back home to an empty house after such an emotional day didn't particularly appeal to her. Starting the car, she drove down the quiet country roads, heading nowhere, just exploring whatever roads she felt like driving down. For a brief moment, she wished she had Dylan's car to properly enjoy the twisty bends and the long straights, something to give her a shot of adrenaline and make her feel alive again.

Struggling with her jumbled emotions, she found herself an hour later driving through a town called Minster Arch. Not familiar with it, she took the opportunity to distract herself and explore the peaceful, pretty community.

As she drove along a side street, she spotted a huge park, lush green grass stretching for what looked like miles. Parking the car under a thick oak tree, she turned it off and hopped out, grateful to stretch her legs.

Picnic tables were scattered around the vast expanse along with dog waste bins and normal rubbish bins. Every blade of grass looked as if it had been carefully preened, cared for, and grown. The rich, vibrant grass underneath a clear, bright blue sky almost painted the perfect scene of tranquillity.

The fresh air and warm spring breeze skimming over her skin helped settle part of the turbulence careering around inside her.

Until she heard the excited yaps of a playful dog.

Kyla loved animals, so to hear one happy brought a smile to her face. However, what she saw beyond the black and tan muscled bundle of a Dobermann stole her brief moment of bliss.

Two figures so close together it was initially difficult to determine where one started and the next began.

But the bright red hair gave it away.
It was her mother.
With Tony.
And two young girls.

CHAPTER 28

AZAZEL RAN DOWN THE stairs to his brother, his mind racing at a hundred miles an hour. As he ran into the living room, he saw his brother sat on the red velvet sofa, whiskey tumbler in hand and a pensive look across his dark features.

"We need to talk," Azazel said. He gave a quick look over his shoulder, checking Mildred wasn't hovering behind him, then turned back to his brother. "But not here."

Balthazar blinked several times, slowly coming back to reality, then turned his attention to his sibling. Downing the remainder of his alcohol, he gave a single nod, stood up, and marched towards the front door.

Following Balthazar outside, Azazel stopped for a second on the threshold, squinting his eyes at the bright sunlight. "It's daytime?"

Balthazar, several metres ahead, stopped and looked back at his brother. "Yes, Azazel. You've been asleep for nearly fifteen hours. It's not just daytime, it's early afternoon."

"That was a good sleep," he said, jogging out to meet Balthazar. "I think I could have slept some more."

"Please," Balthazar said, gesturing towards the house. "Don't let our impending doom stop you, feel free."

Azazel narrowed his eyes at him. "Since when do you do petty sarcasm?"

"Since I became fed up of this life and wanted out."

Balthazar stormed off, not sparing Azazel another glance. After a second or two, Azazel ran after him, falling into stride at his side as the two headed towards the empty pub.

"Is this going to be far enough away?" Azazel asked, eyeing up the old mansion behind the hedgerow.

"You have the same powers as me, Azazel," Balthazar said, pressing the palm of his hand over the lock on the back door. "Figure it out yourself."

The lock sprung open allowing the two demons inside the once thriving building. Balthazar took the lead, heading straight into the kitchen.

"Here will be fine," he said, looking around the empty room. "More than enough room."

Azazel frowned. "For what?"

Balthazar folded his arms across his chest and sighed, meeting his brother's eye contact. "Let's look at some cold, hard facts, shall we? Mildred is a ghost. That's cool, we've met plenty of them before. But she's a lot more 'alive' than she should be, right? And she still has access to her magick. How?"

"I'm guessing it's something to do with that damn pendant hanging around her neck," Azazel replied.

Balthazar nodded. "Exactly. We both know that ghosts aren't normally anything special in the ether world.

They're nothing more than souls without a shell, an engine with no home. And witch ghosts need a physical body to aid their soul to manifest its magickal abilities into physical form, right?"

"Right. But she's got no body. Her bones were laid to rest in the churchyard which is outside the Worthington estate. If the grave was inside the estate boundaries, you might be able to claim she's drawing energy from her brittle old twigs but it's not, so she can't be."

"Her coven," Balthazar said. "The Helios Coven, maybe they have secrets we don't know about? We know they were highly secretive and super powerful. Hence, they took it upon themselves to be judge and jury of this world and the ether world."

"Maybe," Azazel said, shrugging his shoulders. "When they had physical bodies, their power was greater than ours, but when the old hags finally gave up and died, they should be nothing more than a regular ghost."

"Or maybe we have it wrong. She's drawing energy and power from somewhere and she's using it as if she were still physically here. We need to do some research."

Azazel rolled his eyes. "I know exactly what that means. For fucks sake, Balthazar. It's such an arse ache. Do you have to?"

Balthazar ignored his brother, closed his eyes, and relaxed his shoulders. He flexed his neck from side to side and took a deep breath. Summoning objects was not an easy task. Creating them was far easier compared to mentally locating them, handling them, opening a portal, and bringing them back. Even the mind of a demon could wane under the taxing complexities of magick.

Lucifer had a vast library in the cool depths of his basement. Spanning the size of Canada, Lucifer's collection was a golden nugget of information that would never be found by anyone who didn't need to know of its existence. Because the old devil himself suffered with a severe form of OCD, of course never admittedly, the library was a breeze to navigate through.

Like a Kindle Store category selection, Balthazar pictured himself in the library and moved through the different genres and sub-genres to find himself in the right area—History > Ancient History > Magick > Witches > Covens, Societies, and Groups.

The few hundred books assigned to this specific section were going to take a while to sift through, but he could work with that when he physically had a hold of them. The driftwood shelves they were on weren't much bigger than a standard double bedroom so wouldn't take too much manhandling either.

He imagined himself growing big enough to wrap his arms around the section of books he needed. The key point to making transportation work was detail which meant he couldn't be *too* big or he wouldn't be able to transport himself. He then said out loud, "Cogito, ergo sum."

A silver speckled portal began to open in front of him, its yawning, dark abyss enticing him in. Balthazar dove through it, embracing the shelves of books he so desperately needed. Clinging on to his precious cargo as if his life depended on it, Balthazar repeated the same three words before launching himself back out of the portal.

The tiled kitchen floor absorbed the loud thud of his body hitting the floor and the clatter of books falling loose all around him. The portal closed behind him with a 'pop', as if someone had blown a bubble in their gum.

"Thanks for the help," he said, looking up at Azazel.

"You looked like you were more than coping," Azazel replied, bending down to pick up an old red book.

Balthazar jumped to his feet and looked at the heap of old books and encyclopaedias scattered everywhere. He couldn't help but smirk at the thought of Lucifer seeing his precious texts out of order and not being treated like fine china. Balthazar would suffer a punishment worse than being stuck with his obstinate brother for two millennia if Lucifer could see this.

The two siblings fell into comfortable silence as they sifted through the books, speed reading with a single touch whatever they picked up to try and locate the information they needed.

After a dozen or so books, Balthazar came across an A5 sized hardback book with a dark blue cover, the threads between the spine and the front cover the only things keeping it intact. Its pages were yellow and crinkled with age, crinkling like a crisp packet as he flushed through them. It was more than delicate.

Turning it over, he very nearly didn't even bother speed reading it until he spotted the tiniest of symbols on the back cover in the bottom left-hand corner. The tell-tale symbol of the pent-hexagram.

He frowned, his dark eyebrows furrowing together as he looked at the small book. Surely a group as powerful as The Helios Coven would warrant an entire encyclopaedia on its own, not this small, barely noticeable mere few hundred pages.

Placing his right index finger on each page, he absorbed every word within minutes, the words flooded his mind like a tsunami, speaking to him like an audible book on warp speed.

When he finished, he stood still, staring into space for several minutes whilst he contemplated what he'd just understood.

"What?" Azazel asked, glancing quickly at his brother before returning his attention to the current book in his hand. When Balthazar didn't respond, Azazel looked back at him, narrowing his eyes. "Balti? What's up?"

Balthazar, in a daze, threw the book at his brother, not caring for its fragile state now its contents were lodged in his brain, burning into his consciousness with a frightening scar.

Azazel dropped the chunky yellow hardback book he currently held, letting it drop to the floor with a smack. Catching the little book his brother just threw at him, he pushed it against the middle of his chest. Taking a deep breath, Azazel pressed it into his skin, pushing himself forwards against his own pressure. With a little more force, his skin flexed, then broke.

Corner by corner, his bronzed skin parted as if it were a seam being picked apart. Azazel winced, a stream of curse words leaving his pink lips as his face contorted with the discomfort. Once the corners were fully sunken into his flesh, he stilled for a moment, took another deep breath and held it, then closed his eyes.

Two seconds ticked by before, with one swift move, he clenched his right hand into a fist and bashed the centre of the book, sending the entire thing flying into his body.

A heavy ache settled in his chest, sticking in his throat like a bad case of indigestion. He let out an enormous burp, cracked his neck, rolled his shoulders, then flashed his brother a grin.

"Have you quite finished?" Balthazar asked, rolling his eyes. "Why you have to do that is beyond me. There are more painless ways to absorb information."

"For two reasons, dear brother. Number one," he said, flicking his left hand up into the air and holding his index finger up. "It's a challenge and I do love a good challenge. Number two," he said, putting up his middle finger. "I like the pain. It makes me feel alive. Although it's barely a tickle it does resemble something."

"And what exactly have you gained? You know how much it drains your magick and energy to absorb a physical object, let alone the risk of screwing up the fine line between blood and tissue. If you ever get that wrong, Lucifer will flail you with a blunt toothpick."

Azazel clicked his tongue against the roof of his mouth, his eyes glinting with mischief as a sadistic smile curved over his lips. "Oooo, Balti, stop talking dirty to me. It's really not an appropriate time."

Balthazar glared at his brother with a deadpan look that said nothing more than *Are you freaking kidding me?*

"Just to ease your worries," Azazel said. "I haven't forgotten that our demon blood would incinerate anything we absorbed. I've gotten it down to a fine art, we're all groovy, baby."

"Can we get back to the matter in hand?"

"Of course," Azazel said, clapping his hands together and rubbing them with glee. "It seems we have ourselves quite a problem with dear old Mildred, doesn't it?"

"Do you think the witch is working with her?"

"What makes you think that's not her?"

"It can't be. If she had that much power, she wouldn't still be a ghost, would she?"

Azazel waggled his finger at his brother, a cheeky smile on his face. "Thems the brains. That's why I'm handsome and you're clever."

"Azazel, can you just be serious for two minutes, please?"

For a brief second Azazel debated creating a countdown timer for two minutes but figured that might be a step too far right now. "Ok, fine. So, Mildred is getting help. It can't be a coincidence that this witch has appeared right as Mildred is getting more powerful. You know I don't believe in coincidences."

"Any ideas how to find the witch?"

Azazel snorted in disbelief. "Ummm, no. Why would I want to think of a stupidly insane idea that would lead me to the one thing that can whoop my ass?"

"Because you're a demon, Azazel. And we're not afraid of anything, are we?"

"Ha. You speak for yourself." Azazel folded his arms over his chest and said, "I think our history is a clear indicator that we're both afraid of a lot of things."

"What?" Balthazar frowned.

"Come on, Balthazar. We've lived in this weird relationship of ours for two thousand years. You want out so isn't it time to get it all out and bury the hatchet so to speak?"

Balthazar nearly rocked back on his heels. "I'm sorry. Did I step into a philosophy lesson by mistake?"

Completely ignoring his brother, Azazel continued on, the words in his brain just needing out. "Look, the way I see it is I was afraid of losing my identity as a man, hence being away from Cassia so much. When you took her from me—"

"Azazel—"

"WHEN YOU TOOK HER FROM ME," he said, eyeing his brother with a steely glare to keep quiet. "I was then afraid of life without her, and oddly, life without you, even though I wanted to kill you myself. Since we've been like this, I've been afraid that you would leave me, and lo and behold, you've finally taken the first step to do that."

"You hate me," Balthazar said, shrugging his shoulders. "I've had two millennia of our weird dynamics and it's time we go our separate ways. You're never going to forgive me for what I did and that's fine, I understand it, I get it. It doesn't mean we both need to suffer this forever, does it?"

"But," Azazel said, his voice dropping ten decibels. "This is better than the alternative."

Balthazar frowned. "What do you mean?"

Azazel rolled his eyes. "Jesus Christ. You're supposed to be the clever one, remember?" Azazel let out a long sigh. "Alone, Balthazar. I'm afraid of being alone."

Silence fell between the two, stretching on for painful seconds, filling the air with a heavily pregnant pause as each of them tried to work out the shifting dynamics in their relationship.

"But...but you never want me around, Azazel. You kill me at any given opportunity. I don't get it."

"If anyone knows I'm complicated, Balthazar, it's you." Azazel let out a sigh. "I don't want to be alone and I'm also absolutely petrified of finding someone I care for in case...I let them down again, in case I can't protect them when they need me, in case I can't bear the twisted turn of events life may throw at us."

Balthazar stared at his brother, dumbfounded at the words coming out of his mouth. If it weren't for the fact aliens didn't exist, he would have thought Azazel had been kidnapped, cloned, and replaced.

"And you," Azazel said, continuing his speech. "I think you're afraid that you won't ever find your own Cassia, and if you do, she won't forgive what you did. You're afraid of being stuck like this forever, and you're also afraid that I might get my second chance and you'll have to live through all of that all over again."

Balthazar stared at the floor, motionless.

"You're afraid of doing it again, aren't you?" Azazel asked, realisation dawning on him. "You're afraid of me finding happiness, and you wanting my life again, my wife, my child, your own child. You...you can't control yourself, can you?"

"I'm afraid of losing control," Balthazar whispered.

CHAPTER 29

KYLA'S HEART WASN'T JUST in her mouth, it was threatening to leap out of it. The bitter taste of adrenaline swarmed through her, fizzing her veins to the point of trembling. Sweat coated her. The deafening sound of her pulse in her ears soon turned into an annoying thump, one beat indistinguishable from the next.

Nerves, nausea, and shock collided in her stomach in a violent crash. Painful memories seized control of her conscious mind, taking her right back to that fateful moment when everything changed.

The agonising cramps in her belly started, as if Tony were ripping her apart all over again. She could feel each jerky move scraping her womb, tearing delicate tissue and an innocent little egg.

Her arms fell numb from fighting against her restraints, and she could no longer feel her feet from the merciless cable ties either. Each violent stab of pain carved a gully of woeful torment in her mind.

And his face. She could never forget his face.

The empty, blank stare of a ruthless, selfish man guarding his future. His eyes were a hollow window to a soulless creature that deserved not one more breath of oxygen.

Kyla's pleas and screams were nothing more to him than the final squeak of a mouse caught by a snake.

It was when she fell silent, shaking uncontrollably, that his focus seemed to break. The dawning realisation of what he'd done revealed his thoughts as if a pair of bleak curtains had been opened to a summers day. Like the coward he was, he dropped everything and ran.

A gentle whimper pushed Kyla back to the present moment. She blinked several times, needing a second to remember where she was. Looking down to see big brown eyes smiling up at her and the whipping of a tail showing nothing but joy, Kyla saw the Dobermann from minutes ago was now at her feet, begging for her attention.

She bent down to fuss him, and as she did, noticed a few spots of blood on the clean tarmac. Frowning, she glanced over his bulky body, wondering if he'd caught himself on a branch or something.

The friendly little guy nudged her leg with his nose and whimpered again. That was when she noticed it—the blood. It was coming from her. Her lower body was completely soaked like she'd just been dipped in a bath of blood.

Horror overtook her. Kyla bolted back to the car and opened the driver's door, not giving a second thought to her new canine pal leaping onto the driver's seat before jumping over and settling into the passenger seat. She sat down and slammed the door shut, her heart pounding, pulsing fear laced adrenaline around her body.

The car beeped at her about her seatbelt as she struck up the engine. Tyres squealed for grip as she punched the accelerator for speed. Nails dug into leather as her erratic driving had the dog scrabbling to stay upright.

None of it mattered though.

Kyla had opened Pandora's box in her mind again, everything tumbling out like intestines in a disembowelment. The thoughts spinning around and around in her mind were sending her insane and she had no idea how to stop them.

Feeling more than lost and desperate, Kyla could only go to one place to seek some sort of grounding and explanation.

By the time she pulled up at her grandparent's, she had become nothing but a quivering, sweaty wreck. She'd barely brought the car to a stop outside their little cottage before Lily and Malcolm were rushing out of the house. Kyla flung the car door open and hurled herself at her gran, needing a reassuring hug more than anything.

After a brief reassuring embrace of comfort, Kyla stepped back and looked at her grandparents whilst motioning over the lower half of my body.

"What the hell is this?" she asked, her voice trembling.

"It's the result of a living memory," Lily replied. "Come inside, dear. We have lots to talk about."

Malcolm put his hand up in a stop sign and then pointed at Kyla's feet. "Where did you get that from?"

Her canine pal, who had willingly kidnapped himself into the car, stood next to her wagging his tail. He barked at Malcolm which earned him a deep frown from the old man.

"I kinda found him. Then when this happened—" She motioned her hands over her legs "—he jumped in the car before I even realised it. I'll take him to the vets later to get him scanned for a chip."

Lily and Malcolm looked at each other. Their mouths curled upwards in a smile, but their eyes spoke of worry.

What is going on? Kyla thought to herself. *Why isn't anyone telling me any damn thing around here?*

Taking Kyla's arm, Lily walked her inside in silence.

Around an hour later, after a hot bath, Kyla wandered back into the kitchen, clean, revitalised, and ready to learn just what exactly she'd unknowingly been born into. Trotting along at her side, Kyla's new found friend stuck firmly to her side. He'd laid on the bathroom floor the entire time she'd been in the bath.

"If he's not chipped, do you think I can keep him?" Kyla asked, bending down to scratch his ears.

Lily turned around from the worktop, a jug of orange squash in her hand, the ice clinking against the sides as she walked over to the table and set it down. "Let's have a chat first," Lily said, motioning for Kyla to sit down.

Malcolm came in from the living room, his brow furrowed together, and his lips tightly pressed together. He took a seat at the table and poured the ice-cold squash into three tumbler glasses.

Lily cleared her throat, took a seat, and then said, "Well, as your grandad said, I'm a witch and he is a former General of Hell."

Kyla frowned. "Don't you mean 'was'?"

Lily smiled. "He is still a demon, my dear, with all the powers that come with it. He just doesn't live in Hell anymore to retain the title."

Kyla's mouth dropped open. "So you're like Azazel and Balthazar?"

Malcolm nodded. "Only scarier. They're babies in comparison."

"I saw them yesterday." She suddenly remembered Keith's death and froze. "Oh God, I need to see Azazel actually. He kinda did something for me."

"The perverted pub owner?" Malcolm asked, smirking. "How did you—"

"You need to learn to shield your thoughts, Marmalade."

"And how do I do that? I'm not a witch or a demon."

Lily raised an eyebrow. "Kyla, you *are* a witch."

Kyla snorted. "Sure. Of course I am."

Two serious faces stared back at her, not a flicker of jest to be seen anywhere in their emotions.

Kyla took a sip of her drink and swallowed it. "You're not joking."

Lily shook her head. "Magic abilities run in the blood, dear. It was set in stone the moment you were conceived."

"Are you telling me that my mother is a witch as well?"

Lily hesitated for a fraction of a second before nodding. "Does she use her powers?"

Lily shook her head. "She never wanted anything to do with it. Especially after your father."

A twinge of sadness struck Kyla square in the heart. "What do you know of my father?"

"We don't know much," Malcolm said. "All we know is that he wasn't human either."

Kyla's heart lurched, skipping a beat. "What was he?"

Malcolm and Lily shared a brief look before Lily leaned over and placed a hand on Kyla's forearm. "We believe he is a demon."

Sucking in a sharp breath, Kyla let that word rattle around her mind. She knew demons existed of course, her own grandad was one, and she'd very nearly had sex with one just yesterday, but to associate that word, that *creature*, with the blood running through her veins? That was a whole other level she didn't expect.

"Did Mum know? When she met him?"

Malcolm shook his head. "We believe not. Your mother never really said too much about him which leads me to believe he revealed himself to her after she fell pregnant. It was at that point her attitude towards the supernatural and magick in general really turned to something quite hateful. My guess is he tricked her and when she learned of his true nature, she felt angry and humiliated."

"But she couldn't get rid of you, dear," Lily said, squeezing Kyla's forearm. "She loved you from the minute she found out about you."

Kyla rolled her eyes. "From what then happened, Gran, she'd have been better off scraping me out."

"DON'T talk like that," Malcolm boomed, narrowing his eyes at his granddaughter. "I don't want to hear those words ever come out of your mouth again, do you understand me?"

Kyla reached down and touched the dog's head, needing something comforting. The dog nuzzled its nose against her hand in response. "It's true though, Grandad. I wouldn't have felt any pain if she'd aborted me. Look what she's since done to me. I didn't deserve that. She's not a mother. She was a womb donor, nothing more."

"Let's finish this conversation," Lily said, glancing at her husband and then at Kyla. "Before we end up saying things we don't mean. Now, moving swiftly on, let's teach you some basics of magick. Are you up for that?"

"Did you need to ask?" Kyla said, smiling.

"Not really. It's in your lineage. You'll master it easily."

"We'll see."

"You will," Malcolm said. "You have some power in your veins, Marmalade. Embrace it." He cleared his throat and then continued. "Basics one-oh-one for any supernatural creature is to shield their thoughts. Not only does it stop rather private things being sent freely to anyone close by, it also stops other supernatural beings from tracking them which means they know nothing about your true identity either."

"Is that a bad thing? Surely, it'd be nice to mix with others from your own world?"

Malcolm chuckled. "Remember, Marmalade, there is no smoke without fire. Vampires and werewolves—really not so hot on each other. Demons and witches—pretty much the same. All of the teeny-tinies hate each other—pixies, elves, fairies and so on. Ghosts hate everyone and everything. They're stuck lingering here to let go of all their rotten resentment before they can crossover for judgement. Problem is, that makes them madder and the vicious circle carries on and on."

"Oh," Kyla said, her head whirling to try and keep track of all the information. "Sounds about as fun as normal life then."

Lily gave her granddaughter a withering smile. "If anything, it's much more dangerous because of the abilities and power that we can all tap into. Humans tend to battle with words or weapons. Supernaturals are the sort to use a grenade to kill a fly."

Kyla struggled not to smile. Something within her liked that idea. It made a point, showed whose boss, and made damn sure no-one would fuck with you unless they didn't care for their life.

"So how do I shield my mind?"

Over the next hour, Lily and Malcolm taught Kyla how to envision her mind as a bank—a bank of information that needed serious, round the clock protection. She cleared a space in her mind, an empty round room so to speak, that would give her a 'working area' to deal with and process anything that needed specific attention.

Around the edges of this circular room, cast in the shadows of the single lightbulb lighting her 'work area', were the contents of her life—memories, facts, education, subconscious catchments. Kyla arranged everything like a library. Beautiful dark wooden shelves from floor to ceiling encircled her conscious 'work area'. Kyla split everything down into books, and each book then homed in the correct corresponding section.

A two-inch thick Perspex shield sealed them inside their shelves, keeping them from harm as they faced into the centre of the room. Seeing the contents of herself all around her but safely nestled away gave Kyla a sense of organisation in her jumbled mess of a mind.

Behind her mental library sat a six-inch thick wall of steel, interspersed with diamonds. To anyone attempting to hi-jack her thoughts, they would face a gleaming wall of silver thickness combined with shining gems harder than anything on earth.

Cut through that, motherfuckers.

Both of her grandparents tried their utmost to penetrate her defences, but after several unsuccessful attempts, finally gave in.

"You've done a fantastic job, dear," Lily said. "You've caught on very quickly. It will be draining for you, at first, to always be thinking of keeping your shield up, but like anything else, it will become an automatic action soon enough."

Kyla grinned, a sense of empowerment, of being unstoppable, and a force to be reckoned with filling her from top to toe. She knew in that moment that satiating her cravings for revenge would be so much fun now she had all this power coursing through her veins.

CHAPTER 30

"**A**RE YOU STAYING FOR some tea, dear?" Lily asked, looking at the clock. "I need to start preparing something to go in the oven."

Kyla looked at the time, shocked to see it was already past four o clock. She shook her head. "No, thank you, Gran. I should go home. Lots to think about and I need to ring my insurance company as well."

Lily frowned. "What for?"

"That earthquake the other night?"

Lily nodded.

"It was Azazel and Balthazar fighting. The club we were in collapsed. My car was parked outside and well, I'm sure you can imagine what a tonne of bricks does to a car."

"You tell him from me," Malcom said, rising to his feet. "He better rectify that situation real sharp before I rectify his being alive situation."

Kyla smirked. "Like he's going to believe a former General of Hell is my grandad."

"You tell him Malpass said and he'll do it, no questions asked."

"Malpass? That's such an odd name."

Malcolm chuckled. "It's quite normal compared to some of them."

Kyla laughed. "I'll let you know if your message works. I wonder if I can get an upgrade on what I had..."

"You tell him to get you whatever you want. He is capable of it. It's not like demons need money to live on earth. He can make anything happen, Marmalade. Anything."

"Noted," she said, standing up. "I'll bring my new car round when I get it."

"Where are you going?" Lily asked.

"Home?" Kyla replied, frowning.

"We still need to tell you some things before we let you loose back out there," she said, pointing at the chair. "Sit, please."

Kyla sat back down. "I'm worried. Is it something really bad?"

Lily smiled. 'No, dear. I just want you to be fully informed about some things first. You walked into this house human and you're walking out a witch. I think it's only fair you know some family history and at least have some basic control of your powers. Do you agree?"

Kyla nodded. "Of course. Maybe I could have something to eat after all?"

Lily stood up, beaming down at her granddaughter. "As if you need to ask. What would you like?"

"Well," Kyla said clearing her throat. "Seeing as we're going down the nostalgic route today, maybe a crisp sandwich?"

Malcolm let out a deep laugh. "I never thought I'd see you eating one of those again."

"They're good," Kyla said. "It's a quick easy snack when you're peckish but not fully hungry."

Lily walked over to the worktop and opened the bread bin, pulling out a fresh crusty loaf of tiger bread. She sliced off two thick pieces, lathered them in creamy butter, and then presented them on a plate to Kyla complete with a packet of cheese and onion, and a packet of salt and vinegar crisps.

Kyla's mouth filled with saliva. "This is going to be the best thing I've eaten in years."

Lily laughed as she sat back down. "So long as you're happy, dear, that's all I care about."

"You tell that fool from me," Malcolm said. "He'd better take you somewhere decent for a proper meal either before or after he gets you that car."

"I think decent to him will mean KFC, Grandad," Kyla replied, opening the packets of crisps.

"He'll know exactly what I mean when you tell him who said it."

Kyla grinned. "I'm curious how much weight your name has to it." She crushed the crisps in their packets and then tipped them out onto one of the slices of bread. "I think I'm going to really enjoy my next conversation with him."

Malcolm chuckled. "That's my girl."

Kyla put the other slice of bread on top of her mountain of crisps and pressed it down, enjoying the sound of the crunch as the crisps were squashed between the two pieces of bread. When she took her first bite, she closed her eyes and let out a groan of relief. The combination of soft fluffy bread smeared in milky butter with the crisp crunch of the crisps had Kyla floating on cloud nine.

"Oh my God," she said, still chewing. "This is the best thing ever."

Lily poured herself another glass of squash. "Good, I'm glad you like it." She took a mouthful of drink and set the glass back down. "Now, first things first." She looked down at the dog. "Your new little friend there doesn't need taking to the vets. They won't find a microchip nor a home. He is yours."

Kyla swallowed her food and then frowned. "How do you know that?"

"He's your familiar, Kyla, like a guardian spirit. Familiars always appear to their witches in times of great need. Your living memory today was that catalyst."

Kyla took another bite of her sandwich and mulled over her gran's words as she chewed. "So," she said, finishing her mouthful. "Why did he not appear when Tony was doing...you know, what he did? Why did he not appear when I had years of depression and struggling to even bear the weight of living? Why now?"

"It's not quite that simple with familiars, dear. They are summoned through the presence of magic and fear." Lily looked down at the ring on Kyla's finger. "That has certainly been a hindrance in terms of your familiar making an appearance but also the fact that you knew nothing about your powers. You have to be accepting of your place in the world and ready to start your journey as a witch before you can accept the aid that comes your way. Does that make sense?"

Kyla nodded and glanced down at the ring. "What is the deal with this thing anyway?"

A small smile tweaked at Lily's mouth. "Are you ready for a history lesson?"

"Always."

"Back in the thirteen hundreds we had an ancestor by the name of Alice Kyteler. Alice lived in Kilkenny in Ireland. There are obviously no photographs of her but what we do know of her is that she had our trademark fiery red hair and the personality to match."

"Thirteen hundreds?" Kyla asked. She slipped the ring off her finger, lifted it up to eye level, and twirled it around in front of her, studying it. "There's no way this thing can be that old."

"Just listen," Lily said. "Alice knew from a young age she had abilities that other people didn't. It didn't take her long to figure out those 'abilities' were supernatural and she could wield them at will. Not only that, they were powerful. In the small community Alice lived in, she knew that her fellow towns folk would not accept her unusual talents."

"Does this story end with her being burned at the stake?" Kyla asked, setting the ring down on the table. "Because if it does, I'd rather not hear it."

Malcolm chuckled. "No, it doesn't."

Smiling, Lily continued her story. "To protect herself, Alice crafted this ring. Everything in it she chose for a purpose—amethyst, emerald, diamond, gold, and silver—they all have a connection to purity, healing, and balancing your spirit. Alice placed a spell on it for an additional layer of comfort and from that point on, it became like a powerful blanket, an immensely powerful one at that."

Kyla stared at the two teardrop stones, wondering what stories those little gems would have. If only they could talk. "It doesn't look that old."

"It's said that wearing a ring on your middle finger promotes power, stability, and balance so bear that in mind when you wear it in the future."

"But if I wear it, I have no powers, right? I can't do any magic? Does it affect my mental shields as well?"

Lily shook her head. "It doesn't affect your mental shields. It dulls your magic down but you can still use your powers. Think of it like a fire blanket smothering an out of control blaze. The heat and the smoke is still underneath the cover, but the raging power is contained. No one else can see it anymore nor be hurt from it, does that make sense?"

"But I take the ring off and others can sense my power?"

Malcolm nodded. "Especially other witches."

"But you said earlier that all creatures shield themselves from being tracked by others, right?"

"Right. And that applies to all creatures but one, well, two if you count demons. We can sense everything, except werewolves."

"And what's that one exception apart from demons?"

Malcolm shot Lily a quick glance before returning his attention to Kyla. "An elemental witch."

Kyla took a second to put all the pieces together, double checking herself in case she'd read this whole situation wrong. "Are you saying that's what I am?"

Lily nodded. "We're ninety nine percent certain of it. Elemental witches are born from the coupling of a witch and a demon. Not just any witch either, there are distinct bloodlines that have more abilities than others. All elemental witches that have lived have only ever come from those four bloodlines."

"And ours is one of them?"

Lily nodded.

"And my dad is a demon?"

Malcolm nodded.

"So I have siblings out there somewhere? Well, half siblings."

"Potentially, Marmalade," Malcolm said. "But what age they are or where they are is another matter. They might not even share the same father as you. There are many powerful demons in Hell who can father children with witches from these bloodlines."

Kyla let out a long breath and after a few seconds she nodded, as if finally accepting her fate. "Ok, got it. I think. I'm only shielded from others by this ring. Apart from that, I may as well have a massive neon sign above me saying 'elemental witch'."

Malcolm and Lily chuckled.

"Can you tell me what happened to Alice?"

"Well," Lily said, clearing her throat. "No one really knows for sure. We know she fled Ireland in thirteen twenty-four. After that, she disappeared." Lily shrugged her shoulders. "By the year, most would expect her to be dead. I personally don't think she is."

Kyla frowned. "How could she not be dead? What made her leave Ireland?"

"The life of a powerful, elemental witch is only ever over when she's ready for it to be. Alice had a role to play all those years ago and we don't know whether she fulfilled that or not. Or if she did, maybe she's not ready to leave it be. Who knows? As for why she left, we can only guess because she was discovered somehow. Seven hundred years of history buries a lot of secrets."

Kyla picked up the remainder of her crisp sandwich and ate it, losing herself deep in thought as she finished the deliciously weird snack. Her mind raced with possibilities and filled with a million questions. Lily and Malcolm watched her, curious as to what she would say or do.

Wiping her hands on her jeans, Kyla swallowed the last of her food, took a mouthful of drink and then looked at her grandparents. "Ok, question one. How many siblings could I potentially have? Or rather, how many other witches like me will exist?"

"There are only ever four alive at any one point," Malcolm said.

"So if Alice is still alive, there are only two others?"

"Alice won't be alive like how you're thinking," Lily said. "She won't have a physical body. From that perspective, there will be three more of you alive somewhere. They could be sixty or sixteen, we don't know."

"And our purpose is for what exactly?"

Lily shrugged her shoulders. "No one knows. But once the first of that quartet has passed, the others have to die before a new quartet can come into being. On that basis, you could be looking at a good hundred years in between each living quartet of elementals."

"My ring," Kyla said, lifting it from the table. "Why did it affect you so much when I took it off?"

"My talent is being an empath," Lily replied. "Do you know what that is?"

Kyla nodded. "You're sensitive to other people's emotions."

"Yes," Lily said. "Especially witches, and especially my own blood. Everything you've endured whilst wearing that ring balled itself up inside your magick. When you took it off, it released everything like a blockage that had finally been freed. You need to remember that your emotions feed your magick as well. I felt everything all at once, like you'd hit me with a grenade. But now, now it's all normal. I'm tuned in to your energy and soaking it all in steadily, as usual."

"My last and final question for the day—when do I get to learn what my powers actually do?"

Lily and Malcolm smiled at each other before Lily turned to Kyla and replied, "Let's step outside, shall we dear?"

Kyla stood up and went to grab her ring.

"No, no, no, dear," Lily said. "Leave that where it is if you want to see the world as you should."

CHAPTER 31

B ALTHAZAR AND AZAZEL HEADED back to the Worthington mansion, their frank heart to heart having worn them both down mentally. They both wanted a pint of whiskey and they both wanted to sit in front of the fire and contemplate their worlds since their chat.

Walking up to the front door, Azazel grabbed the door handle only to be greeted with a short, sharp electric zap, as if the handle had been electrified. Shaking his hand for a few seconds, he took a hold of the door handle again only to receive another but more powerful buzz of electric.

"Ow," he said, frowning and jumping back. "Mother fucker."

Balthazar stepped around his brother and tried the handle as well only to be greeted with the same jolt of electric. Taking a step back, he took measures to an extreme and kicked the door in, smiling with satisfaction as it bust wide open.

As he lifted his foot and placed it over the threshold, a powerful surge of energy bounced back at him, sending him flying back six feet through the air.

"What the fuck?" Azazel said, walking up to the threshold. He held out his index finger and inched it across the doorway, finding the point at which resilience met him. "It's a shield," he said, turning to see Balthazar already back on his feet.

Balthazar picked up a fist sized rock from the driveway and hurled it at one of the upstairs windows. He watched in disbelief as the energy shield surrounding the mansion seemed to bend like a trampoline before throwing the rock back away from itself. To Azazel's amusement, the chunk of rock bounced right back at his brother, smacking him square in the forehead.

"I could have told you that would happen," Azazel said, chuckling.

Balthazar rubbed at his head, a deep frown creasing his forehead. "That actually hurt."

Before Azazel could come back with a sarcastic response, the air around them filled with the sound of tinkles, as if a million cats with bells on their collars were running around.

"Hello, gentlemen," Mildred said, shimmering into existence just the other side of the threshold. Close enough to touch but no way of doing so. The air around her pulsed with a sky-blue energy, her eyes gleaming with triumph as her body seemed to vibrate with life. "I'm terribly sorry for this minor inconvenience. Unfortunately, I have something very important to do this evening and I can't have any distractions or interruptions. Perhaps you could seek some alternative accommodation elsewhere?"

Azazel snorted. "I think you may perhaps fuck off. This is our damn house."

Mildred gave him a bone chilling stare, her eyes empty and devoid of emotion. The sinister smile that then tweaked at the edges of her thin lips turned the air around the three of them icy cold. "I think it would pay you dividends to be very careful what you say to me, Azazel."

"I think it would pay you dividends to remember who the fuck we are, Mildred. You're a ghost, you mean nothing here."

"Let's revisit this conversation in a few hours, shall we?"

Balthazar walked back several metres, away from his brother and Mildred and their battle of words. Bending down to touch the ground, Balthazar closed his eyes as he splayed his palm out across the earth. In his minds eye, he pictured himself as a bird, soaring over the entire expanse of the Worthington estate. The same vivid sky-blue energy throbbing around Mildred flooded the earth around them.

Flying up higher, Balthazar tried to see the edges of this power, to see where its limitations reached, but to his shock, it reached out for miles and miles, filling up all the ley lines, telluric lines, and water lines. It swallowed at least half the county from what he could see.

Pages from the book he'd read on the secretive coven Mildred had been a part of sprung forwards, filling his consciousness with the words.

A witch can easily alter her physical state for a long-term period of time. Should the witch lose her previous physical body, i.e. she is in a state commonly referred to as 'dead,' the witch can inhabit the physical body of only another witch.

However, such a transfer can only take place under the exact measures of the following three circumstances:

1. *The witch (from here forwards referred to as 'A') wishing to inhabit the physical form of another witch (from here forwards referred to as 'B') will need to be in a position to take control of B's body before B's soul leaves the physical form.*

2. *'A' will need to have the required energy levels, strength levels, and skill levels to perform this transitioning merge outside of her group's powers.*

3. *'B' will need to be fully complicit and fully understand that no reversal can take place. 'B' will essentially be replacing 'A' in the ether world.*

It must be understood that no general witch can perform, undertake, nor survive such a complicated, delicate practice, nor is it permitted. This course of action is strictly to be used only if a member of The Helios Coven is in dire need of being in physical form once again.

N.B. It is highly recommended, for power and strength purposes, that an elemental witch be persuaded to aid the event. If such a feat is accomplished, and 'A' is of sufficient stature, this could be attempted single handed, although no such event has ever been recorded.

!WARNING!

An elemental witch cannot be threatened, coerced, or forced in any manner to aid any member of the order. All actions must be fully of their own choosing. If a situation arises where an elemental is a part of such a task, 'A' will need to be capable of controlling and harnessing the raw, wild power of the elemental. Failure is almost certain. Destruction of the elemental is also a distinct possibility.

Balthazar's heart stopped dead. The penny dropped as to what exactly Mildred was up to. He ran to Azazel, grabbed his arm, and as Azazel was mid-sentence describing how he would eviscerate the old maid, Balthazar ferried them out of there in a protective layer of ectoplasm.

Travelling them across town to the woods surrounding Sam's house, Balthazar closed the portal, leaving both of them covered in white goo.

"What the fuck...?" Azazel said, scraping the sticky substance off his face. "You know I hate this stuff!"

Ignoring his brother's curses, Balthazar smacked him around the back of his head. "Did you want her to track where we went? Shut up and actually pay attention to that damn book you absorbed. Page sixty-six."

Azazel, with a handful of ectoplasm, flicked it all in his sibling's face as he raced through the details Balthazar had just realised the complexity of.

"I see," Azazel said, moments later. "That could be quite problematic."

Balthazar gave him a withering look. He then raised each hand in the air and rubbed his thumbs over each fingertip several times. Slowly separating his fingers apart, a tennis ball sized hole appeared in front of each hand. Almost immediately, a haze of shimmering blue and yellow colours flooded through each mini portal. The two sparkling masses joined together before moving around Balthazar's body like a bee hunting for pollen.

"Creepy little mofos," Azazel said, shuddering. "Still don't understand how you can have them all around you like that. Urgh."

As the hundreds of tiny pixies hovered around Balthazar like pea-sized blue and yellow honeybees, they sucked his skin and clothes dry of the disgusting ectoplasm. In less than twenty seconds, he was sparkling clean with the pleasant aroma of peppermint emanating from him.

Balthazar laughed. "Because they absolutely love the stuff, it helps them with their fruit farms, and it creates good allegiances."

Azazel muttered to himself about spiders and pixies being from the same alien planet as he used his own method of cleaning. He stripped his clothes off and then held his right palm above his head like a shower head. A fine mist of water fell from his hand and as each droplet touched his bronzed skin, it tripled in size. As the water slid down his body, it cut through the goo like a hot knife through butter.

"Some warning might be nice," Balthazar said, scowling and turning away from his naked brother. "Or maybe just using the pixies, Azazel. For goodness sake."

Grinning to himself at annoying his brother, Azazel took a second to debate a mid-afternoon 'treat' in his handmade shower.

"Don't you fucking dare," Balthazar said, all but growling at him.

"What?" Azazel replied, looking down to make sure he was clean in the most important place. "It's been a while. We've been here nearly a week already and I've had no action. None. That's a record for me, Balti, and not one that I'm proud of either."

"Can we perhaps focus on the task in hand please?"

Flicking his hand dry of water, Azazel took his left hand and stroked it over his skin. The warm heat from his palm dried him as if it were a hair dryer. As he debated what clothes to produce, Balthazar threw a pair of dark denim jeans and a white cotton shirt over his shoulder at his naked brother. He couldn't bear to be this close to Azazel in his birthday suit a second longer.

"The task in hand?" Azazel asked, checking out the clothes his brother threw him. "Oh, you mean going after the elemental witch that could essentially banish us to Hell for all eternity? Or trying to stop the crackpot ghost witch, whatever she is, that's trying to perform some sort of weird resurrection thing?"

"Both, actually."

Azazel pulled the clothes on and grumbled. "Why? Aren't we supposed to enjoy watching catastrophes unfold? We're demons, remember. Not Batman and Robin."

"Well," Balthazar said, daring to open one eye to check on his brother's state of dress. "Today, we are. Deal with it."

Jade green eyes lit up with excitement. "Does that mean I get to drive—"

"No."

"But—"

Balthazar sighed. "Do you not think it's going to be difficult enough to keep the current goings on under wraps without driving around in the bat-mobile, Azazel?"

"But that's what compulsion is for."

"No. Compulsion is only to be used in dire circumstances if our identity is compromised."

Azazel grinned. "To you, maybe." When he saw his sibling's eyes narrow, he sighed and tutted. "Alright, so 'powers of persuasion' then."

Folding his arms across his broad chest, Balthazar gave him a curious look. "Please explain to me how you intend to 'powerfully persuade' an entire town that they haven't seen the bat-mobile?"

"Well...it could be that they're filming a new movie and—"

"No, Azazel." He lifted a finger to stop Azazel when he opened his mouth to interject. "And if you carry on, I'll make you dress up like Robin."

Azazel pouted and let out a big sigh. "Fine. You win. This once. Anyway, back to the task in hand." Balthazar rolled his eyes. "What's the point of going after the elemental witch anyway? What are we, or rather you, planning to do once we find her? Or him?"

"We befriend them and figure out why their power is only just coming to life now. Is there something bigger going on here that we don't know about? Keep your friends close and your enemies closer, Azazel. You should know this."

"Yep," Azazel said, popping the p. "That's why I had you chained to my side for two thousand years."

Balthazar gave his brother a sideways glance. "You really viewed me as your enemy?"

"Of course I did. How could I not?"

A streak of pain rushed through Balthazar's dark eyes, followed by sadness and realisation. "I never wanted that, Azazel. I'm sorry. Really, I am."

Azazel studied his younger brother for a good minute or two before he gave him a simple nod. "I know it wasn't your intention." He sucked in a deep breath and then said, "But I can't help but feel hesitant that if I find my someone again, history will repeat itself."

An arrow of pain hit Balthazar square in the chest. The truth hurt, he knew that, but it didn't lessen the pain of hearing it any less. "It can't if I've found mine, can it?"

"And have you? Considering the words you spoke when you brought us here?"

Balthazar nodded. "I'm convinced it's Sam."

Azazel raised an eyebrow. "And what makes you think that?"

"Just a feeling," Balthazar replied, shrugging his shoulders. "I can't explain it. I just know I'm supposed to be with her."

"She knows what you are?"

He nodded. "And she's not entirely human either."

"What?" Azazel asked, narrowing his eyes. "What is she? Because whatever she is, her pesky jealous brother is one too."

"Werewolf."

Azazel closed his eyes and sighed, letting out a stream of curse words. "For fucks fucking sake. Of course he fucking is. Jesus Christ." Opening his eyes, Azazel said, "Are you prepared to claim her? You know what that means right?"

Balthazar looked down at the floor. "I don't know," he whispered. "What if she rejects me?"

Azazel licked his lips and said the words he really didn't want to. "At least you'll be out of your misery permanently. Is she worth dying for?"

Balthazar glanced back up at his brother and nodded. "Completely."

CHAPTER 32

T HE SECOND KYLA STEPPED outside of her grand-parent's cottage, she felt as if she were seeing the world for the first time.

Everything she now looked at harboured a beautiful mirage of colours surrounding it. Everything from people to animals to plants had its own aura that she could now see. The colourful shimmers roughly outlining each living thing constantly changed according to what they wanted, needed, or felt. It fascinated her.

When she closed her eyes, she felt a level of peace and serenity encasing her heart, filling her with warmth and love.

Kyla took her familiar and headed home, her entire world new and refreshed, as if she were born again. Once back home, she wandered out into her back garden to the old willow tree at the bottom. Its colourful aura held a tinge of grey around the outsides which overshadowed the other colours, dulling its beauty somewhat.

The tree had been there ever since Kyla could remember and its size only spoke of its old age. With its age came roots that ran deep and for a long way. Walking up to the tree, Kyla pressed her palms flat against the thick trunk and stilled as a groan vibrated through her mind, almost like an old door complaining of being opened.

She closed her eyes and quietened her mind, allowing the floods of colours to flash through her minds eye, the ever-changing mix of greens, browns, reds, and blues masked with the darkening grey of a slow death. In that instant, Kyla understood that this tree was dying, cell by cell, in a painful undignified death only humanity could bestow upon it.

Kyla imagined its roots, sliding through the dark earth beneath, stretching out like fingers searching for nourishment. Following the vine-like lengths, she skimmed down the veins coloured with red. The closer she came to the ends, the more the groans turned into shrieks of agony, piercing her peaceful mind with shrill echoes of long held pain.

As she came to the open ends of the roots, she saw an array of bright greens and yellows spurting out like an arterial bleed of wonderful energy colours. Beyond that lay nothing but concrete, inches and inches of grey concrete. She understood in that instant that this tree had half of its roots severed when the ground had been dug up to lay the foundations for the houses surrounding it, making Kyla an unknowing accomplice to this tree's tortured drawn-out end.

Kyla drew a deep breath and let it out slowly. She had the power to fix this tree, and every other living thing around her. This world carried such beauty, yet humans could do nothing but destroy it.

Envisioning herself picking up the root ends and hold-ing them in her hands like a bundle of straws, Kyla said aloud in her mind *telluric currents*. Instantly, her mind flooded with a grid map intricately detailed with green, blue, and yellow lines.

Following her gut instinct only, she tried not to focus on what the hell telluric lines were and followed what felt nat-ural and right. With great care, she laid each broken root down onto a new telluric line. As each one nestled into its new home, the screams of agony in her mind lessened as the roots immediately spurted with growth, burrowing into the earth along its new line.

The shades of red around each injured root dissolved and by the time she'd rehomed each cut root, the aura of the tree had lost its grey shadow. When she finally opened her eyes and took her hands away from the tree, she swore she heard a sigh as it seemed to straighten to new heights.

Kyla took several steps back and looked up at the tree, grinning as she realised the depths of her new magical talents. Staring down at her hands, she wriggled her fingers and turned her hands over, wondering if they could be equally evil as they seemed to be healing.

Twelve hours ago, she'd known nothing of this and now, now she had the powers of Mother Theresa and of a nu-clear bomb, all accessible through the sheer will of her mind.

Kneeling down on the grass, Kyla pressed her hand against it and closed her eyes as she let out a long breath. Thinking again of the telluric currents, she retrieved her map from moments ago, this time millions of lines all criss-crossed like a crazy spaghetti junction, the jumble of colours and twists and turns almost giving her a headache.

Gran and Grandad, she thought to herself.

In the blink of an eye, a bright purple pulsing ball of energy around the size of a marble shot along the telluric current from Kyla and zig zagged its way through the earth before settling at a point a few miles away that Kyla knew without a doubt was her gran and grandad's house.

A sinister smirk tweaked at her lips.

Mother, she thought to herself. *Tony.*

The purple throbbing marble dashed from her grandparents house along the various lines, twisting and turning around the bendy lines. After a good minute or more, it came to a stop at a point that Kyla didn't recognise.

Street name, she thought.

In her minds eye, a white street sign with black letters flashed before her, spelling out *Acorn Drive*.

Number?

Two golden numbers of thirty-eight danced underneath her closed eyelids.

Kyla took her hand from the grass and stood up, pulling her phone from her back pocket. Opening Google maps, she typed in Acorn Drive and hit 'Go'.

The map zoomed in on Minster Arch and pinpointed a horseshoe shaped road with a large green park at the back of it.

Realisation hit Kyla like a sledgehammer. When she'd found her familiar, she'd not only been metres away from them but also their house.

A gentle whine snapped her back to reality. Kyla looked down to see her new friend sat at her feet, looking up at her with big brown eyes full of love and adoration.

"I have to do this," she said, scratching him behind his ears. "And afterwards, we'll think of a name for you. When I'm free of all this and my head is clear. Ok?"

He whined again and licked Kyla's hand.

"You can't come with me. You don't want to see what I'm about to do."

He jumped to his feet and let out a sharp bark, stopping his wagging tail instantly.

"I am doing this. You don't get a say in it. Got it?"

He dropped his head and turned around, tucking his tail between his legs as he trotted back towards the house. Kyla followed him inside, settled him on a blanket with a bowl of water, and grabbed the car keys, her body filling with the false hope of freedom as she drove towards her target.

Chapter 33

S AM COULDN'T STOP THINKING about Balthazar. Not only because of what had happened in the woods but because of the draw she felt to him. Something inside her felt as if it had clicked into place, as if she were suddenly at peace and settled. She would even dare to say she felt content. The fact he said he felt that too unnerved her in one way but excited her in another.

The problems he'd hinted at that they would face piqued her curiosity. What could possibly be more problematic than their supernatural statuses? What if she fell for him and something prevented them from being together? It would be a waste of her time and would break her heart. He seemed too good to be true right now and usually when something seemed too good to be true, it was always that way.

His words had left somewhat of a taint on the rest of the day, she couldn't deny that. He'd taken her into town for a milkshake after their kiss, but he'd seemed distant and lost to his thoughts, his smiles not reaching his eyes, and his mind wandering.

When he'd dropped her off at home, he'd given her a polite kiss on the cheek and left without a further word.

Sam traced her fingers over her lips, remembering their passionate kiss in the woods before he'd backed away. Why had he done that?

Her bedroom door burst open, bringing her back to reality. "Hey," she said, frowning at her brother. "I could have been naked in here. A bit of courtesy wouldn't go amiss."

"Oh, get over yourself," Dylan replied, rolling his eyes. "What I have to say is so much more important than you wearing clothes or not."

Sam raised an eyebrow and cocked her head to one side, waiting. When Dylan didn't reply after a few seconds, she said, "And? Are you going to tell me or just stand there like a gormless moron?"

"I was just making sure you were interested. After all, this affects you the most."

Sam's heart stopped and flipped over backwards. "What? What are you talking about?"

Dylan's face unfolded into a huge grin, his eyes shining bright and his pearly white teeth on full display. "We have an elemental witch in town."

Sam sucked in a sharp breath. "What? Seriously? Where? Who is it?" She uncrossed her legs and leapt off her bed. "How do you know this?"

Dylan folded his arms across his chest and leaned back against the doorframe. "Suddenly you don't care if you might be naked or not, huh?"

"Stop being an asshole," Sam said, throwing a pillow at him. "Tell me."

"It was so weird," he said. "I was just at the gym, doing some reps, you know, pushing the kilos up..." He glanced down at his biceps, smiling.

"Dylan, I don't give a shit about how much you bench press. Tell. Me. About. The. Witch."

"I'm setting the scene," he said, looking back at his sister and shrugging his shoulders. "Do you want the story or not?"

Sam sighed. "Fine. Carry on."

"So I'd just pushed my best record yet, one-fifty, and thankfully just set the bar back down in the cups when this almighty scent hit me like a bottle of smelling salts. It nearly knocked me out with the power I felt from it, it was like a wave but with the power of a block wall. Anyway, I ran outside and Mum called. Her and Dad felt it too. They were with Granny and she said she's only ever smelled that scent once before and that came from an elemental witch."

"Are you sure it's not just Granny and one of her old tales? You know she's getting mixed up with her memory lately."

Dylan shook his head. "Definitely not. Dad said he'd never smelled anything like this and you know how many witches he's been around."

Sam's heart started racing as her mind spun with millions of possibilities. This elemental witch could be a lifesaver, they could end her family curse, finally stop the torment that three generations of women before her had endured, and that she was enduring now.

"How do we find them?" Sam asked. "Is it just one? Where are they?"

"Granny thinks they're close. I don't know if it's just one or not. But she said the strongest scent is coming from just outside of town. Whoever it is, they're within reach, Sam. Are you ready to grab the bull by the horns? Or rather, the witch by the broomstick?"

"How are we going to find them?"

Dylan tapped the side of his nose. "Using my superpowers, of course."

"Walking or driving?"

Dylan shrugged his shoulders. "Either or. How old school do you want to be?"

"We don't have time for old school. If we have an elemental in town, we need to get there yesterday. I'll even suffer your crazy driving for it."

Dylan grinned. "That's what I like to hear."

Sam followed her brother out of her room, excitement jingling together with anxiety as the heady mix coursed through her veins. This witch could be an angel of mercy without even realising it.

Jumping in the car with Dylan, Sam didn't fuss at all over his crazy driving or the insane speeds he reached as they hurtled closer towards their prize.

As Dylan raced around the country lanes, following his nose, Sam took in the scenery whizzing by the window, a familiar feeling of having been here before creeping up over her.

"I've been here before," she said, frowning, as Dylan threw the car around a corner, the tyres squealing for grip.

She focused on her memories, trying to pull forwards how she knew these small little lanes.

"We're literally in the middle of nowhere," Dylan said, frowning. "I've barely even got any phone signal."

Driving past a large crooked willow tree, Sam gasped as the memory hit her. "I know where we are," she said, grabbing Dylan's forearm. "Kyla's gran lives around here. That can't be a coincidence."

Dylan let off the accelerator instantly. "What? Are you serious?"

Sam nodded. "It's been a long time since I've been around here but yes, I'm sure. I remember that willow tree and all it's twisted branches. We used to spend hours climbing it."

"This elemental witch could be Kyla's gran?" he asked, the reality of that sinking in slowly.

Sam nodded. "Looks like it."

"Well that's only a good thing, surely? It can only guarantee the fact she'll help you."

Sam shrugged her shoulders. "Not necessarily. I've not seen her for years. She probably doesn't even remember me."

Dylan let out a long breath and pulled up outside an idyllic little cottage. "This is where my nose has brought us."

Sam nodded. "This is it."

Before either of them could move, Lily appeared in front of the car, her arms folded over her chest as she stared at Sam and Dylan. Seconds later, Malcolm burst through the garden gate, standing at his wife's side, ready for action if needed.

"Hi, Lily," Sam said, stepping out of the car. "I don't know if you remember me. I'm Sam—Kyla's friend."

Lily cast her piercing blue eyes over Sam, roving them up and down. Then, seconds later, she burst out into a wide smile. "Sam! It's been a long time. You look so different now you're all grown up. How are you? What brings you here?"

Dylan opened his car door and jumped out, standing at his sister's side. "Hi," he said. "I'm Dylan, Sam's brother."

Malcolm eyed him up and down, taking in every muscled bit of him. "Malcolm," he said. "Lily. What can we do for you?"

Sam and Dylan looked at each other, not sure how deep to go with this.

"We were kind of looking for something and it lead us here..." Dylan said, testing the waters without giving away too much.

Malcolm raised an eyebrow. "What exactly were you looking for?"

As the two siblings hesitated over their next words, Lily stepped forwards and said, "Rose is your grandmother, right?"

Sam nodded. "You remembered well."

Lily gave her a tight smile before replying, "Rose is not human. Just like me. Which means you're well and truly involved in our world. Am I wrong?"

Dylan inhaled sharply before looking across at his sister.

Sam shrugged her shoulders at him. "No," she replied, looking back at Lily. "You're not wrong."

"Ok, good, we're all on the same page. So what are you looking for?"

"We're werewolves," Dylan said, keeping his voice quiet and low. "I smelled an elemental in the area and it led us here. Is it you?"

A wry smile tugged at Lily's lips. "No, it most certainly is not me. What do you want with an elemental?"

"My family, well, more the females in my family, have an old curse on them and we understand we need an elemental to break it. We were kind of hoping, if it was you, that you might help us."

Malcolm started chuckling, his broad chest vibrating. "It's neither of us, dear. You might want to have a chat with your best friend."

Sam gasped and stumbled back a step. "Kyla? Kyla's the elemental? When did she find this out?"

"Today. You've just missed her actually. She left about ten minutes ago," Lily replied.

Sam turned to Dylan, horror flooding her in an instant. "We have to go find her. Now."

"What's going on?" Lily asked.

"Kyla has been really unstable lately. I fear she's on the verge of another breakdown. If she's just discovered she's an elemental witch, she's going to go nuclear with that."

Lily and Malcolm shared a look, their expressions saying a thousand words.

"I can track her," Dylan said, tapping his nose.

"Go, go," Lily said. "We'll follow you."

Dylan threw Sam his car keys and said, "I'm shifting. I can find her faster. Give me five minutes and I'll call you to tell you what direction to head in."

Sam nodded, her heart racing. Suddenly, her family curse mattered no more. What was now priority was making sure Kyla didn't do anything she might regret.

CHAPTER 34

Anna-Rose Wilkins had learned a lot in her forty-eight-year life. Especially that the grass is definitely never greener on the other side.

But also that karma always takes its debts back. The longer it waits to call, the bigger the debt is to pay.

Holding her phone in her hand, the monotonous tone of a dead line penetrating her eardrums, Anna-Rose Wilkins went over and over the words her mother had just said to her before cutting the line.

"I had a visit from Kyla today," Lily had said. "And she told me the truth, Anna. In fact, when I touched that ring, I felt every little thing you put her through."

Anna had no words. She had never dreamed her parents would discover the truth. As she struggled to grasp a hold of any coherent words, her mother continued.

"Kyla is an elemental, Anna. Malcolm hasn't seen power like this since Alice and Amelia. She will come for you."

With that, the line had gone dead, and she knew she was on her own. Her mother had all of her power, as did her father, but she knew without even asking where she now stood with them.

With her heart pounding against her rib cage like a mad man trying to beat his way out of a padded cell, a cold sweat trickling down her back, and every cell within her trembling with fright, Anna-Rose Wilkins knew that her karma bailiff was about to call.

In less than a minute, her life had been turned upside down, shaken, stirred, and pulled inside out. The most difficult thing to swallow was the fact that there was absolutely nothing she could do about it.

Throwing her phone down on the coffee table, she walked over to the fireplace and stared at the photo of her and Tony on their wedding day. For the first time, her wonderings if she had done the right thing came forth fully forged without doubt that she had not done the right thing, that she had monumentally fucked up by fathoms no one could gauge.

Her time with Tony had been great in the beginning. She'd felt truly treasured and like she was 'the one' for him. What it took her time to realise was that Anthony William Cecil Wilkins had all the charisma any man could ever wish for. If he set his sights on a particular specimen of the opposite sex, that poor woman was already doomed before she even laid eyes on the lanky streak of piss.

He wasn't good-looking in the general sense of the term. He didn't have a six-pack, high cheekbones, dark skin, or even the rough look of a 'bad boy,' but what he did have was a brain—one that functioned independently of his penis. Tony knew that all women wanted was to be listened to, to be made to feel like they mattered, like they were the sole affection of their partners world and would

never have any cause to suspect anything unto-
ward—even the smallest of things like lying about liking
their wife's cooking.

Marrying an older woman gave appeal to his support-
ers. To then start a family with that woman, after she
already had a child, just painted him in an even better
light. Anyone who knew of his and Kyla's relationship
had been paid off and wrapped up so tight in NDA's,
they dare not even mutter Tony's name, let alone anything else.

Anna-Rose had fought against her better instincts all
along. She'd ignored her daughter, cut her out of her
life like the cancer Tony had said she was, and blindly
followed her lust as he led her into the unknown.

For a thirty-six-year-old woman, who had been duped
to the extent she had and left alone with a demon-born
daughter, it was nothing but a dream come true when a
man suddenly paid her attention. He made promises that
he kept, he gave her orgasms she'd never experienced, and
he put her on a pedestal she'd never been privy to.

The fact he'd discarded her daughter like rubbish to
then bless Anna's life with such rich fruits was a means
to an end. Cruel, yes, but that was the way of the world
and very nature itself.

But as time went by, Anna-Rose couldn't shake her
uneasy gut feeling. So when she discovered Tony's
frequent visits to paid-for services offered by certain
women, she struggled to keep it together.

But she did.

Just.

Now starved of the ecstasy ridden orgasms her husband had once blessed her with, Anna-Rose was nothing but a bored, frustrated housewife expected to play happy families. For the sake of her two young daughters, aged ten and eight, she did. But not without contempt, nor making the slimy bastard aware she knew of his 'activities'.

Whilst she thought this was the biggest blow she'd have to face in the wrath of karma and her past sins, Anna-Rose had never dreamed in her wildest of dreams that her mother would call her one day, saying the words she said in that call—letting her know that her debt to karma was far from paid.

But now, as the doorbell rang and her heart galloped to new speeds, Anna-Rose regretted all of her life. She knew who stood the other side of that white door. She knew what was about to happen—she could feel it in her gut.

But as a tiny piece of karma to her bastard husband, she kept her mouth shut.

CHAPTER 35

S EEING THE LOOK ON Tony's face when he answered the door was a moment Kyla would relive over and over again, for the rest of time.

His pink cheeks literally drained to a ghostly white, his green eyes filling with fear and trepidation as she smiled back at him. As she stared at him, not saying a word, she watched with nothing but sheer satisfaction as his aura turned from a multitude of colours to a wishy-washy grey.

"Well, hello," she said. "Long time, no see."

He opened his mouth, but no words were spoken, almost as if he were choking on his own thoughts.

Appearing behind him, Anna-Rose peered over her husband's left shoulder, standing a good six feet back from the door. Her piercing blue eyes paled to a dull, watery grey, the sheet white colour of her porcelain skin stood out against the dark shadows around her eyes.

Kyla grinned. Her mother knew exactly what was going to happen next. She knew her time was up. "Hello, mother," she said, almost spitting the word out of her mouth. "How lovely to see you looking so...dreadful."

Anna-Rose dropped her eye contact and stared at the floor, not sure what exactly to say.

Before Kyla could say anything more, a young girl with long black hair skipped up behind Tony and peered around his side. With her fair skin, brilliant blue eyes, and red pouty lips, she could have easily been named Snow White and no one would have questioned it.

"Hi," she said, smiling at Kyla. "I'm Lina. Who are you?"

Kyla looked down at her half-sister and smiled. "I'm Kyla. Nice to meet you. How old are you, sweetheart?"

"I'm ten," Lina replied, giving Kyla a proud smile.

"Don't you talk to her," Tony said, his voice sounding nothing but weak and feeble. "Whatever you wanted to achieve today isn't going to happen. Go away. You're not welcome here."

Kyla took her eyes from her younger sibling and fixed Tony with a steely glare. Cocking her head to one side, she asked, "And how old would our child be now, Tony? Do you remember that?"

Tony pressed his lips together and shuffled backwards a step. "That is the past, Kyla. You have no business bringing that here."

Kyla ignored him and looked down at Lina again. "Did your daddy ever tell you how he tried to murder your brother or sister?"

Lina frowned, her dark eyebrows furrowing together as confusion and horror spread through her eyes. "Mummy..." she said, her voice shaking. "What is she saying?"

Anna-Rose lifted her eyes from the floor and stared at her daughter. The second her eyes locked with Kyla's, Kyla's mind flooded with her mother's voice.

Please don't hurt the girls. Please, they are innocent in all of this. Please, Kyla, for the love of God, don't hurt them.

Kyla narrowed her eyes at her mother. "God himself couldn't help you even if he was stood right here."

Tony shoved the door, trying to close it in Kyla's face. Kyla stuck her foot over the threshold, keeping her eyes on Tony's as the door bounced back off her shoe.

Tony moved forwards a step in an attempt to close the door again, this time piling all his weight against it.

Don't you dare move, Kyla thought as she stared at him, not even blinking.

The air filled with a deep rumble followed by splintering wood. Seconds later, thick brown vines ripped through the floor of the house, their pointed ends snaking around Tony's legs, coiling around him with dark menace.

"Mummy!" Lina cried, running to Anna-Rose and throwing her arms around her waist.

She started screaming and crying, tears streaming down her face, streaks of snot falling from her nose as she gasped for breath in between her pitiful sobs.

Kyla rolled her eyes, stepped into the house, and closed the door behind her. "Stop that noise," she said, staring at Lina. "Before I make you."

"You don't have any control whatsoever, do you?" Anna-Rose asked, her voice quiet.

"What's that old saying? 'Like mother, like daughter'?"

"You don't understand," Anna-Rose replied, her eyes washing over with water. "They'll use you, Kyla. All for nothing but their own gain."

Kyla facepalmed herself and then gave her mother a sadistic smile. "Well, fuck me if this really doesn't sound familiar. Talking about yourself in the third person really isn't healthy, Mother."

Anna-Rose let out a high-pitched scream that could have easily shattered Kyla's head if it were made of glass. "Shut up about me and him. This is nothing to do with that. I'm talking about the witches. The highest, most powerful order of them all. They need an elemental's power to achieve their aim, Kyla. Centuries have passed without any elemental giving in to the dark side, but if you do this, you're nothing but a lamb to the slaughter."

Kyla narrowed her eyes as her curiosity won over. "What are you talking about?"

"The Helios Coven. Did Gran tell you anything about them?"

Kyla stalled for a second, wondering why her gran wouldn't have mentioned this if it was so important. "No."

"They are the crème de la crème of witches, Kyla. Except, none of them ever have been an elemental. Not one. But they are at the top of their game. Everyone thinks they're all dead but they're not, they're very much alive, Kyla. All they need is the power of an elemental to regain their leader. She is not a nice person and not someone you want to be responsible for bringing back to life."

Kyla frowned as she took in her mother's words. "If it was that bad and that drastic, Gran would have told me. I don't believe you. It's just more lies to stall what's about to happen."

Anna-Rose shook her head. "No, Kyla. I know what's going to happen and I know nothing will stop that. But that doesn't mean I can't pass on what I know. Gran wouldn't have said anything to you because she doesn't believe they're still around. To her, they're not a risk."

"And if they are a risk, what have they got to do with me?"

"Elemental witches are granted their powers because they're not susceptible to particular persuasions or manipulations, they are their own free spirits. God himself knows you are definitely the definition of that. But, if an elemental is tempted to do bad things driven from ill feeling, this could make them vulnerable to being kneaded in certain directions because their free spirit is compromised by negative emotions."

"For someone that wanted nothing to do with magic and the supernatural, you seem to know a hell of a lot about it. That only begs the question of how much of this is bullshit?"

"It's not bullshit, Kyla. I'm trying to help you. Just because I never practiced magic, it doesn't mean I wasn't aware of rules and laws. Your gran brought me up in this world don't forget."

Kyla let out a sigh. "I'm afraid it's too little too late and I don't believe you. I think I'm more than enough of my own person to decide when, where, and how to use my powers. No one can manipulate me differently."

Anna-Rose reached out and grabbed Kyla's forearm, digging her nails in to the point of fetching blood. "You're not getting it," she said, all but hissing. "You're not in control. All you have to do as an elemental is think something and it happens. That's why you must have complete control at all times. You leave one gap, the smallest of gaps in your mind, and they're in. Then that's it. You're done for." She dropped her hands from Kyla's arm and gestured at Tony. The mud brown vines had worked their way around his entire body, even covering his mouth. "You are clearly *not* in control."

"Maybe I like it," Kyla replied. "I want things to happen just from thought alone. Go with the flow, see what happens." She shrugged her shoulders. "I can't know my limits if I don't push myself."

"This isn't maths or running on track. This is the fate of the world, Kyla. If they get what they want, that's it—the New World Order is going to be happening faster than you can say your own name."

"Well, maybe that's not such a bad thing. It's hardly as if the world is a marvellous place as it is, is it?"

Anna-Rose sighed and ran her hands through her shoulder length strawberry blonde hair. "Just promise me you'll bear in mind what I said."

"I'm promising you nothing."

Anna-Rose turned and walked into the living room, Lina still clinging to her side. Kyla followed, glancing around the bland, cream coloured room. Various family pictures hung on the walls and cute ornaments were dotted about on shelves.

Kyla watched her mother collapse into a brown coloured leather chair and seemed to deflate, as if all the life had been pushed from her. She stared into the distance, fixated on nothing in particular but clearly lost in her own thoughts.

"Liiiiiinnnnaaaaa..."

The chirpy, giggly voice of a young girl floated through the air, singing her sister's name repeatedly. Kyla turned her head towards the doorway and waited for the child to appear. Right on cue, a small girl with sunshine coloured hair, porcelain skin, and piercing blue eyes appeared. With her little blue dress, she really did resemble a miniature Alice in Wonderland.

As soon as she saw Kyla, she stopped dead. When she turned her attention to her left, to see her father covered in earthy vines that had broken through the floor, she let out a piercing scream.

"Arana, come here, sweetheart," Anna-Rose said, leaning forwards in her chair and holding her hand out.

Arana ran for her mother, sobs and heaving cries taking control of her little body.

Kyla looked at Tony, staring him straight in the eye. "You've got a miniature Snow White and a miniature Alice in Wonderland," she said. "I wonder what ours would have looked like. Cinderella, maybe? Or maybe Aurora? Or perhaps she'd have had my trademark red hair and been a miniature Ariel or Merida?" Kyla sighed. "But we'll never know, will we?"

Arana, now sat on her mother's lap, stopped her cries long enough to ask, "Who is she?"

Kyla, upon hearing that, turned her attention to her younger sister and walked over to her. "Hello, sweetie. I'm your older sister, Kyla. It's lovely to meet you."

"You never told me you were *my* older sister," Lina said, narrowing her eyes at Kyla and sticking her hands on her hips with a defiant tilt to her chin. "I think you're lying."

Kyla raised an eyebrow. "My, you've certainly got some sass. I think we could get along just fine."

"I don't like liars so no, we won't."

"That must mean that you don't like your mummy or your daddy then, sweetheart, because they are both liars. Very big, very bad liars."

"No, they're not. You're lying," Lina replied, shouting, and stamping her foot for effect.

A gargled noise cut through the exchange, taking Kyla's attention. Tony's eyes had glazed over with a hardened stare, anger and hatred oozing from them. Spit rolled down his chin from where he'd tried to talk through the grip of the vine.

"I can't quite hear you," Kyla said, tapping her right ear. "Have you got something to say?"

Tony strained against the vines, grunting at the effort of trying to wriggle free. The more he struggled, the tighter they held him.

Kyla looked back at her mother who cradled Arana against her chest, resting her chin on top of her daughter's head, gazing off into space.

She never held me like that, she thought to herself, a spike of jealousy hitting her square in the heart and spreading through her veins like poison.

The creaking of the vines curling around a struggling Tony took Kyla's attention back to him. In a moment of spontaneity, she decided she wanted to hear what he had to say, more curiosity than anything. With a carefree flick of her wrist, the vine around his mouth slithered free, scraping its rough surface against his flesh. Dots of blood sprang to the surface and trickled down his skin, hypnotising Kyla instantly.

Her heart raced to new speeds, pumping adrenaline through her veins at the sight of spilling Tony's blood—just like he did hers. As Kyla realised he was finally feeling pain at her hands, just like she did at his, a strange sense of relief seemed to lift itself from her soul but at the same time, urged her to do more. To avenge herself and then some.

Tony needed to know the depths of the excruciating agony he'd left her in. He needed to linger in the bottomless abyss of gloom that she'd been left to live in, alone.

But he wasn't the only guilty party.

Anna-Rose needed to experience all of that too.

CHAPTER 36

W ITH TONY HAVING THE power of speech back, he begged and pleaded for his life. "Kyla," he said, his eyes full of pleading. "Please. Come on. What's done is done. It's in the past. I'm a father now. Don't scar my children forever."

Kyla stared at him, poker faced, taking his words in one by one and deciding how to reply. "'What's done is done'. Is that really how you think about what you did to me? What you did to *our child*?"

"I did what was best for everyone involved," he said, straining against the vines holding his wrists.

"Did you? Who told you that? Because I certainly disagree that you did what was best for me."

"You were too young to have a child. You needed to live a little first, enjoy life, be without burden."

Kyla tilted her head back and laughed, a proper deep guttural laugh that shook her stomach and vibrated through her chest. Seconds ticked by as her laugh bounced off the walls of the silent house, the children, Anna-Rose, and Tony all watching her, waiting, wondering what she would do next.

When she finally eased her laughter, she lowered her head and glared at Tony, her eyes sparking with hatred. "Enjoy life? What's your definition of that Tony? Because being told at the age of eighteen that I can't have kids, being pushed from psychiatrist to psychologist to therapist because no one could help me, battling with depression, anxiety, trust issues, and trying not to kill myself on a daily basis is *not* my idea of enjoying life."

Tony stared back at her, mute, unable to say a word. He knew in that moment how much he'd fucked up. Fucked up royally. After nearly a minute of staring each other out in tense silence, he finally whispered, "I had no idea."

"Of course you didn't," Kyla yelled, throwing her arms up in the air in exasperation. "Because you were too busy running away with and fucking my mum!"

"What's fucking?" Lina asked.

Kyla turned around, seeing her younger half sibling staring at Anna-Rose, expectantly waiting for an answer. "Please," Kyla said to her mother. "Indulge her. Tell her what that is."

Anna-Rose looked up at her daughter, her eyes full of water. "Please, Kyla. They're innocent in all of this. Don't force them to face the same horrors you did."

Kyla raised an eyebrow and considered her mother's words for a second. More like a split second. "Why not? If it was good enough for me to endure, dear mother, it's more than good enough for them to also endure. You can't have favourites now, can you?"

"You heartless cow," Tony shouted. "You're a fucking heartless bitch."

Kyla whirled back around to face her former lover, pure ire flowing through her veins, splashing against her insides with a dire need to be let free. "Quite the opposite, Tony. If I had no heart, I wouldn't be feeling all of these things inside of me, now would I? I wouldn't still cry at the sight of pregnant women or lose myself in depression for days at the sight of a baby, would I? That if anything proves that I do have a heart. However, if you wish to see a heartless cow, or a heartless bitch, I can indeed show you that."

"You're a nasty lady," Lina said, her voice full of scorn. "You'll never get into Heaven."

Kyla turned her head and smiled at the little girl. "Who said I wanted to even go there?"

Lina sucked in a sharp breath and grasped a hold of Anna-Rose's arm, clinging onto her like a koala onto a branch. Arana still sat on Anna-Rose's lap, holding onto her mother like a baby monkey.

"I think I've heard enough out of you for now," Kyla said. Lifting her right arm, she pointed her index finger over to the corner of the room. "Go and stand over there and take your sister with you."

Lina shook her head and huddled closer to Anna-Rose.

"Do it now, before I get my viney friends to drag you over there. Your choice."

Lina glared back at Kyla, not moving, her blue eyes filled with defiance yet tinged with fear.

"Fine," Kyla snapped. "You had your chance."

Kyla moved her right arm and pointed it at Lina. In that instant, the living room floor began to creak and rumble. Seconds later, the floor burst open, thick brown vines snaking through the jagged hole in the middle of the room.

Lina screamed. Arana sobbed. The vines flew through the air, heading straight for their ankles. As the tip of one wrapped itself around Lina's leg, she yelled, "Ok. I'll do it."

Kyla dropped her arm, the vines retreating back to the hole in the blink of an eye, peeking through the opening, waiting for the next command.

Lina grabbed her sister's hand and tugged at her. Arana shook her head and continued to cry, only holding on harder to her mum.

"Come on, Arana. Do you want that thing to touch you?"

Arana shook her head.

"Then you need to come with me."

Arana nodded, then several seconds later, she finally released her grip on Anna-Rose and followed her sister like a lamb over to the corner of the room.

"Good," Kyla said, giving them a small smile. "Now, what happens next is for your own good. *All of it.*"

Kyla envisioned in her mind exactly what she wanted, watching with nothing but sheer satisfaction as the vines responded, giving her her desired result in less than ten seconds.

The vines coiled around the two girls tightly, covering every inch of them, save for a small gap for their noses and their eyes. Hot tears fell from the girls' eyes as their muffled screams and pleads were almost drowned out by the thick vines keeping their mouths shut.

"They're terrified," Tony said. "What is wrong with you?"

Kyla rolled her eyes and turned her attention back to him. "I'm bored of you now. Time for you to be quiet." With a flick of her wrist, a thick vine slid back across Tony's mouth, silencing him once again.

Moving to stand in front of her mother, Kyla folded her arms across her chest and smiled at Anna-Rose. Anna-Rose looked up at her daughter, the emptiness in her eyes telling the world she'd resigned herself to her fate.

"Not even a tear to shed?" Kyla asked, cocking her head to one side.

"I'm not going to give you the satisfaction," she replied. "I want you to hate yourself forever for this."

Kyla dropped her folded arms and squared her shoulders. "Do you hate yourself for what you did to me?"

A second of hesitation passed through Anna-Rose's eyes before she replied, "Of course."

"You're a bad liar."

Anna-Rose sighed and looked down at the floor. "If I hadn't done what I did, Kyla, I wouldn't have Lina and Arana. I don't regret having them—"

"Fucking wow," Kyla said, a fresh stab of pain searing through her heart. "You are unreal. What did I ever do to you to make you hate me so much?"

"If you'd let me finish, I was going to say but I regret the situation that happened that made their lives possible. You're my daughter, Kyla, how could I ever hate you? Every time I look at you, I see myself."

Kyla snorted. "Don't you fucking dare. I would never do to my own child what you did to me. Not that I'll ever have a chance to prove that."

"I'm sorry, Kyla. Really, I am. I'm sorry I made a terrible error in judgement, that you suffered like you did, that we lost each other, that you feel you have to do this to quiet the anger in your soul. I'm sorry."

Kyla felt her breath catch in her throat, a lump lodging itself as tears started to prick at her eyes. She couldn't deny she was angry, so very very angry. She'd spent so many years, *lost* so many years being full of hate and bitterness. An entire decade of her life had been robbed from her.

Squeezing her eyes shut, Kyla pushed the rising emotions away, focusing on what brought her here. Seconds later, she opened her eyes, marched over to her mother and grabbed her by the throat, yanking her to her feet.

Anna-Rose didn't make a single noise nor resist. When garbled noises from Tony filled the air, she still kept her eyes on her daughter, wanting to keep the eye contact, to force Kyla to face the reality of what she was doing.

"Now," Kyla whispered, her eyes glazing over with a hardened stare. "Seeing as you apparently care for me so much, it's only fair I share my pain with you, right?"

Staring her mother straight in the eyes, Kyla placed her free hand on Anna-Rose's stomach. Her mind flooded with memories from that fateful day, from when Tony had almost caused her to bleed to death. Kyla channelled all of her fear, all of her agony, and all of her desperation into her energy, her palm tingling as the heat from her magic flowed out of her.

Within a few seconds, Anna-Rose crumpled, clutching at her stomach, her eyes scrunched shut as she screamed in pain. Kyla tightened her grip on her mother's throat, forcing her to straighten up. Kyla could feel her mother's pulse beneath her skin, the racing beat, the slight sheen springing to the surface of her skin.

"Are you feeling it?"

Kyla pressed her hand harder against her mother's abdomen, against the loose skin that had once been stretched by her own limbs as she grew inside that stomach. Now though, that meant nothing. All she could think of was the cold, thin metal being forced inside her, ripping through her delicate tissue, tearing her to pieces.

The memory of that day had been burned into her mind but now, now she imagined it wasn't her laid on her bed, spread eagled to a cruel tormentor, but instead her mother. In her mind's eye, she built up a huge shovel, like a snow plough, and pictured every speck of emotion and feeling from that day being pushed out of her and into her mother.

Anna-Rose began to tremble, her knees struggling to support her as the overwhelming emotion from Kyla flooded her body, breaking her down chunk by chunk.

As Kyla's festering emotions poured into her mother, the heat from her palm began climbing up her wrist, then seeping into her forearm, each second she kept the touch on her mother notching the temperature up a degree.

When the heat emanating from her reached borderline scorching, Kyla let out a frustrated scream. She wasn't done ploughing her mother's quivering wreck of a body with all her pain and fear. She would make sure she sucked up every last drop whether she liked it or not.

Letting go of her throat, Kyla placed her other hand on her mother's stomach, wanting to share the load between both hands. The instant she did this, it was as if a dam wall had been broken—everything flowed out of her at twice the speed.

Anna-Rose wailed like a child. Tony continued making noises, the girls muffled screams almost drowning out his grunts of protest. Anna-Rose collapsed, her legs buckling beneath her.

As quickly as Kyla wished she had some support to hold her upright, the vines from the hole next to her sprung to life, coiling around Anna-Rose like a snake, stretching her into a standing position. Her entire body from head to toe shook violently as Kyla continued her outpour of hatred.

Finally, after another minute passed, Kyla felt her palms turn ice cold. She knew then that it was all gone, all of her seething, fermenting negativity, all of her excruciating agony, she had finally shared it with the one person who deserved to feel it.

Stepping back, Kyla bent over and placed her hands on her knees, taking in big deep breaths. Every part of her felt as heavy as lead, like all of her energy had been sapped away, leaving her nothing but a body stumbling around.

But at the same time, she felt light, like a shadow had been lifted from her soul, the heavy weight of old scars and painful memories dealt with and packed away. For good.

Standing up straight, she smiled. *This* was what she'd been waiting for. And boy was it worth the wait.

Looking at her mother's face creased with anguish, her eyes screwed shut as she hung limply by her neck, the vines taking all of her weight. She began shaking violently, blood trickling from her groin. Seconds later, the trickle turned into a flood.

Anna-Rose turned a sickly shade of grey and in that moment, Kyla knew she was *there*, right in that moment when she knew Tony had caught the little foetus and tore it from her womb. Anna-Rose's light denim jeans were staining dark red, a stream of blood coming from her, pooling onto the floor beneath.

At this point, Kyla had passed out, during the real thing, but of course, her mother wouldn't be given the same mercy. Kyla narrowed her eyes, ready to prick at Anna-Rose's consciousness to keep her awake if necessary.

Seconds later, her mother vomited, the acidic stench of bile seeping through the air. An almost clear, runny liquid dripped from her chin onto the vines wrapped around her neck.

She opened her eyes and looked at Kyla, tears leaking from her eyes. "I'm sorry, Kyla. I had no idea."

Kyla raised an eyebrow. "It shouldn't have taken this to get an apology." Anger bubbled in her veins, the reality of the situation overflowing yet again. Kyla couldn't help but let it out in a scream so loud, her voice box cracked with the exertion of her yells. "I didn't even want an apology back then—I wanted my fucking mother!"

Anna-Rose dropped her eye contact and turned her face away, her tears now soaking into the vines around her neck to the point of changing their colour.

"You can think on that whilst I continue," Kyla said, whirling around to face Tony.

She grinned at him. She knew this one would be particularly fun.

CHAPTER 37

W HEN SHE TURNED TO Tony, Kyla knew she'd lose all restraint. Even if she tried her best to hold herself back, she knew it wouldn't happen. The man had caused her far too much pain and suffering for her to not release it all.

She stood in front of him and folded her arms over her chest as she cocked her head to one side. Letting a slow, sinister smile spread over her lips, she stared at him in silence, watching with nothing but pleasure as his eyes filled with fear.

"I'm treating this like a spot squeezing exercise," she said. "You know? Where you need to get all the pus out before the hole can heal and disappear."

Tony didn't make a noise, he didn't even blink, he just stared back at her, blank and impassive.

"You understand that you're my pus, right?" She laughed and waved a hand through the air. "Of course you do. You're not that dumb. But then again..." She clicked her tongue against the roof of her mouth "...look at what you did, thinking karma wouldn't come back to get you."

Kyla lifted both of her hands and rotated her wrists, imagining in her mind at the same time exactly what she wanted. The vines holding Tony moved with fluid ease, tilting him onto his back. Moving her hands apart from one another, the vines spread-eagled Tony's legs.

Seconds later, the stench of ammonia filled the air as a dark patch grew on Tony's jeans.

As urine dripped down onto the floor, Kyla sighed and rolled her eyes. "You really are one pathetic man, Tony. What I ever saw in you is beyond me. And what on earth *she* ever saw in you to warrant the mess we're now in is something I will never understand."

Lifting her right hand, Kyla clicked her thumb and index finger together, smiling as a bright orange flame sprang to life. Carefully placing it on the edge of Tony's right trouser leg, she took a deep breath and blew on the flame. Just as she wanted, the flame shot up the inside of Tony's leg, burning away at the seam.

Hearing strangled noises now coming from Tony sounded like nothing but music to her ears. As the flame reached his damp crotch, it faltered, making Kyla frown. She walked between his legs, the apex of his thighs at her eye level, and lifted her right hand, facing the palm towards him.

Seconds later, a ball of fire streamed from her hand, blasting his clothes with such intense heat, it dried the dampness in a matter of seconds.

Tony squealed, his whole body rocking and tensing as he tried to fight the vines holding him. The small flame she'd set along the inside seam carried on round, making its way back down his left leg. With his jeans burned open and flailing like a pair of unzipped chaps, Kyla focused her thoughts on what was to come next.

"You wait there," she said, patting Tony's calf. "I'll be right back."

As she turned to leave, a thought suddenly crossed her mind. The flame that had taken care of his jeans had extinguished, leaving only a red mark on his skin. Reigniting it, she set it back on its path, like a train track, pushing it along the imprint it had already made once.

Tony groaned and fought the vines as the flame bit at his skin, the rancid smell of burning flesh quickly filling the air.

Kyla smiled to herself and headed upstairs, looking for one thing and one thing only.

The house itself was quite nice, new, modern, simplistic decoration in each room. With four bedrooms upstairs, the girls had a room each, painted in pastel pinks and purples. Pictures of unicorns were dotted around, several shelves on the walls holding dozens of adorable fluffy animals. They each had a double bed with matching double wardrobes and a set of drawers. TV on the wall complete with a games console underneath, the girls had led a privileged life so far.

Kyla had had nothing but a mattress on the floor until she turned ten. Bitterness and jealousy clashed together inside her, sparking her rage with a newfound wave. Perhaps if she'd been spoiled to this extent, she would be a completely different person to who she was today.

But then again, would she want to be?

The smallest room appeared to be an office. With all four walls painted white, with a matching white desk, white computer, and a cream-coloured leather swivel chair, the room actually felt sickly more than anything.

Turning her attention to the next room, the master bedroom, *their* bedroom, Kyla found herself surprised to see it was as bland and uninteresting as a hotel room. Dark grey and burgundy colours stretched across the bed, a stark contrast to the magnolia walls.

Across one wall, to her left, sat a built in, sliding door wardrobe complete with floor to ceiling mirrors. She slid the doors open and looked for her prize—a wire coat hanger.

Sliding her mother's purple wrap-around dress from it, she took the coat hanger and headed back downstairs, twirling it around in her hand.

When she stepped back into the living room, her eyes fell upon her mother. Anna-Rose looked nothing but dreadful. Sweat and tears had mangled together on her face, streaks showing in her foundation along with black lines of mascara. Whilst no more blood fell from her, the exhaustion of the physical torture had clearly taken its toll on her. For a brief second, Kyla debated keeping her alive in this very state for the next decade, just so she could feel all the mental pain too, but ultimately, she didn't have the patience for that.

Turning her attention back to Tony, she stood in between his legs, trying to ignore the putrid smell of burning skin lingering around her. The flame had run its course in reverse and extinguished whilst she had been upstairs.

Tony's eyes were red, bulging like golf balls, his cheeks wet with tears. Kyla smiled. Tapping the vines, she lowered him down so she could see his face, his groin level with her stomach. Ready with her weapon of choice, Tony's lower half burned free of clothes, Kyla found herself once again staring at the dick she'd happily ridden for months.

Back then, she'd loved it, couldn't get enough of it. He was well hung, a good eight inches with a thick girth to match. For a brief second, she had a fleeting moment of sympathy for her mother. After years of no sex to then be offered something like this, no wonder she'd given in.

But she had still more than crossed a line.

Kyla took a moment to rethink her plan. Her initial idea had been to lift his balls up out of the way, to get that sweet spot right underneath his scrotum, but the thought of touching his genitals now made her want to be sick.

"I'm not going to lie, Tony. I don't particularly want to touch you there again so I'm afraid I'm having to adjust my initial plan. It unfortunately means you'll suffer a bit more pain but what's a tad more in the grand scheme of things, hmmm?"

Kyla held her hand over the edge of the coat hanger, where the shoulder of it curved around into the bottom rail. Picturing the curve elongating to a sharp tip, she couldn't help but grin as she watched her thoughts coming to life right before her eyes.

Using the new tip of the coat hanger to start her hole, she stabbed straight through his ball sack and into his flesh. He jerked and jolted, the creaking of the vines telling her how much he strained against them. A mangled cry shouted from his throat but she paid little attention to it—it was nothing but background noise.

As screams from the girls echoed around the room, Anna-Rose stayed silent, staring straight ahead into nothingness.

Kyla, happy and lost to herself, started whistling as she worked a jagged hole through Tony's flesh, not caring for the blood and bits of muscle she tore away.

The beautifully bone chilling sound of Twisted Nerve by Bernard Herrmann mixed with Tony's gargled screams. Kyla held her coat hanger with both hands and pushed, hard. Like a boat gliding through a pond full of underwater reeds, it eased its way up inside his body by a good five inches. Hearing the fibres of his muscles shredding like meat being pulled from the bone, Kyla couldn't help but grin. Blood gushed back at her, spilling out of him like a red river.

Tony's eyes fluttered as a streak of blood trickled out from underneath the vine wrapped around his mouth.

"No, no, you don't," Kyla said, taking her left hand and slapping the inside of his thigh. "You're staying awake for this."

His eyes sprung wide open, an almost startled look crossing his features as the unexpected shot of adrenaline coursed through his body.

"No checking out until I say so. I've yet to show you your heartless cow. You can't miss that."

A shiver ran down Kyla's spine, a feeling of unease settling in her stomach. When the hairs on the back of her neck stood up, she turned her head towards the window, frowning when she saw the blinds still turned. No one could see in. So why did she feel like she was being watched?

Shaking her head and ignoring it, she tilted Tony upright, so he had a full view of what she was about to do to Anna-Rose.

Keeping the vines around her mother's neck, Kyla brought forth two new vines, using each one to curl around both of Anna-Rose's wrists and stretch her arms out like Jesus on the cross.

"This is going to be something of an experiment. It's theoretically possible but we'll see how it goes." Kyla looked over her shoulder at Tony. "Are you watching?" The ire burning through his eyes only made Kyla's grin even bigger. "I love how much you hate me right now." She shuffled to the side and smiled back at him. "I didn't want to block your view."

Rubbing her hands together, Kyla stood at her mother's left side, hovering her left hand over Anna-Rose's chest, around three inches above where her heart would be. Closing her eyes, Kyla put her everything into concentrating on this. This would be her piece de resistance.

Seconds later, Kyla could hear her mother's heartbeat in her head, the erratic rhythm telling Kyla exactly what her eyes weren't giving away. Imagining her palm as a magnet and Anna-Rose's heart as a piece of metal, Kyla slowly inched her palm away from her mother's chest.

Nothing happened for the first few seconds, then in her minds eye, she could see all of the veins and arteries stretching, bit by bit, to support the new position of her heart.

When her heart came within millimetres of touching her ribcage, Kyla pictured a bone cutter in her mind, slicing through the sternum, freeing her ribs. Like a poacher's trap in reverse, her ribcage flung open, tearing through her flesh, spraying blood, skin, and muscle all over the walls and floor.

Muffled screams from behind her alerted Kyla to the girls still being a good audience and not hiding from the scene unfolding in front of them.

Anna-Rose let out a moan, her eyes closing as her head lolled to one side. Kyla touched her forehead with her right index finger, flooding her nervous system with a shot of adrenaline. Anna-Rose jolted awake, sucking in a deep breath, her eyes wide and scanning in the room as she took in what was happening.

Tony wriggled and squirmed, his cheeks turning red as he fought against his restraints. Every move he made squirted more blood from between his legs, the coat hanger knife still in place.

Kyla knew the human body shut down in cases of trauma but in this instance, neither of them deserved that respite, especially when she had the means to take it from them. Plus they couldn't miss out on such a fantastic climax. Passing away with this as their last memory would be the cherry on the cake.

With Anna-Rose's chest now wide open like something from a butcher's shop, her beating heart elevated a few inches above where it should be, Kyla turned her attention back to the task in hand.

Moving her left hand closer to the heart, she slowly drew it away from Anna-Rose's body, the smile on her face only growing bigger as the veins and arteries stretched with it, fighting not to let go. Seeing the tiny, intricate veins clinging on to the heart reminded her of how she'd felt so many times over the last decade, like she'd been dangling from a cliff, clinging onto the edge of sanity with her fingertips, desperate for someone, her mother over all others, to put their hand over for her to grab on to and never let go.

Kyla reached out and took the heart in her hand. The warm throbs drove home how callous this woman actually was. There was no emotion in that organ—it was nothing but a blood pump. She squeezed her hand, digging her fingernails into the pulsing muscle, scoring blood from it.

Looking over at Tony, burning her glare into him, Kyla asked, "Are you ready to see your heartless cow?"

The muffled shout grating through his voice box turned into a scream.

Treating her hand like a vice, Kyla closed her hand harder around her mother's heart. With her right hand, she took Anna-Rose's face between her thumb and forefinger, forcing her eyes to stay locked on Kyla's as she took every last bit of life from her.

When she felt her fingernails scraping against her palm, she knew it was only a matter of seconds. With one final push, the heart finally exploded, signalling the end of Anna-Rose's existence.

Shaking the remnants of mangled organ from her left hand, Kyla tapped her mother's forehead, flooding her brain with a last bout of adrenaline, just to keep her awake for as long as possible as her oxygenated cells slowly gave out all of their life.

Anna-Rose choked, blood spurting from her mouth, the gargling noise in her throat like music to Kyla's ears. Kyla kept her eyes on her, refusing to drop her eye contact until she'd taken her last breath.

"I'll see you in hell," Kyla whispered.

Anna-Rose gasped, then her eyes shuttered as her head fell backwards.

She was gone.

Kyla's heart sped up as she soaked in her new reality. She'd killed her mother. The woman that had given her life was gone, existed no more. A sense of relief hit her, freeing her soul. She felt...light.

Just as she turned to her left, about to drop Anna-Rose's lifeless body on the floor, a wave of tiredness washed over her, turning her limbs to lead. She felt as if a pin had just been stuck in her body, instantly deflating her.

Then she saw it.

The twinkle in her mother's eyes shining back at her. Except the way her lips twisted in a sardonic smile resembled nothing of her cowardly mother. Her mind flooded with power, raw power—her own power—washing away her mental defences like they were nothing but sandcastles under a tsunami.

Kyla collapsed, her mother's body hitting the floor only a second before Kyla fell on top of her. The body was dead, not responsive, but her eyes were very much full of life.

A brief flicker from a *Chucky* movie pinged through the chaos in her mind as she watched those eyes focus intently on her like they were trying to suck the very soul out of her.

Then it came.

With her mental barriers gone, Kyla was wide open and susceptible to anything supernatural heading her way. When the image of a pleasant old maid filled her mind, she frowned. The maid did nothing but stare back at her, cackling like the wicked witch of the west. In her mind's eye, Kyla watched as the maid grew bigger, like someone had pressed the zoom button a million times, but at the same time, she felt herself shrinking in comparison. It felt as if the maid was filling Kyla with herself, pushing her way into Kyla's body.

"No!" Kyla screamed, clutching at her head.

Feeling the weight of the maid pushing her down, squashing her into the blackness yawning beneath her, Kyla had not an ounce of energy to fight back, to stop herself from drowning in the nothingness waiting for her.

As her eyes closed, her mind filled with images of swirling jade green eyes comforting her as she fell into the darkness.

CHAPTER 38

A ZAZEL AND BALTHAZAR HAD no time to spare. Focusing on the ley lines, they teleported to the heart of the energy within the blink of an eye.

The instant they appeared outside the stereotypical family home, they both took in their surroundings. And set eyes on Sam's car at the same moment.

"Sam can't be the witch," Balthazar whispered, his mind running riot. "It's not possible."

Azazel pulled his lips into a thin line. "That's Sam's car. But she's not had it since the incident the other night." He quirked an eyebrow up as he looked at his brother, wondering when the penny would drop.

"Kyla," Balthazar replied. He looked towards the house, the metallic scent of blood already tinging the air. "It can't be her, surely?"

"No!" Kyla screamed.

Azazel raced towards the house, Balthazar close behind. Bursting through the front door, ripping it off its hinges, Azazel rushed into the living room just in time to see Kyla collapse on the floor. She locked eyes with him a split second before her eyelids fluttered closed.

There were few times in Azazel's life where he willingly admitted he was wrong or made an 'error in judgement' as he preferred to call it. However, this current moment, of seeing Kyla unconscious, surrounded by her murderous activities, was something he realised he had gotten totally wrong. He'd seen something dark and lurking in her but too afraid of scratching his own wounds, he'd ignored it.

Now, that old shrew, Mildred, had made her move, exactly as he and Balthazar had feared. Now they were too late.

Sitting on the floor, Azazel lifted Kyla up, pulling her away from her mother's body, cradling her head in his lap. The fact that she had tortured her own tormentors intrigued him immensely. Not only was he fascinated by the sheer depravity her imagination went to, but he found himself contemplating the situation with Balthazar.

Sure, the pair had had their fair share of fights, but the fact they knew they would never fully die surely played a part in the frightening carousel of their sibling war. How would things have panned out if they both knew the kill would be it, the final cut?

Despite everything that had happened, would he prefer a life without his brother? Mulling it over, he decided no, he wouldn't. He and Balthazar had endured times darker than most relationships, and in all honesty, that was something to be proud of. They still bickered, but that was no different to any other friendship or relationship in the universe.

Somehow though, in Kyla's case, all this murderous chaos seemed to be healing something inside her. Was that normal or did it just mean she was different?

"Azazel!"

Balthazar's shout of despair cut through the demon's ponderings in an instant.

"Yeah?" he said, still slightly dazed by his deep thinking.

It was when he registered his brother hurtling towards him at full speed that he realised he'd lost the moment.

"Fucking move!" Balthazar yelled, pelting towards him.

Seconds later, Balthazar flew back through the air, crashing into a wall. Before Azazel could even think, a huge weight knocked him flat on his back. Looking up, Azazel wasn't surprised to see the huge furry head of a mahogany brown wolf, its dark eyes boring straight into him, its front paws on either shoulder, pinning him to the floor with its weight.

"For fucks sake, Dylan," he shouted. "I'm trying to help her. Get off."

A dinner plate sized paw smacked Azazel around the head, leaving him stunned and with his ears ringing. To top things off, the beast used him as a springboard to hurl himself back at Balthazar.

Meeting one another in a mid-air bear-hug, the demon and the wolf wrestled for a few seconds. Grunts sounded from both sides until after a few seconds, the sound of a body being thudded against the earth signified a winner.

It wasn't Balthazar.

As three more wolves hurtled past Balthazar and his temporary captor, the squealing of car tires and dirt being scuffed filled the air.

"Dylan, no!"

That sweet, honey laden voice caught Balthazar's attention immediately. He fought with the oversized dog to see if what his ears told him were true—Sam was here. Sure enough, like an angel in the midst of darkness, there she was.

She ran towards him, her golden hair streaming behind her like a ray of sunshine. The wolf jumped off Balthazar and put itself between Sam and the demon. Not caring for the family ties, Balthazar could think of nothing but eliminating the threat that could keep him from his demi-soul. He would die a thousand times before losing his one shot of happiness.

Leaping onto the beast's back, Balthazar held onto its wild bucks, twists and turns like a cowboy, all the while shouting at Sam to get away.

Azazel, still recovering from his belt to the head from the damn wolf, sat up and looked around him, dumbfounded. When he saw Sam, stood a few feet away from him, smiling, he frowned, and said, "Well that escalated quickly."

"Get your ass up," she hissed. "I knew something wasn't right with you two. Do you have any idea how complicated you've just made all of this?"

"Me?" Azazel said, struggling to believe he was being blamed. "I'm the good guy here."

"You should have told us from the outset what you were, dammit. Could have avoided all of this."

Azazel snorted. "I doubt that, sweetheart. You lot might have the roles of peacekeepers, but you're just as dirty as the rest of us. The only difference is you have a righteous mask to hide behind."

"You're an asshole."

"Actually, for the first time ever, I'm quite offended. By rights, I don't have to do anything. Heck, I don't even know why the fuck me and him are getting involved anyway. The only motivation for me right now is being on the good side of your best friend so I don't get zapped to hell for the rest of eternity. Aside from that, you can keep your stupid politics."

Sam's mouth dropped open. Her emerald eyes looked past Azazel, trying to focus on what had happened in the room. Anna-Rose lay on the floor, her chest cavity wide open, her heart missing, but her piercing blue eyes roving with a wild glare only a possessed person could muster. Blood was sprinkled everywhere, like Tinkerbell had been in here and sprayed glitter dust for decoration.

She saw the bundle of thick, brown vines in the corner, two sets of fear filled eyes watching everything happen in front of them.

Tony, held by vines, blood streaming from between his legs where the glint of metal reflected back at her, blinked furiously at her, as if trying to communicate something to her. The stench of burnt flesh and urine singed the hairs in her nose, making her want to vomit.

"Are you fucking kidding me?" she asked, narrowing her eyes at him. "You almost killed her scraping your baby from her but then you go and have two kids with her mum? What the fuck is wrong with you?"

Tony stared back at her, not a flicker of regret or remorse.

"You're a piece of shit. I can't wait until we're in hell together for all eternity."

A loud crash followed by a deathly snarl caught her attention. She whirled around to see Dylan holding off Balthazar and Azazel as the other three pack members Dylan had called in had their jaws locked around Kyla's body—one on each wrist and one around the throat. Blood dripped from the wounds already and judging from the growls vibrating each of their bodies, whatever the hell was going on with Kyla was life threatening.

Sam gasped, covering her hands with her mouth as she watched her friend's vibrant red hair turn darker by the second, streaks of black lining her hair like tiger stripes.

"She's being inhabited," Sam said, desperation flooding her in an instant.

"I know," Azazel replied. "That's why we're here. We were going to stop it."

Sam folded her arms over her chest and glanced down at Kyla. "Cracking job."

"I don't see you doing much."

Sam quirked an eyebrow up. "My pack members are stopping it from happening. If you two back off and let Dylan help as well, this would all be over with much sooner."

"MOVE."

The deep bellow froze everyone, even the wolves who were wrestling with Kyla's unconscious body.

Azazel turned around to see his brother stood behind him, ash white, like he'd seen a ghost. When he looked at the gigantic figure blocking the doorway, and heard that voice, Azazel resisted the urge to run in fear.

"Malpass?" Balthazar said, his voice trembling.

Two steely-grey eyes settled on the mild-mannered demon. A twisted, unnerving smile flashed across the old man's face.

"Let me at my grandbaby. NOW."

Azazel nearly choked. "She's your *what*? Kyla is *your* granddaughter?"

Malcolm fixed Azazel a deadpan stare. "Best remember that for when she wakes up, *Zay Zay*. You owe her a new car and a decent meal."

Balthazar sniggered. A muscle in Azazel's jaw ticked as he scraped his teeth together in an effort to keep his mouth shut.

Seconds later, an older lady walked through, carrying a neatly folded purple cape. Neither demon needed to ask who she was. The piercing blue eyes, the quiet determination, and the general presence of her intimidating nature spoke volumes about her role as Kyla's grandmother.

She looked at the scene around her and allowed a stray tear to roll down her cheek. "We can fix this," she said, her voice barely a whisper. "But I need the wolves to let go."

Dylan growled and shook his head.

Sam gave Lily a look of despair. "They're the only thing stopping her from being fully inhabited."

"I know, dear, but I can't do my job if they don't let go."

Sam nodded and glared at her brother. He curled his top lip back and snarled in response.

"Have some respect," Balthazar said, stepping in front of Sam to face off her brother again.

Dylan snapped his jaw and took a step forward.

Balthazar narrowed his eyes at him. "You wanna go again, big boy? Come on then."

Before the wolf or the demon could do anything, Malcolm leaned down, picked Dylan up by the scruff of his neck, Balthazar by his ear, and threw them both out of the door. Several seconds passed before the thud of bodies hitting the floor sounded their new destination.

The wolves holding Kyla looked at Sam, finally retreating when she nodded for them to let go. Sam glanced at Azazel, expecting some kind of explanation for his sudden submissive role.

"Malpass," he said, shrugging his shoulders. "The General of Hell. Even I'm not stupid enough to piss him off."

"Do you need any help?" Sam asked, moving to Lily's side.

"No, dear. Thank you. Just some space and a bit of time."

"What are you going to do?"

"Have a little fun. Malcolm—can you hold her next to *him* please?"

Doing just as his wife asked, Malcolm scooped up the limp body of his granddaughter and held her in his arms next to the worthless piece of shit that was Tony.

Lily unfolded the purple cape she'd been carrying. Tying one end around Kyla's throat, and the other end around Tony's throat, she stood up, excited to be performing some old school magick after so many years out of the game.

"I do believe," Lily said, smirking. "This will be the first trans-gender body possession."

Azazel chuckled. "Interesting. Shall I record it or something?"

Lily scrunched her nose up. "Probably not. It's not like he's going to live to tell the tale." She leaned forwards and retrieved two daggers that were tucked under Malcolm's waistband. "I need you to listen to me very carefully," she said, looking at Sam. "The soul escapes the body through the throat. That old witch is buried deep enough in Kyla to—"

"No, no, no, no, no," Sam said, shaking her head. "I know where you're going with this. No way. No. I can't believe you're even contemplating this after everything she's been through."

Squaring her shoulders, Lily glared at Sam. "These are soul knives," she said, lifting the two knives up in the air. Their six-inch-long curved serrated blades reflected light off them, the amethyst and ruby jewelled handles hypnotising in their beauty. "There are only six of these in existence. They're incredibly powerful and used in the right way can literally channel a soul anywhere. Could you imagine the havoc he could cause with one of these?"

Azazel held his hand up, like he was in class. "Can I just say that—"

Malcolm narrowed his eyes at Azazel, silencing him immediately.

"You promise," Sam said, tentatively taking one of the knives. "That this will work?"

Lily nodded. "But we need to act quickly."

Glancing at her unconscious friend, whose hair colour would now rival that of any raven, Sam realised she had no choice but to slit her best friend's throat.

CHAPTER 39

KYLA FOUND HERSELF LOST, trapped in a nightmare happening in her own head. Her surroundings such a pitch black she couldn't even see her hands in front of her face. The only sound echoing around her being the haunting cackle of the old maid trying to overthrow her.

Fear froze her to the spot, full well knowing that the witch was looking for her, wanting to extinguish her to jet-black oblivion forever.

"I bet your dear old gran never expected this," she called out, her voice high pitched, full of mocking.

Footsteps echoed around Kyla, bouncing all around, making it impossible to pinpoint exactly where the old hag was. Kyla tried to block out the maid's taunts of her gran but she was ultimately done for—she had no mental barriers protecting her thoughts anymore—the rotten bitch was a *part* of her thoughts now.

A sudden ice-cold breeze blew across the back of Kyla's neck sending a violent shiver down her spine. Dread pooled in her stomach. She knew she'd been found.

"I must say, you really are quite powerful. I never expected this much raw energy to be inside one of you." A flash of bright blue streaks lit up the darkness like lightning before two frightening eyes stared back into Kyla's. "I think we're going to get along just fine. Don't you?"

"Just kill me already, you old bitch."

The maid cackled, the chilling sound howling around Kyla in such a way, goosebumps popped up all over her body.

"My dear girl, what would be the point of that? It's you that has all the power. You're like the nuclear reactor of a submarine. I'm merely the driver."

"And what makes you think I'm going to do anything for you?"

"Because if you don't, I'll kill all your friends and family, which of course to the outside world is actually you. I don't need magic for that, my dear. Then, when you're all sad and alone, rotting in prison, I'll set up my next body and leave you to a life of loneliness, misery, and guilt."

"You need help."

"No, my dear. I think the one in need of help is actually you."

"Actually," came a third female voice. "It is you that needs help, Mildred."

Silence. A long, strained silence filled the empty dark void. Kyla sucked in a sharp breath. She didn't recognise the new voice at all. However, the underlying threat and promise of danger in her tone of voice could not be mistaken. If it weren't for the voice being female, Kyla would have sworn the words came from her grandad.

"Impossible!" Mildred hissed.

A flash of blue streaked across Kyla's vision before darkness plunged around her again.

A girly giggle filled the space around her, the sound not too dissimilar to a young girl being tickled. "You should know more than anyone that nothing is impossible."

"I watched you die," Mildred yelled, her voice wavering with anxiety. "I saw your throat slit open like the Grand Canyon."

"Ah," came the reply. "But what is life if not but a state of mind? A mere perception of being?"

A sharp gasp sounded from behind Kyla. "No," whispered Mildred. "No..."

Kyla watched, her eyes widening, as a dot of white light appeared in front of her. Like a zip being opened, the dot then widened into a huge horizontal line, bright light streaming through like someone had just allowed the sun to shine.

Consumed only by fear and a dire need to escape, Kyla ran towards it, desperate for freedom. After all, light meant good things, right?

As she took off, a hand clamped down around her forearm, holding her back, keeping her pinned to the spot with that one touch.

"This is not for you," the voice said. "You will stay."

Kyla stood, rooted to the floor, watching in nothing but utter fascination as through the light came a long purple cloth. Its fibres reached down towards her, teasing her to take a hold and follow it back up, like a rope of life from the lifeguard when lost at sea.

Just as she debated lunging for the cloth, Mildred screamed, a deep guttural scream that pierced Kyla's ears and curdled her blood. Cringing, Kyla covered her ears, not able to listen to that animalistic noise.

Strange Latin words started filtering in, reverberating all around her. With each word spoken, Mildred found herself dragged closer and closer to the purple tendrils dangling from the light. The instant Mildred involuntarily touched the cloth, she was whipped back to the light.

The instant she disappeared, the light vanished, but her screams still resonated around Kyla. Wondering what would happen to her next, in the darkness, Kyla held her hands out in front of her, hoping to find the source of the strange voice, wanting something, someone, to hold on to, to make sense of this reality, to ground her, to bring her back.

Inch by inch, the darkness began to fade, light slowly creeping in from her peripheral vision. She then realised she was growing again, filling out her own body. Mildred was gone, Kyla was back. Tears swam over her vision.

As the last of the shadows faded, the tingling of her limbs alerting her to an outside presence, she frantically looked around for the owner of the mystery voice, wanting to thank her, needing a face to remember as she found herself grateful for her life.

"Wait!" Kyla yelled. "Who are you? I need to thank you."

No words came but instead a picture filled Kyla's mind's eye.

A picture of the ring she'd received on her seventeenth birthday.

CHAPTER 40

S AM POISED THE KNIFE at Kyla's throat, the tip around an inch to the left and just under her voice box. She closed her eyes, her entire body shaking, her mind whirring with nothing but the fact she was about to slit her best friend's throat.

"I can't," she said, her voice trembling. She opened her eyes. "I can't do it."

Lily turned her head and fixed Sam with a hardened stare. "If you don't do it, she dies. I can't do both. I need to be in charge of the body that takes the spirit, which means *you* need to be in charge of the body who loses the spirit." She quirked an eyebrow up. "Do you understand me?"

"Let him do it," Sam said, inclining her head towards Azazel.

"I just told you why he can't touch those knives."

Sam let out a whimper. "But he's not going to do anything with him around, is he?" she said, motioning her head towards Malcolm.

Lily looked up at Malcolm, a silent exchange passing between them for a few seconds. "Can you?" Lily said, flicking her attention over to Azazel.

"You're sure this will work?" he asked, stepping forwards, his eyes fixed on Kyla. He couldn't ignore the 'what if' scenario of this not working that rolled around and around his mind. Surely fate wouldn't be so cruel as to take his demi-soul from him before he'd even asked her for her heart?

Lily rolled her eyes. "WHY," she yelled, then took a deep breath. "Is no one trusting me?"

"I'll do it." Dylan's deep voice came from the open doorway. He strode forwards and held his hand out, moving his fingers in a 'come here' motion. "We need to get this done. Give it here."

Sam let out an audible sigh of relief and moved away from Kyla, handing the knife over to her brother. Balthazar followed him inside the room, taking his place next to Sam.

"You don't need to do the whole neck," Lily said. She pointed to where Sam had had the knife. "Go from here to here, that's more than enough," she said, dragging her finger under Kyla's voice box, stopping just over an inch to the right of it. "On my count. Got it?"

Dylan nodded. He took the knife, held it against Kyla's creamy pale skin and focused on the task in hand. Now was not the time to think of what could happen beyond this. Things like this had to be tackled in stages.

First stage, knife. Second stage, make the cut. Third stage, get the witch out. Fourth stage, heal Kyla. Fifth stage, process what had just happened.

"You get ready to take my knife," she said, giving Azazel a quick glance. Making eye contact with Dylan, she gave a single nod. "One. Two. Three."

In unison, Lily and Dylan cut the throats of Kyla and Tony. Sam gasped and closed her eyes, turning her back as she watched her best friend's life force pour from her throat. Balthazar wrapped her into a tight hug, whispering into her ear not to worry. Azazel sucked in a deep breath, wincing as he kept his eyes glued to Kyla, checking her constantly for signs of life. He could hear her heartbeat, steady and strong.

Lily all but threw her knife at Azazel. Once both of her hands were free, she took the purple cloth and placed one end over Kyla's gaping wound. Stretching the long fabric towards Tony, she settled the other end over his open throat.

Dylan took hold of one of Kyla's hands, noticing the cold, clammy feel to her palm straight away. He made brief eye contact with Azazel who pulled his lips into a thin line as her heartbeat slowed.

"Ego praecipio tibi," Lily said, closing her eyes and hovering each hand over each throat. "Oriri ad lucem. In nominee omnium spirituum. Non habitabis. Tu in lucem cades. Et absolve animam tuam."

Upon hearing the Latin words, Sam dared to turn around and look at what exactly Lily was doing. Seeing the end of the purple cape turning a dark red as Kyla's blood soaked it through sent a cold shiver down her spine. It was only when a blue wisp of energy, like a thick fog around twelve inches long, floated through the purple fabric that Sam stilled and ignored the horror currently unfolding.

As Lily repeated her words, Sam's mouth dropped wide open as she watched the energy glide across the length of the cape before slipping back through the cloth and into Tony's throat.

"Dylan," Lily said. "Heal Tony's wound please. Azazel, you need to heal Kyla. She will take to demon blood better than werewolf blood."

Dylan dropped Kyla's hand and moved to Tony, biting into his wrist and tearing a chunk of flesh from it. Pressing the open wound against Tony's mouth, he used his free hand to open the man's lips and force his blood in.

Azazel rushed to Kyla, lifting his palm to slit it with the soul knife.

"NOT with that," Lily yelled. "For goodness sake, boy. Give it here." Azazel glanced down at the soul knife and back at Lily, confused. Before he could even think another word, she snatched it from his hand. "Unless you want your soul transported somewhere?"

"Not today, thanks," he replied, grinning.

Tearing into his wrist exactly as Dylan had done, Azazel allowed his blood to flow into Kyla's mouth, silently wishing with every drop that she would be fine and that this would work, that she would come back like a shiny new penny.

Lily removed the cape, carefully folding it to keep all the blood from dripping everywhere. Not that it would make much difference given the current decoration.

Less than ten seconds passed before the wounds on both stopped bleeding. Another ten seconds passed before the gaping holes were gone, no trace of anything having ever happened to either of them.

Tony came back to life, his eyes possessing a rabid wild stare as he stared around him. After a couple of seconds, a high-pitched shriek left him.

"You old bitch," he shouted. "I'll kill you for this. I'm not done, Lily. I will be back."

Lily gave Malcolm a brief look.

"Take her," Malcolm said, handing Kyla over to Azazel.

Azazel took her, gladly, keeping her close to his chest. Dylan narrowed his eyes, spikes of jealousy coursing through him at a rate of knots.

"Not the time, boys," Malcolm said, moving to Lily's side in two steps.

Lifting one of his giant hands, he tapped Tony in the middle of his forehead. "You still in there, fucker?"

Lily rolled her eyes and stepped away, going to Azazel to check on Kyla. She pressed the back of her hand to Kyla's forehead. "How is her heartbeat?"

"Still weak," Azazel said.

"She drained herself doing what she did to her mother," Lily replied, casting an eye over the devastation that was her daughter's body. "I shouldn't have let her out of my house until she had learned some real magic." Lily shook her head, tears clouding over his vision. "I had no idea she would come here and do this. Not this quickly."

Azazel pressed his lips together, trying to think of an appropriate response. "She's been very haunted by what happened for a long time. I think she just wanted it over with. As soon as she had the means to do it, she grabbed the opportunity with both hands."

"Are you listening, Tony?" Malcolm said, slapping the man's face. "I hope you're seeing me, you sick little bastard. I might even take a special return trip to Hell just to tear you apart for the next century."

The corner of Lily's mouth quirked up into a half smile. "He will do that," she said, glancing up at Azazel.

Azazel nodded and grinned. "I know he will."

Malcolm thumped his right hand against Tony's chest, his palm flat against him, his fingers splayed out. "I hope you feel every second of this, you miserable oxygen thief."

Digging his fingers into Tony's chest, he forced his way through the skin, grabbing at his ribs, crushing them as he clenched his hand into a fist.

Pulling his hand back out, he threw the handful of tissue and bone across the room before going back into the bloody hole and punching his way through the sternum, accessing Tony's heart. In the blink of an eye, he ripped it out, pressed it to his lips, and bit a chunk out of it before then spitting it in Tony's face.

"You're mine now," he said, pointing his index finger at Tony right as the light of life left the man's eyes.

Throwing the heart across the room, Malcolm wiped his hands on his trousers, rubbed his mouth clean on the bottom of his jumper, and then turned around to Lily and Kyla.

"Is she awake yet?"

Lily shook her head.

Dylan moved over to Kyla, Malcolm's presence making him feel somewhat restrained towards Azazel. Standing at her head, Dylan began stroking her hair softly, in a calming rhythm, as if he were comforting a young child.

After a couple of minutes, he leaned down and pressed a kiss to her forehead, his eyes closing as his lips lingered against the coolness of her skin.

Azazel watched Dylan, the tenderness in his touch hard to miss. A shred of guilt clenched at his heart as he realised just what Kyla meant to this man. There would be a lot worse fates for Kyla than being with a man like Dylan, hell, a werewolf like Dylan. Azazel knew the man would fight for her until his last breath, he could see it in him. After all, it was exactly how he'd felt about Cassia.

Suspecting what he did about his and Kyla's ties, Azazel didn't know how to process this. How would he have felt had some random guy come along and professed to Cassia that she was his demi-soul and needed to be with him?

Kyla's fingers twitched, pulling him from his thoughts. When she let out a soft moan, her lips parting as she stirred in his arms, Azazel couldn't help but wish that when she woke, his name would be the first on her lips, even if that would push a dagger of pain into Dylan's gut.

Dylan leaned down and kissed her forehead again. "It's ok," he whispered. "We're all here. You can come back to us now."

Kyla opened her eyes, blinking several times. Then she said, "Azazel?"

Chapter 41

THE INSTANT KYLA SAID his name, Azazel couldn't help but want to smile. His egotistical male pride burst through his veins in an instant making him want to grin like a Cheshire cat at anyone who looked his way.

However, upon seeing the instant rigidity in Dylan's shoulders and feeling the tension in the air grow as thick as mud within a split second, Azazel somehow, by the grace of God, managed to restrain himself.

"Steady," Lily said, pressing a hand to Kyla's upper arm as she peered over to look at her. "How are you feeling? You ok?"

Kyla blinked several times, then turned her head to the left, taking in the sight of her gran. "Gran? What are you doing here?"

"Easy, Marmalade," Malcolm said, moving to her feet and looking up at her. "Take a minute to readjust and then we'll fill you in."

"Uh-hum."

The sound of a deep, sarcastic cough stole everyone's attention. Azazel lifted his eyes to the source of the noise, then rolled them as he swore under his breath. Malcolm let out a sigh. Sam shrieked and jumped backwards, bumping into Balthazar who gladly slipped an arm around her waist and pulled her close.

Kyla settled her eyes on a tall, broad-shouldered man. With jet black hair, jet black eyes, and an air of arrogance she'd never seen on anyone, she knew whoever this was would be a force to be reckoned with.

"You could have waited," Malcolm said, folding his arms over his chest.

"I prefer to strike whilst the iron's hot—you know that better than anyone, Malpass," the man replied.

Kyla watched her grandad, his shoulders square and stiff, his eyes narrowed, and a muscle in his neck twitching. He was angry. Why? Who was this?

"What's going on?" Kyla asked. "Azazel, put me down, please."

"Are you ok to stand?"

Kyla glared at him. "I don't know if I don't try, do I?"

Biting his lip to keep himself quiet, he gently lowered her to her feet. "You good?"

As Kyla took her weight, she nodded. "I'm fine. Thanks."

"Let me introduce myself," the man said, stepping forwards from the doorway and into the blood soaked room. His jet-black eyes gleamed with a streak of red as echoes of shouts and screams of agony whispered in the background, a wall of shadows surrounding him.

Seconds ticked by with no further indication of words coming from the man. Kyla folded her arms over her chest and raised an eyebrow. "That's it? That's your introduction?"

The shadows lifted and the background noise ceased. The man smirked, his eyes returning to normal. "I would have thought that little skit would have been enough for you to guess who I am."

Kyla flashed him a sarcastic smile. "Oh, I've guessed that alright. What I mean is, are you going to tell me how to address you? Or do I just guess? Is it Lucifer, Satan, Krampus, Beast, Lord of the Flies, the Antichrist? Or perhaps Santa Clause depending on the time of year?"

"Kyla...," Malcolm said. "Be very careful."

The man shrugged his shoulders and stared at Kyla. "Well with Easter right around the corner, why not just call me the Easter Bunny?"

"Whatever takes your fancy," Kyla replied, not dropping her eye contact with him.

The two stared each other out for several seconds before the man narrowed his eyes and took a step forwards. "Lucifer, Kyla. You address me as Lucifer."

"Ok, no problem," she replied, giving him a sickly-sweet smile. "Would you care to explain why you're here, Lucifer?"

Flicking his eyes over to Azazel, and then Balthazar, he returned his attention to Kyla. "Since you were about to become a serial killer, you caught my attention. As Azazel and Balthazar will tell you, serial killers are escorted down to Hell by me personally. It used to be your grandad's job, but we all know how that one turned out."

"Ok, understood. However, I only killed one person so that kind of doesn't warrant you being here."

Lucifer lifted his right hand and waggled his index finger from side to side. "Ah ah. It's your intentions that count, not what actually happened."

Kyla snorted. "That's ridiculous. That's like letting a bomb off to kill one person but end up killing thousands and then saying 'its fine, only meant to kill one'."

He dropped his hand to his side and said, "Well in that case I would make an exception, so I guess what I'm really saying is I'm not making an exception for you." He flashed her a lopsided grin. "Nothing personal. Just good business."

"Business? Since when is there a business in taking souls to Hell?"

"Ah," he said. "Now that is a whole other story that we don't have time for today. Now—" he clapped his hands together "—shall we skip to the teary goodbyes? I've got a cannibal in Canada I need to catch before dinner."

"Err, no. I'm not going anywhere with you."

"Marmalade, don't fight him. You will lose, trust me."

Lucifer grinned. "Wise words spoken from the General of Hell himself. When are you coming back to visit us, Malpass? We miss you."

"I think what you meant to say was that you bend the rules to however they suit you," Kyla said, tilting her chin up in defiance.

Lucifer settled a steely glare on Kyla, quirking an eyebrow up at her. "My, my. You do have some balls. I guess you inherited those from your father." He shrugged his shoulders and smiled. "But yes, you're right. I am judge, jury, and executioner so I can change the rules as I see fit."

Kyla gasped. "What did you just say?"

"Ooops," he said, slapping a hand over his mouth in mock horror. "Did I just let a little secret out of the bag?" He held one hand in front of the other and jokingly slapped the back of it. "Naughty boy."

Malcolm took a step forwards, clenching his fists at his sides. He gave Lucifer such a hardened glare that it would have made anyone else wet themselves in an instant. "You told me you didn't know who that was."

Lucifer shrugged his shoulders. "Well, at the time you asked me, I didn't."

Malcolm widened his eyes. "Are you telling me you found out at some point?"

"Perhaps..."

"Why didn't you tell me?" Malcolm bellowed.

Lucifer lifted one shoulder in a casual shrug. "You never asked again."

"You slimy good for nothing mother—"

"Leave it, Malcolm," Lily said, placing a hand on her husband's forearm. "It's done with and all in the past. You know how he works."

Lucifer grinned. "Yes, Malcolm. Listen to the wife. Now there's a good boy."

Malcolm narrowed his eyes at his former boss. "Mary would be ashamed of you."

In a split second, Lucifer's eyes turned blood red, shadowed by black circles. He grew by four inches in height and width as his fingernails sharpened to knife points. He opened his mouth to reveal four-inch-long razor sharp teeth from one side to the other, top and bottom.

"Speak her name in my presence again, I dare you," Lucifer boomed, his voice deep and full of authority.

Malcolm, still in his human form, folded his arms over his chest and smiled. "When you don't react like this upon hearing her name then you can shower me with jibes about my wife all you like." Malcolm took another step towards him, closing the gap between them. "But not a minute before. Do we have an understanding?"

Seconds ticked by, the tension in the air thickening with every millisecond. The two demons stared each other down, neither flickering nor giving in.

Lucifer took his eyes from Malcolm and flickered them towards Kyla. "Fine. We have an understanding." He looked back at Malcom. "But don't expect to pull rank over her, too."

"Why are you so interested in her? You don't normally bend the rules for something as small as one murder."

Lucifer closed his mouth, his size slowly shrinking to its previous state, along with his teeth and fingernails. "She's an elemental, Malcolm."

"I'm well aware of that. You've never been too bothered about them before, Lucifer. So what's going on?"

"I couldn't possibly share that information with an ex-employee."

Malcolm rolled his eyes. "Stop being an asshat and tell us what you know."

Lucifer sighed, his eyes returning to their former jet-black depths. "Fine. Abaddon is her father. If you bothered to do your research on elementals, you'd realise that every single one of them has a mystery, unknown father. Can you guess who father's them all?"

Lily gasped. "Of course. Now it makes sense. That's why if one dies, they're not replaced—none of them are replaced until that foursome is all dead."

"Them's the brains," Lucifer said, fist-pumping the air. "You got a keeper there, Malpass."

"I'm sorry," Kyla said, holding a hand up. "But who the hell is Abaddon?"

Lucifer burst out laughing. "Oh, sweetheart. Think of me as the CEO and Abaddon as the MD."

Kyla didn't know what to say to that. "Oh."

"Quite so, hmmm? What a lineage you have—my MD Abaddon for a father, a general for a grandfather, and a prince for a demi-soul. Who would have thought?"

Kyla's mouth dropped open. "What? A what?"

Azazel scrubbed his hands over his face and stifled a groan. This was not what he wanted to happen right now.

Dylan looked at him, worry flooding him in an instant. "What is he talking about?" he whispered. "What the fuck is going on?"

Malcolm looked over his shoulder at Azazel and then back at Lucifer. "You have got to be kidding me?"

"Unfortunately," Lucifer said, clicking his tongue against the roof of his mouth. "I'm really not." He looked over at Balthazar and said, "Why don't you tell him, Balthazar, what little spell you cast for this year's holiday destination for you both?"

Malcolm turned his attention to Balthazar, eyeing him up as he waited for his answer.

Balthazar looked down at the floor, feeling more than a little foolish. "Amor aeternus," he said, his voice all but a whisper.

"You moron," Malcolm said, balling his fists. "You purposefully brought that idiot into *my* granddaughter's life?"

"Hey," Azazel said, taking a step forwards. "It's not like either of us knew that Kyla would be involved in any way, is it? Hell, I didn't even know he was doing that until I heard him cast the words."

"Erm," Kyla said, tentatively holding a hand up. "What the hell is a demi-soul?"

"Soul-mate, honey," Lucifer said. "The other half of you—the part that completes you. And lucky for you, you have my finest prince, Azazel. Ta-dah!"

Kyla turned to look at Dylan, watching the sheer horror flood through his eyes. His skin paled ten shades of white and he moved his eyes to stare at the floor, his shoulders hunched. A little piece of her broke away.

"Don't they make such a cute couple?" Lucifer said, his eyes lighting up with life.

"You're an asshole of the highest degree," Malcolm replied. "You know what needs to happen first. I can't believe you're putting her in this position after what she's just been through."

"No time like the present," Lucifer said. He rolled his left wrist over, checking his skull shaped watch. "Speaking of, I must dash. Now, you two," he said, looking at Azazel and Balthazar. "You know what you need to do." Lucifer held his hands out, palms facing up. Seconds later two red roses materialised, one on each hand. "Hopefully, I'll see you both at the end of your holiday. If not, well," he shrugged his shoulders. "Been nice knowing you."

With the click of his fingers he vanished into thin air, leaving the two red roses to drop to the floor. Almost a minute ticked by as they all stared at each other in silent shock.

All of a sudden, Lucifer reappeared, chuckling to himself. "Silly me. I got so caught up in all your family drama I forgot why I was even here." He turned to look at Kyla and said, "Now, dear, given who your granddaddy is, I'll give you a bit of leeway. You can come down to Hell when these two boys return. Well…" he looked at the roses on the floor "…if they don't perish beforehand that is. If so, consider June twenty first your last day on dear old earth. I can't wait to tell Abaddon who you're hitched with. Them two—" he motioned his hand over to Azazel "—are like this," he said, crossing his fingers with a mischievous grin on his face.

Kyla eyed the demon up for a second before deciding to try her luck. "What if you could have a trade?"

Lucifer quirked an eyebrow up. "A trade? I'm listening."

Kyla looked over to the corner of the room where her two half-sisters were still quivering inside the tree. "You take those two instead of me."

Lifting his nose in the air, as if trying to smell them, Lucifer motioned his hand at them. Like a curtain being dropped on stage, the vines fell away from the two sisters who were still huddled together, clutching onto each other for dear life.

"Yes," he said. "I could be interested but only if I see them as beneficial to me in some way." He roved over their bodies with his eyes several times, like a hungry lion deciding which part of the gazelle to go for. "They have their own abilities, I can smell it in their blood, although it's somewhat dampened by that festering human DNA." He struck a pose, tapping his index finger against his chin. Then his eyes lit up with a streak of red. He turned to Azazel and said, "I think they could have a use. What do you think, *Zay Zay*?"

Azazel scraped his teeth together as his jade green eyes speckled with black. "I think they could be very good additions."

"Excellent," Lucifer said, clapping his hands together and smiling at everyone. "It's a done deal. Now I really must dash. Kyla, see you soon, sweetheart."

With a further single clap of his hands, he vanished again, taking Kyla's two half-sisters with him.

CHAPTER 42

"**I** THINK WE ALL need a good cup of tea and a rest before we try to wade through what's just happened," Lily said. "And Kyla especially needs some time to process everything."

Kyla nodded, the events of the past couple of hours running riot in her mind. "Can we reconvene tomorrow or something? I just want a hot bath, a pizza, and to think about nothing."

"You can have whatever you want, Marmalade," Malcolm said, running a hand up and down his granddaughter's back. "Do you want to stay at ours tonight? So you feel safe?"

Kyla shook her head. "No, thank you. I want to be in my own space. Besides, the dog is at home."

Sam frowned. "Dog? What dog?"

Kyla sighed. "Long story. I'll tell you tomorrow."

Sam nodded. "Ok. Go home and get some rest."

Kyla glanced across at Dylan. "Can you take me home please?"

Dylan's heart skipped a beat, warmth and pride filling him in an instant. Whilst her saying Azazel's name as she came around had hurt like hell, he knew she'd been drowsy and also in his arms as she woke up. However, after the demi-soul bombshell, he couldn't shake the little niggle in the back of his mind that it was something more.

Despite all that, Dylan couldn't wait to hold her in his arms and keep her safe by his side. The memory of slitting her throat played over and over in his head like a horror movie mini trailer on repeat. He knew he had to do it, it was a means to an end, but he'd never imagined he would have to do something so horrific to the woman he loved more than anything else on earth.

Upon hearing Kyla's words to Dylan, Azazel's heart sank, disappointment flooding him. Realistically, he knew she would turn to the safest comfort but the fact she'd said his name when she woke had planted a seed of hope inside him.

Trying his best to ignore his feelings, he walked over to one of the red roses and picked it up, twirling it around in his fingers. "We need to have a conversation about this tomorrow."

Kyla stared at it for a few seconds then looked over at her grandad. "Do we?"

Malcolm nodded. "Lucifer has just handed the pair of them a death sentence." He held his hands up and smiled. "But don't worry about it now. Go home, rest, and we'll revisit all of this tomorrow."

"We'll, erm, take care of this," Azazel said, motioning his hands out at the room.

Kyla offered him a genuine smile, truly grateful at his offer. "Thank you." She dug her hands into her pocket and fished out the keys for Sam's car. "I'm sorry, I'm just not up to driving. I can barely process my own name right now."

Sam took the keys from her and then wrapped her friend in a warm, crushing hug. "Don't you apologise for anything. Now go home and chill. And I do mean chill. Not Netflix and chill."

Kyla laughed. "Definitely not Netflix and chill." Kyla looked over at her gran and smiled, tears glazing over her vision. Rushing to her, she embraced her in a bear hug as she whispered, "Thank you. I love you."

Lily hugged her granddaughter back, her own tears already falling. "No need to thank me. I love you, too."

Taking a deep breath, Kyla broke the hold and headed towards the door, forcing herself not to look back at her mother's carcass. Dylan pressed his hand to Kyla's lower back, guiding her out of the house.

Dylan rushed forwards to the car, opening the passenger door for her. Kyla slid inside, offering him a tight smile as a thank you. He shut the door, giving her a precious few seconds of time to herself before he joined her in the car. In those few seconds, her only thought was *Should I have asked Azazel to take me home?*

Settling in the driver's seat, Dylan struck the car up and pulled away, desperate to get her as far away from her demi-soul as possible. He knew that eventually Kyla would find her way to Azazel, it was written in the stars, already designed in fate. How could he stand in the way of that? If anyone tried to be in the way of him and Kyla, if she were his demi-soul, he would end them without a thought.

Yet, here he was, about to spend the night with another man's demi-soul. How must Azazel be feeling right now, watching Kyla walk away with him?

Dylan shook his head and reached over, placing his hand on Kyla's knee. He couldn't afford to get lost in his head right now. Kyla needed some stability and comfort, not him second guessing himself and putting some demon's feelings before his own.

Kyla sat her hand on top of Dylan's smiling at the warmth seeping through her skin from his singular touch.

Leaning her head back against the head rest, she began to process everything right from the moment Mildred had invaded her.

She'd never felt so scared or lost in all her life. In those minutes she was trapped in utter darkness with a psychopathic old hag, Kyla had never felt fear like it. Fear of helplessness, fear of life being done, fear of looking back on her time and not feeling satisfied or accomplished with what she'd spent her time on. In those moments, Kyla felt nothing but grateful that she'd never managed to achieve her aims of suicide.

Kyla realised that in order to live life to its fullest, to succeed in a happy, successful life, she needed to trust. She needed to open her heart and let people in, or *someone* at least. To live a life scared, full of anger and bitterness, would get her nowhere. That wasn't the way to be. After all what is life if not but a state of mind? A mere perception of being?

"Are you ok?" Dylan asked, glancing over at her. "You look lost in thought."

Kyla sighed and smiled. "Just a lot to process. I don't really know where to start."

"You don't have to process anything right now. You just need to rest. Worry about all of that after a good sleep."

She nodded and fell silent, losing herself in thought again.

"What's this dog?" Dylan asked, trying to keep her mind in the present.

"He's my familiar," Kyla replied. "Gran said witches get their familiar when they go through a traumatic event."

Dylan frowned. "But you went home before you came here, right?"

She nodded. "I'll tell you about it tomorrow. He's nameless at the moment. He's a Dobermann."

"Nice. They're good dogs. Very intelligent, agile, protective. He could be a good friend for you."

"I hope so. I have no food for him though. I kind of just abandoned him at home before I drove...here."

"I'll stop at a shop and pick him some stuff up, don't worry," he said, smiling at her and patting her knee. "I'm just glad you're alive. I thought you were lost for a moment."

"So did I," she whispered, tears hazing over her vision. "I've never felt so helpless." She turned her head to look at Dylan. "I thought I was done for." She swallowed the lump in her throat then said, "I heard you telling me to come back. I've never felt so relieved to hear your voice." Squeezing his hand, her heart backflipped. "Thank you for being there."

Dylan's heart swelled with a heady mix of hope and love. "I told you I'm always going to be there for you. No matter what." He licked his lips and let out a sigh. "I love you, Kyla. You're my world."

Hearing those words come from him twenty-four hours ago would have sent her into a whirlwind meltdown. Now, however, hearing those words come from him made her tears spring free and her heart fill with joy and endless possibilities.

"I know. Thank you." She gripped his hand tighter and wiped her cheeks with her free hand. "I can't say it back yet, Dylan, I'm sorry. I'm just..." she let out a breath which came out as a huge sob "...I'm so overwhelmed I don't want to say anything because I'm emotional. I want to say it because I genuinely feel it, in a normal moment." She gave a half laugh, half sob. "If that makes any sense."

"You have nothing to be sorry for. I just don't want to hold back any longer on how I feel about you," he said. He pulled up to a stop outside a pet shop. "I don't care if you never say it back, I want to tell you every day, remind you, that *I* love you and you have someone in your corner. Always."

Kyla closed her eyes and nodded. "Thank you."

"I'll leave the car running. Turn the heater on, you still feel so cold."

Kyla shivered and switched the heated seat on before cranking the heater up to high. Minutes later, Dylan reappeared with a massive frozen bag of tripe and a huge bag of dried food. Dumping it in the boot, he sat back in the driver's seat, taking Kyla's hand once more as he pulled away.

Dylan made senseless chit chat about the latest on his TV show *The Tudors.* Kyla listened, grateful for the distraction that kept her from losing herself in her head again. By the time they arrived back at hers thirty minutes later, Kyla felt relaxed and like nothing had happened today. It all seemed like a lifetime ago.

Listening to Dylan chat about King Henry the eighth and Anne Boleyn's passionate love for each other kept Kyla in the present just enough for her not to think about today. By the time he pulled up on her driveway, she actually found herself wanting to watch the show herself.

Dylan took her keys and unlocked the house, taking a tentative step in as he prepared himself to meet Kyla's familiar. When nothing appeared to be launching itself at the door, he opened it fully and stepped inside, ushering Kyla in.

"Here, boy," she called out, letting out a whistle.

Instantly, the sound of scrabbling nails on tiles filled the air. Seconds later, a huge chunk of muscle bounded through the kitchen, galloping towards Kyla. As he reached her, he sat down, his dark eyes bright and filled with happiness, soft whines coming from his throat.

"Hey, boy," Dylan said, leaning down and offering his hand for the dog to smell.

The dog jumped back a step, his previously wagging tail now still and quivering between his back legs. He took several steps back, cowering behind Kyla as he kept his eyes pinned on Dylan.

Kyla looked up at Dylan and frowned. "What the hell?"

Dylan froze. His and Sam's secret had been outed to everyone—whilst Kyla had been unconscious. She still didn't have a clue about their true identities.

Glancing down at the floor, Dylan lifted a hand and scratched the back of his neck, buying time as he tried to form the right sentence to say to her.

Kyla reached down and stroked the dog's head, giving him some kind of reassurance. Feeling the tremble through his whole body, she looked back up at Dylan again. "Dylan, what's going on?"

Letting out a huge sigh, Dylan dropped his hand, lifted his head, and met Kyla's enquiring eyes. "You're going to find out sooner or later so it's best you hear it from me first, right?"

Kyla frowned again. "Are you asking me or you?"

Sucking in a deep breath, Dylan replied, "Sam and I...well...our whole family actually, we're um...kind of like...werewolves."

Kyla stared at him, seconds ticking by as she processed his words. The Kyla from yesterday would have exploded at him for lying to her and keeping secrets. Would this Kyla be any different?

Kyla let out a long breath and then nodded, pursing her lips. "Of course you are." She shrugged her shoulders. "It explains a lot." Turning to look down at her familiar, she scratched his ears and smiled before looking back at Dylan. "For the rest of today, no more supernatural shit. Deal?"

Dylan grinned. "Deal."

CHAPTER 43

For the first time in their relationship, Kyla and Dylan managed to share a bed and not have sex. After her energy draining ordeal, she wanted nothing more than to fall asleep held in a pair of strong, arms that encased her in a warm hug.

The fact those arms belonged to a bad ass werewolf made the deal even sweeter, but she wouldn't tell Dylan that.

When she woke the next morning, refreshed and buzzing with energy, she rolled onto her side, looking down at her dog, who had slept by the side of the bed all night, and smiled. "I think he looks like a Dylan," she said, biting her lip to stifle her smile.

Dylan shot straight up in bed. "What did you just say? You'd better not name your dog after me."

"Why?" she asked, innocently shrugging her shoulders. "He wants my love and affection, just like you. He's cute, I want to pet him all the time. I think it's a good fit."

Dylan put his hand on her shoulder and forced her to turn to face him. "Don't you dare," he said, narrowing his eyes as he looked down at her. "You can call him anything else but my name."

Kyla grinned up at him. "I think it's up to him what his name is." She turned back to the dog and said, "What do you say, boy? Do you like the name Dylan?" The dog barked and jumped to his feet, wagging his tail eagerly. Kyla looked back at Dylan. "I think he likes it."

Dylan rolled his eyes and then rolled out of bed. Glaring at the dog, he said, "No."

The dog whined and sat down, his big brown eyes filling with sadness.

"You're so mean," Kyla said.

Dylan lifted his chin and said to the dog, "Oscar." The dog leapt up and barked twice before spinning around in a circle. "There you go," Dylan said, folding his arms over his chest, a triumphant gleam in his eyes. "That's his name."

"Oscar," Kyla said, sounding the name out. "I like it. How did you come up with it so quickly? Does it have a meaning or anything?"

"I believe it has some Irish roots that means God's spear or champion warrior. I think he's definitely going to be your protector when I'm not around."

Kyla turned to look at him. "How do you know it's meaning?"

Dylan kept quiet for a few seconds and then said, "It's my middle name."

"Dylan Oscar Mohun," Kyla said. "That's quite a nice name." She paused for a second, then said, "Wait. Your initials spell DOM."

He grinned. "Yes, they do. And don't you forget it," he said, winking at her.

Kyla giggled and dragged herself out of bed.

Around an hour later, after breakfast, feeding Oscar, and getting ready for the day, Kyla decided it was time to visit her grandparents and talk about yesterday. As Dylan drove them both towards her grandparents' house, Kyla phoned Sam, asking her to join them there.

After she put the phone down, Dylan gave her the side eye and sighed. "What about the guys?" he asked, his voice low and quiet.

Kyla's heart backflipped in her chest at the thought of the handsome demons. Quirking an eyebrow up at Dylan, she replied, "I didn't expect you to ask about them."

Dylan pulled his lips into a thin line, staring straight ahead. Seeing an entrance to a field on the left, he swung the car in and came to a stop. Turning his full attention to Kyla, he took a deep breath and said, "I need to get something off my chest. When you woke up yesterday, the first thing you said was Azazel's name."

Kyla held her breath and looked down at her hands, wringing them together as she tried to calm her racing pulse. "He was the last thing I saw before I fell unconscious. He literally rushed in right as Mildred pulled me under."

Dylan reached over and took one of her hands. "Hey," he said, his tone quiet and gentle. "Look at me."

Kyla peeked up at him from beneath her lashes, her mind whirling as to what he would say next.

"I am not blaming you for anything, let me just get that clear. You had been through a hell of an ordeal, he was the first person you saw when you woke, considering you were in his arms." Dylan took a breath, those words leaving a sour taste in his mouth. "It hurt like hell, I won't deny it, but I believe it happened because of the circumstances. What concerns me is…"

Kyla waited a second or two for him to finish his sentence but as his eyes drifted away from hers, she took a guess at where those words had been going. "The fact he's my demi-soul. Apparently anyway."

Dylan glanced back at her and nodded.

"Do you want me to be honest with you?"

Dylan swallowed a lump in his throat, then nodded. "Always."

"I can't deny that I don't feel a pull towards him." Kyla took a breath and let it out slowly, picking her next words carefully. "I can't explain it, it's weird…like he's a magnet and I'm a paperclip."

Dylan chuckled, trying to ignore the ache in his heart at her words. "What an analogy."

Kyla smiled. "I know that's not what you wanted to hear. I'm sorry, but we've battled through so much over the years, the least I can do is be honest with you."

He nodded. "I appreciate the honesty so thank you. I guess I'm just worried about what happens next. Is this where you run off with him into the sunset playing happily ever after?"

She shrugged her shoulders and stared out of the windscreen. "I don't know, Dylan." She looked back at him. "I'm sorry but I just don't have those answers yet."

"What are we in the meantime?"

Kyla studied him for a few seconds, scanning her eyes over his. "Is it selfish of me to ask for everything to stay as it is until we figure all of this out?"

Dylan relaxed somewhat, grateful she wasn't telling him to give her space until she knew her place with Azazel. "Not at all."

Squeezing his hand, she said, "I'm worried that you'll end up being hurt at the end of this though. Is it kinder to just cut it off now?"

Something in Dylan's chest constricted, an arrow of panic shooting him straight in the heart, coursing through his body at a rate of knots. "No," he said, shaking his head. "I'm ok, don't worry about me. I'm as tough as old boots, you know that."

"Maybe you'll find your demi-soul soon."

Dylan gave her a small smile, appreciating her optimism. "There was a reason I had no idea what a demi-soul was," he said, his voice almost a whisper. "Wolves don't have one."

Kyla frowned. "What? How? Why? Maybe you're just not aware of it?"

"It's complicated," he replied. "Werewolves are seen as the peacekeepers of the supernatural world. That's why we're big and tough and take a bit of rough and tumble. We're like guards. If we had a weakness, such as a soulmate, it would compromise our position. Our duty takes precedence over anything else. As such, we can choose freely to be with who we please."

Kyla frowned and shook her head. "I don't buy that. It doesn't make sense. If all the supernatural creatures have demi-souls, then you being with any of them means you're with someone that isn't technically yours."

"That's why we tend to be with humans or wolves. You won't find records anywhere of wolves being with any other species."

Kyla thought over his words for a few seconds, then said, "We need to get to my grandparents. Once we have some solid facts, then we can make decisions and figure things out, right?"

Dylan lifted her hand to his mouth and brushed a kiss over the back of it. "Good point."

Easing the car back onto the road, they continued on in silence, each lost to their own thoughts. Kyla kept replaying yesterday over and over, specifically the part with Lucifer where he mentioned demi-souls and then presented the brothers with two red roses. What was that?

She needed them at her grandparents, they had questions to answer. Wondering if she could reach them with her mind, Kyla took a deep breath and closed her eyes. Picturing Azazel in her mind, focusing on his jade green eyes, she thought *I need you* and then showed him an image of her grandparents' cottage.

After repeating it three times, she opened her eyes and bit her lip as she debated if it was as simple as that to call a demon to her aid. Was it as easy as willing yourself to communicate with someone?

Minutes later, as Dylan rounded the corner to Lily and Malcolm's house, Kyla couldn't stop herself from grinning as she saw Azazel and Balthazar waiting for her outside the cottage.

Maybe it was that easy after all.

CHAPTER 44

KYLA EXPECTED DYLAN TO be his usual possessive arsehole self when seeing the two demons again. However, much to her surprise, he shook both of their hands and greeted them both with a smile, albeit a tight lipped one.

When Sam pulled up seconds later, she jumped out of her car without even switching it off and launched herself at Kyla, giving her a hug so tight, she all but squeezed all the air from her body.

"I'm so glad you're ok," Sam said, finally stepping back. "Do you feel ok?"

Kyla nodded and smiled at her friend. "Better than ever." She motioned with her head towards the cottage. "Come on, let's get this sorted."

Lily and Malcolm had prepared a table full of coffee, tea, biscuits, cakes, and of course a specially made crisp sandwich just for Kyla.

Giving her grandparents a kiss each on the cheek, Kyla took a seat next to her gran, waiting for the others to find their seats around the large table. Sam sat down on Kyla's left, Balthazar then sitting next to Sam. Azazel took his seat opposite his brother, leaving Dylan to sit opposite Kyla and on the right of Malcolm, who sat opposite his wife.

The empty space between Dylan and Azazel spoke volumes to everyone present. Kyla clicked her fingers to Oscar and pointed at the chair. He jumped up without hesitation, sitting between the two men like some kind of referee. Every few seconds, he would give Azazel the side eye, as if sizing him up.

"Please," Lily said, gesturing at the display of food. "Help yourselves. We have lots to discuss."

"That's your dog?" Sam asked Kyla, staring at the handsome face looking at her from across the table.

Kyla nodded. "Oscar," she replied, flickering her eyes across to Dylan with a smirk. "He's my familiar."

Sam lifted an eyebrow. "Your what?"

Kyla grinned and then recalled her story from the day before when Oscar had appeared to her, along with her gran's explanation of what familiars are.

"That's so cool," Sam said, looking at Oscar again. "He won't attack me or anything, will he?"

Kyla frowned, confusion swirling through her eyes. "What? No. Why do you ask?"

"Dogs tend to not like werewolves much. Specifically, females who don't have full access to their powers yet."

Kyla frowned. "Why? Dogs are descended from wolves. I don't get it."

"They're fine with alphas, or those who are destined to be next in line," she said, nodding her head towards Dylan. "But females that aren't quite human but aren't quite wolf they see as a threat, we're an unknown quantity."

"How are you not quite human but not quite wolf?"

"We don't have access to our full powers until we're a mum. I can't shift, I don't have super speed, a better sense of smell or super strength either. I heal quickly, see better, and have enhanced hearing." She shrugged her shoulders. "Not quite human, not quite wolf."

Kyla picked up her crisp sandwich and bit into it. As if that broke some kind of seal on the others, everyone reached for food and drink, filling their plates and cups in a comfortable silence.

"Surely then," Kyla said, finishing her mouthful of crisp sandwich. "We just need to get you pregnant and then boom, you're all wolfy, right?"

Sam gave Kyla a small smile. "Not quite that simple."

"Why?"

"Right," Malcolm said, clapping his hands together. "Sorry, Sam, but I think we have more pressing matters to discuss than your potential babies."

Kyla raised an eyebrow and looked at her grandad. When he refused to meet her eye contact, she kept quiet, not wanting to press the matter any further. It was clearly a discussion for another day. Or perhaps for her and Dylan later on.

"Yes, of course," Sam said, picking up her cup of tea. "Sorry, Malcolm."

He nodded his head once and shared a brief look with Lily, a wordless exchange passing between the two.

"Azazel, Balthazar," Lily said, turning her attention to them. "I think it's time for you both to explain what happened just before Lucifer left yesterday."

Azazel stared across at his brother, not wanting to take the lead on this one. Balthazar glared back at him, cursing him mentally for leaving him to pick up the short straw.

"You heard Lucifer speak about demi-souls," Balthazar said, his voice quiet. "And obviously the spell I cast for our vacation this year."

Malcolm narrowed his eyes at the demon, not needing reminding of his transgression.

Balthazar cleared his throat. "Once we recognise our demi-souls, we have to approach them with the truth and ask for their acceptance of our souls. We do this by presenting them with a red rose. They take the rose and are shown all of our..." he took a breath "...all of our wrongdoings. They can choose to accept us, warts and all, or they can reject us."

"What happens if you're rejected?" Dylan asked.

Balthazar hesitated for a second before he replied, "We die."

Kyla's jaw dropped. "What? Are you serious?"

Balthazar nodded. "In Lucifer's eyes, if not even our other half wants us, then why would anything else want us?"

She let out a low whistle and shook her head. "That was a risky game you pulled doing that. You knew that though, when you cast the words? That you'd either have your demi-soul or die?" Turning to her gran and grandad, she asked, "Did this happen for you guys? Did you have to give Gran a red rose?"

Malcolm nodded. "Yes, I did. But your gran and I had a good foundation behind us before I even approached the subject. I was very lucky with my timings. Lucifer was otherwise engaged which meant he wasn't really paying attention to me and what I was up to. If your gran had had the ritual sprung upon her within the first few weeks of meeting, well, I don't think you'd exist, Marmalade."

Lily rolled her eyes and tutted at him. "You don't know that. Stop being so dramatic and trying to scare the poor girl."

"I still remember the hesitance before you accepted," Malcolm said. "It was the longest seven seconds of my life."

Lily sighed. "Are you ever going to let those seven seconds go?"

Malcolm flashed her a toothy grin. "Never."

"Wait, wait, wait," Kyla said, glancing over at Azazel. "Lucifer gave two red roses. One for you, and one for Balthazar, right?"

Azazel nodded.

"So that means Balthazar has met his?"

Sam coughed and tentatively raised her hand. "That would be me."

Kyla widened her eyes as her best friend's words rattled around her head. "What? How long have you known that?"

"Only a couple of days. With everything that happened yesterday, I obviously didn't get chance to tell you. Plus, it's all so new with me and him, I just wanted time to process it all before I tried to make you understand the connection we have."

Kyla sat up straight and leaned forwards. "Like he's a magnet and you're a helpless paperclip?"

Sam tipped her head back and laughed. A couple of seconds passed before she met Kyla's eyes and nodded. "Exactly like that."

Kyla let out a sigh and looked across at Azazel. "So what you're telling me is that if I reject you, you die?"

Azazel nodded.

"Wow, no pressure or anything then," she said, letting out a long breath.

"Ultimately," Azazel said, biting down on a strawberry cupcake. "You hold the power as to whether you think I have a right to live any longer. If there's something in my past you can't deal with, that could swing your choice the wrong way. Or the right way, whatever your perspective on that is."

Kyla shook her head. "I can't do that. I can't have that power of someone's life."

"But you do," Dylan said. "And you need to do what feels right for you. If you don't feel comfortable having that power, then there's only one choice, isn't there?"

Kyla couldn't ignore the sadness swirling around in his chocolate eyes. She could only guess at the pain he must have been hiding in order to say those words. "But, if I see all of his wrongdoings, and think he doesn't deserve to live any longer, that he needs stopping from being a menace to society, then there's only one option, isn't there?"

Lily placed a hand on Kyla's forearm with a gentle touch. "Your grandad had some very dark secrets that I discovered when I took that rose, dear. If his soul is redeemable, so will his be," she said, motioning her head towards Azazel.

Kyla wet her lips with her tongue. Covering her gran's hand with her own, she then said, "It's not just that, Gran. It's that if I accept, what that then means from there." She glanced at Dylan and then back at her gran. "It makes everything much more complicated."

"Can I just say," Azazel said, holding his hand up as he grabbed a biscuit with the other. "That neither option is good for us. We either die or become human and lose all our powers."

Sam sucked in a sharp breath. "What?" She looked at Balthazar, her eyes filling with tears. "Is that true?"

Balthazar nodded. "Yes, it is."

"Why? Why would you want to give up eternal life and all your power just to live a few decades of nothing and then die?"

Azazel clapped his hands together. "Thank you!" He took a bite of the biscuit and looked over at Lily. "Amazing biscuits, Lily." Glancing back at Sam, he said, "That's exactly what I said but that buffoon couldn't see past his idealistic views of romance."

"No, no, no," Kyla said. She looked at her grandad. "You still have all your powers, right?"

Malcolm nodded. "I know where you're going with this, Kyla, but the deal I cut with Lucifer in order to keep my powers was a one off. He won't grant them two the same."

"How do you know? You never know unless you ask, right? You taught me that."

Malcolm pursed his lips and let out a sigh. "Kyla, just trust me on this one, ok?"

She narrowed her eyes. "What did you do? What was your deal?"

Lily, still with her hand on Kyla's forearm, patted her granddaughter and said, "That doesn't matter. What matters is now. These two don't want either option they are left with so what can we do?"

Kyla looked over at Azazel. "What's the lesser of two evils for you? Death? Or living as a human?"

"Death," he replied, with no hesitation. "I would rather die than live life in any other way than what I am doing now."

Kyla's heart skipped several beats. The thought of Azazel being no more, and being no more at her will, sat uneasy in her chest.

"And you?" she said, looking at Balthazar.

"I'm happy to live as a human."

"Well, you're sorted," she said, looking at Sam. "It's just me left with the shit decision. Again."

She put her elbows on the table and rested her head in her hands as she raced through options in her mind. The glaringly obvious thing to her was that she couldn't force Azazel to live a life he didn't want. How would that be fair to him just to save her own conscience? If he wanted to die, it's not like he would hate her for doing it—he wanted it. Therefore, it would just be her own peace to make with his decision.

But it wasn't just that.

He was her demi-soul. Was death really preferable to him than being with her? A small whisper in the back of her mind told her she had her answer to her mess with choosing between Dylan and Azazel. However, even though he willingly wanted death, she didn't like it.

She wanted him alive.

She needed him alive.

"Kyla," Lily said, rubbing a hand over her granddaughter's back. "Are you ok?"

Kyla sucked in a deep breath and looked up, straight at Azazel. Her decision was made. She held out her left hand, palm up, and motioned with her fingers for him to pass something. "Give me the damn rose."

Azazel froze. He hadn't been expecting that. A fizz of adrenaline shot through his veins. Was this it? His death? Would it hurt or would he go peacefully? Would Lucifer take his soul, or would he just float around in nothingness for all eternity?

"Kyla..." Dylan said, his voice all but a hiss. "What are you doing?"

She met Dylan's eyes, nothing but determination rolling off her in waves. "I can't live with this going around and around in my head until frickin' June, Dylan. I want it over with now. Short, sharp, done. That's it."

Balthazar glanced at Azazel, a wry smile playing on his lips. "I told you you'd met your match, didn't I?"

Azazel took a gulp of his tea, reached over for a chocolate cupcake, peeled the wrapper off and stuffed it in his mouth in one go.

As everyone watched him chew, in silence, Kyla knew her decision already. She had this.

Finishing his mouthful, Azazel stood up, his chair scraping back against the kitchen floor. Pulling a thorny red rose from his back pocket, he held it between his thumb and forefinger. "Are you sure you're ready for this?"

Kyla rolled her eyes. "Don't second guess me. Give it here."

"Very well." He glanced at Balthazar and smiled. "See you on the other side, brother. It's been a pleasure."

Chapter 45

As Azazel reached across the table, offering Kyla the rose, she snatched it from him, impatient to get this over and done with.

Wrapping her hand around the stem, several of the thorns pricked her skin, drawing blood. She gasped, looking up at Azazel.

The second their eyes connected, their whole world shifted entirely.

As her gran's kitchen faded from her reality, Kyla could do nothing but watch in utter fascination as a new world shimmered into existence. A sandy cobbled road stretched before her, stone buildings lining the edge of the street either side. Bright blue skies above, not a cloud in sight, beaming sunshine baking the earth beneath. Bright green trees littered the landscape, standing metres tall, shouts and screams of children playing echoed around her.

On the horizon, a huge mountain reached high up into the sky, lush green grass and thriving vegetation reaching halfway up its side.

A woman appeared from a house on Kyla's right, dragging a bright red and white patterned rug out into the street. Her long brown hair was tied up into a high bun, leaving only a few wispy bits framing her delicate face. Her white dress wrapped around her slim frame, held in place by a red and gold threaded rope cinching her in at the waist.

She turned to Azazel, on her left, and said, "Where the hell are we?"

He closed his eyes and pressed his lips together for a few seconds. "Here we go again," he whispered. Opening his eyes, he looked at Kyla, his jade green eyes brimming with tears. "This is a glimpse of my human life before I became...well...me." He took a breath, his Adam's apple bobbing up and down as he swallowed the lump in his throat. "Balthazar and I lived in Pompeii before it...you know the rest."

Kyla's jaw dropped. She drew a deep breath as she glanced around her, taking in the odd shaped stones underneath her feet, the columns supporting the corners of each building, and the old but peaceful feeling surrounding her.

"I...oh my God. Can they see us?"

Azazel shook his head. "No. Thankfully. I think I'd slit my own throat if that were the case."

"What happened here, Azazel?"

He lifted an arm and motioned for them to walk down the street. "I'll show you." He took a moment and then said, "I've been back here many times, torturing myself over what happens next. I haven't been back for at least five hundred years—I realised it was doing me no good to keep rehashing things that had once been. But it's still just as raw as if it happened yesterday."

Kyla's heart sped up, pumping a heady mix of adrenaline and anxiety through her veins. What on earth was going to happen next? "Is…" she wet her lips with tongue "…is what happens next what turned you into a demon?"

He nodded, glancing down at the street, his features glazed over with sorrow.

The warm yet fresh air enveloped Kyla in a serene hug, making her want to stay here and explore. Smells of baking bread, cooking meat, and herbs and spices invaded her senses, making her stomach grumble.

They walked past a few shops that sold everything from pottery to clothing to paintings. Men and women hurried around the streets, going about their day. Kyla couldn't help but feel a sense of sadness as she flickered her eyes towards Mount Vesuvius, wondering how she would have felt knowing her impending doom was slithering towards her and she couldn't do a thing about it.

"Am I about to see that erupt?" she asked, nodding her head towards Vesuvius. "I don't think I can handle watching thousands of people and animals be turned to ash."

"No," he whispered, leading her off the main street and down a side alley. "That's about another five months from now."

So enamoured with her startling temporary reality, Kyla paid no attention to the rabbit warren of streets Azazel led her through. She walked with the pace of a three-year-old, staring at every building they passed, drinking in the magnificent old buildings and wishing she could witness how they built everything to last so many thousands of years.

When Azazel finally came to a stop, Kyla bumped into his solid form, her attention taken by staring high up at the roof of a shop and the exquisite markings carved into the stone.

"Sorry," she said, heat rushing through her in an instant.

Azazel offered her a small smile, ignoring the bolt of electricity that shot through him when their skin touched. "This was my home," he said, nodding his head towards the building in front of him.

Kyla took in the front of an exquisite villa. Two huge columns, easily eight feet tall, stood away from the front door, supporting a flat, block roof that appeared to be some sort of balcony with its linear metre high edging. Along the front of it was a beautiful artwork of a lion and an eagle, following a two-horse chariot into battle. The vivid reds, whites, and golds were absolutely breathtaking.

"This was my human life as Lucius Maximus Valens. I was a general in the army." He took a deep breath and pointed to the villa next door. No grand entrance, just a modest double oak door hinting at being an entrance. "Balthazar lived there. He worked in politics. He had the name Octavio Maximus Valens."

Kyla felt her heart skip a beat, stealing her of breath for a second. *Where is this going?*

"Let's start here," Azazel said, motioning for her to head towards Octavio's front door.

Opening the front doors, Azazel led them through a shaded entrance way, closing the doors behind them. Straight in front of her sat a picturesque courtyard, edged by the stone of the house, but a thriving green garden complete with a fish ornamental fountain, water spouting from its mouth.

Azazel headed them to the left, taking her into a large kitchen, an open fire on one side, the light-coloured bricks charred black from smoke, shelves of pots, pans, and herbs littering the walls, and thick wooden benches dotted around for food preparation.

As he led her through the house, each room linking to the next like a line of rooms, Kyla took in everything she could—ancient paintings of gods and goddesses on the walls, intricate patterns in expensive mosaic flooring, colourful motifs on the walls depicting various scenes from eating to orgies.

By the time they'd done a complete tour of the rectangular home consisting of a kitchen, four bedrooms, two bathrooms with small pools in each, and a reception room, Kyla found herself speechless.

"This is incredible. I'm blown away." Standing back in the shaded entrance way overlooking the garden, Kyla thought back over the rooms she'd been through. "I don't get the feeling of a family being here though. Nothing hinting at kids." She looked over at Azazel, noticing the anguish lingering in his eyes. "Was a woman's touch even a thing back then, back here? If it was, I don't see it."

Azazel shook his head. "You won't see it. Because he was unmarried, he was alone."

Kyla raised an eyebrow and looked around her again. "Why would he need something this big if he was all alone?"

"Times were different back then. You lived in a home according to your status in society, not according to the size of your family."

"But if he had a high status, he must have had women wanting to be with him?"

Azazel nodded. "He wanted nothing more than a wife, really. I can't deny him that truth. The problem was he was always too picky, finding something wrong with even the most beautiful of women." He closed his eyes as he ran shaking hands over his face. "I only wish I had realised why."

Kyla watched his hands as he let them fall to his side, the tremble in them still glaringly obvious. Her mouth ran dry as a ball of dread churned in her stomach.

Azazel led them inside his house, the layout identical to Octavio's, just on a slightly larger scale. Walking through the rooms here, it was hard to miss that this was a family home. Various items of clothing strewn around, marbles littered the floor, a couple of wooden swords and some handmade chariots, clearly a child lived here.

The clattering of pots and pans combined with the sound of a cheery female voice singing had Azazel walking straight to the kitchen. He went through the doorway and stopped dead, holding his breath.

Kyla came to a stop at his side, her eyes widening as she took in the sight of Azazel as a human, as Lucius. Crisp white robes settled against his bronzed skin, his muscled arms flexing as he wrapped his arms around a brunette beauty. She ran a small hand through his blonde hair as she stared deep into his eyes, her whiskey-coloured eyes full of love for her husband. With her silky-smooth skin, red lips, and high cheekbones, the woman was the epitome of beauty. Her own white dress clung to her body, held in place by two horse brooches decorated with gleaming gems.

"Cassia," Azazel whispered, his eyes glazing over with a forlorn look.

A young boy with blonde hair and high cheekbones ran through from the inner courtyard, his bright green eyes gleaming with joy as he tugged on Cassia's robes. "My vegetables are growing," he yelled, jumping up and down in excitement.

"That's amazing," she replied. "Why don't you show me?"

Lucius let his wife go, taking a long, velvet red robe from a nearby bench and swinging it over his shoulders. Grazing Cassia's cheek with a kiss, he departed, leaving his smiling wife and child to head out into the garden.

Kyla heard a hitch in Azazel's breathing and turned to look at him. His whole body shook from head to toe, his lips pursed into an O as he tried to regulate his breathing. "Hey," she said quietly, gently placing a hand on his forearm. "Are you ok?"

A couple of seconds passed before he blinked and turned to look at her. "I never thought I'd watch this again. Let alone with..." his voice cracked "...with my demi-soul. I don't want you to see me like this, Kyla. Say the words, say you reject me, and you won't have to see what happens next." He squeezed his eyes shut, a solitary tear rolling down his cheek. "And I won't have to relive it again either."

Emotion rose in Kyla like a tidal wave. Knowing what she did of Azazel so far, to see him so open, so vulnerable, so sensitive, struck a chord in her. She knew these raw emotions, the damage they did when you drowned in their depths for too long.

"Maybe," she said, sliding her hand down to his and interlacing their fingers. "Maybe this will be the visit that heals you. That finally gives you closure."

He opened his eyes, nothing but walls of water staring back at her. "How?" he whispered. "I've been back here thousands of times, Kyla. And I mean thousands. I once spent an entire month here, just reliving it over and over again. There will never be a moment of closure for me."

She squeezed his hand. "Maybe you're looking in the wrong place for closure."

He blinked at her a few times, confusion and surprise filtering through his jade green depths. "Maybe."

They moved to stand out in the street watching as time sped forwards, the hustle and bustle of town life quietening down as twilight settled in the sky, the glittering of stars giving the dusky landscape a priceless picturesque view.

A swishing sound caught Kyla's attention, making her turn around. She saw Cassia walking out of the house down the street towards Octavio's home. Carrying a dish in her hands, she hurried along, her pretty face set into a look of determination.

"The streets were no place for a woman after dark," Azazel whispered. "She knew I didn't like her being out after dusk." He swallowed. "But she also knew how much

Octavio hated his slaves cooking so whenever we had left-overs, she took them to him."

Azazel moved to walk behind Cassia, ushering Kyla along with his hand hovering over her lower back. Holding the door open for her, he let Kyla take the lead and follow Cassia through the house.

Heading straight into the dining room, Cassia set the dish down on a wooden table, various burn marks across the surface of it. Sat in a carved wooden chair was Octavio, dressed in his white robes with a gold eagle brooch at his shoulder. His dark eyes held an unnerving stare, a paradoxical mix of emptiness but at the same time full of emotion.

"You're so kind to me," he said, looking up at Cassia. "I cannot understand why."

Cassia moved towards him, placing a delicate kiss on his cheek. "You're my husband's brother, Octavio. I will always care for you."

Kyla felt her mouth go dry. She sucked in a breath and held it, each second that ticked by feeling like it stretched for eternity.

"I can't watch this again," Azazel said, closing his eyes and turning around.

Kyla spared him a glance, but her curiosity won out. She needed to know what happened next.

As Cassia turned to walk away, Octavio grabbed her wrist, yanking her back to him. Surprise and fear mixed together in the woman's eyes. Standing up, Octavio reached up with his free hand and caressed Cassia's cheek, the aching tenderness in his expression sending barbs of panic right through Kyla.

"Will you ever feel anything for me, Cassia? Anything more than just care and goodwill?"

"Octavio," Cassia replied, her voice quiet and calm, despite her rapidly paling colour. "I am married to Lucius. To your brother. I love him. We have a child together. I will always love you, Octavio, but only as my husband's brother. Out of respect for yours and his relationship I have said nothing to him, but you need to stop this before I say something to him. This has gone on too long."

Tears started welling in Kyla's eyes as she forced herself to watch the scene unfold. As Octavio's face clouded with hurt and rejection, he lunged at Cassia. She jumped back but found herself restrained by the grip he still had on her wrist.

Pulling her back towards him, he swung them around and pressed her back against the wall. With her free hand, Cassia slapped at him, screaming at him to let her go, to stop.

Octavio released her wrist, giving the woman both hands to now push back at him. However, seconds later, he grabbed both of her hands in one of his. Pushing them against the wall, he rested them on the top of her head, keeping them in place with his fingers whilst using his palm to push against her forehead and keep her head still.

Realising all she had left was the use of her legs, Cassia kicked out at him, yelling at the top of her lungs for him to take a moment and think about what he was doing.

Locked in some kind of trance, Octavio ignored her completely. When she next kicked a leg out at him, he pushed his thigh against her, trapping her leg between him and the wall and placing himself right between her legs.

As he fiddled with his robes and then lifted Cassia's, Kyla felt her heart go into overdrive. She knew what was coming, why the brothers were now demons, there was only one way this could end, but a small part of her still hoped the woman would fight her way out.

Kyla shut her eyes and turned away, her legs trembling as her tears spilled down over her cheeks. When Cassia fell silent, Kyla *knew.*

Hearing a loud grunt a minute or so later, Kyla choked back a sob. When she felt an arm slide around her shoulders, she screamed and scuttled sideways, opening her eyes to see Azazel staring at her. "I'm sorry," she whispered. "I thought..." she looked over at the scene still playing out before them. "I thought it was him."

Octavio released Cassia. Without even giving her another glance, he turned and stormed away, his shoulders tense and his back ramrod straight. Cassia collapsed onto the floor, sobbing her heart out as she quivered all over.

The agony piercing Azazel's eyes made Kyla want to kill Balthazar for him, and for what he did to Cassia. The woman had shown him nothing but kindness.

"Let's go," Azazel said, holding his hand out for Kyla.

She hesitated, not sure what she would see next. So far, the only demonic act had come from Balthazar. What had Azazel done to deserve being a demon?

Placing her hand in his, they walked back out into the street, time flashed by them, day blurring into night over and over. Heading them back into his house, Azazel stood them in the entrance way.

Kyla watched as a tired looking Lucius appeared, his face thinner but his muscles more defined, his clothes dirty and dishevelled. He'd clearly been away at war. "How long after is this?"

Azazel sighed. "About four months."

Kyla's heart stopped. *No,* she thought. *No, no, no.*

Lucius strode into the kitchen, his handsome face creased into a huge smile. Upon seeing her husband, Cassia ran at him, throwing her arms around his neck.

"I love you," she cried, burying her face in his neck as tears poured from her.

Lucius pulled back from their embrace, his eyes scanning over her. "What's wrong, my love? Don't cry. I'm home now."

Cassia, like a floodgate had been opened, let everything pour out of her, all the emotion she'd kept bottled since that fateful night.

Taking her into their bedroom, Lucius settled her on his lap and coaxed her to tell him what was wrong.

"Something awful happened. A man came in the night..." She recalled the events of that night to him without telling Lucius who the man was.

Lucius, visibly raging at his wife's tale, shook all over, his hands clenching into fists as his face turned bright red. "Who was it?"

Cassia bit her lip. "I don't know. I couldn't see him."

Kyla sucked in a sharp breath. "What?"

"She didn't want to ruin our relationship," Azazel said. "Even to the end she was nothing but selfless."

"Lucius," Cassia said, placing her hand on his cheek. "I'm bearing his child. I don't want it. You need to kill me."

Kyla whirled around to face Azazel head on, her eyes wide. "Tell me you didn't kill her."

Azazel dropped his eye contact, staring at the ground. "Watch."

Lucius picked Cassia up, set her on the bed, planted a kiss on her forehead, then grabbing his sword, marched out onto the street, demanding people tell him who dared to violate his wife. Women screamed, children ran. Men came towards him, trying to calm him down but no one offered him an answer.

Seething in the revelation from his wife, Lucius saw red. Any man that dared come within the swing of his sword felt the full wrath of Lucius Maximus Valens. Hands were lost, arms cut off, blood drawn from spilled guts.

As the men rallied round, trying to calm the seasoned general, Lucius took two hits from arrows, one in his left calf, the other in his right shoulder blade. Completely numb to anything but his own grief, he paid no attention to his wounds, slaying anyone who dared to come near him or not give him his answer.

The dusty street stones turned red with blood as the bulldozer of a man carved his way through the streets, driven by his need for vengeance. As someone called for the soldiers, Lucius, with a heaving chest and tired arms, stumbled towards his brother's villa for help.

Busting through the front door, Lucius dragged himself into the kitchen only to find Octavio dead by his own sword through his gut, a scrawled message in his blood written on the floor admitting his guilt.

Lucius let out a cry of agony. Cassia ran in, their son clutching onto her, fear consuming him at the sight of his father's breakdown.

"Why didn't you tell me?" Lucius cried.

"Because of your love for him, Lucius. He was still your brother."

Lucius fell to the floor, his sword clattering onto the floor next to him. "They will kill me for this." He looked up at Cassia. "You know that?"

She nodded, her face streaked with tears. Lifting a small dagger from beneath her robe, she pressed the handle of it into Lucius' hand. "Please, Lucius. I would rather die than bear another man's child."

Lucius shook his head and pushed her away. "No."

A flash of pain and rejection ran through Cassia's eyes. She took the dagger back and without hesitation she drove it straight into her abdomen, letting out a primal scream as she did.

Their son screamed, covering his face with his hands, his robe darkening with liquid as he wet himself.

Cassia fell to the floor, her breathing laboured as her white robe started to turn red, her blood leaking from her at a rate of knots. "Put me out of my misery, Lucius," she said, staring up at him. "Please."

Lucius sobbed and crawled to his wife, pressing his lips to hers. "I love you," he said, taking the dagger from her hand. With a shaking hand, he took the dagger from her hand and moved it to her throat, poising it at her artery. Closing his eyes, he let out a sorrowful howl as he drew the blade across her porcelain skin, fracturing her forever.

Forcing himself to open his eyes, Lucius watched as her whiskey-coloured eyes dimmed with life. "I love you, Cassia. For all eternity."

Her head lolled to the side, the gaping wound on her neck staring at Lucius, reminding him of what he'd just done.

"Loreius," he said, motioning for his son to come close. "We must join your mother in the afterlife."

The boy took tentative steps towards his father, the gravity of those words sinking in the closer he came. Taking his son by the hand, Lucius sat him on his lap and repeated the same action he'd just done to his wife.

As his son gasped and gurgled for air, Lucius pressed his lips to the side of his head, his hot tears wetting the boy's hair. When he fell limp, he laid Loreius next to his mother before submitting himself to the same fate.

CHAPTER 46

KYLA STOOD, DUMBFOUNDED, LOOKING at the family of three slain by Lucius's hand, their blood staining the floor around them. She watched fascinated, as Lucius's blood spread over the stones, slowly inching towards Octavio's body. Was that coincidence or perhaps something more that even in death the brothers had a link?

Turning to Azazel, she took both of his hands in hers and squeezed them both. "I am *so* sorry you lived through that. That was horrific. I don't see what you did that warrants you being a demon."

"I killed a child, then committed suicide." He shrugged his shoulders. "It doesn't matter why I did what I did, it only matters that I did it. In Lucifer's eyes anyway."

Kyla's head was whirling at a million miles an hour. "I don't know what to think...I'm shocked. I can't believe he did that...he seems so different." She let out a sigh. "But then I guess everyone has a side we don't know about, right?"

Azazel shrugged his shoulders. "I guess."

"And he's Sam's demi-soul." She shook her head. "I can't let her be with him. I just can't. She'd be horrified to see this."

"That's not a decision for you to make. That's *her* decision to make."

Panic started crawling through Kyla like poisonous ivy vines. "I can't not tell her, Azazel. Jesus, look at what he did!"

"I am perfectly aware of what he did, Kyla. You can't make your friend live a life she doesn't want to. If she wants him, that's it. You can't do anything about it." He lifted his left hand, palm flat, the dreaded red rose sitting on top of it. "Now you need to make your choice. You've seen the worst of me as a human. I'm a murderer and a coward. Is that really what you want from your demi-soul? As much as I hate to say this, that werewolf of yours would be much better suited to you than me. He slit your throat without a second thought, anything to save your life. *That's* the kind of man you need."

Kyla dropped his hands and took a step back. "I don't call murdering your son cowardly. That took an immense amount of strength not many people would have. You didn't want him to grow up without his parents, I get it. Yes, you murdered people, but it was also kind of your job." She shrugged her shoulders. "I don't see the issue. I think you've vilified yourself in your own head more than you should have." She took a breath and then said, "Dylan did *what*?"

"He had to," Azazel replied. "For the ritual to get Mildred out."

Kyla fell silent, thinking back over what she'd just witnessed Lucius do to Cassia. Had Dylan tortured himself over doing it to her? What if the ritual hadn't worked and she'd died at his hand? How would he have handled that? Would he have killed himself?

"Time is ticking, Kyla," Azazel said. "Make your choice."

Pulling herself back to reality, Kyla looked up at him. "There is no choice. I knew before I even took the rose back in Gran's kitchen that I would accept."

Azazel gasped, his eyes filling with tears.

"I accept you for *you*, Azazel. And everything else," she said, motioning at the scene behind her. "Is just trivial. There's a reason we've been bound together. I've no idea what that reason is but I'm certain I want to find out."

Azazel's heart thudded against his rib cage. Was this the closure he needed on his old life? Had Balthazar unwittingly done them both a favour by casting those words and bringing them their demi-souls?

"And your werewolf?" Azazel asked, his eyes scanning across hers.

Kyla shrugged her shoulders. "We'll figure it out." She reached up and took the rose. "If you thought this was going to be impossible to get past then surely anything else will be a breeze."

He nodded and smiled at her, his mind racing with thoughts, anxiety pricking at him for his life as a human. Would this really be the countdown to his last eighty years alive?

The rose shrivelled up in Kyla's hand before burning up and turning into ash, blowing away on the wind and scattering over Pompeii.

As their world started to shift again, returning them to Gran's kitchen, Kyla reached out and grabbed Azazel's hand. No, Dylan wouldn't like it, but after what her and Azazel had just been through, the demon needed her more right now than Dylan.

Shimmering back into reality in Lily's kitchen, a collective sigh of relief sounded from the table as the pair reappeared side by side, in front of the Aga.

"Thank goodness," Lily said, rushing forwards to her granddaughter. "Are you ok?"

Kyla nodded. "I'm fine."

Malcolm eyed Kyla for a few seconds before saying, "You accepted."

"How do you know that?" Kyla asked.

"Because if you hadn't, you would have returned alone."

Kyla flickered her eyes over to Dylan. Their eyes met for a brief moment before he looked away, grabbing a biscuit from the table.

Azazel dropped her hand and moved back to his seat, Oscar still sat in the chair as he had been before they left.

Heading back to her seat, Kyla sat down next to Sam and glared at Balthazar over her friend's shoulder. "I don't recommend you doing what I just did."

Balthazar's brown eyes filled with fear, and he froze, waiting for Sam's response.

Sam patted Kyla's leg and smiled. "I appreciate your concern, really, but I'm a big girl I can handle it."

Kyla shook her head. "No. You don't understand—"

"I don't need to. I know what I want, Kyla. He's my answer to everything. I don't need to know what he did however many years ago. It matters what and who he is now. Everyone changes over time."

"Sam, at least take until the deadline to think it through and get to know him. *Please.*"

Sam shook her head. Turning to Balthazar, she held her hand out and said, "Give me the rose."

Balthazar sucked in a sharp breath. Azazel's eyes widened. Was this the moment he'd lose his brother forever? If Sam saw what Kyla just did...she would come back alone.

"I think you should listen to Kyla," Balthazar replied. "You need to think this through."

"No, I don't. I don't need to think about anything when it concerns my demi-soul. We're in this together, no matter what."

Balthazar turned to Azazel, his face nothing but a paling picture of shock and fright.

Azazel shrugged his shoulders. "Give her the rose."

Balthazar, his breaths now quickening, stood up and held his hand out, the rose materialising on his palm.

Sam stood up, looking him straight in the eyes. "I don't need to see anything to accept you," she said. "I know we're meant to be together and that's all I'm worried about." Reaching for the rose, Sam picked it up by the petals, never taking her eyes from Balthazar's. "I accept you."

Kyla dropped her head, her insides filling with dread. What had Sam just done?

"You silly silly girl," Malcolm said, his voice deep and full of disapproval. "Very smart not to touch the thorns but you have no idea what you've just agreed to."

The rose shrunk before setting itself alight and turning to a pile of hot ash. Balthazar walked outside and blew it off his hand. When he walked back in, the relief filtering through his eyes was impossible to ignore.

Going straight to Sam, he curled his arms around her waist and drew her into him for a hug. "You are one incredible woman. I've waited a very long time for you."

Kyla looked over at Dylan, his eyes trained on his sister, a muscle in his jaw twitching. Flickering her gaze over to Azazel, their eyes met, a buzz of adrenaline piercing her heart. She couldn't help but wonder what lay in store next for her as she stared into those familiar swirling jade green eyes.

A Note from the Author

I hope you enjoyed Kyla's story. If you did, I would be eternally grateful if you could leave a review to let others know how much you enjoyed it. Even one sentence is fine. Thank you so much!

Kyla, Dylan, the delicious demonic duo Azazel and Balthazar, and Sam will return in book 2, Vampires and Vendettas. This is planned for a December 2024 release.

If you want to follow me and keep up to date with all my latest goings on, visit www.cjlauthor.com and sign up for my newsletter, or look me up in the places below:

www.facebook.com/CJLaurenceAuthor

www.instagram.com/cjlauthor

https://www.bookbub.com/authors/c-j-laurence

I love hearing from my readers and will always reply to you!

Also by this Author

Want and Need
Cowboys & Horses
Retribution
The Red Riding Hoods – The Grim Sisters Book 1
Game Changer – Hell's Rejects MC Book 1
Angel of the Crypt
The Twisted Tale of Saffron Schmidt
Love, Lies & Immortal Ties
Love, Lies & Blood Ties
Love, Lies & Eternal Ties
Love, Lies & Family Ties
The Golden Winged Horse
Blue

Made in United States
Troutdale, OR
11/16/2024

24909046R10249